He

Praise for Sarah Harrison's previous novel,
That was Then:

'Sarah Harrison shows herself to be more than equal to the complexities of her plot, handling its developments with impeccable timing' Christina Koning, *The Times*

'A work of extraordinary fictional daring … assured … always convinces' *Weekend Telegraph*

'Harrison does not disappoint … [her] integrity as a writer translates into a funny and touching account of self-discovery' *Mail on Sunday*

'Moving and funny' *YOU Magazine*

'Written with Sarah Harrison's usual verve, this story offers new insights into the dangers of a mother's overdependence and the absolute necessity of letting go' *Good Housekeeping*

'*That was Then* is written with Sarah Harrison's usual perception and telling eye for detail. A warm, moving and believable read' *Home & Life*

'A nice dry wry style – but a gut wrencher for mothers of sons. You who have tears to shed, prepare to shed them now'
Northern Echo

'This author's light touch and witty, thoroughly modern approach make for a very enjoyable read and a worthy successor to her last novel, *Flowers won't Fax*'
Beverly Davies, *The Lady*

Heaven's on Hold

Sarah Harrison

FLAME
Hodder & Stoughton

First published in Great Britain in 1999
by Hodder and Stoughton
First published in paperback in 2000
by Hodder and Stoughton
A division of Hodder Headline

A Flame Paperback

10 9 8 7 6 5 4 3 2 1

A CIP catalogue record for this title is available
from the British Library.

ISBN 0340 76658 1

Printed and bound in Great Britain by
Caledonian International Book Manufacturing Ltd, Glasgow

Hodder and Stoughton
A division of Hodder Headline
338 Euston Road
London NW1 3BH

For Patrick

Chapter One

It was drizzling when David left work, and the unmanned roadworks outside Border and Cheffins, with their muddy waterlogged troughs, bell tents and precarious boardwalks were reminiscent of the trenches of the Somme.

He'd omitted to bring any sort of coat with him that morning, so by the time he'd negotiated the planks and walked the few hundred yards to the car park he was obliged to use while the pipe laying was in progress, he was distinctly damp. The fact that the Volvo had acquired a parking ticket was grimly in keeping with everything else. It had been a distressing week and the bloody ticket — he ripped it off the windscreen and stuffed it in his pocket as another warlike metaphor sprang to mind — put the tin hat on it. The commuters of King's Newton were to parking what German holidaymakers were to sunbeds, and even if his own office hours had been less pleasantly civilised he would have refused to compete. Though strictly speaking the Volvo was not in a marked bay, neither was it causing the slightest inconvenience or obstruction to anyone else, and he had paid the full daily rate.

A woman unlocking her own car nearby made a sympathetic noise.

'Bad luck.'

He shook his head, embarrassed by his scowl. 'It's the complete lack of any discretionary judgment, you know?'

'Jobsworths.'

'Exactly. Well,' he tried for a debonair grin which probably manifested itself as a gargoyle's grimace, 'they can whistle for it.'

'Power to your elbow,' said the woman.

It was only three o'clock and muggy in spite of the rain: the inside of the car was stifling. He shrugged off his jacket and slung it on the back seat. The parking ticket, the sullen weather, not to mention the attrition of the week gone by and the challenge of the days to come, conspired to make him thoroughly out of sorts. He wondered if, after years of taking his health for granted, his blood pressure might be high.

It was therefore not unexpected, though no less infuriating, when he forgot he was not going straight home, and took the wrong turning at the lights on the edge of town. This would have been easily remedied had it not been for yet more roadworks — they seemed to be using the holiday season to tear King's Newton apart — which ensured he was stuck in a single-lane diversion for the best part of half a mile, before being politely returned to his original, wrong, route.

Fuming, David decided to cut his losses, and rather than retrace his tracks make for the God-awful dual carriageway which encircled the town. At his usual time the ringroad would have been out of the question, a log-jam of crawling cars, but in the middle of the afternoon he considered that speed would compensate for the slightly greater distance involved.

The traffic was moving freely and he congratulated himself on his decision as he accelerated briskly down the slip road and moved into the middle lane. The knots in his shoulders, and his brain, loosened a little and he turned on the radio. There was one of those pleasant talk-for-talk's-sake discussions going on, ostensibly about the role of teachers 'in society' (as though there were any other place for them to have a role). The voice of one of the women reminded him of Annet's — husky, with that thing she did of sounding both drawling and incisive. It was one of the first things that had attracted him to her, the voice she used when she pointed out that her name rhymed with 'dammit'.

His wife was a bit of a verbal dominatrix: he liked to think of her wiping out wimps at meetings with a couple of well-chosen, smokily-delivered put-downs.

These more spirited thoughts prompted him to pull into the outside lane. He must have been doing nearly ninety, but in no time some idiot in a performance car zoomed up from nowhere, practically nudging the tailgate before falling back, and then repeating the process, as though the Volvo were a tiresome obstacle in his path.

David put up with it for a bit, maintaining his speed and trying not to look at his tormentor in the rear-view mirror. After all, he was already breaking the law and there was no reason on earth why he should compound the misdemeanour by going any faster. But the car – it was white, with sit-up-and-beg headlamps and a rear spoiler – surged again, hovered menacingly and fell back with a poor grace to let him get out of the way. Which in the end of course he did, telling himself it was the mature thing to do. He didn't hurry, but signalled and pulled over in as measured a way as was commensurate with a dangerous lunatic breathing down his neck.

He forebore to give the driver anything more than a pointed look, and was shocked to discover that it was a woman. Her impassive profile shooting past was as painfully humiliating as a kick in the groin. It was with the greatest possible difficulty that he restrained himself from pulling out and giving her a taste of her own medicine. Only Annet's voice in his head prevented him. 'Testy ...!' she'd jeer in these circumstances: 'Testy!', implying that the word had its roots in 'testosterone'.

His mood swooping to a new low he remained where he was, in the middle lane. That was it of course: he was irredeemably middle-of-the-road. And middle-aged, middle-class, middle-management – men didn't come more middling than him. If he wasn't careful, he'd be subject to a kind of living death by mediocrity. The voice of the woman on the radio, he now considered, didn't sound a bit like Annet's but was the usual circumlocutory, mid-Atlantic psychobabble. He switched it off.

Glum drizzle continued to smear the windscreen. The sign for his turn off loomed up, the left-forking arm like that of an admonitory policeman: This way for a major upheaval.

He was a few minutes late, and in keeping with the theme of the day was unable to find a parking space. Mindful of the ticket crunched up in his pocket he circled the lot a couple of times, but the thought of Annet pacing the floor and fretting finally prompted him to park on the end of a row. Someone else had done the same thing just in front, and he told himself he was doing both of them a favour, making it look as though the rows actually extended to this point. The law of averages stated that he was unlikely to be nicked twice in one day.

In the foyer he debated whether to buy Annet a small present by way of apology, but decided against because it would only have to be carried straight back down again and she would almost certainly regard it as a waste of money. In the lift on the way up he realised he was sweating – why were these places always so airless?

On the second floor he followed the helpful painted footprints along the short route which must surely now be engraved on his heart. Expecting to walk straight in, he gave his wrist a nasty jolt trying to push open the swing doors which were in some way jammed. Rubbing his arm and blushing with embarrassment it took him a second or two to realise that a slightly hectoring disembodied voice was addressing him.

'Who are you visiting?' He glanced around, trying to locate the source of the voice. It wasn't something he'd encountered before, but then he'd normally been here in regulation hours.

The voice repeated itself with ponderous patience. 'Who are you visiting please? Gentleman at the door – who are you for? Hello?'

He peered through the glass at the top of the door. At the desk in the central bay halfway along the corridor there were a couple of nurses, and a couple more standing around: none gave any indication that she was the owner of the voice, which now sounded again, with a distinct rasp of irritation.

'Who are you for please?'

David had tracked it down now to a small strip of louvred metal to the left of the door, towards which he now stooped slightly and spoke into.

'David Keating. I've come to collect my wife.'

'Just the one of you?'

Absurd as the question was he still found himself glancing briefly over his shoulder. A harsh buzz in his ear prompted him to push the door, which this time opened. As he passed, the nurse behind the desk said: 'I hope you're going to take both of them with you, Mr Keating.'

'I'm sorry?'

'You said you were going to collect your wife, but we'd appreciate it if you could take that daughter of yours too.'

'Oh ... yes!' Their laughter had been friendly, his was a little nervous. 'Yes, don't worry, I plan to.'

'They're all ready for you.'

The antiseptic air of the ward could not altogether mask the feral, hormonal odour that so disturbed him. Like the proceedings he'd been obliged to witness in the labour room, the smell was a little too primitive for his taste: he shrank from it, and rather regretted not having brought some more flowers, like a plague nosegay, to waft it away.

It was a relief, as he came round the curtain that had been drawn across by her neighbour, to catch the spicey tang of Annet's Nina Ricci scent.

Her greeting however was characteristically terse. 'At last, what kept you?'

'Sorry, stupid lapse of concentration. I took the turn for home by mistake and then got dragged all round the houses by those palsied roadworks. My life's been plagued by pipes and sewage systems all week.'

'Mine too,' she said drily.

Annet rose from the chair by the locker where she'd been

sitting. She wore the clothes he had been instructed to bring in yesterday, and was immaculately made up. Her handbag and case were on the ground at her feet. The baby – thankfully asleep – was neatly strapped into her carrier car-seat thing on the bed.

David and Annet kissed, on the mouth but politely. David was keenly aware of the new dimension to their relationship: parenthood. Dutifully he bent over his daughter and touched her cheek with his finger. To his alarm she convulsed, and her tiny hands jerked upwards.

'My God, have I—?'

'Just made her jump, I think.' They both looked down, frowning anxiously, but the baby already looked as if she'd never moved.

'Come on then,' said Annet. 'Let's get out of here, I'm stir-crazy.' She picked up her bag and glanced at David. 'I'm not supposed to carry darl, can you manage the case and her?'

'Easily.'

The baby, he noticed as they walked down the ward, was much lighter than his wife's suitcase. The nurses at the desk smiled at their approach, though he thought he detected something knowing in the smiles. Annet said, very much en passant:

'I won't pretend I'm not glad to be going, but thanks for everything.'

They assured her it had been an absolute pleasure and the two younger ones advanced to admire the baby.

'Aah ... she's lovely.' The girl looked up at David. 'Have you got a name for her yet?'

'We haven't actually.'

'So she's Fred for the time being, is she?'

'Something like that.'

'Bye bye Fred ...' They stroked and patted the baby unselfconsciously while Annet waited, one hand on the door. David felt large and wooden, like a telegraph pole around which a couple of finches fluttered and cheeped. He feared he could never begin to match the unforced affection which these two relative strangers showed to his daughter.

'Come on then,' said Annet, opening the door. 'Out into the big bad world.'

He edged awkwardly through with his twin burdens. 'Wide.'

'What?'

'It's wolves that are big and bad. The world's big and wide.'

She moved past him to the lift. 'I know what I mean.'

'Ah,' said the youngest nurse again, 'it's lovely to see an older couple like that with a first baby. The dad's really sweet, isn't he?'

The older staff nurse leaned across the desk. 'More than sweet, girls — gorgeous.'

'Do you think so?' The two younger ones giggled at this sign of weakness in a wrinkly. 'Do you really?'

'He's a bit mature for you two I grant, but he looks like the film star Gregory Peck.'

They looked at each other, then at her. 'Who?'

To his relief, there was no retribution exacted for this, his second parking infringement of the day, but the new dispensation made itself felt at once. The babyseat apparently had to go in the front, and Annet sat in the back, leaning forward anxiously (and dangerously, David considered) to keep it under observation.

'You should put a seat belt on.'

'In a minute. I have to gaze obsessively, it's my job.'

He moved off with extreme caution. 'Will she always have to travel in the front?'

'I don't suppose so. Of course not. But at the moment it's safer for her to be facing towards the back, so if she was actually in the back we wouldn't be able to see her.'

'I see.'

Annet prodded his shoulder. 'Not miffed, are you darl?'

'Not in the least, just wondering.' He put up his hand to

touch hers, but she'd leaned back and was clicking her belt in place. Glancing in the mirror he was shocked at the unguarded tiredness of her expression. 'How are you? Are you OK?'

She pulled a what-sort-of-question's-that? face. 'Nothing Mother Nature won't take care of in time, I'm sure.'

'How was last night?'

'Eventful.'

'Poor darling. At least now you're home I'll be able to help.'

'I'm feeding, remember.'

When she mentioned it, he did remember, but now that Annet was no longer pregnant it was hard to get his mind round the idea of his wife's fit, overworked body providing nourishment for another. Would she, he wondered, even be able to sit still for long enough?

'Well – even if it's just moral support,' he added.

'I'm sure we can think of something,' she replied. 'And anyway I'm going to have to get her on to a bottle fairly soon so that she can be handed over to the admirable Lara.'

David thought about this. Where the nanny question was concerned he detected in himself a quite irrational ambivalence. It had had to be addressed of course, it was the only way, their combined incomes could well afford it, and it would keep Annet sane. But the unreconstructed traditionalist in him still resisted the idea. It was not that he wanted Annet to be chained to the pushchair and the washing machine, far from it, but that he could not quite resign himself to the handing over of their first (and, Annet was resolved, their only) child to a relative stranger, no matter how admirable. He glanced down at the tiny form in the car-seat and realised how stupidly selfish these reservations were, considering how little he knew – or even at this stage felt – about his own daughter.

The journey home took longer than usual because he was exercising such care. As they came into Newton Bury and obeyed the injunction to 'Drive slowly through the village', he noticed that Annet's head had fallen sideways and she was asleep, but by the time they reached Gardener's Lane she'd woken and collected herself and he made no comment.

There was a bay tree by the gate of Bay Court which Annet deemed only one-up from a monkey-puzzle, but which they'd kept because of the house. He turned into the horseshoe-shaped drive and parked next to the door. After undoing his own safety belt, he tried to release the baby from her seat harness, but he was all thumbs and the flat clasp remained intransigent. Annet, already out of the car, opened the passenger door and took over. She simply dove in, with no greater expertise than him but with a great deal more force, and bent the thing to her will. David banished as unworthy the notion that this served as a metaphor for their entire relationship. He fetched Annet's bag from the back seat and held out his hand for the car-seat.

'Here, let me.'

At the front door, while he found the key, he put down the bag but thought it might seem disrespectful to do the same with the baby.

'After you.'

Annet went in and straight through to the back of the house to open the windows and the garden doors: she hated stuffiness. He was glad he'd arranged for Karen to come yesterday, so everything was clean and tidy. Bay Court was as close to the house of his dreams as their combined incomes would allow, an ample, solid, bourgeois Edwardian residence, the only one of its kind in the village – a city villa gone walkabout. The very bricks and mortar, the rooftiles, the cornices and light bosses, the picture rails, the fireplaces and window frames, promised comfort and security, and inspired in David the same sense of confidence which he was sure the builder had had in creating them, before the old world ended in 1914.

A confidence he sadly lacked as he contemplated his own new world. He put the bag at the foot of the stairs and followed Annet with the car-seat. She was sitting at the wooden picnic table on the terrace, her chin resting on her hands.

'You OK?'

'Yes thanks.'

'Cup of tea? Coffee?'

'Tea sounds good.'

He tried to see her face. 'Sure you're all right?'

'I'm fine ...!' she protested, still without looking at him and with a scratch in her voice.

He retreated to the kitchen and placed the car-seat in the middle of the kitchen table. He was sure there were probably all sorts of strictures on this matter, but it was a large table and the baby was tiny and sound asleep.

He filled and plugged in the kettle. Everything felt very strange. It was unusual for them both to be at home at five-thirty on a weekday without some specific reason. But then – he glanced anxiously at his daughter who now seemed to be moving slightly – they did have a reason. It was just that he didn't know what the prescribed actions were. He and Annet, two intelligent, assertive adults in late and early middle age respectively were on hold, waiting to react to the demands of this minute and (to them) alien, lifeform. Since her birth four days ago he'd experienced moments of pure elation during which he shouted silently: 'I've got a daughter!' But they had always been when he wasn't with her – to do with the idea and the future, rather than the reality and the here and now ....

Annet came in as he was pouring the tea. In spite of the mugginess of the day she had her arms folded as though she were cold.

'Oh – she's waking up.'

'She did seem to be twitching a bit.' He handed her her mug and they sat down at the table with the car-seat between them: its tiny occupant, rather elevated, seemed to dominate them in what David couldn't help seeing as a symbolic manner. In an attempt to get into the spirit of things, he asked: 'Does that mean it's time for a feed?'

'I should think so. Yes – it certainly feels like that.' Annet touched her breasts speculatively as she said this and David felt a wholly inappropriate pang of desire. It was the first time he'd allowed himself to notice how impressively swollen she was.

'Is it uncomfortable?' He was unable to keep his voice completely steady.

'Yes,' she replied. 'Hard and lumpy.'

He stretched out his hand. 'May I?'

'Be my guest.' She took his hand and placed it over her right breast. It was taut, and hot to the touch – like so much, different from before. 'See what I mean?'

'I do . . .' He permitted himself a tentative stroke. 'Poor you.'

'A perfectly natural state, as I keep telling myself. What women throughout history have had to put up with.'

There was a stain of bitterness in her voice, and although she hadn't pushed his hand away he withdrew it, rebuffed by her mood, the desire anyway quite gone. The baby began to make little testy grunting sounds, and its face beneath its small round hat became red. They sat staring at her over their half-finished tea. Annet glanced at her watch.

'I haven't a clue what there is for supper.'

'Don't worry about that, there's stuff in the freezer.'

'Not that I'm hungry . . . .'

'You must eat properly.'

She closed her eyes and placed her finger and thumb against her lids. It was a gesture he recognised, of mild exasperation. 'David . . . .'

'Sorry, didn't mean to treat you like an invalid.'

'It's OK. What I'd really like is a stonking great gin and tonic.'

'Have one!' he said, eager for normality.

'I'm not sure it's a good idea – I shouldn't be feeding mother's ruin to our infant daughter.'

'Haven't I read about nannies dipping dummies in brandy, or something?'

With her hand still to her eyes she gave a short laugh. 'I don't know . . . have you?'

'Something like that. It'd probably just help her to sleep.'

As if in protest the baby let out a cry, wavering but imperious: a terrifying expression of utter frailty and need. Which they, David supposed, were there to assuage. To his enormous relief Annet took charge, standing up and unfastening the harness. The baby flexed and writhed between her hands as she lifted it, its face crimson. When Annet took off its hat David could see a pulse beating strongly between the still-open plates of its skull, beneath a tissue-thin covering of pink skin and downy hair. The cries intensified.

'Anything I can do?' he enquired.

She gave him one of her dark, gimme-a-break smiles. 'I don't think you have the technology, darl.'

'I suppose not.' He couldn't keep the relief out of his voice.

'I'm going to sit in a comfortable chair, if you don't mind.'

'You do that.' He got up too, trying to look and feel more energetic than he really was. He felt completely exhausted, with no good reason. The day had been trying, but it had at least been short, and unlike Annet he'd had four nights of uninterrupted sleep. He was at a loss to know what was wearing him out.

'I'll organise supper,' he said.

'Good plan.'

She stopped on her way out of the room. 'Do we have any stout?'

'Stout?'

'Guinness, that sort of thing? That's supposed to be good for nursing mothers.'

'Not that I know of. Want me to get some in?'

'No, no, it doesn't matter ... It was only a thought, I'm not that desperate for alcohol.'

She went. The baby's cries receded as she carried her into the drawing room, and then ceased as, presumably, it fed. To take his mind off this David assembled some things for supper – a packet of smoked salmon, three eggs, some single cream, a granary loaf. He went out on to the terrace via the back door and snipped off some parsley and chives from the clumps growing in pots under the kitchen window. He was a perfectly adequate cook, acknowledged by both of them to be rather better than Annet, whose strong suit was not in the domestic arts, and yet he felt slightly nervous. It was as though some ancient unreformed biological chauvinism ruled their house, with Annet the undisputed female life force, secure in her fecundity while he 'a mere male' – how he hated that expression – dithered in the kitchen. He was all thumbs, he seemed to be able to hear at least half a dozen clocks ticking, in different rooms in the house. His own territory felt strange to him.

To cover his awkwardness and fill the silence he turned on the radio. It was tuned to the local BBC station (a sign of the times, Annet didn't care for it) and there was a phone-in in progress about a proposed halfway house for the mentally ill and whether it would mean local children were at risk. The ignorance, prejudice and poor command of English displayed by the callers were nothing short of lamentable. He was embarrassed, by them and by his own snobbishness, but he left it on as he chopped chives and beat eggs, and soon there was relief in the form of the excellent Marti Webb singing 'Tell Me on a Sunday'.

Or it would have been relief had he not been swept by a completely unexpected, rush of emotion. 'Take me to a park all covered with trees . . .' was the precise moment at which he felt his Adam's apple lurch and his whole face suffuse with a rising tide of tears – something he hadn't experienced since childhood. (Not even, he reminded himself, at his daughter's birth, when so many younger, braver fathers had warned him he would be completely unmanned.) He wasn't at all sure what had caused it now. The peculiar purity of the singer's voice, the lilt of the tune, the wistful stoicism of the words – the power, he conceded, blowing his nose on a sheet of kitchen towel, of cheap music.

What he needed to do was to go and embrace his wife and baby, instead of standing here in an emotional taking over the chopping board. It was Annet who had introduced him to this song, and the eponymous album of which it formed a part. Ages ago, when they first met. He turned it up slightly. 'Take me to a zoo that has chimpanzees . . . .'

He walked firmly to the drawing room. His wife's dark head rested on the back of the sofa. 'Remember this?' he said. 'The closest we came to having a song.'

But with that filmic, cartoon-quality that real life so often had she was asleep, and the baby too, its tiny, perfectly chiselled mouth encircling but not holding the nipple from which a bead of translucent greyish liquid emerged. Rebuffed, yet again, by the perinatal imperative, David delicately drew his wife's shirt over her nakedness, being careful not to cover the baby's face.

Back in the kitchen the beaten eggs had developed a sticky film and the butter in the saucepan had become a fizzing, tarry slick.

Two hours later the baby and Annet awoke, in that order. By that time David, having fielded several phone calls from exuberant friends and relations and fended off potential visits for the time being, had all but fallen asleep himself on a hard kitchen chair. With the cup of rest dashed from his lips, he felt utterly dire. Thick-headed and dry-mouthed, he wiped out the caramelised contents of the saucepan and prepared to launch a second attempt on the scrambled egg.

He heard Annet going upstairs and called: 'Everything all right?'

'Yup . . . just going to change her.'

'Anything I can do?'

'Come and keep me company if you like – see how it's done.'

'Good thinking.'

This time he checked that everything was switched off, and placed the smoked salmon, and the egg bowl (covered with a plate) in the fridge before going up to the baby's room.

They'd spent quite a bit — in his private view an outrageous amount — making this room nice. Their thinking had been that it shouldn't be a nursery as such, with all the twee frightfulness which that implied, but their child's room, in which their own taste would prevail in a custodial capacity for the time being. The dominant colour was a pleasing wedgwood blue and David had done up the Victorian washstand which had been sitting in the garage, and bought a willow-pattern bowl and jug — repro, but none the worse for that — to go with it. On the bottom shelf were all the tubes, jars and bottles which the baby industry insisted were necessary for the maintenance of infant hygiene. In the hearth, with its Arts and Crafts tile surround there were dried cornflowers and grasses, and the curtains were a blue and terracotta print. The divan in the corner was covered in a large (it puddled on the ground), and beautiful Afghan throw in shades of indigo. It had been impossible to find any infant bedding not covered in wince-making bears or moppets, so Annet had persuaded her sister Louise to make up some small duvet covers, and a lining for the Moses basket, in the same colour scheme.

The only picture in the room was one of David's own, a pencil portrait of Annet done not long after they married. He liked the drawing for the very reason that Annet wouldn't countenance its being displayed downstairs: it conveyed something of her fierce, well-disguised vulnerability. He wasn't even sure how he'd achieved it, but it was there, something to do with the mouth in particular . . . .

However, as he entered the room this evening the tranquil adult decisions and choices of the past months seemed a ridiculous irrelevance. Reality was biting, and likely to draw blood. The baby, now yelling fit to be tied, was on a plastic mat on the divan bed, while Annet struggled to mop up what looked like several pints of runny mustard with handfuls of wet wipes. It was one of those laugh-or-cry situations, but there was no doubt to which Annet was closer.

'Could you get me something to put this lot in?'

He glanced round. Their forward planning had not included

the capacious pedal bin demanded by the situation. There was a wicker wastepaper basket, but without a lining.

'David—!'

'Hang on.'

He ran down to the kitchen and unwound a series of bin liners from the roll in the drawer, the baby's persistent screeching sawing at his nerves as he did so. He returned to find Annet standing with her hands held up like a surgeon waiting for operating gloves. She pointed with her foot at the pile of stained debris on the floor.

'There you go,' she said, 'present for you. Can you keep an eye while I go and wash my hands?'

'Of course.'

With extreme caution he turned one of the binbags inside out, picked up the rubbish using the bag as a glove, and turned it back out the right way. The baby's rasping complaints continued. She seemed to be in some sort of furious altered state from which it would be impossible to retrieve her. Annet had replaced the disposable nappy, and greatly daring he picked her up. It was only the third time he'd done so and her squirmy smallness unnerved him all over again. He tried cradling her in his arms, but this most traditional of attitudes didn't seem easy for either of them. The baby was too tiny to cuddle or grip firmly and her unrestrained arms and legs waved about like those of an upturned beetle. When he lifted her to his shoulder her head lolled back, then forward, on its pliable stalk of neck, prompting first the fear of injury, then that of stifling her against his chest. When Annet re-entered the room he was holding their daughter in front of him on his palms, like a tenor with a musical score. Her crying was unabated.

'So what do we think?' he asked in what he hoped was a reasonably light-hearted way which didn't confer the whole responsibility on his wife. 'Hungry again?'

'I can't believe that. And she's clean. Their needs are simple and few at this age.' She sounded far from confident. 'I think I'll wrap her up and put her in the basket.'

To his intense relief she took the baby from him, swathed her in a primrose shawl – he believed it was the one crocheted by the mother of Karen, their cleaning lady – and laid her in the Moses basket. She seemed to rest on the narrow mattress like the pupa or chrysalis of some giant and extremely vocal moth. Annet stood with folded arms gazing down, and he went and laid his hand on the back of her neck. He felt an inexpressible tenderness for his wife's uncharacteristic anxiety and lack of competence.

'How about you?' he asked gently, rubbing her neck with his thumb. 'You hungry?'

She gave a little shrug.

'Well,' he went on, 'you said there isn't much else we can do. Why don't I go and get supper going, we could both do with something to eat.'

'OK.'

He went to the door. She hadn't moved. 'You are coming down?'

She nodded. He escaped.

Downstairs he poured himself a Scotch. It was reviving just to get a little further away from the crying. But he couldn't quite enjoy it until Annet joined him a couple of minutes later. She had brushed her hair and it was damp at the roots where she'd splashed her face.

'I'll get some Guinness in tomorrow,' he said.

'Mackeson would be even nicer.'

'Mackeson it is.' He stirred the eggs. 'Anything for now?'

'Just this.' She filled a lager glass with tap water. 'Got to keep my fluids up.'

He stirred. Annet drank thirstily, and refilled. Upstairs, the baby cried.

The eggs reached a critical stage, that point where he could turn the heat off and they would finish cooking on their own. He took the saucepan off the ring and sprinkled in the chives and parsley; removed the smoked salmon from the fridge and divided it out on their plates. Bread and butter, knives and forks and napkins, he had already laid out on the table. Annet watched him, but her air was fretful and distracted, and as he was about to dish up she left the room, saying abruptly:

'I'm sorry, I can't leave her like this.'

So the Moses basket sat on another of the kitchen chairs between them while they attempted to eat. Or at least, he did. Annet managed a few small, uninterested, intensively-chewed mouthfuls before picking the baby up and putting her to the breast once more. David continued manfully, but the food might as well have been sawdust. The clock proclaimed it only eight o'clock, but the three of them seemed to inhabit some parallel dimension, separated from friends, relations and all the signs and landmarks of normal everyday life. It might have been any time, any season, any meal. He was relieved when the phone rang again and he had a reason to leave the table.

He took the receiver off the wall mounting near the kitchen door.

'Hello?'

'So how's the paterfamilias? Changing nappies like a goodun?'

It was his younger brother Tim, wealthily wived and four times a father in Chichester. It was a measure of David's state of mind that he was actually quite pleased to hear his voice.

'Hello Tim. We're all fine, thanks for asking. But then we haven't been back for more than a few hours.'

'I know, I know . . .' Tim chuckled. 'But it feels like a lifetime, right?' Tim's eldest was sixteen, and he affected some of the verbal mannerisms of the young.

'I wouldn't say that.'

'No, because Annet's probably within plate-chucking distance.'

'Not at all. She's feeding at the moment as a matter of fact. We all are.'

'Am I disturbing?'

'Not me, I've finished.'

'Good. No, look, I'm really pleased for you. Mags said I was a lazy bastard not to have called before and she's quite right – by the way she wants to know did Annet get the flowers?'

'Yes – I'm sure – hang on.' He turned to Annet. 'They want to know did you get the flowers?'

'They were great. I'll be writing.'

'No need for that,' said Tim in his ear. 'Early weeks are enough of a bugger without bread and butter letters. Anyway, Mags intends coming up for a private view as and when.'

'Of course. You too I hope.'

'I do as I'm told. You and I can nip off for a pint of best while they talk post-partum politics.'

David felt suddenly bruised by Tim's well-meant blokiness. 'Maybe. Anyway, give us another ring before you come.'

'Christ no, we won't turn up unannounced. And we won't bring the kids either, you'll be relieved to hear—'

'Not at all—'

'Because there's another half hundredweight of baby kit Mags want to unload on to you, and there won't be room for anything else in the car.'

'That's kind.'

'It's called clearing the loft, if you ask me ... No that's not true, it's all good stuff and we want you to have it. If it's not to Annet's taste she can rock round to the Oxfam shop, it's hers to do what she likes with.'

'Thank you.'

'How is the new arrival, anyway?'

'Very well, as far as I can tell. I'm not much of an expert as yet.'

Tim chuckled. 'Nor do you want to be, take it from me. It's like cars, know too much and you'll have nothing more to do with them.'

David felt uncomfortably caught between his instinctive resistance to this theory, and the paucity of his experience compared to that of Tim.

He hung up just as Annet disengaged from the baby and adjusted her complicated bra and the front of her shirt.

'Let me take her while you finish your supper.'

'Would you?'

'I'd like to,' he lied.

'Hold her sort of up, if you can, there'll be some wind.'

He managed much better this time, and even enjoyed the silken feel of his daughter's eggshell skull against his neck, and ventured a kiss.

'Tim was doing his battle-scarred veteran number,' he said.

'I guessed. Yuk, this is cold.'

'Let me do you some more egg.'

'No, I'm not all that hungry . . .' She put down her fork. Her shirt was still unbuttoned to the waist, and the unaccustomed depth of her cleavage with its pulsing tributaries of blue veins was in contrast to her drawn and exhausted face.

'Anyway,' she said, 'it's not some sort of competition. Tim and Mags are Tim and Mags and we're us, and this is our daughter, and our home, and our business.'

'Of course. You gathered I didn't retaliate.'

'The thought of being patronised by Mags . . . I think I'd spontaneously combust.'

'I know. But she won't. Her heart's in the right place.'

'Yes —' She looked away for a moment and he knew she was struggling. 'I'm just worried in case—' Another working silence.

'In case what?'

The silence stretched. The baby belched up a puddle of curds and whey on to his lapel, there was a faint, cheesy smell. He held her against him with one hand and placed the other on his wife's shoulder.

'Darling?'

She shook her head, and when her voice came out it was a shaky whisper. 'In case my heart isn't.'

'It will be,' he said, awed by the bleakness of her honesty. 'Of *course* it will be.'

The baby was quiet, so they went to bed, with the Moses basket on the ottoman in the bay window. They both felt it was a little soon for her to be far away in her own room. David wrapped his arms around Annet, who remained armoured in her nursing bra, and they fell asleep quickly.

When David was disturbed by the baby's agitated grunting he had no idea what time it was nor how long they'd slept for. They'd brought the electric nightlight through from the baby's room to obviate the need to turn on anything more, so the bedroom was bathed in a crepuscular half-light. He looked at his watch. It was just after eleven. They'd only lain down an hour ago. He told himself sternly that there were parents the length and breadth of the country sharing this moment with them, that it was perfectly normal and natural and no one ever needed as much sleep as they thought — but it was still a miserable shock.

Annet stirred. 'Oh God ... I'm coming.'

'It's all right, I'll bring her.'

'Thanks ....'

The baby was hitting her stride, beginning to cry in earnest. David almost tripped on the collection of cushions which Annet had cleared from the top of the ottoman. He moved them aside with his foot, but missed one and picked it up. For a moment he stood paralysed, clutching the cushion, looking down at his daughter's furious face that seemed two-thirds mouth. It was difficult at that moment to imagine that he might ever draw her portrait. Or, indeed, that he would ever draw again ....

'David — what are you doing?'

'Nothing,' he said. He dropped the cushion. 'Coming right up.'

Chapter Two

It was David's intention to stay awake while Annet fed the baby, to provide some moral support. He began well, propping up the pillows so that they could both sit comfortably, and putting his arm round her shoulders. But the faint, rhythmic sucking sound, and the comforting knowledge that crying would be out of the question while a nipple occupied their daughter's mouth, acted as a soporific. The third time his head dropped heavily forward he was unable to lift it again, and sleep engulfed him.

When Annet nudged him awake he was ashamed to discover his head resting against her shoulder, his mouth open, like a baby himself.

'Damn—!'

'That's all right, would you take her while I have a pee?'

'Yes, of course . . . .'

She swung her legs out of bed. 'You can change her if you like.'

'I don't—'

'You saw, it's not difficult.'

It wasn't, in principle. The design of the disposable nappy was an exemplar of functional simplicity, and his daughter had mercifully not produced another mustard-like evacuation, but was only damp. And yet he made a complete hash of it. He couldn't seem successfully to unite the inert pad with its self-stick strips to the baby's tiny red body and jerking limbs. He squeamishly avoided touching the scabby stump of her umbilicus, and sprinkled powder from a great height as he'd seen Annet do. After applying thick, white goo to her private parts he found he had so much still on his fingers that the strips wouldn't stick. He removed that nappy and wiped his fingers clean on it; put another one beneath her only to discover she'd peed on the mat; all was awash.

Annet appeared in the doorway.

'All right?'

'I will be,' he replied without conviction. The baby emitted a querulous squawk.

'Just wrap her up loosely and lie her on her side in the basket.'

'Got it.'

She disappeared and he heard the enviable flop and rustle of her getting into bed and pulling the duvet round her. So vividly did he empathise with these comfortable, comforting actions that he might almost have fallen asleep standing up, if his daughter hadn't begun to cry in earnest.

Even more cack-handed in his anxiety not to disturb Annet he nonetheless got the next nappy on. It seemed huge and ill-fitting, but once he'd pulled the baby's nightdress down over her purplish feet, that didn't show. When he picked her up he noticed the back of the nightie was slightly damp, but decided against attempting to change it. Babies of this age were used to a certain amount of dampness, surely, it went with the territory.

The crying found another gear and took on that persistent, nerve-fraying quality he was beginning to recognise. Annet's voice came from the bedroom.

'David — what's the matter?' There was no mistaking something accusatory in her tone.

'Nothing I can't handle.' What was he saying?

'Bring her in here.'

'I will in a moment. You get some sleep.'

'She was feeding for ages, she can't possibly be hungry . . . .'

'Exactly. Don't worry about us.'

Annet tailed away on a token protest, somewhere between a mumble and a moan. Clasping the baby against him with one hand David closed the door, and then picked up one of the new, smoothly folded cellular blankets from the bar cot. He dropped it on the divan, spread it out, then laid the baby on it and wrapped her up. With her wriggling fragility contained and bulked out by the blanket she was more manageable and even cuddly. Holding her with greater confidence he began to hum tunelessly against the side of her head, 'Take me to a park, all covered with trees, Tell me on a Sunday please ...' There was a recitative-ish bit in the middle of the song that was quite beyond him, so he just kept repeating the chorus. Lots of people, Annet included, had told him he was tone deaf, but his faint nasal sounds seemed not only not to bother his daughter, but positively to soothe her. He stood near the window, swaying and humming, and over a period of about ten minutes the pattern of her crying changed, the tone became less furious, the interstices longer. It became of paramount importance to him to quieten her completely, to be able to lay her in her basket contented and asleep. He pictured himself telling Annet: 'She was a bit crotchety, but I got her off ....'

After a further fifteen minutes she was quiet. Her head drooped passively in the crook of his neck. His sense of triumph was, he knew, quite out of proportion to the scale of the achievement. He had after all done no more than thousands of lone teenage mothers in tower blocks with a fraction of his advantages did on a regular basis, and yet he was full of a tender elation. He was reminded of something he'd read, long forgotten till now, about how people trained birds of prey, a process known as 'watching'. The falconer and his charge would sit together through the night, the man remaining resolutely awake until the exhausted bird at last fell asleep on his wrist. The trust implicit in this was the basis on which all subsequent training took place ....

Problems remained however. In his haste he had failed to clear up as he went along. There were two discarded nappies on the floor, along with the used wipes, and a puddle of urine lay on the changing mat, only contained by the mat's raised edge. He was fearful of putting the baby down in case he broke the spell.

Gingerly, he scooped the two sides of the mat together in his right hand and lowered it to the floor. Then he picked up the wipes and the nappies and dropped them on top. It was the best he could do for the moment.

He switched off the light and crept back to the bedroom, rolling each foot heel-to-toe and carefully avoiding the one and a half weasel floorboards on the left centre of the landing.

Annet seemed to be sound asleep, but as he came in she asked in a fairly normal voice: 'Everything under control?'

'Yes.' He whispered, wanting, in every sense, to keep the peace.

'Thanks, darl.'

'My pleasure.'

He knew she was probably less awake than she seemed. Even when sleeptalking she sounded fearsomely incisive, and at busy times he'd known her organise whole phantom meetings in her sleep, asking for chairs to be moved and so forth. As her breathing signalled unconsciousness, he slipped into bed, still holding the baby. It was one a.m., but the long night, which had appeared such a threatening prospect, now seemed warm and protective, he almost didn't want it to end. He felt he had achieved some kind of personal breakthrough. In bed with his sleeping wife and child, he considered he was performing the proper function of the paterfamilias, keeping watch over their slumbers.

And curiously, he was no longer tired himself, but calm and alert. For the first time, he allowed himself to look back over the events of the day at work.

The girl had to go, but that hadn't made it any easier. Telling someone they weren't up to the job was not something he relished, and to make matters worse she was a lovely girl – nice, well-mannered, pretty in an unfashionably rounded, wholesome, pink-and-white way. She ought to have been called something like Joyce, or Trish, but her name, improbably, was Gina: Gina King. The sort of name you glimpsed on dog-eared cards in London phone boxes. He knew when he'd said his piece as gently as he could, and closed the door after her, she would just about make it to the Ladies before bursting into tears. And she hadn't even been around long enough to have acquired a real office friend, male or female, to whom she could unburden, and who would take her part, and exult in rubbishing him from arsehole to breakfast time. He suspected she still lived with her parents, and very probably had a boyfriend of whom they approved, but who had so far failed to shake her composure. According to his scenario both parents and boyfriend would be sympathetic to her plight in a vague, uncomprehending sort of way.

In the great scheme of things at Border and Cheffins her dismissal was no great shakes. She was full young and had simply failed to come up to scratch during the probationary period. He'd had far more agonising confrontations when he'd been involved in 'human resources' (horrible term) at his previous, larger company – honourable, hardworking victims of downsizing in their middle years, who had every right to expect security . . . high fliers who'd come a cropper over gender politics . . . people sitting there telling him they'd found out they only had a limited time to live, and wanted to spend it with their family . . . All stuff for which he'd had neither the stomach nor the aptitude and which had got him in the end . . . But it was a long time since something had affected him as much as the letting go of Gina King. With this girl he had a sense of someone who had lived till now a dim life of sensory deprivation and who had, through the unlikely agency of Border and Cheffins, Country Property Agents, experienced an unprecedented degree of movement, light and colour. Even as he uttered his carefully chosen words of dismissal – thanking her for her contribution, emphasising the positive, wishing her well in the future – he'd known he was banging the lid back down on the tank.

The situation wasn't helped by the knowledge that he had selected Gina King from a shortlist of six, all of whom on the face of it might have been better suited to the task. Charmed, he had stuck his neck out and cast against the role, and this unpleasantness was the result.

Doug Border had warned him, sort of. 'It's those hand-knits, isn't it? You can't beat a nubile figure in lambswool.'

They were having a drink in the Marquis of Granby after work on the day of the interviews, and the remark had touched a nerve.

'That had absolutely nothing to do with it.'

'Well you may be a man of iron, David, but I plead guilty to susceptibility.'

'She struck me as having some nice qualities—'

'Oh she did, she did.'

David pressed on. 'She was polite and softly spoken, and whatever you say about the jumper she was smartly and appropriately dressed. And she really wants the job. There was a kind of—' he sought the right word – 'a kind of *respect* about her that you don't get so much of to the pound these days.'

'Respect?' Doug raised an eyebrow over his glass. 'She liked you.'

'No, it wasn't that ... I mean I wouldn't know if she did or not, and anyway it's irrelevant—'

He was stopped in his tracks by Doug's chortling laughter.

Annet, of course, had asked him about his choice at the time.

'Did you find someone?'

'Yes.'

'And will she do? Silly question I suppose, you wouldn't be taking her on otherwise.'

'She'll more than do. Basic skills at least as good as the rest, computer literacy fine, and a very pleasing manner.'

Annet darted him one of her scowly amused looks. 'Which means – what?'

'Pleasant and polite,' he replied firmly, determined not to be wrong-footed again. 'Not as fearsomely self-aware as some of these young women. Interested more in other people than herself. A little old-fashioned, which is no bad thing.'

'What a paragon. Sounds too good to be true.' Annet had kissed him to show she was teasing. 'Right up your alley, darl.'

And so it had proved, at least for a week or so. Gina moved about the outer office not terribly quickly, but quietly and to good effect, leaving a faint trace of wholesome cologne on the air – violets or lily of the valley. At lunchtime she took a tupperware box from her desk drawer and disappeared outside somewhere. Border and Cheffins had a small back garden but it was strictly for show, and there was no park nearby, David couldn't think where she got to. On the Friday of her first week, he couldn't resist asking.

'Have you found somewhere congenial to have lunch? This is a nice area but not exactly packed with green spaces.'

She actually blushed. 'I go and sit by the fountain.'

He was puzzled. 'I didn't know there was one.'

'In the Formby Centre.'

'Oh yes!' He nodded. The Formby was the local shopping mall, about a quarter of a mile away. 'Good idea.'

He wasn't well acquainted with the Formby, but he retained an impression of the central plaza (as it was grandiosely known) as a meeting place for booze-ravaged down-and-outs and those underage hangers-on in training for the job. The knowledge that Gina King took her lunch there redeemed it somewhat in his eyes, and the following Monday when he needed to draw some cash, he found himself heading for the building society hole in the wall in the Centre rather than the slightly closer one at his own bank branch.

On his way in as he crossed the plaza, Gina was nowhere to be seen. There were two rheumy-eyed chaps with fiery complexions sitting on the ground, their backs against the wall that surrounded the fountain, and a fat girl singing a cappella – 'The water is wide' – with a mongrel lying on a greasy anorak at her feet. A spotless elderly couple sat on a nearby bench consulting a map of the town. In spite of her unpromising appearance, the girl had a nice voice, true and resonant, and he dropped a pound coin on to the anorak, which she did not acknowledge.

On his way back from the cashpoint he saw that the girl had joined the two tramps on the ground and they were sharing a bottle of cider. The dog on the anorak had its eyes rolled soulfully their way, as if hoping for a drop. So the singing had just been a ploy. David hoped he hadn't unwittingly and with the best of intentions added to society's problems, then reprimanded himself for his pedantry – he'd put his money down because he liked the song, its use was nothing to do with him. The neat couple had gone, leaving the seat empty. It was only as he walked on that he spotted Gina King from the corner of his eye: she was perched on the wall on the far side of the fountain, eating from a bag of crisps, the tupperware box open on the wall next to her.

He must have looked for just a second too long, because that sixth sense made her turn and see him. He called 'Hello there!' self-consciously and she gave him a childish wave, arm raised, hand wagging back and forth sideways from the wrist. Blushing again, unless he was much mistaken.

He had to see clients at their property in the afternoon, but when he got back he said breezily: 'You're right, it's quite a good spot by the fountain there.'

'I like it.'

'You can watch the world go by.'

'That's right.'

By the end of that week, things were beginning to go wrong. Gina's inadequacies were beginning to catch up with her. The polite, respectful manner, it seemed, was a kind of camouflage to disguise her lack of savoir-faire. A couple of important messages got scrambled, another failed completely to get through, a potentially valuable deal was put in doubt. It was clear she'd been to great lengths to cover up her mistakes, and in doing so had compounded the difficulties. It upset David to think of her secretly suffering in the outer office, getting in a muddle and not asking for help. For a while he colluded in her efforts at concealment, pretending he hadn't noticed, slipping her hints and giving her the chance to correct what had gone wrong. But one by one the chickens came home to roost, and once Doug cottoned on there was no escape.

This time he wan't joking. 'She's a nice enough girl, David, but she can't cut the mustard.'

'It's early days.'

'Damn right and she's made enough cock-ups to last years.' He was in David's office, and the door was closed, but here he lowered his voice significantly. 'Joking apart David, you've had your bit of whimsy, it's time to recall one of the harpies off the shortlist.'

David demurred. He disliked Doug in this thrusting, company-comes-first mode, he wouldn't allow himself to be tainted by association.

'I haven't even had a talk with her yet, I've been standing back and giving her a chance to sort things out.'

'Well don't stand back any longer or we'll go down with all hands!'

'That's a slight exaggeration.'

'You think?' Doug gave him a bellicose glare. 'Look, who cares? The job market is awash with smart cookies dying to better themselves, give me one good reason why B and C should run some kind of charitable institution for misfits.'

David had begun to sweat slightly with an uncomfortable mixture of anxiety and anger.

'We've always tried to run this company on traditional, principled lines. I'd like to talk to Gina before we simply discard her.'

'It's up to you,' said Doug. He went to the door and opened it wide, so that David could actually see Gina sitting at her PC, the unwitting victim of their deliberations. 'But a word to the wise – don't be too long about it.'

That evening he'd asked Annet for her opinion. It had only been ten days ago, she was massively pregnant, in her last week at the office. But just as cooking was more his bag than hers (though they pretended otherwise), so the trials, triumphs and tribulations of the workplace were her province. She was more savvy, more *au fait*, metropolitan to his provincial, a go-getter to his wait-and-see-er.

She listened to him with unblinking, plain-faced attention, a person consciously closing herself off from his underlying agenda of persuasion and entreaty. When he'd finished she picked up her drink and said:

'Well, darl, you won't be surprised to learn that I'm with Doug on this one.'

'What, boot her out, just like that?'

'No point in prolonging the agony.'

'But a lot of people are thrown off their stroke in their first weeks in a new job.'

'Some do, but the good ones are proactive in looking for solutions. She should have come to you, apologised, asked your advice, showed an immediate and significant improvement – a steep learning curve. From all you've told me this girl's bumping along the bottom.'

David sighed heavily. He'd got exactly what he asked for – his wife's unbiased opinion, and if it wasn't what he wanted to hear he had only himself to blame.

'Oh, darl, I'm sorry ...' Her tone was contrite, she got up and came to sit on the arm of his chair, her arm round his neck, hand stroking his cheek. 'Hm? But you asked and I'm not going to flannel you. Cruel to be kind time.'

'I suppose so.' He caught her hand and kissed the palm. 'I'm sure you're right.'

'I think so.' She turned his face up to hers and they kissed.

He put his arms right round her and rested his face on her bulging stomach.

'I love you,' he told her.

She clasped his head and rocked him slightly. 'You have no idea how glad I am about that.'

He'd put it off a week, and then the baby's tumultuous arrival had enabled him to postpone it another few days. Gina had left a card on his desk – a big card with a picture of a pink bassinet pavilioned in lace and garlanded with roses. Inside was a not-too-cloying rhyme about the joy occasioned by a baby girl, and Gina's own message in loopy, forward-leaning writing:

'To Mr and Mrs Keating, many congratulations on your new baby, with love from Gina K. xx'

Shell-shocked as he was, he could still see that the two rather sweet childish kisses on the end were not wholly appropriate. It was the first time he'd been able to view what had to be done with any sort of equanimity. In the end he'd actually been able to use his impending paternity leave as a buffer.

'I shall miss you, Gina,' he said, more truthfully than she could know. 'But this is a sort of natural break for both of us, so perhaps that will make it easier.'

'Yes,' she said, with heart-rending docility, adding for good measure: 'And I'm really sorry I messed things up.'

'Not at all, nothing serious, no harm done, but I'm quite sure you'll find something more suited to you.'

'I do hope you find someone more suited as well.'

'We'll see.' He tried to make it sound as though that would be hard, if not well nigh impossible. It was then that he got up from his desk and went over to open the door for her, touching her upper arm briefly and gently as he did so. It was a gesture of reassurance and comfort, for himself as much as for her, but he was aware even as he made it that in the present climate men in his position had been dragged through the courts for less. The only reason he felt safe in venturing it now was because the poor girl was going anyway. After she'd left the room he developed a tremendous headache.

Just before he'd left to collect Annet from the hospital, Doug slapped him on the shoulder.

'Cheer up, you can get off home to the little family knowing you did the right thing.'

'I hope so.'

'Give my love to Annet, and enjoy the baby – they're not small and sweet for long.'

Bearing this in mind, David had slipped Gina's card into his briefcase as he left.

Sitting in bed in the half-light at – he turned his wrist and peered at the small green numerals – two a.m., it was hard to believe all this had only taken place less than twelve hours ago. If ever he'd needed proof that time was relative, the past week had provided it. Parts of it had been so momentous that in his memory they occupied huge chunks, while other periods of a day or more seemed to have slipped by almost unnoticed, time in parenthesis. Yesterday afternoon came under the former heading. Dismissing Gina King, which in reality had taken no more than half an hour, was a great expanse in his mind, with every detail clearly recalled. Conversely, the preceding couple of days were a blur, but the birth of his daughter stood out like a small lifetime, not necessarily for the right reasons. He'd found himself envying earlier generations of prospective fathers who had been banished by fierce midwives to pace the corridors with a supportive friend and a hip flask until such time as they were presented with their respectably swaddled offspring, when they could repair to the nearest telephone and spread the happy news . . . .

He'd been baffled by Annet's refusal of pain relief. She had written a characteristically lucid 'birth-plan' with numbered bullet points, declaring that she wanted analgesic only if it would assist the chances of survival of herself or the baby in a life-threatening situation. The whole exercise had seemed pretty life-threatening to David. He didn't like to see Annet, who was always so rational and in control, reduced to a heaving, pain-wracked, cursing delivery system. And then when it all got too much, and had gone on for too long, and she agreed to an epidural, he felt her humiliation and disappointment keenly.

'You're doing wonderfully, my darling,' he said, kissing her reddened cheek and smoothing her damp, sweat-smelling hair, but she wasn't to be comforted.

'It's not what I wanted . . . .'

'But it's for the best.'

'Only because I'm too old and too bloody feeble to go on under my own steam.'

'Nonsense, no one could have done more.'

She was always so determined to do things right, and in the most rigorous way. Sometimes he thought she would never know how much he loved and admired her, because she never believed she had quite come up to scratch by her own exacting standards. Her gallantry was among her most appealing qualities, but he knew what it was she feared: weakness, letting go, loss of control. This fear was what he'd captured in his drawing of her. Only in the very extremity of lovemaking did she lose herself for a moment and afterwards she was herself again in no time, speaking in a perfectly collected voice, of everyday matters. Because he adored her he would have liked more – or indeed any – whispering, inconsequential intimacy, but for the same reason he accepted that it was not to be.

In view of what she perceived as a failure in her performance at the birth, he knew it was doubly important for her to succeed – in her terms – now. He understood, anecdotally and from reading, that she might be rather wobbly for a few weeks, prone to tears and so on. That he was prepared for, and believed she was too. What he could not countenance was the thought of her despair if things actually went wrong – if the baby failed to thrive, or became ill, if she (or he) dropped her in the bath, if the nanny was a disaster, if she herself went into a clinical depression ... it didn't bear thinking about.

This train of thought brought him full circle. Another half an hour had passed and his arms were getting a bit stiff. He wondered if he dared risk putting the baby back in her basket. Annet was deeply asleep now, the only movement was the tremble of a strand of dark hair with each slow exhalation. Gently he moved the strand aside, and touched her cheek with his fingers. He felt held in a still, steady circle of love. It was a spell that he was loth to break by moving. When he did, he was swept by a tender melancholy, and kissed his daughter lightly on the forehead as he lowered her into the basket.

Stirred by new feelings and haunted by old ones it was another hour before he fell asleep. He put a careful arm round Annet and felt what had been a wife's and was now a mother's body – the soft slack of her stomach, the taut breasts encased in that infernal bra ... a feral dampness that had seeped through to the front of her nightdress ....

The curtained rectangle of the window was turning a dull grey and the birds were emitting their first tentative cheeps as his eyelids drooped.

Less than an hour later the baby woke up again. This time David could manage no response. He was dimly aware of Annet lurching out of bed, going to the basket and returning, and then of the sounds of sucking which meant it was OK to sleep. But the room was getting lighter and the heartless birds noisier, so that after a short interval the next outburst of crying was harder to ignore and he struggled dutifully, miserably, back into consciousness.

Annet wasn't in the bed, the crying was coming from the other room. He squinted at the clock and stifled a groan of anguish: it was five-fifteen. There followed a brief struggle with his conscience during which he told himself that Annet had slept soundly while he dealt with earlier crises. But conscience won and he shuffled over the landing.

Annet said without looking at him: 'Stupid of me, I should have done this first.'

'What difference would that have made?'

'She might just have drifted contentedly off. Now I'm having to disturb her.'

He nearly said that worked both ways, but stopped himself in time. 'Shall I make us a cup of tea?'

'What time is it . . . ? Jesus wept. I'd say coffee, but it's not a coffee time of day.'

'I'll make a pot.'

The crying continued at full strength and he hesitated. 'What's up, do you think?'

'God knows.' Annet completed the nappy and picked the baby up. 'I hope she's all right.'

He went over and touched the back of the baby's head, but had no reassurance to offer that would have carried weight with his wife.

For the next two hours they sat groggily in the kitchen, then in the drawing room, putting the baby down and picking her up again. Annet kept putting her to the breast with a desperate and exhausted air, as though stuffing a dummy in her mouth.

'Can she be – I mean, is there an inexhaustible supply?' he asked.

'They say the more you feed, the more there is.'

'Fair enough . . .' In that case, he wanted to ask, could he have a suck? But the likelihood of anything so sensuous seemed remote. As in the delivery room, biological imperatives ruled, the role of his wife's body had changed for the forseeable future and he would never have dreamed – or dared – of importuning it in full cry.

Tired unto death the two of them kept watch: a watch not so much of wondering love, as of confusion and anxiety.

At about seven, with the sun climbing, the milk on the doorstep, the *Independent* on the mat and the *Today* programme dishing out its customary stick to political spokespersons, they rallied. And their daughter, worn out, fell into a profound and peaceful sleep in her Moses basket.

With the bright morning, the sights and sounds of everyday life, the knowledge that the rest of the world was once more going about its business, a sense of normality returned. They even, as they ate toast in their night things, ran baths and took occasional wary peeps into the basket, experienced a holiday mood. This was enhanced by flowers arriving at the door. 'From Doug and all at B and C' read David off the card. 'Welcome home to all three, have a good week.'

'That's nice of them,' said Annet. She took the flowers and stood them in the sink. Following her bath she'd put on a pair of black trousers — normally evening wear but they had a drawstring waist — and a white shirt, with the sleeves rolled up. With her hair brushed and her make-up on she looked ready for anything, and David could no longer resist putting his arms round her, his hands resting on her bottom.

'Have I told you lately that I love you?'

'No, but I shan't hold it against you. There doesn't seem to have been much time for that sort of thing.' She placed her own hands on his cheeks and drew his face down for a kiss.

'Well anyway I do,' he said. 'More than ever.'

She pulled back to look at him. 'And why is that?'

He hesitated, wanting to give not just the right, but the truthful answer. But she misinterpreted his pause and added mockingly: 'Because now I'm a fully paid-up woman?'

'Your words, not mine.'

'Close though.' She gave his cheek a quick kiss as if saying that was that, but he held on to her.

'We've been through something together, something momentous. A rite of passage.'

'Correction darl,' said Annet. 'I went through it.'

Rebuffed, he let her go.

Just as they were now middle-aged parents who'd sworn they'd never start a family, so they'd been resolute elective singletons who'd confounded everyone by getting married.

David had been forty-two when he'd met Annet ten years ago, and she'd just turned thirty. Curiously, as it now seemed, it was he who'd been the veteran of several reasonably longstanding relationships, none of which had resulted in any domestic arrangement, while she at the time was living placidly with a man named Seth in Bayswater. But then again, he hadn't known about Seth to begin with, any more than she'd known he was on his own and out of work. These two conditions were not unconnected. Redundancy at his age had knocked him for six and left him winded, angry and demoralised. His lady friend at the time, a divorcée slightly older than him, had pretty soon tired of his depression and formed a jollier liaison with her tennis partner, leaving David plagued by self-doubt to face months of job applications and assiduous, time-filling self-improvement.

On the day in question he'd forced himself to put on a suit and cart into London to attend the national AGM of the only good cause he formally supported, a charity for the homeless. The state of dispossession, whether from country, beliefs, home or family, was one with which he found it surprisingly easy to identify, and he feared it. In his present situation, in spite of a mortgage paid off and a perfectly healthy bank balance, it seemed only a step away. He knew that at every city soup kitchen and among every cluster of cardboard boxes there was probably at least one man pretty much like him, well-spoken, well-educated, middle-class – alone. Situations such as his, occurring at what was anyway a tricky time of life, were profoundly unbalancing, and though he was very far from being unable to cope he needed the salutary reminder of what not coping in its most extreme form could lead to. But as well as these secret fears his unprecedented attendance at the AGM was informed by less complicated self-interest – it was something to do, and he might meet someone interesting. He had read that most romantic liaisons began in the workplace, and while that particular avenue was currently closed to him, this was the next best thing.

The meeting was held in a suite of rooms in a perfectly respectable middle-rank hotel off Gower Street. There were perhaps seventy people there. He wasn't actually seated next to Annet – there was an empty seat in between them occasioned by a no-show – but they exchanged a few pleasantly ironic asides during the rather dull first half, stood together in the queue for coffee and biscuits in the interval and introduced themselves. She was dark and intense, a little on the thin side, with good legs and a ramrod-straight back. In the meeting she'd paid close attention, but did not clap when everyone else did. His first impressions were that she might be either a journalist or perhaps a political animal of some sort. Strikingly attractive, not his usual sort. As they drank their coffee near a window (so that she could smoke) he offered, by way of trade, his own reasons for being there.

'I'm a patron of this charity, but to my shame I've never been to one of these before.'

'No shame in that.' She shrugged one shoulder. 'It's your money they're after.'

'Perfectly correct, but it's only sensible to acquaint oneself with where the money's going.'

'True.' She cast him a tough oblique look which he would soon recognise was typical of her. 'And are you any the wiser?'

He laughed. Even then he was acutely, almost embarrassingly, smitten. 'I shall be, when I've read the bumf.'

'Dream on,' was her comment.

'You're very cynical.'

She put her cup down on the windowsill. 'Yup.'

'May I ask why? I think we should be told.'

In answer she put another question. 'That bumf you place

so much faith in, all that glossy colour printing, how do you think it's funded?'

'Fair point, but surely there are bound to be running costs in any organisation ...?'

'If this lot were directors of a company you'd say they were creaming the profits.'

He smiled to show that what he was about to say wasn't personal: 'You seem to be making quite a serious allegation.' Another small shrug, but he determined not to let her off the hook. 'Do you know something the rest of us don't?'

'The company I represent have supported this outfit till now.'

'But you're thinking of withdrawing that support?'

Another cowboy look. 'We might be.'

He was amused by what seemed to him to be her *faux* poker face, and yet there seemed to be a real coolness there too – a learned behaviour on top of an inherent quality. She was like a bright, shiny stone, complete in itself.

'I can understand,' he said, 'why a company would want to feel that its donations were being well spent, but it would hardly seem worth my withdrawing my support of a few pounds a year given for highly idiosyncratic reasons. In fact it would seem unnecessarily grand. Unless of course we're talking fraud on a massive scale.'

He allowed this suggestion to hang in the air between them, for her to take hold of or ignore as she chose. She blew it away with her last mouthful of smoke, and stubbed out her cigarette in her saucer. 'No, no, no ... Just rank incompetence. No one'll be called to account for it except the poor bloody homeless.'

David could almost feel his wrist stinging, a sensation which he found nicely combined pleasure and pain. And it was at some point in this conversation that he essayed an 'Annette', thinking, because it was familiar, that that was what he had heard, and she broke in on his subsequent remark to correct him: 'No, it's *Annet* – like dammit.'

At the end of the AGM he asked her if she would join him

for a drink, but she declared, without hesitation or glancing at her watch, that she was afraid she couldn't. No excuse or reason was offered, but perhaps inspired by her example he was equally direct.

'Another time then? You could rattle a few more of my innocent assumptions.'

For the first time she'd laughed in a way that told him he'd got through.

'All right – end of the week after work?'

By the time he met her again he already suspected he was in love with her, but would have to play a canny waiting game if he were to stand any chance at all. He was reminded of the words of a song: 'The difficult I'll do right now, the impossible may take a little while . . . .'

There was Seth, for a start, whose presence he learned about in the wine bar where they shared a bottle, and the price, of a recherché red far more expensive than anything he'd have chosen himself.

Seth was introduced into the conversation simply as 'the person I share with', so he allowed his interpretation the latitude he felt it deserved. This was jolted slightly when Seth himself, a cord-trousered academic journalist in his twenties, arrived an hour later for what was obviously a prearranged supper date and was greeted with a kiss on the lips. David watched them go with a sinking heart, and had been hugely surprised and gratified to receive, a fortnight later, a scribbled invitation to another drink with Annet so that in her words she could say 'I told you so'.

Over this second meeting, which they rounded off with a Thai curry, he began to gain a correct perspective on Seth. Seth was Springboard Man. In fact it would not have been too much, or too unfair to say that Seth was one of Nature's Springboard Men. From everything Annet said it was clear that they had been together in a low-wattage kind of way for several years, during which time she had outstripped and outgrown him. Just the same, David couldn't help but feel a certain fraternal sympathy with Seth, and would not have presumed to move things on had

not Annet said casually but clearly, that she was in the process
of looking for a flat to buy on her own.

Three months later when his whole life had changed and
they had bought the house in West Hampstead which preceded
the one in Newton Bury, she had told him in bed one night
that the decision to acquire the separate flat had been made as
she opened her mouth to speak.

It was the closest she ever came to saying she'd fallen in
love with him, and it was lucky it was night, because he wept.
Her head, dark and mysterious-smelling, was tucked beneath
his chin, so she never knew.

Chapter Three

They had a plan, of course, because Annet always did. They were to have a week at home together between the baby's arrival and David's return to work; and a few weeks later, when Annet went back, he would have a week looking after the baby on his own before the New Zealand nanny arrived.

While he agreed wholeheartedly with his wife's analysis that being a full-time father for a few days would provide not only useful experience but also a sound frame of reference by which to judge Lara the Kiwi (whom Annet had taken on unilaterally), David was more fearful about this undertaking than he cared to let on.

He eventually moved to confide in Tim when he and Mags came up for the day on the Sunday after Annet got back. It wasn't something he'd wanted to do, being slightly fed up with Tim's been-there-done-that attitude to child-rearing, on the other hand they found themselves alone together in the kitchen after lunch, charged with stacking the dishwasher while the baby fed, and the opportunity presented itself.

'She's great,' Tim said generously. 'We'll let you keep that one.'

'Thanks. Yes, we think so.'

'Giving much gyp generally? I mean you can speak freely now.'

David added detergent and closed the door of the machine. 'A bit – I don't know. I don't have a yardstick.'

'Just as well.' Tim picked a bit off the cold chicken, stuffed it in his mouth and wiped his fingers on a tea towel. 'So when do you get her christened?'

'I don't know.' David hoped not to be pressed on this one, a mild bone of contention between him and Annet.

'More to the point, *what* will you get her christened?'

'We're not sure about that either. Annet's drawn up a short list.'

'Give us a clue.'

'We both quite like Freya ....'

'Different,' conceded Tim, 'without being embarrassing. Go for it.'

David pulled out a chair. 'Tim—'

'Yup!'

'Take a pew why don't you.'

'That can be arranged.' Tim swung the chair round and sat on it back to front, an attitude which for some nameless reason David found disheartening. 'What can I do for you?'

'Nothing in particular. It's just we don't often get an opportunity to talk like this.'

'Don't we? Like what?'

David suspected that if he wanted to hang on to any dignity at all he mustn't be drawn into the arena of what constituted Big Talk. Instead, he tried to make his question sound as if it sprang from simple man-to-man curiosity. 'I'd be fascinated to know just how confident you were with your first. With Josie.'

'With Jose? Christ, not at all, I was the original hapless, hopeless male. I wanted the whole thing to go away if you must know. If we could have had the film rewound so that she went straight back where she came from I'd have pressed the button myself.'

David was suddenly reminded of times when their mother had soothed a boyhood argument with the assertion 'You love each other *really* ...' Perhaps they really did. 'Yes, but Tim, were you able – to manage on your own?'

Tim frowned quizzically. 'Sorry, bro, you've lost me.'

David tried hard not to sound exasperated. 'Were you able to look after her on your own when occasion demanded?'

'I suppose so. Just about, when I had to, which wasn't often. It didn't involve much, if memory serves me. Mainly ongoing surveillance at that age.'

David considered the tenor of his domestic life over the past few days in the light of this observation. 'A bit more than that, surely.'

'Certain amount of disturbance, I grant you. Anyway, why? Is Annet planning to shove you into the front line so soon?'

'We agreed that I'd stay at home to look after the baby for a while when she started work again. Before and until the nanny arrives.'

'Sort of induction session.'

'No,' said David firmly, not to be sloppily traduced, '*this* is the induction session. That will be ops in the field.'

'Point taken. You'll be fine.'

'You think? I'm assured she'll be on the bottle by then.'

'She may not be the only one.' Tim snorted briefly. 'Sorry, someone had to say it.'

And it had be you, thought David.

'You'll be fine, bro,' said Tim again. 'It's all common sense. Just look at the people who do it and then ask yourself, how hard can it be?'

David didn't care to let on that he'd hoped Tim would answer this question in full; nor that the contemplation of other more disadvantaged but perfectly successful parents only increased his sense of inadequacy. He did however take some comfort from what had passed between them, especially his brother's generous admission of his own incompetence with Josie. At least something of value had happened between the two of them. He just hoped that Tim would see it in the same light, and treat the exchange with the discretion and gentleness it deserved. He could almost hear Tim saying jovially to Mags before they'd even hit the main road, 'Poor old David, he's going to be on solo fathering fatigues and he's scared shitless ....'

Perhaps it was this that made him say boldly, as they rejoined their wives.

'Right, we've been talking and we think she should be called Freya.'

'OK,' said Annet. 'Suits me.'

There was no doubt in anyone's mind that Mags was one of the kindest women imaginable, a good sort who would give you the shirt off her back and the food off her plate if need be, but this did not alter the fact that she was a *summa cum laude* graduate in getting up noses.

Generally speaking Annet could afford to be tolerant, since she reasoned that Mags had the sort of life that she would pay a king's ransom to avoid. But today, with the roles temporarily reversed, there was no hiding place. With the men loading the washing machine, and the baby latched on as though this feed were her last, there was no option but to grit her teeth and take her medicine like a man.

'How are you finding the breastfeeding?' asked Mags.

'She seems to be getting something.'

'Oh, *definitely*,' agreed Mags. 'Regained her birthweight?'

'So I understand,' said Annet.

'The midwife's been round, I take it ...?' Mags smiled brightly to show that this was a purely casual enquiry and nothing to do with checking things were being done properly. 'With her infernal machine?'

'Yes. Twice.'

'One sort of resents it, but it's also a comfort, don't you think?'

Annet shrugged. 'I don't resent it. They're the experts.'

'Now *there* I beg to differ.' Mags bridled. 'You're the expert on your own baby – never forget that.'

'I'll try.'

'There's so much advice about these days, so much so-called expert opinion on what ought to be perfectly natural common-sense things, we're in danger of losing our instincts.'

'I think,' said Annet, 'that instinct is overrated.'

'Ah! There speaks the modern woman.'

Annet felt her blood beginning to heat rapidly. 'I certainly hope so.'

'No, I mean we're all modern women, but that is a very typical modern anxiety.'

'It's not an anxiety, it's a fact. If we were all dependent on some atavistic, earth-mother set of instincts we'd still be out hunting in packs while the alpha male lounged under a tree.'

She realised at once that she'd played into Mags's hands. 'Annet – have you been to Tesco's on a Friday?'

Fortunately for Mags's health and the baby's digestion the men walked in at this point, and David said:

'Right, we've been talking and we think she should be called Freya.'

Out of relief, she agreed.

A walk was decided upon and they loaded Freya into her backpack, and the backpack on to David. It was the first time they'd used this particular piece of equipment and Mags commented quietly that it was not what she'd have chosen.

'And why's that?' asked Annet, who was standing behind David struggling with the fastenings. She spoke in a tone intended to repulse a detailed answer.

'Need you ask?' Mags smiled ruefully. 'Too complicated.'

'It's not actually,' said David over his shoulder. 'We're just a bit new to it, like everything else.'

'This is but the test drive,' agreed Tim. 'Can I help?'

David was glad he couldn't see Annet's face at this point, but equally glad when Tim's intervention proved successful.

They set off on the easiest of the bridleways that led out of the village, on to the gentle billow of the arable land to the south.

It was one of those fine, wind-blown late summer afternoons with high cloud and a long view and the merest teasing hint of autumn in the air. Most of the fields had been harvested but not yet ploughed, so what with that and the set-aside they were soon able to leave the bridleway and take a less-used footpath that afforded a good view of the church spire, sheltered housing, Grade II listed buildings, sympathetic council development and assorted roofs and aerials of Newton Bury.

'It's nice round here,' declared Mags indulgently, perhaps aware of having pushed her luck earlier. 'Not as picturesque as our part of the world, but much less occupied. More real, in a way.'

'Being dastardly commuters I'm not sure we're qualified to comment,' said David, 'but we like it.'

'I don't see Annet rearing marrows and making featherlight sponges for the annual show!' agreed Tim jovially, placing as he did so a pally — and David thought somewhat ill-judged — hand on Annet's shoulder. But as with the business of the name, she seemed too distracted, or more likely too bone-tired to brush him off, and replied instead:

'Er — no. But I did go along to that palsied parish meeting and kick up a bit of a stink about the parking near the shop.'

Tim raised an eyebrow at David, who confirmed: 'She did.'

'Poor sods.'

'To good effect?' asked Mags.

Annet pulled a wry face. 'My comments were noted.'

'I bet they bloody were,' said Tim. 'Which way, chief?'

They'd reached the top of a rise and were confronted with a variety of choices.

'We've got a short circuit, a long circuit, or a straight out and back,' replied David. 'Short circuit's about a mile, long one's about two and a half, the out-and-back is however long you want to make it.'

'Out and back thanks,' said Mags, 'then I can turn for home when it suits me and the rest of you can strike out for the horizon.'

'Please,' said Annet, 'forget it. I shan't be doing any striking out.'

'That's decided then.' Tim made a grand pointing gesture. 'Wagons roll!'

They set out along the chalky cart track and fell into twos, the men at a slightly quicker pace in front, the women bringing up the rear. Far to their left a combine harvester churned through a few remaining acres of wheat in a nimbus of greyish dust and chaff. It was far enough away not to be heard, but every so often when the fluttering wind dropped for a second they caught the distant growl of its engine.

'So,' said Mags, approaching her favourite subject from a different angle. 'David seems every inch the proud father.'

Annet grappled with this. 'Does he?'

'It's really lovely to see – I'd say at his age, but it's not as if he's that much older than the rest of us—'

'But old to be a first-time father,' supplied Annet, 'yup?'

'Yes. Sweet,' added Mags with an appropriate *moue*.

'And I'm a bit of an elderly party in those terms as well.'

'Well, I don't know, women have so many more options now, and more and more of them seem to be waiting until they've done whatever it is they want to do with their lives before starting a family.'

Annet humphed. 'Is that what you think I've done? Achieved my career goals and moved on to the next thing?'

'That's not quite how I'd have phrased it.'

'Well, however you want to say it that's not how it was.'

'You're not saying—' Mags's face was a study in contained anticipation – 'you're surely not saying the baby was unplanned?'

'No, rather the reverse – she was a long time coming.'

'Oh, I *see* . . . ! And just when you thought it was safe to – yes, I get you.'

Annet thought grimly that the day Mags got her was the day she'd pack it in. She'd never taken the view that relatives had some special right to affection and this was even more true of those belonging to her husband. She'd married David, and David only. She could appreciate that the baby's arrival had occasioned a small fraternal rite of passage between David and Tim, but she resisted the idea that a similar sisters-under-the-skin thing should take place between herself and Mags. Who was now, right on cue, enquiring about what she called 'the nanny situation'.

'I suppose you won't really know till she's started and you've seen her in action? I mean obviously not actually seen her, because by definition you won't be there, but seen how she gets on.'

'Obviously.' Annet allowed herself a withering put-down on the assumption that Mags would interpret it as an echo of her own remark, and the assumption proved a safe one.

'Who was she working for before?'

'An American family in London. They gave her glowing references. But she's a country girl at heart I gather and wanted to move out. Not to us, I hasten to add, she's renting a maisonette in town.'

'I gather,' said Mags, 'that the strapping Antipodean lass has taken over from the English rose as the must-have nanny.'

'Really? I wouldn't know.'

'I suppose they're more flexible, more sort of user-friendly . . . ? After all who wants some uniformed virago telling you what you may or may not do with your own baby?'

'Quite.'

'What does she look like? I'm eaten up with curiosity.'

Annet had a shrewd suspicion where this line of enquiry was heading and answered accordingly. 'She's tall and attractive.'

'Heavens!' Mags giggled in a way that conveyed both dismay and delight. 'Is that good or bad?'

'Good for her, I imagine Mags. Not that she's likely to have that vibrant a social life in King's Newton, but she'll certainly set a few bucolic pulses racing round at the Anvil when she takes Freya in for a jar.'

'Goodness . . . What exactly *will* she do with her time off?'

'Go up to town. She's got a Metro, on us. And there's a perfectly good commuter line if she intends getting ratted. Provided she turns up on time and isn't a pathological clock-watcher her social life is not my concern.'

'Still, it's a bit different to living in London.'

Annet felt her jaw tighten with the effort of remaining polite. She was glad to see that the men had stopped and were standing and talking to let them catch up. 'Of course, but she didn't have to take the job. It's a seller's market in the nanny trade these days, they decide whether they like the look of you just as much as the other way round.'

'It makes my blood run cold ... What does David think of her?'

Annet permitted herself a note of exasperation. 'He took her for a deceitful, child-hating, alcoholic sociopath, of course, that's why we snapped her up.'

Mags slapped her own wrist. 'Sorry!'

Annet did not tell her it was all right. They caught up with the men. Freya's eyes were now open and her face had lost the porcelain pallor of sleep.

'How you doing, girls?' asked Tim.

'Fine,' replied Annet.

David put out his hand towards his wife but she had moved out of reach. 'Do you want to go on for a bit?'

'Why not. As far as the line of trees.' A row of well-spaced poplars, listing with the prevailing wind, marched across the fields about half a mile away.

In a spontaneous act of self-regulation they regrouped, with Tim and Annet now walking briskly in front, David and Mags bringing up the rear. David liked Mags but realised that in this context she represented the short straw. He sensed that Annet had escaped and that it might be up to him to do a little making good.

'How's she looking?' he asked, jerking a thumb over his shoulder towards Freya.

Mags peered. 'Very bright and beady.'

'Not winding up for a paddy?'

'No, she just seems to be taking it all in.'

'Good,' he said, with feeling.

'She's an alert little thing, isn't she?'

'She must take after her mother.'

'Now don't undersell yourself,' said Mags, patting his arm – she had a soft spot for David. 'How are things at work, by the way?'

'A little fraught, when I last looked. Hiring and firing is not something I enjoy. I had enough of that with my last outfit.'

'You're too nice,' declared Mags. 'You take everything too personally.'

'It's how the other person takes it that bothers me.'

'That's what I mean.'

'Anyway . . .' he tried to dismiss that and change tack, 'much as I dislike the idea of going back it'll be a relief to be sorting out the problems myself. Empty desk syndrome, you know . . . .'

'Let's be honest—' Mags made a gosh-better-keep-our-voices-down face – 'you'll be glad to go back for a rest!'

He acknowledged there was some truth in this.

'Give Tim a couple of days in sole charge of hearth, home and offspring and he's a gibbering wreck.'

'Yes, I shall never again underestimate the hard work involved in that. Even with one small baby there doesn't seem a lot of time or space to spare. But it has been nice. Being together – I mean Annet and me – has been a rare treat.'

Mags looked a shade crestfallen. 'Yes, I can imagine, you both work so hard.'

They trudged for a bit in silence. As the village came back into view Annet turned and cupped her hands round her mouth.

'We're going round by the church!'

He nodded and raised an arm in acknowledgement, then asked Mags: 'Are you happy to do that? The church is rather fun actually.'

'Is it miles out of our way?'

'A few hundred yards.'

'And fun you say – go on, you talked me into it.'

Neither David nor Annet were regular churchgoers, and Annet refused even to write the despised 'C of E' on forms, preferring a dismissive dash or an assertive 'None', depending on her mood. But All Saints was acknowledged by even the ungodly as the jewel in the crown of Newton Bury, and David had been known to slip in at the back of evensong from time to time for what he thought of as broadly cultural reasons. He liked entering beneath the jerky tumble of bells, rung by a keen team of peripatetic campanologists, and once in he was profoundly susceptible to the stillness of stones which had stood on this chalky soil for five centuries. He liked the message of continuity in the repetition of local names in the plaques and memorials around the walls, particularly Fox-Herbert, that of the local landowners. The Fox-Herberts had presided over Newton Bury, more or less benignly, since the Reformation, and many of the beauties of All Saints – the elaborately carved pulpit and priest's stall, and the stained glass in the west window for example, bore testament to centuries of discriminating pillage on the other side of the channel. Added to which the present incumbent, Maurice Martin, was a likable, literate man, a dramatomane since his Cambridge days and someone who with his garrulous wife Della was a fully paid-up member of the local social scene. Annet – stern as only a non-believer could afford to be – took a drolly censorious view of their preparedness to break bread with sinners, but had never yet refused an invitation.

She and Tim were already inside when he and Mags got there. The door at the far end of the porch stood half open, and all beyond was darkness, though David knew that once they'd entered it would not seem dark at all. He held the door for Mags. Freya was beginning to make the small sounds, no more than vibrations really that he felt through his back, that would become fretting. The font, huge and rough-hewn on its white-washed pedestal, greeted them. For the first time since some prep-school sermon David remembered the significance of the font being near the door: the beginning of life's journey. From there one went (though less frequently these days) up the aisle to the chancel steps to be married; and from there back into the churchyard for burial. For what he recognised as fanciful personal reasons he would have liked his daughter to be christened in this old, wise watchful place – but not enough to have a fight with his wife about it.

Mags had gone to join the other two who were standing at the top of the south aisle near the lady chapel. Annet was pointing upwards, telling them about the bats which flitted and swooped inside on summer evenings. The empty building made her already resonant husky voice reverberate, and when Tim laughed the sharp sound seemed to shoot up and bang back and forth between the roof-beams of the nave.

David went to the table near the north porch where the Book of Remembrance lay open in its glass case. The last entry in the immaculate black calligraphy of the church warden was that of someone called Robert Tertius Townsend who had died only a week earlier, aged (David quickly calculated) only sixty-two. So the church had seen a funeral only recently, and somewhere in the village a family was bereft. Or it would be comforting, in a perverse way, to think so. He hoped it hadn't been one of those bleak, unattended rites of a poor chap who had died alone and uncared for. Because even in a small rural community like Newton Bury where such things weren't supposed to happen, they occasionally did. And there was something doubly chilling in a death going undetected for several days in a supposedly neighbourly environment. For the same reasons that David had supported the charity for the homeless he feared the indifference evidenced by such brutal oversights. How terrible to be known, or at least recognised, and yet so friendless that one could die and not make a jot of difference in anyone's life ... A contingency that was in sharp and ironic contrast to the bats, both in the church and elsewhere, which were now fiercely protected and even a lively topic at local dinner parties among householders whose lofts had become bat-friendly and conversion-averse.

Freya's small grunts had become more vocal, she would soon be crying. Annet was treating her listeners to a caustic summary of the Fox-Herberts' historic pilfering. She was one of those atheists with a kind of scornful but consuming interest in the more disobliging aspects of the church, and was pretty much of a walking guide book on All Saints. Not wanting to disrupt her set piece he wandered back in the direction of the north porch. It occurred to him that a lonely death such as the one he'd been contemplating would probably not have occasioned a copperplate mention in the Book of Remembrance. Perhaps there would be a freshly-turned grave and fond flowers in the churchyard to confirm a happy ending.

There was a good break in the cloud, and the bright sunlight, along with the breeze, seemed to have a soothing effect on Freya. It was funny, he thought, how quickly a name became an integral part of its bearer. It was only a couple of hours since they'd made their decision, and yet now he could not have contemplated changing it. Freya was no mere appellation, it was who she was.

As they strolled round towards the eastern buttress of All Saints, the names on the grave stones reinforced this view. Thomas Butcher ... Ellen Hargreave and Samuel Hargreave, devoted husband of Ellen ... Edward Mason, aged six weeks, Reclaimed by God ... Louisa Chaffey, beloved wife of John, taken in childbirth ... a whole rake of solid, prosperous Beechams, but only one Fox-Herbert (admittedly housed in a huge Victorian tomb flanked by appropriately chinless angels), the majority being commemorated in comfort inside the church. But almost all, David reflected, so long gone that they lived on in name only. He found the graves not morbid but companionable, standing in quiet testament to those whose names they bore.

As they came round to the north side of the church they were out of the wind. In the sudden stillness it was quite hot, with the sun beating off the walls and glittering on the diamond-paned windows. David saw, with a little thrill of recognition, the new grave with its shining headstone and garlands – he thought of them as garlands, though of course they were wreaths – of colourful flowers. He went over to it.

Close to, you could see the flowers had been there for two or three days – many of the petals had curling brown edges and the oasis, visible between the stems, was beginning to take on a pale and crumbly appearance. But the cards on their little plastic forks, were not yet faded. 'To my darling Robert, I'll see you in Heaven, yours for ever, Mary'; 'Dearest Dad, rest in peace at last, all our love, Mandy and Sue'; 'Dear Granddad, miss you loads, Jessica and Justin'; 'To Bob, with grateful thanks and fond memories from all at the Cricket Club'; 'To RT, with many happy memories, from your friends and colleagues at Micasol'; 'To dear Mr Townsend from Pam' ... And there were more. So, far from being lonely, it appeared Robert Townsend had been blessed with a rich life full of love, friendship, rewarding work and fruitful leisure. David felt quite put in his place by the abundance and breadth of the wellwishing.

As he turned to continue his circuit of the church he caught sight of a woman sitting on a bench beneath one of the chestnut trees which stood between the north of the churchyard and the field beyond. The trees had their roots in the field, and the woman shared their shade with a couple of somnolent horses standing end to end on the other side of the fence, their tails switching. David couldn't make out much about her – she wore a print dress of no fixed fashion, and a floppy-brimmed cotton sunhat, but from her attitude – hands clasped on lap, head slightly averted – he formed the impression she was waiting for something.

Of course, he thought, his cheeks suddenly hot with embarrassment, she'd come to be at the graveside. This might be Mary – or Mandy, or Sue, or Pam, or any one of dozens of others with a right to visit Robert Townsend's last resting place, and she was waiting politely for him, a mere idle gawper, to get out of the way.

He quickened his pace, but as he went round the end of the building he stole a last look, and she was still sitting there, in the same position, in half-profile, her face shielded by the brim of her hat.

The minute he rounded the corner it was as though the peaceful, sunlit interlude on the other side of the church had happened in another dimension. Here it was cooler, and there was a breeze, and a long, deep shadow shot out from the church tower, making him shiver, and there were the others walking towards him, pointing and exclaiming – where had he been? they'd been looking for him! And Freya, startled, began to cry. Against this background Mags commented enthusiastically on the beauties and historic features of All Saints – 'It's enough to make you want to join the faithful!'

'You speak for yourself,' said Tim.

'Here, I'll take her.' Annet went behind him and freed Freya from the papoose. He slipped the straps off his shoulders, but she said, 'It's OK, it's not far, I'll carry her.' So he dangled it in one hand. Tim, for some reason, strode ahead and stood beneath the lychgate with his hands in his pockets, staring into the road. Mags walked alongside Annet, clucking over the baby. David brought up the rear, the papoose bumping against his leg.

As he walked down the path towards the gate he glanced over his shoulder. He could see Robert Townsend's colourful grave, and another couple of paces revealed the seat beneath the tree as well – but the woman had gone. He found himself hoping that their intrusive presence hadn't driven her away.

Against a background of Freya's bawling, Tim became suddenly restless, worried about roads, and having time to 'get his head together' before work the next day. When Mags demurred about leaving earlier than intended he became tetchy.

'Mags, I'm sure these people have had quite enough of us.'

'Not at all,' said David stoutly. 'A cup of tea, surely . . . .'

'Yes, *surely*,' echoed Mags.

'A quick cup, then—' he glanced at his watch – 'time marches on.'

'Don't worry chum,' said Annet, filling the kettle one-handed. 'we want you out as well. And this isn't a cake-on-the-go sort of household, though we might rise to a chocolate suggestive, take a look darl, would you?'

'I'll see to this,' David told her. 'You go and do whatever needs to be done.'

Annet retreated to the sofa and the yelling ceased. Mags went into the hall to phone home and give, as she put it, 'an ETA in case the mice are playing'. Once again David found himself in the kitchen with his brother.

'Sorry to rush things,' said Tim.

'Not at all, I'd do exactly the same in your shoes.'

'You're a pal.' He addressed Mags as she returned from the phone. 'How are things back on the ranch?'

'No reply, the machine was on. I left a threatening message.' She patted David's hand as he picked up the tray. 'You've got all this to come.'

He caught Annet's eye as he entered the drawing room, and was sure she'd heard this last remark, and equally sure that they were both grimly calculating how old they would be when 'all this' happened.

Freya, disturbed, Mags suggested, by all the untoward goings-on, continued to cry after her feed, and showed not the least interest in either eating any more or going to sleep. David was beginning to recognise this as the low point of the day – this queasy shift from late afternoon into early evening. Just at the time when in the old days (he tried not to think of them as 'good') he and Annet would be leaving work, travelling home in pleasant anticipation of a stiff drink and supper together, the pressure was winched up. Freya was too little, as Annet's mother kept telling them, to be into a proper routine, and anyway demand feeding militated against it. Besides, she added, six p.m. was when babies traditionally played up. This mystified and apalled David, with its implication that there was some dark, biological conspiracy among infants the world over. What hope was there if babies were immutably pre-programmed to make life hell between certain hours? He could almost have wished back Mags and Tim with their comfortable, comforting child-weariness to make it all seem less sinister.

Mags gave a little sighing laugh and shook her head. 'The poor things. I do feel for them at their ages. Particularly David. It can't be easy.'

'They're doing OK,' Tim said flatly. His thoughts were turning fondly towards the office and real life.

'Of course they are, I never meant to imply ... But you must admit they do look exhausted.'

'Well – remember what we were like? I kept falling asleep in meetings.'

'Yes ...' Mags laughed again, silently, but bouncing her shoulders up and down which Tim found dire. 'Poor old David ...!'

Tim shot her a cold look which she didn't see. So she fancied David – so what? There were at least half a dozen women he saw every day about whom he fantasised, and of those at least three would not have thrown him out. His wife's elephantine coyness annoyed the hell out of him.

'Don't you worry about David,' he said. 'He'll live.'

Between six and nine David and Annet passed the baton back and forth. He cleared up while Annet fed Freya. He bathed the baby while she threw stuff in the washing machine. Bathing, though he had done it before, terrified him – his arm and wrist were throbbing with the effort of supporting his small, slippery daughter in the correct way, and when he'd finished the tension in his back took several minutes to unlock. Aching all over, he looked on as Annet fiddled about with their daughter's vest and nightie and wondered exhaustedly why the designers of such garments thought so highly of minute ribbons.

'You'd have thought they could have come up with something better.'

'Sorry?'

'Other than those fiddly ribbons. For doing up baby clothes.'

'Such as?' She raised her voice pointedly over Freya's yells.

'I don't know ... Buttons? Poppers? Velcro?'

'Beastly uncomfortable, darl – think of having a button sticking into you if you couldn't move. And velcro's horrible bristly stuff. Tapes are baby-friendly.'

'I suppose so.' He decided this was not the moment to suggest that parent-friendliness was also desirable.

'Anyway.' Annet wrapped Freya in her yellow shawl, picked her up and held her out unceremoniously for him to take. 'All done.'

It wasn't, not by a long chalk. The screeching continued for the best part of another two hours, ceasing only during those periods when Annet fed her daughter with an increasing air of desperation, muttering, 'I hope to God they're right about demand dictating supply.' As soon as each feed was over it seemed only to have added to Freya's agitation. During one of them David lit a fire in the drawing room. It was far too early in the year for one, really, but the evening had turned chilly, and besides he saw the cheery flames as a promise of comfort and relaxation to come. But as soon as the nipple popped out of her mouth Freya started up again.

'*Integris viribus ...*' he murmured to himself.

'What?'

'Nothing.'

Annet tapped brisk, edgy fingers on Freya's back. 'You know darl, either I'm going deaf or you've started talking to yourself.'

'Sorry.'

'No, what did you say just then?'

'*Integris viribus*. It was forever cropping up in Caesar's Gallic wars. It means "with vigour unimpaired".'

Annet gave her dark grin. 'Who were they talking about – Caesar?'

'No, the poor bloody infantry. They were always sent back into the fray *integris viribus*—' he pointed – 'like that young lady.'

'And her poor bloody parents!'

It was another one of those borderline moments and he knew which way his wife would go unless he rescued her.

'Here's an idea,' he said. 'You go and run yourself a big hot bath. There isn't another thing you can do for her. I'll walk her around and catch some of the news. She might even fall asleep.'

'If you say so.'

He took the baby, knowing that Annet's snappishness was as close to weeping as she would allow in front of him. When she'd left the room he began walking up and down, up and down in front of the fire trying to impose some order and rhythm on the confined chaos of their lives. Freya's crying remained resolutely out of sync. His own pacing reminded him of a zoo animal's sad, mindless stereotyping, but having once begun he was afraid to stop because it might, just might, have an effect in the end. Even when the fire needed a log he managed the operation in easy stages. Two paces, bend the knees, take the log out, two more paces, turn. Two paces, bend the knees, put the log in place, two more paces ... He remembered reading in some magazine, back in the sixties, that this was how bunny girls were taught to serve drinks, to avoid over-presentation of breasts or buttocks. Some bunny – he laughed sniffingly to himself.

Incredibly it worked. Or perhaps inevitably – Freya would have fallen asleep anyway out of sheer exhaustion. In any event, David felt a warm surge of satisfaction as his daughter's head rolled gently against his collar bone as he continued to walk. With extreme care and delicacy he looked at his watch, and saw that nearly half an hour had passed.

Being careful to maintain the same pace he went upstairs. The bathroom door was open and the light still on. A steamy fragrance hung in the air of the landing. He switched off the light and walked across to the nursery. Annet had tidied it — it bore none of the traces of the evening's skirmishes — but she wasn't there.

He re-crossed the landing to their bedroom. He was satisfied with this, his second small triumph and wanted Annet to share in it.

But she was spark out, on the bed. She wore her pale blue towelling bathrobe and a pair of white sports socks. Her hair was damp. She lay on her side with both arms stretched out in front of her, her nose between them, like a cat.

It was odd, after the bustle and stress of the day and the clamorous exchanges of the evening, to be standing here in the still, silent house, awake while his wife and daughter slept. He felt a pang of loneliness, but also of quiet pride: this was what it meant to be the head of a family.

He savoured the sensation for a moment and then carried Freya back to her bedroom and laid her with exquisite care in her Moses basket. The crucial moment, he knew, was when her face separated from the warmth of his neck — he could almost feel the cool emptiness himself. But she made only one involuntary bend and stretch, her face growing pink for a second, before she relapsed into deep sleep. He lifted the blanket from the foot of the basket and laid it lightly over her, tucking it down the sides of the thin mattress.

Going back downstairs he ran, as though sprung from a trap. He'd been worn out, drooping with fatigue, but not any more. He fetched himself a beer from the kitchen. In the drawing room the fire burned merrily, and he switched off the TV and put on some Bach, storming with energy and detail.

Conscious, almost guiltily, of being truly happy for the first time in days, he went to draw the curtains. The back garden was full of a windy, flickering darkness. Dry leaves skittered across the pool of spilled light beyond the window, and disappeared.

There were no visible stars, only a lurid peep of light between ragged clouds.

The drawing room ran from the front to the back of the house. The village was on the whole poorly lit, but on the corner opposite, its head bashfully half-hidden between the branches of a large chestnut, was a streetlamp. As David was about to draw the curtains he noticed a figure standing beneath the lamp. There was nothing remarkable in the figure except its stillness – the shadows of the branches streamed across it like waterweed over a stone.

Briskly, he closed the curtains.

Chapter Four

David had heard the phrase 'separation anxiety' – a smart new expression, he considered, for good old-fashioned homesickness – but not experienced it until that first morning he went back to work.

He was wrong, he discovered, it wasn't homesickness. It was a malady which began afflicting him before he'd left home, and evaporated once he'd gone. They both tried to make light of it, to treat it as though it were nothing more than a partial return to the status quo. But everything had changed and they both knew it. He'd not been aware of a new routine developing, but now it appeared that it must have done, because as he showered and shaved and put on shirt, tie and suit he felt himself the odd man out. The shock of the new had blended into custom without his noticing. It was he who was pulling away, doing something different, breaking stride. This was most apparent when he went to say goodbye to Annet. She was feeding the baby in the kitchen, with Radio Four in the background, the cafetiere on the table between his empty mug and her half-full one, and was wearing her dressing gown. Next to her soft, worn towelling, his suit made him feel stiff and armoured, though against what he was by no means sure.

'This is weird,' she said.

As she said this she didn't raise her head from contemplation of her task, so David bent his own awkwardly to place a kiss on her mouth, and to drop another on Freya's head. 'It is rather.'

'What am I going to do here all day on my own?'

'You're not on your own.'

'You know what I mean.'

'She's kept the two of us fairly busy so far.'

He had intended this to be consoling, to mean that Annet wouldn't be at a loose end, when that was what she hated most: as he pulled out into Gardener's Lane he realised it might have sounded like an awful, smug warning. On the other hand, he calculated, his wife was the most formidably capable person he knew, so it was hardly likely she would be overwhelmed by the responsibility of looking after a tiny baby.

It was still odd to be leaving her there. There was a passing-place on the single-lane road that climbed the hill out of Newton Bury towards the ridgeway, and he pulled over for a moment and looked down at the village. From this distance the place had a Tiggywinklish aspect, the rooftops tightly clustered and peeping between trees, the aerials and satellite works invisible. Although he couldn't make out Bay Court he could pinpoint its position, and tried, unsuccessfully, to picture Annet down there going about her maternal business. It was impossible. As he rejoined the road again he reflected that with all due respect to the dignity of motherhood, the stage it provided was simply too small for her. He was a traitor for going, and a bastard for feeling relieved.

He must have left a tad early, or driven a tad fast – whatever the reason, he beat the eager beavers to pole position in the car park, and was at his desk by eight-thirty.

The moment David had left, Annet was poleaxed by loneliness. She had never, since they moved out of London, confronted a day completely alone in the house, or at least not a day over whose direction she had no control. She knew that in theory she could do as she liked – she was demand feeding, she had a car, she had no one to answer to except herself – and yet she felt buried alive, abandoned. She cried.

She cried non-stop for about five minutes, and when she did stop it was not because she'd pulled herself together, but because she was all cried out. Throughout this humiliating episode Freya, sated, slept tranquilly in her arms. When the storm had passed, Annet put her in her basket and carried the basket upstairs to the baby room while she had a bath.

Gazing at herself stretched out in the water beneath an archipelago of bubbles she determined to get back in shape. You couldn't do it all at once, she realised that, the Canadian Airforce programme would have to wait, but first steps must be taken. She'd been given a leaflet before leaving hospital with a regime of 'mums' muscle-tighteners' that had made her lip curl with scorn, but once out of the bath and back in her dressing gown she dug out the leaflet and followed its instructions. Dismayingly, she found several of them quite difficult. particularly those pertaining to the pelvic floor. She was shaken by her apparent feebleness. Would these weakenings and loosenings be permanent? Would David no longer sigh with pleasure on entering her, and cry out in ecstasy at the end? Did motherhood signal the end of her as a sexual being? A reference to 'stress incontinence', especially prevalent it appeared in older mothers, caused her to go cold with apprehension. Was she then to wet herself every time she coughed, or laughed, or ran for a cab ...? The dismalness of these possibilities nearly started the tears again, but she fought them off by redoubling her efforts.

She was composed, dressed and wearing eyeliner when the arrival of Karen exactly coincided with Freya waking up.

'This is what I've been waiting for – may I come up and see?' called Karen, already halfway up the stairs.

'Be my guest.'

Annet went out on to the landing to meet her.

'Here she is. Karen, Freya. Freya, this is Karen.'

Karen's welcoming grin was almost as wide as her out-stretched arms, giving Freya up to her seemed the most natural thing in the world.

'Hello Freya, aren't you gorgeous, look at all your hair,

just like your mummy . . .' Annet watched a little wearily as Karen chirruped and fondled with practised ease. Karen, Mags, her mother, not to mention an entire monstrous regiment of friends and colleagues waiting in the wings, knew that here was an area where their own experience far exceeded hers, and they were going to make the most of it.

'Want a coffee before you start?' she asked, only slightly pointedly.

'Lovely . . . is there time?' Karen followed her down the stairs, still doting away. 'Ah, bless, she's so beautiful, what does your husband think?' In his absence David was always referred to in this way rather than as 'Mr Keating'. Annet had pulled just sufficient rank to remain 'Mrs Keating' on notes and messages, but this appellation was never used to her face.

'He's delighted. A little nervous, of course.' She was in all fairness about to concede that they both were, but Karen jumped in on this familiar territory.

'They are, aren't they?' she agreed, swaying comfortably from side to side while Annet put the kettle on. 'I remember Don, he used to hold Julie out in front like a tray, like this—' she demonstrated – 'but he got over it. You wait till you're on number three . . . only joking!'

Karen was a couple of years younger than Annet, though she didn't look it, and already a grandmother (courtesy of Julie), which she also didn't look. She was a cheerful, energetic, uncomplicated woman with good legs and a sound marriage to Don in spite of the mocking way she talked about him. She was a voracious reader of every kind of fiction from schlock romance to Booker hopefuls and had a Rita-ish propensity to put them all on the same level. Issues about comparing like with like did not concern her – it was enough for Karen that they were all books. Annet thoroughly approved of this attitude, and they'd had some lively discussions when Annet was at home packing reading matter for an overseas trip. Karen's all-time favourite was *Wuthering Heights*.

'So what are her other names, then?' asked Karen, as though Annet were deliberately withholding information.

'She hasn't got any at the moment.'

'Never mind, Freya's lovely — is that Scandiwegian?'

'Yes, I believe so. It's one of my husband's choices.'

'Goddess or something, right?'

'Probably.'

'Well,' said Karen, handing the baby back in order to take delivery of her coffee, 'you might as well aim high. Now then, where would you like me?'

There seemed to Annet that there was both too much to do and not enough. She supposed that this was what people meant when they talked of parenthood being tiring. She was moving more slowly and less frequently than she would have done, say, at the office, but her legs were heavy and her brain sluggish. There were far fewer demands being made on her time and energies, and yet the one that existed was absolute, so she was in a continuous state of low-level alert, quite different from her sharp, proactive work mode.

Listening to Karen bustling about, and staying out of her way, she wondered why she'd asked her to come back so soon — she should be doing the housework herself. Last week, wanting to be left in peace, she and David (mainly David) had seen to it. On the other hand, it was boring as hell, and in her present state she wouldn't have got round: Bay Court was a big house. Plus, and here she was guilty of the professional woman's self-interested manoeuvring, she didn't want to lose Karen, so it was probably better not to mess her about.

In spite of, or perhaps because of, the background domestic activity, Freya slept and slept. Annet put washing in the machine, answered some mail, and finally gave in and called Major Events in Bayswater.

'Hello!' exclaimed her junior colleague and court jester Piers, as if she were calling from some obscure foreign country (which in a sense, she thought grimly, she was). 'How's it going?'

'Fine. Well – different.'

'I bet!' Piers was the super-efficient scion of a lord lieutenant, with the amiable unsinkability and camp manner of one who had no need to work. 'Lady of leisure, is it?'

'I wouldn't say that. It takes a bit of getting used to, being the first resort.'

'God, I can imagine. Or rather, I can't. I do remember my mother saying the first one was utterly dire—' he pronounced it 'dah' – 'and she's not a woman given to exaggeration.'

'Freya's no trouble really—'

'Freya? Is that what you're calling her? That is just so fab!'

'We like it. Piers – what's the in-tray looking like?'

'Surprisingly OK. You are indispensable, of course, but it's still silly season so only the occasional letter is flooding in. The world of conferences and exhibitions is holding itself in readiness for the great autumn push. Or your return, whichever comes the sooner.'

'Just the same,' said Annet, 'I want to be kept in touch. Will you please make sure to call me if there's anything I could or should be handling.'

'Trust me.'

'In fact, Piers, perhaps you'd give me a ring every day where possible around this time, and touch base – let me know what's come in.'

'I will, but are you quite sure you wouldn't rather be left in peace?'

'I'll be more peaceful if I'm kept in touch. Trust me.'

'OK, whatever, oh God I wish I could see Freya, does she have hair?'

'Quite a lot, darkish.'

'Like you!'

'David's dark as well.'

'I suppose he is . . .' Piers spoke musingly. 'I can't wait any longer, I'm going to have to dash out to Baby Gap at lunchtime and buy something fetching.'

'Don't go mad,' said Annet, 'with your hard-earned bunce. Please.'

'It's not particularly hard-earned,' replied Piers unguardedly, adding as an afterthought, 'with you away. And I shall go as mad as I like. Are you having a christening?'

'No.'

'Why ever not?'

'None of your business.'

'Quite,' agreed Piers. 'And I've got too many godchildren already. Still it's a crying shame to pass up the party opportunity – all the more reason to buy the poor little mite a present.'

Border and Cheffins was the most upmarket property agents in the district, and its premises reflected its status. Not for Border and Cheffins any breezeblock business-park monstrosity, or high-street shopfront: their offices occupied a gracious Georgian house in an area too spacious and leafy to be called town centre, too smart and central to be a suburb. Secluded but within easy reach of amenities was how Doug Border would have put it. In the case of Border and Cheffins the garden had been left at the back – though the herbaceous borders had been replaced by low-maintenance shrubs – but levelled to create (currently redundant) car parking at the front. Other than this, and a discreet brass plaque in the porch, there was nothing to advertise that the house was now offices. Even functional blinds had been eschewed in favour of elegant and expensive curtains, the choice of Doug's wife Marsha.

Doug was grandson of the original Border, and ran the show. He had inherited a comfortable, established business and made it fabulously successful. David told himself that he did not, in the main, envy Doug his millions, but he did envy him his easy entrepreneurial flair, a flair which had skipped a generation after his grandfather Lionel, and returned in its fullest form in the grandson. Doug's father, Gordon, had been a plodding, consolidating presence; it was Lionel who had been the instigator and moderniser. Doug himself had the acumen to see that the way to a brilliant future was to emphasise the qualities of the past – hence the house, the curtains, the whole decor with its rose reds and cinnamon browns, its watercolours and old maps and trailing plants in jardinieres – its real fire in the hallway, forsooth, through the winter months. The term 'estate agent' was proscribed – Border and Cheffins had started life as a land agents and was now simply a land agent gracious enough to take on the *crème de la crème* of county property. As practice got if not sharper then at least more combative and profit-driven, so the ambience in which it was conducted became mellower and more gentlemanly.

David could see for himself how admirably all this worked. Border and Cheffins' clients, people who bought and sold property for monumental sums, were among the most hard-nosed imaginable, but liked to see themselves as toffs. And it was the genuine toffs who struck the hardest bargains. Though it was nominally his administrative skills for which David had been employed it was in his unassumingly patrician manner that his value to the company lay. He was without personal vanity where work was concerned, but he had gradually become aware that his was an emollient presence and made the clients feel that they were engaged in transactions that were gentlemanly rather than, as was in fact the case, dog-eat-dog. Only last year, when the rock star Chris Harper (a little past his sell-by date but still worth millions and coining in the royalties) had been bidding for a beautiful house with private fishing rights and a deer park, David had almost single-handedly smoothed the hackles of the local landowners, calmed and reassured the threadbare, aristocratic vendors and brought home the bacon and the sale at a price in excess of everyone's wildest dreams.

Doug had whooped, slapped his shoulder, popped champagne, dragged him and Annet out to dinner and declared to anyone who would listen that David was his main man, and if he only midwifed such a deal once a year it would take care of them all in the twilight of their years.

On the way home in a minicab afterwards Annet was sceptical about Doug and his enthusiasm. 'He's jolly enough, but he's a user. I'd watch your back if I were you.'

'I wasn't born yesterday,' had been his reply as he'd taken her happily, drunkenly, in his arms, but even through the euphoria he'd been able to hear the faint sound of a cock crowing. Because compared to his wife he had been born yesterday, if not later, and they both knew it. It flitted across his mind that she might be the tiniest bit jealous, and the last thing he ever wanted was to upstage her. That wasn't how it was with them.

He was less vulnerable than he appeared, she more, a fact tacitly acknowledged between them: the delicate balance of their relationship depended in large part on this tender collusion.

When he arrived this morning there was a temp in the outer office. She introduced herself as Jackie — a neat, plain, unflappable, young woman with a slightly censorious manner. He had only to think something and it was done.

'Good girl though,' said Doug in the gents' washroom at lunchtime. 'No nonsense. Might invite her to apply.'

'I shall reserve judgement.'

Doug chortled. 'Reserve it as long as you like old boy, after last time.'

'Yes.' David frowned. 'I felt bad about that.'

'Why? We're still standing.'

'No, about the girl. If she was employed beyond her capabilities that was my fault.'

'Forget it,' said Doug. 'I bet she has.'

Forgetting it was easier said than done. Jackie's terse competence was a constant reminder to David of how patently unsuited her predecessor had been to the job. To make matters worse there was a letter from Gina amongst the afternoon post: he recognised the round, carefully-formed handwriting. It had 'Personal' written across the corner of the envelope, so thankfully Jackie had not opened it, but placed it on the top of the pile.

He set it aside and left it till last. Even then he was too self-conscious to read it in the office and only took it out of his pocket when he'd reached the car park and was sitting behind the wheel. She really shouldn't be doing this, he told himself. He'd read it now it was here, but then it would be incumbent on him to choke off any further communications.

'Dear Mr Keating,' she said. 'I do hope you and the family (!) are well. I realised that you would probably be back in the office this week, and so am taking the liberty of dropping you this line to ask if you would be prepared to give me a reference. I realise this sounds a bit strange when your company let me go, but you were kind enough to wish me well, and I believe that the position I have applied for would be ideal.'

He imagined she must mean that she would be ideal for it.

'I am writing not ringing so as not to put you on the spot! but I would be so grateful if you could say yes. You can contact me by phone or letter at the above. Perhaps I should say that I have sent off my application today, so I need to have references ready just in case. The father of a friend who is a methodist minister has also agreed. As I hope you will, you were so understanding when I had to leave.

　　With very best wishes,
　　Yours sincerely,
　　Gina C. King.'

He read this several times before restoring it to his jacket pocket and starting up the car. What on earth, he wondered inconsequentially, did that pretentious middle initial stand for?

He found the tone of the letter as a whole hard to place. In spite of the apologies and the gratitude, there was something importunate that lingered in the mind after reading. Some would have said the letter's mere existence was an impertinence, but no, he didn't feel that, you could hardly blame the girl for trying, when he himself had made it so abundantly clear – and she had remembered – that he wished her well. He was in no doubt what his response should be. He should bin the letter and leave it at that: if she had any sense she would infer that no reply meant no dice.

Turning all this over in his mind he drove slowly, but without due care and attention. Approaching a T-junction on the edge of town he completely failed to see a cyclist coming from his right and turned out into the woman's path. Fortunately for them both he didn't hit her, but she wobbled dangerously, put one foot down to stop herself and dropped the bike so that it scraped her leg. Being a big woman and no longer young she then fell forward over the bike in an undignified way, her skirt hitched up and her backside in the air. To his chagrin, when he leapt out to help her she apologised to him.

'I'm so sorry, I wasn't looking.'

'Really, the fault was all mine.' With some difficulty, and aware of the excoriating disapproval of other road users, he took her weight as she righted herself and disengaged from the bicycle. 'Is your leg all right?'

Still clutching his arm she peered down at the sticky graze on her shin. 'Oh, it's only a scratch, I'm more bothered about my stupid old stockings.'

'Yes, what a shame.' He steered her with one hand, the bike with the other, on to the pavement, and leaned the bike against the street sign. 'You must at the very least let me get you some more.'

'Goodness, don't be silly ...' She was handsome in a downright, unadorned way, with sad, serious eyes. David thought how odd it was that when a woman of Annet's generation wore stockings it was generally a sexual signal, whereas in this woman's case her sturdy support hose were probably something she'd moved into without having passed through the intervening phase of tights.

'And what about your bike?' he asked hastily. 'Let's have a look.'

'It's fine, it'd take more than that I promise you. Built to last, like me.'

David was no expert but the bike did, to his relief, seem undamaged.

'May I give you a lift home – or to wherever you were going?'

'Absolutely not!' She shook her head and held up a hand to prevent further discussion. 'It was my own silly fault.'

'Well, I tell you what, let me have your name and address so I can get in touch.'

He saw what he was sure was her split-second conditioned response about not giving her name to strange men – and found it touching, both for its old-fashioned good sense and its implied girlishness. Instinctively he glanced at her left hand – no wedding ring.

'Just so I can check you're all right,' he added. 'For my own peace of mind.'

'Yes, of course.' Having for no particularly good reason decided to trust him, she gave him a six-figure number, of which the first three were common to all the numbers in the town, and the second three easily consigned to memory.

'Thank you.' He held out his hand. 'David Keating, by the way.'

'Jean Samms.'

'And again my apologies. That was exactly the sort of thing that gives car drivers a bad name amongst pedestrians and cyclists.'

She reclaimed the bike and he returned to his car, where he scribbled the number on the corner of an old car park ticket, and allowed her with a smiling gesture to cross the road in front of him. As he started the engine he saw her put her left foot on the pedal, scoot for a few yards, and get back in the saddle — a brave woman, considering.

Shaken by this mishap, and the knowledge of how much worse it might have been, he concentrated hard for the remainder of the journey home.

He usually arrived back at least three quarters of an hour before Annet, so it was strange to open the door to the sound of the radio — and Freya's complaints — and the smell of cooking. This, he supposed, was how millions of men half his age expected to be greeted at the end of a day's work.

He went into the kitchen. The baby was in her basket on the table and Annet, in jeans and sweatshirt, was at the stove, turning noodles and whatnot in a skillet, with her hair in a ponytail. Her backview was like that of an eighteen-year-old, but when she turned round she looked tired and fierce.

He took her face in his hands and kissed her. 'Hello, how's it been?'

'We have missed you, if that's what you mean.'

'Good.' He bent to kiss her again, but she moved tensely, quickly away. 'Have you got a drink? There's still some stout.'

'No, but I'm all right at the moment, would you pick her up?'

'Of course.' He craved a drink himself, but it didn't seem right to pour one before taking charge of the baby. He removed his jacket and hung it over the back of one of the chairs, and then lifted his daughter out of her basket.

'So what on earth is the problem?' he said. It was meant to be rhetorical, affectionate, of no consequence, but Annet answered sharply:

'What do you think? It's gripe time.'

'Fair enough.'

'Which began about—' she consulted her watch angrily — 'two hours ago?'

'Poor darling. You must be frazzled.'

'You could say that.' She stirred, turned the heat off, stood holding the wooden spoon with both hands. 'Frazzled and ...' She added something which, what with her dropping her voice and Freya squawking in his ear, he couldn't hear.

'And what?' He tried to put his hand on her shoulder but she twitched away.

'Nothing.'

'I'm the one who's had it easy. Just tell me what I can do now.'

She put the spoon down on the side and walked out of the kitchen. She'd been making one of her fail-safe, standby Chinesey things – chicken, water chestnuts, spring onions, it looked appetising. From habit, he placed the lid on the skillet and followed her. He was conscious that with Freya screech-screech-screeching away, his presence, no matter how good his intentions, was less than soothing.

'Please,' she said, as he entered the drawing room. 'Please, darl, don't bring her in here. I honestly can't stand another second of that.'

'Fair enough.' Suddenly he remembered something Tim had said. 'Tell you what, I'll take her out in the car for a bit. That'll give you a break and with a bit of luck it'll send her to sleep.'

He was rewarded by the sight of her face softening, warming, in gratitude. 'Oh, darl, would you? It doesn't have to be for long, but I can't tell you ... could you stand it?'

'Very easily.' It was true. Nothing would be too much trouble if it could achieve such an effect.

'You have to take my car, it's got the carrycot straps.'

'No problem. You pour yourself a drink and take it easy, promise?'

'No problem. David –' He paused in the doorway. 'I do love her, truly.'

'I know.'

'What I hate is feeling as if I don't.'

'Yes.' He understood.

*   *   *

80

Annet's Toyota was small, mean, sporty: not as comfortable as the Volvo, but equipped with drop-dead acceleration. As the engine pounced into action he had to remind himself that what he was engaged in was the late twentieth-century equivalent of the lullaby: so much available speed was a real temptation. But his heart-stopping getaway, lurching pauses and swooped corners had only a beneficial effect on Freya, who was asleep within two minutes of pulling out of the drive.

He'd decided on a six-mile circuit of the village, taking in the hill which led to the ridgeway, but then branching off and heading due east, then south and round. It had been an indifferent day weatherwise and with the dull cloud cover it was almost dusk as he drove along the top of the escarpment, with Newton Bury beginning to light up like a minor constellation beneath him. His spirits rose, and with it his speed. He might as yet be an anxious and inept father, but the opportunities fatherhood afforded to be of service to his wife made it all worthwhile.

When he got back to the village he was almost afraid to stop in case Freya awoke. He slowed down on the approach to Gardener's Lane, and once round the corner actually paused, with the engine idling and home in sight, savouring the peace – both his, and Annet's, behind the warm curtains of Bay Court. It was astonishing the extent to which either tumult or tranquillity were dependent on the baby's sleep patterns. He remembered with shame those times when he'd glanced censoriously at harassed mothers yanking on the arms of toddlers while clutching a buggy in which a screaming baby writhed and yelled incessantly. In a peripheral way he had assumed both stroppy toddler and screaming baby to be consequent upon the mother's bad temper. Now he realised all too clearly that it was the other way about. The mere sight of his daughter's sleeping form was enough to slow his heart-beat and steady his breathing, so that ease stole through him.

To confirm this pleasant sensation he turned to look at the Moses basket, held by its straps like a lifeboat by davits. All he could see of Freya was one minuscule fist resting motionless on the pale quilted lining. The gentle thrum of the idling engine was like a heartbeat. Outside another heaving autumn wind had got up, and the lane ahead was no more than a tunnel of stirring darkness in which the lights of houses, his own included, were like those of boats at anchor on a restless sea. A handful of large, random raindrops spattered on the windscreen. Almost wistfully, he prepared to move off.

His foot was already hovering over the accelerator, and he was glancing automatically in the rear-view mirror when he glimpsed someone about to cross the road behind him. A pale, startled face looking out from a hooded jacket, an arm flew up – perhaps the person thought he was about to reverse – and then, presumably for the same reason whoever it was stepped back out of sight. David paused for a moment, hoping by not revving the engine to reassure the pedestrian and give him or her time to cross over, because the rain was intensifying. But whoever it was didn't reappear, and he almost wondered whether he'd imagined it. Except that his heart was beating at the narrowness of his escape from a second accident in one day.

Annet opened the front door and watched as David unstrapped the Moses basket with excruciating delicacy, closed the car door in the same manner, and covered the intervening distance in two long, loping strides to avoid the rain. He put his finger to his lips, pointed into the basket and then mouthed the word: 'Where?'

She in turn pointed to the drawing room, where she'd left the fire low and one lamp lit.

A couple of minutes later he reappeared, announcing: 'Out for the count.'

'Thanks, darl. I appreciate it.'

It was the moment when she might have returned the kiss he'd tried to give her earlier, but she couldn't quite bring herself to do so. She was simply too tired to face the full release of his love at what was the nearest they'd had to a real opportunity since the baby was born. So the moment she'd spoken she turned away to pick up plates, pretending not to have seen the dawn of expectation on his face. It was like hitting a puppy, but it was still easier for her than the alternative.

'I know you're not supposed to keep this stuff hanging about,' she said briskly, putting the skillet on two mats on the table, 'but a few congealed noodles are a small price to pay for a whole half hour of peace and quiet.'

When she'd dished up, she asked: 'So how was the day? The in-tray from hell?'

'No, all quite orderly really. I've got a temp for the time being, rather robotic, but efficiency on legs.'

'Sounds good to me. And Doug?'

'Fine ... We had lunch. He sent his love.'

'Bullshit. He doesn't like me.'

'What makes you say that?'

'How long have you got?'

Annet was always brought up short by David's obliviousness to certain attitudes and behaviour, even though she knew this was a characteristic he shared with many others of his gender. For a man who was quite painfully sensitive about his relationship with her, he could be almost wilfully obtuse about others.

'Come on,' he said now, 'he thinks you're great!'

'No he doesn't.' She knew he was cheerful because she was more like her old self: stroppy, contentious. Of such strange stuff, she thought, was marriage made. 'That's what he pretends,' she went on, keeping him happy in the only way open to her, 'but I annoy the hell out of him.'

'I'm sure that's not true. He admires you.'

'Exactly.'

David said: 'That's too complicated for me.'

'Look who he married,' Annet pointed out, and then wished she hadn't.

'Marsha? How do you mean?'

'She's a very nice woman but you wouldn't call her independent-minded.'

'Well, no,' conceded David. 'I suppose not, but then opposites agree.'

That left them even stevens, thought Annet, because he probably wished he hadn't said that, either.

David changed the subject. 'Something awful happened on the way back just now. I knocked a woman off her bicycle.'

'God, David!' She seemed genuinely shocked. 'How is she?'

'All right actually. I say I knocked her off but that isn't quite true. I popped out at a junction and didn't see her, and we both had to stop rather abruptly. She was quite elderly and fell off her bike. There was no actual contact, but it was entirely my fault.'

'Poor woman. She must have been shaken.'

'She wasn't the only one,' he said ruefully. 'It's the sort of thing that makes your life flash before your eyes.'

'I should think so indeed.' Annet put down her fork and subjected him to a narrow-eyed look. 'It's not like you though, what on earth were you thinking of?'

'I don't know ... bit dazed, first day back ... looking forward to seeing you, who knows?'

'Flannel,' said Annet, standing up to put the plates on the side, but must have been satisfied, for she went on: 'So the woman wasn't injured at all?'

'She had a nasty graze on her leg where the pedal scraped her. Don't worry, I'm going to get in touch. I feel very bad about it.'

'Did she make a scene?'

'No. On the contrary, she apologised.'

Annet snorted. 'Dear oh dear.'

'Shock, I suppose,' he said

*   *   *

Freya slept and slept. They went to bed early, carrying her gingerly up the stairs and placing the basket on the divan in her room, sure that at any moment the spell would break. When David came out of the bathroom he found Annet standing bent over the basket, staring fixedly at its occupant.

'Everything OK?' he whispered, joining her.

'I suppose so — what do you think?'

'Looks fine to me. Famous last words, let's leave her to it before she decides to wipe the silly smile off our faces.'

As he said this, he put his arm round her shoulders. She was wearing her dark blue satin nightshirt, and the warmth of her skin beneath the slippery material reminded him of how long it had been, and how much he wanted her.

'Come on.'

Without looking at him she laid a hand on his chest to detain him, but she left the hand there as she spoke.

'She's been asleep for such ages.'

'She had some ground to make up, let's face it.' To soothe and oblige her he stooped over the basket. Freya was pale and still as a boxed hothouse flower lying there, but he could just make out the faint tremor of the downy hair over her fontanelle. 'She's asleep,' he said, and putting his arm once more around his wife, drew her out of the room. 'Come.'

After they'd made love, Annet fell asleep at once, but he was wide awake. It wasn't the best sex they'd ever had — she was still sore, and they were both a little tense and wary — but it had nonetheless marked the beginning of their return to each other.

His stomach rumbled: he hadn't eaten much at supper, and now he was ravenous. He slipped out from under the duvet, pulled on his dressing gown and padded downstairs to the kitchen. He lifted the lid of the skillet and considered the remains of the noodles, but that wasn't what he was after. Fuel. He needed fuel. He replaced the lid, cut a couple of slices of bread and put them in the toaster, and then filled a bowl with cornflakes, added plenty of milk and too much sugar and stood under the strip light eating them while the toast was making. When it popped up he slathered on injudicious amounts of butter and some slices of Cheddar, and wolfed them down, still standing up. Childishly, the pleasure of this simple orgy was intensified by the knowledge that if his wife could see him she would voice her most wasting disapproval: 'Well, it's your heart, darl,' or something like it.

When he'd finished he put the crockery in the dishwasher. Crossing the hall he noticed that they'd omitted to replace the fireguard, and went into the drawing room. When he'd dealt with the guard something prompted him to go to the window overlooking the road and part the curtains.

The rain had stopped, and there was no wind. Neither was there anyone about on this Monday night in Newton Bury.

Midnight and all's quiet, he thought to himself as he closed the curtains and went back up the stairs. Which was tempting fate, because as he reached the landing Freya snickered into life.

Chapter Five

Annet didn't want to visit her mother, but she knew she if she didn't take Freya to see her now while she was off work it was something that would have to be squeezed in with more difficulty – and even less enthusiasm – in the course of a precious free weekend.

Karen took time out from the kitchen surfaces to come and see them off. She stood by the car with her arms folded, watching with a hint of indulgent *schadenfreude* as Annet fixed the babyseat in place.

'Have fun!' she instructed. 'Be careful on those roads.'

'I shall certainly do the second,' said Annet. 'The first's asking a bit much.'

She was pretty sure she saw Karen shake her head in mock despair as she went back into the house. It was all very well – Karen's own mother was a great grandmother at not yet sixty, and appeared (from what Annet understood, she'd never actually met her) to have been in training for the role all her life. Whereas one thing her daughters were agreed upon was that Marina Holbrook was not one of nature's nurturers.

The drive from Newton Bury to the outer London suburb where Marina lived took one and a half hours, and Freya was lulled as always by the car, so Annet had plenty of time to reflect on the difficulties. There was no doubt Marina had got worse since the girls' father, Miles, had died fifteen years ago. At the time Annet was working as a secretary for the World

Women's League off Piccadilly, and sharing a large gloomy flat in Bayswater with a churchy young woman whose dispiriting tights dripped endlessly into the bath and who had a framed postcard of the crucifixion on her bedside table. Annet would return from the ageing but still-feisty Fabian glories of the WWL to find Ellen presiding over a glum Bible-study group at the gateleg table in the living room. Partly, though not solely, for this reason she tended to retire to the bath for half an hour with a glass of wine and the radio at full-blast, prior to going out again. It was pre-Seth and she'd had no regular boyfriend, but there were two or three ex-Sussex University friends with whom she pursued evenings of dedicated drinking and clubbing, culminating (more often than she cared to remember) in nameless one-night stands.

During this period Louise, who was seven years younger, was still living at home and in her second year of A-levels at the local grammar school. Louise had been pretty and amiable and popular and successful, none of which epithets could at the time have been applied to Annet. It went without saying that Miles's death from a massive and richly-deserved coronary hit Louise the harder of the two sisters, and Annet had returned home crossly, dutiful but dry-eyed, to find her mother and sister weeping enough tears for all three of them.

Louise was at least understandably shocked and saddened by her father's death, but Marina was sorry only for herself.

'We were lovers!' she keened embarrassingly. 'Right to the end we were lovers! We weren't ready to say goodbye – whatever shall I do without him?'

Under the circumstances Annet refrained from saying 'Settle up with the off-licence and get a life', but by the end of that week she'd developed a migraine from the effort of not saying it. It astonished Annet that her mother could persist in the notion that she and Miles had enjoyed a lifelong romance, when his only love affair had been with himself. Their father had been a large, amiable, floridly handsome man who had never found anyone or anything half so deserving of passionate devotion as what he saw in the mirror, and who was hugely content with this monogamous relationship.

When she'd finally aired her views to Louise, her sister was as always more inclined to be forgiving. 'But if she's happy thinking that—'

'Happy? The woman never stops weeping and wailing!'

'You know what I mean. If she finds that consoling, why worry?'

'I don't *worry*, it annoys the hell out of me to see her deluding herself.'

'Then don't let it. After all, marriages work in different ways, and if Mummy was deluded then it certainly kept them together.'

'OK, that was when Dad was alive, but now he's gone I suppose I hoped a little honesty and realism might peep through.'

Louise laughed. 'You'll wait a long time – now he's gone he's taken honesty and realism with him to the grave.'

This much was irrefutable, but for a long time it was the spectre of her parents' horribly successful charade of a marriage that put Annet off contemplating such an idea herself. Her mother's arch fantasies, her father's blind, jovial complacency, it was all too ghastly. Equality, truthfulness, mutual independence were what she aspired to in a long-term relationship.

She'd got very drunk after Miles's funeral, and she was a combative drunk. Marina's display of frail, tremulous pluck, and the mawkish comments it provoked, made her gorge rise. She had to keep escaping the rheumy stares, clutching hands and egg-sandwich breaths of the mourners, and retreating to the back garden to smoke furiously.

It was during one of these interludes that Marina had come out and stood nearby, but at a little distance, like a character in a play. Annet wanted to tell her for Christ's sake to cut to the chase and get it over with, but it was a pregnant minute and a half before Marina said in her most wistful, whispy voice:

'Your father always loved this garden.'

'Did he?' replied Annet.

'Oh *yes*. You remember, he and I used to sit out here on summer evenings and he always used to say the same thing – "This is happiness, my darling".'

'Really?' Annet knew she was being ungenerous, but she felt she simply couldn't stand another second's vacuous sentimentality.

And anyway Marina wasn't going to notice, she was well away. 'He knew how to be happy. It's a great gift, perhaps the greatest, and he had it.'

'If you say so.'

'I only wish—' There was a pause, during which Annet could all too clearly picture the brimming eyes, the delicate hand raised to the working mouth . . . She couldn't bring herself to ask what her mother wished, when what was certain was that she would be told anyway.

'I only wish,' Marina murmured brokenly, 'that he'd passed it on to you.'

Now Annet was genuinely dumbstruck: that was the last thing she'd expected. She had so deliberately distanced herself from these proceedings and her mother's performance in them, confident in the assumption that no one, least of all her mother, would notice. And here she was with the spotlight suddenly upon her.

'I'm sorry?' She made herself look at Marina, whose face was puckered into a parody of maternal concern.

'I wish you were happy, Annet. Or even that you *wanted* to be happy. Daddy and I used to worry so much about you.'

This was too much. 'Mother!'

Her outrage did nothing to shake Marina's sickly intrusions. 'You're not happy, are you?'

'That's a fatuous question, predicated on the idea that people go around consciously being happy. They don't—'

'We did.'

'Well bully for you, but most people don't, take it from me.'

She was close to boiling point, and conscious of the occasion, reined her voice back in. 'I know when I'm *not* happy, which incidentally is now, and the rest of the time I'm too busy to think about it.'

'Now you're angry with me,' said Marina. She was closing in: Annet could smell her sweet scent and hear the small, confiding creak of her black patent court shoes. 'Please don't be. Today of all days.'

'I am not angry!' hissed Annet furiously.

'You don't know how proud he was of you.'

'No.' Annet shrank inside her jacket, hoping, no, praying, that her mother wouldn't touch her. 'No, I don't. Was he?'

'He thought the world of you, but he was afraid you'd never find happiness.'

'Mother.' Unable to stand any more, Annet turned to face her. 'Enough. I'm not angry, and most of the time I'm not unhappy, very far from it. At this precise moment I'm just getting through today like we all are, as best I can. As for Dad being proud of me, I'm glad if he was, but he never said anything to me.'

'But he would have done. If he'd – That's why I'm telling you now.'

'Thanks,' said Annet. 'I appreciate it. Excuse me, Mother, I'm going to go round with the bottle.'

She went back into the drawing room with a cold, set face, but she was on fire inside – hating herself for behaving badly, hating Marina for always making her do it, hating (at his funeral, for heaven's sake!) her father, for having talked a lot of bullshit and then buggered off leaving the rest of them to cope.

Not long after that, she'd taken up with Seth, and Louise had passed her A-levels with rather less brilliant grades than expected and opted for what came to be known as a gap year. Weirdly, in Annet's view, she spent this working as a playleader at a community project in Catford, while living at home. The gap had extended indefinitely. Louise had met Coral, a tall, red-haired, local government officer, who was now her partner, and whom she looked after beautifully in a nice garden flat not a mile from Marina's house. Marina herself seemed resolved to see nothing unusual in the domestic arrangements of her younger, prettier, happier daughter, and it was never discussed, but this particular form of wilful blindness was one which Annet was prepared to overlook in the interests of her sister's wellbeing.

Louise and Coral were not politicised in any obvious sense: indeed, being with another woman had seemed to give Louise permission to be the old-fashioned wife she was so perfectly qualified to be. Their flat had the comforting feel of a place run along traditional role-specific lines, with napkins in named rings, a cake always in the tin, and a cat, Porridge, on the hearthrug. Annet half suspected that Coral crossed the threshold each evening with a 'Hi honey, I'm home!' Theirs was the setup for which the phrase domestic bliss had been invented, and which in a heterosexual couple might well have given rise to accusations of smugness.

Marina, meanwhile, played the heartbroken widow, and the field. With her lifelong romance safely behind her she could move about the cocktail and conservative club circuit making men behave like gentlemen while feeling like goats. Annet, still smarting from the 'wish you were happy' exchange found this behaviour profoundly irritating. She knew she should be pleased that her mother had moved on and made a new life for herself, but was this, then, what it took to be happy? Or what it meant? She despised Marina's vanity and her small hypocrisies, to an extent which Louise couldn't understand.

'Look at it this way, Annie, if she's out having fun she's not bothering us.'

'I know, but that doesn't stop me wanting to give her a good shaking.'

'Be grateful. Don't let it get to you.'

'She's such a silly woman!'

'Well, yes ...' Louise had agreed, and then added gently but pointedly: 'In her way.'

The 'as we are in ours' did not need to be articulated. But

Annet had been more surprised to find that the redoubtable Coral took a similar view.

'The old dear's entitled to some fun — it may not be our idea of fun but she's still entitled to it.'

'It's not what she does ...' Annet sought the right words to convey her feelings.

'It's the way that she does it?' suggested Coral.

'Something like that. The untruthfulness of it all.'

Coral smiled. 'You're a stern critic. Who's truthful?'

'You and Lou, for instance.'

It was a dirty trick which still failed to rattle Coral's composure. 'We do our best — so far as each of us knows. It's all an act of faith.'

The perfect, easy reasonableness of this assertion coud not be denied, but had nothing to do with the conduct which made Annet want to wring her mother's neck.

Falling in love with David had been a shock, because it was so unexpected. On first meeting him at the charity AGM she had formed the impression that he was nice and intelligent enough, but risk-averse, an observer rather than a doer. And yet there'd been something seductive in his watchfulness. It conveyed sufficient admiration to be flattering, and enough detachment to be discriminating. She had also always liked that brand of looks — tall, rangy, slightly languid — and was attracted in spite of herself by his slow smile and his confiding way of speaking, in that crowded room, with his head bent slightly towards her. Her bold invitation to him to join her for a drink had been a sort of test — she was fairly sure he would decline, scared off by her forwardness. When he not only accepted but ran, as it were, with the ball, she was charmed in spite of herself. After Seth's dour predictability (which to be fair had been exactly what was needed at the time) to come across a man who was not all what he seemed was a pleasing novelty. Of course she'd done her best to conceal her interest. She remembered with a cringe her bullish attitude on that first date — insisting on an expensive wine, taking her jejune opinions out for a walk, failing utterly to elicit his. Just the same, something happened.

David had told her he was in love with her as they were coming down the escalator at Holborn after seeing a play at the Aldwych. He leaned forward – she was standing on the step in front – and simply said: 'Safe journey. I love you.' She hadn't replied, or even turned round. They'd exchanged a quick kiss on the lips at the bottom, as the impatient travellers poured round them, and then they'd gone in their separate directions. The force and the significance of what he'd said only hit her as she strap-hung amid the rattle and roll of the southbound line. He loved her? He loved her! Overcome by a helpless smile, she caught the eye of a youth in combat trousers who stared back with withering indifference.

Looking back, she assumed that at some point she must have said 'I love you, too' to David or that, if she hadn't, he must have inferred it from her ready acceptance of the situation. She, who had long since decided she would never marry, now entered into marriage with a sort of passionate pragmatism. If this was what it took to be with David Keating for as long as they both should live, then this was what she would do. With David she felt herself to be, if not a nicer person herself, then at least a person redeemed by the understanding of one who was. His strength was in letting her be the strong one. The ten-year age gap between them gave an extra dimension to this arrangement: it allowed Annet to feel comfortable with David's support. With Seth, who was her own age and who had watched her find her feet, she had in the end felt only impatience and irritation. She was also mindful of the fact that David had gone even further down the road of life without marrying, and was therefore taking an even greater step than her.

As she considered this, and with the journey half over, she glanced at Freya, still spark out in the seat next to her. And now they were three. Quite distinctly so. She could not subscribe to the view that a baby was an extension of oneself and one's partner. For her, the opposite was true. Freya had been almost shockingly her own person from the moment of her birth, that was one of the reasons they were rocked back on their heels. They were old to be having a first child – when they were gone their daughter would still have most of her life to live, and who on earth knew what she would do with it? Would she and David, confused novices that they were, be able to exert any influence during her formative years, let alone any that would extend into the future? Annet took leave to doubt it. She had the greatest difficulty in picturing herself passing on pearls of wisdom about life and love to her growing daughter. After all – she pulled a wry face to herself – what wisdom? It was less difficult to imagine David involved in a similar exchange: he, after all, was a listener *par excellence*, his strength as a father would be in absorbing the shocks, finding a way through. She wondered how they would be remembered as parents.

This line of speculation brought her back to her own mother. Marina had ostensibly been thrilled to bits with Annet's marriage to David. After all, here at last was concrete evidence of the right sort of happiness, involving a man, a woman, and romantic love. At the same time it ever so slightly queered Marina's pitch. During the long years when Annet had so signally failed to be happy, and Louise (poor lamb) had made the best of a bad job, Marina's crown as the great romantic had been secure. With the arrival of David, it received a nudge which their subsequent ten childless years had done much to restore, though Annet was by no means sure which posture her mother would be adopting today.

It was soon made clear. As she unfastened the babyseat she heard the series of little wails, somewhere between a coo and a moan, which indicated the most intense approval tinged, perhaps, with a slight wistfulness that this was the first time she had seen her granddaughter and since she did not expect to see her all that often anyway . . . .

'. . . let me see, let me see, let me see! Oh – look at all that *hair*, and she's so like you darling – hello darling – may I take her out of this horrible thing?'

'It's a very useful thing, I don't know what I'd do without it,' said Annet. 'Hello mother. Let me carry her in in this and then you can do what you like.'

She walked steadily towards the open front door with Marina bobbing and weaving alongside.

'But she's so good – not a sound, not the tiniest peep!'

'That's the car. She can yell, believe me. As you're probably about to find out.'

'We-ell . . . She needs to give her lungs an airing from time to time, don't you Freya? And that's such a pretty name, whose idea was that?'

'David's. He and Tim cooked it up in the kitchen when they came to visit.' She didn't say that the name was one that had been on their list, she was feeling scratchy and uncharitable – the Marina effect.

'So they've been up to see you . . . How were they?'

Only Annet, or perhaps Louise, could have detected the smidgen of resentment in the first half of this question, and the hasty regrouping in the second. But even though the pushing of the guilt button had been on this occasion inadvertent, Annet was programmed to react at once to its minute, precise pressure.

'Mags had got a pile of baby stuff together for us,' she said as she put the seat down on the circular rug in the drawing room. 'I think they wanted to get rid of it as much as anything, still, it was kind of them.'

She needn't have worried about Marina, who was already battling with the clip and in serious danger of chipping a nail.

'Here, let me, it's a sod to undo.'

As she took Freya out of the harness she awarded herself a pat on the back for disturbing her daughter – and so by definition herself – in her mother's interests. But curiously Freya didn't wake up, and gave every appearance of being content with the old-fashioned rocking treatment she was given.

'Goodness, you have no idea how this takes me back, Annie, you were a dark little stranger just like this ... but she's so *pretty*, at such a young age ... prettier than you were, do you mind my saying that? Of course you don't, you're her mother ....'

Annet, perched on the arm of the sofa and dying for a drink, did mind. It was pathetic, but as with everything Marina said there was an underlying agenda which she found it impossible to ignore. A remark which in a different relationship might have been taken as an affectionately frank and teasing compliment to the next generation, was here a small calculated slight of the kind to which Annet was habituated but not hardened.

'Mind if I get a drink?' she asked.

'Do, do, how remiss of me. I haven't got any wine I'm afraid, but there's plenty of everything else, and splits in the fridge.'

This was another thing. Marina was the last person in the home counties, if not Great Britain not to have been touched by the wine revolution. Whether through choice, indifference or sheer affectation (Annet favoured the last), Marina still regarded wine as something one ordered with a meal in a restaurant or in the unlikely event of holidaying abroad. At home the available drinks, kept on a glass trolley in the living room, were sherry, spirits, or squash (fresh fruit juice and bottled water had been considered pansy extravagances by Miles). But whereas Annet kept in a supply of gin and dubonnet for her mother, the compliment *vis-à-vis* wine was rarely returned.

'Thanks, I'll get a G and T. Do you want your usual?'

'Actually, I've got one on the go,' said Marina without looking up from her granddaughter. 'It's on the side near the stove.'

On the way to the kitchen Annet noticed the table in the dining room laid for four people. There was an appetising stewy smell in the kitchen itself, and potatoes lay immersed in cold water in a saucepan on the stove. A tumbler containing a good quarter of a pint of reddish liquid stood nearby as indicated.

She returned with this, and a tonic from the fridge, to the sitting room and put it down on one of the RSPB coasters on the occasional table next to the sofa where Marina had taken up residence with Freya. As she poured her own drink at the trolley she asked: 'So who else is coming to lunch?'

'Louise and Coral, you don't mind do you?'

'Of course not, it'd be nice to see them. And,' she added pointedly, 'Louise will be able to tell me if Freya looks bigger.'

This was intended to remind Marina that Louise had visited her in hospital, but Marina chose to place a different interpretation on the remark.

'Why, is she not putting on weight? You know there's no shame in a bottle, you can always—'

'No, she's feeding fine, I surprise myself. And yes, she's been weighed and she's gaining all right. It's just that she's probably changed since Louise saw her.'

'Oh, of course, of course she will have done ...' Marina wasn't giving an inch, her face was alight with grandmotherly feeling, held in place, Annet knew, to repel further awkwardness.

She hadn't actually expected her mother to accompany Louise. Marina didn't care for hospitals – a common and understandable aversion in someone her age – but cared even less for occasions of celebration where the centre of attention was not herself. She would have liked an invitation to visit (hence the miff about Mags and Tim), but Annet preferred to take the mountain to Mohammed on the basis that it was easier to escape. Perhaps, she thought grimly, they deserved each other.

'So has Coral taken the day off specially?' she asked.

'I think Lou said she was having a long weekend anyway,' replied Marina dreamily. 'Something to do with redecorating the bathroom.'

Yet more evidence, reflected Annet, of the solidly conventional nature of her sister's relationship. She could neither remember nor conceive of, a day when David had taken a day off on account of grouting.

'Louise made some beautiful baby stuff for us,' she said. 'She is clever.'

'She is,' agreed Marina. 'She always had nimble fingers. A clever auntie, your Auntie Louise,' she told Freya.

'That reminds me,' said Annet, 'I think we shall probably dispense with titles.'

'What, no aunties and uncles?'

'Not unless they want to stand on ceremony, no.'

'Well I'd like to be good old-fashioned Granny,' declared Marina, taking a sip of her gin and dubonnet as if to dispel the least notion of old-fashionedness.

'Fine. Grannies are different.'

'And I'm the only one after all, aren't I,' continued Marina, 'and Freya's my first grandchild. And probably my last!' She gave a worldly, resigned laugh, but Annet didn't take the cue. 'So I have the field all to myself.'

This was too chilling a prospect to contemplate so Annet filled the vacuum with the first remark to hand. 'David sends his love.'

'Yes, how is David?' Marina's brow furrowed in sympathy. 'How's he coping?'

'He's at work, mother. Business as usual.'

'Has he been able to be of some help? Has Daddy changed a nappy yet, I wonder . . . ?'

'Of course he has. He's perfectly competent, as you'd expect.'

'Oh-ho, *I* wouldn't expect *anything*, darling, after Miles. New men hadn't been invented then, and even if they had he'd never have been one. I'm afraid your father was a man's man to his fingertips.'

'That's true,' agreed Annet.

This topic was Marina-heaven. 'But he was a strong man. If anyone had ever done anything to hurt me he'd quite simply have killed them. I truly believe that.'

'Do you?'

'Yes I do. I know it. I suppose what I mean is that somehow we all get the person who meets our needs—' she'd been talking to Coral again – 'And I needed someone forceful and strong.'

Annet struggled to reconcile this Heathcliffe-ish picture with her own memory of Miles: a large, florid man whose massive selfishness was only imperfectly disguised by his affability. It seemed to her that what Marina chose to characterise as the romance of their partnership was its essentially infantile quality. Each was prepared to accept, without question, the interpretation the other placed on themselves and to play along with it. Most of the time it was the man's man and his popsy, but Marina seemed retrospectively to be shifting towards something more heavy duty and even less obliging.

'I think we're waking up,' said Marina. 'Yes, we are! And violet eyes, just look at them.'

'I think they all have them at this age.'

'They're very often blue,' conceded Marina, 'although yours were more grey. But these are an astonishing colour, a true violet – like Elizabeth Taylor.'

It was on the cards that, after such a long period of undisturbed sleep, Freya would go from nought to full-belt in record time, and she didn't disappoint. Marina handed her over with a show of reluctance announcing that the others would be here soon so she had better attend to her culinary duties.

'Will you be all right in here?' she asked. 'Or would you like to be somewhere more private?'

'In here's fine,' said Annet.

'Are you sure it won't disturb you if the others come trooping in?'

'There's only the two of them, mother.'

Marina fluttered her hands in apology. 'I don't want to be held responsible for a colicky baby on the drive home.'

The thought of Marina being held responsible for anything was beyond Annet's compass. 'You won't be, I promise.'

When Louise and Coral arrived five minutes later Marina greeted them with much important shushing which Annet put a stop to by calling out:

'We're in here, come and say hello!'

She was holding Freya against her shoulder as they came in, and Louise at once said 'May I?' and laid claim to the baby. This carried none of the disturbing implications of the same proprietary gesture in Marina. Annet was struck afresh at the unforced femininity of her sister, so unlike Marina's archness.

Coral put her arm round Louise's shoulders and said: 'Mind if I join the fan club? Lord ... how did you manage to spawn such a princess?'

Louise nudged her. 'Good gene pool, stupid.'

'Silly me.'

Louise went to the window the better to admire her niece, and Coral plumped down on the sofa next to Annet. She was a big-boned, tousled redhead with pale, transparent-seeming eyes. Before their steady beam Annet felt that she too became transparent. She was sure Coral was an excellent social worker, able to predict and analyse problems long before they arose.

But all she said was: 'She's great. You must be chuffed.'

'We are.'

'When do you go back to work?'

'Four weeks. David's going to have a week looking after her on his own.'

'Good for him. You can tell him if he needs any support, moral or otherwise, he knows where we are.'

'I'll do that.'

From the kitchen Marina sang out: 'Won't be long!'

'Let's go and see how Granny's doing,' said Louise.

Coral hadn't blinked. 'Looking forward to going back, or blissfully addicted to motherhood?'

'I don't know.' Annet realised she hadn't thought about it in those terms. Returning to work was a given factor. 'Neither of those, really. But I certainly feel different.'

'I can see that.'

'It shows?'

'Oh yes.'

She didn't enlarge, but Annet's curiosity was piqued. 'In what way?'

'You look ...' Coral narrowed her eyes ... 'softer. A bit bruised. More vulnerable. Rounder – nice.'

Annet always sensed that Coral threw in these occasional suggestive remarks to test her – to see how she would react. It made her wonder in what terms they discussed her in private. Louise had always been a model sister – unselfish, dignified, unfailingly kind and discreet – and yet there was, as Coral proved, another side to the paragon.

She said: 'The roundness is going, as soon as I'm allowed back in the gym, believe me.'

'I bet David likes it.'

'I wouldn't know.' Coral raised an eyebrow. It was the most she'd moved since sitting down on the sofa. Annet met her eyes squarely. 'It's not what he fell for in the first place.'

'True.' Coral glanced around. 'Dare I risk a fag?'

'No.'

'The nicotine fascists have it too much their own way, you know that?'

'It's not that, it's not good for the baby.'

'Now you're talking. That argument hits home.'

'Which?' said Louise, from the doorway. 'Don't tell me she's conceding a point.'

'Here,' said Coral, bouncing up. 'Let me have a hold, it's my turn.'

'And lunch is ready,' added Louise, relinquishing Freya, 'so you'll have to put her down again.'

Annet brought the car seat and sat it on the Parker-Knoll in the corner of the dining room. Demurely lidded Coalport vegetable dishes sat on Redoute rose table mats on either side of matching salt and pepper shakers. Coral pulled a chair back from the table and sat down on it with the baby still held in front of her.

'Marina!' she called, without taking her eyes from the baby's face. 'OK if we open our bottle of wine?'

'Of course! I'm no good with the blithering corkscrew, but if any of you girls can manage it . . . .'

'Go on,' Coral jerked her head, 'what are you girls waiting for?'

Louise went out to the kitchen. Annet said: 'Good thinking.'

'Well you have to, don't you? And what's more we take the leftovers with us.'

'You don't . . .' Annet was impressed. 'Do you?'

'Sure. She makes it perfectly plain this is a wine-free zone, and she makes a point of never touching it as though it's an invention of the devil or something, so we think it's only polite to go along with her.'

'I gave up bringing it because it was only me that drank it and since I'm driving—' Annet shrugged. 'When in Rome.'

'When in Rome,' said Coral, 'do as the Italians do, I say.'

Marina dished up, and held court.

'Isn't this fun, all girls together? Even little Freya . . . we're quite a sorority.'

'Men, who needs them?' agreed Coral mischievously.

'Oh, I never said *that*.' Marina wagged a finger. 'I would *never* say that.'

'Of course not.'

Louise turned to Annet. 'Do you think she'll be a real Daddy's girl?'

'Miles was always—' began Marina.

'Probably,' replied Annet, 'if only because I suspect older fathers are more indulgent. So I shall be left with the unenviable role of Wicked Witch of the West.'

'You've got the looks for it,' said Coral.

Louise sucked her teeth. 'Honestly. What sort of remark is that?'

'It was a compliment. Bad girls are always the sexiest.'

'*Anyway*,' interjected Marina, smiling fixedly to show that she was taking no notice of the sex talk but wished to put a stop to it nonetheless, 'this little one will be able to wind David round her little finger, you may be bound.'

'Speaking of which,' said Louise, 'how's your social life, mother?'

This was a question which Annet would never, on principle, have asked, and she could not bring herself to look up from her plate as Marina answered.

'Quite hectic, believe it or not. I'm a Friend of the Arcadians now, thanks to Geoffrey and Phyllis, which entitles me to all sorts of jolly things.'

'Translate please?' said Coral.

'The Arcadians, you know,' said Louise. 'Local amateurs but quite good. They put stuff on in the Masonic Hall.'

'Why on earth don't we go?'

'I didn't know you were interested.'

'Interested?' exclaimed Coral. 'Interested? How can you say such a thing, of course I'm interested. The tender green shoots of artistic endeavour should be nurtured wherever they appear. Particularly around here. You really must get me along to these things.'

Annet bit on a smile.

'Yes you should, you really truly should,' agreed Marina. 'They are quite wonderful. I mean darling, you describe them as amateurs and I suppose in the strictest sense they are but the *Salad Days* they did in April would have stood comparison with anything in the West End.'

'*Romans in Britain, The Blue Room* ...?' murmured Annet subversively.

'See what we missed?' said Coral to Louise.

'So mother, what do you get for being a friend?' asked Annet. Coral gave a snort, which she ignored. 'Priority booking, I suppose.'

'Priority booking, discounts, social evenings, workshops—'

'Workshops? Do you do those?'

Marina gave a flirtatious smile. 'There's no need to sound

so surprised. Geoffrey and Phyllis were signed up for the one on verse speaking and Phyllis wasn't well so I took her place and I found it quite fascinating.'

'And did you?' asked Annet. 'Verse speak?'

'I had no intention of doing anything in public, but everyone had been told to take a piece of verse along and since I'd inherited Phyllis's mantle I was bequeathed her poem.'

They looked at her expectantly. Coral said: 'You have us in the palm of your hand Marina.'

'Oh, it was something terribly tricksy and difficult and pretentious about a hawk.'

'"The Windhover"?' suggested Annet.

'Some such thing.'

'Who he?' Coral asked.

'You know,' said Louise. 'Manley Hopkins. "My heart in hiding stirred for a bird".'

'Means nothing.'

'It didn't, as far as I was concerned,' said Marina triumphantly. 'It wasn't my cup of tea at all, I couldn't make head or tail of it but fortunately I have a few old favourites rattling around in here—' she tapped her coiffure – 'so I recited one of those.'

Once again Louise obliged where Annet would not have done. 'So which one did you give them?'

'Lovely old John Masefield. Rhyme, rhythm, and something to say.'

'"Cargoes"?' asked Coral. 'Please say it wasn't "Cargoes".'

Marina laughed, too pleased with all the attention to perceive any slight. 'No, no, not this time.' She raised her right hand, palm uppermost, like a priest invoking the holy spirit, and tilted her head to the eau de nil pleated lampshade hanging from the ceiling. '"I must go down to the sea again, to the wild sea and the sky, And all I ask is a tall ship and a star to steer her by ...."'

It was, reflected Annet, altogether more than flesh and blood could stand.

When she'd finished, Coral led the clapping which woke the baby up.

Thereafter, Freya didn't settle. It might have been the long sleep that morning, or the new surroundings, or Annet's humour – but whatever the cause she embarked on a campaign of noisy complaint which effectively sabotaged the rest of lunch. Annet attempted further feeding, which only seemed to make matters worse. Having unwisely speculated about the wisdom of drinking gin when breastfeeding, Marina neglected her main course in order to walk about doing a lot of ineffectual patting and jiggling. While Annet seethed, Coral and Louise cleared their plates and dished up the chocolate mousse.

Annet took Freya back while Marina made coffee, and they drank it against a background of unabated yelling. She was tiring rapidly, straining at the end of her tether, entering that now familiar but unwelcome zone where the forcefield of new motherhood separated her from normal human intercourse. The thought of the drive home was intolerable, but as the only escape route it had to be faced. Anything was preferable to this awareness of other people's tolerance, and their pity – it was not too strong a word – for her plight.

'Right,' she said. 'Enough already. I'm out of here.'

'Oh, darling,' said Marina, 'must you? None of us minds a bit of crying.'

'Maybe not, but I do.'

'I mind it,' observed Coral, 'a bit. It's disturbing to hear such a small person in such a taking. If the car makes her happy, who are we to disagree?'

'Thank you,' said Annet, with feeling, getting up and leaving Freya with Louise as she fetched the basket.

Marina continued to argy-bargy gently, in the tone of one who is satisfied to have behaved impeccably, but to whom peace, nonetheless, is soon to be restored.

'. . . turning my words against me as usual, Coral. I want

Freya to settle more than anyone, but it seems a shame for Annet's day to be cut short when there might be something the rest of us could do.'

'There isn't, really,' said Annet. 'The two of us need to get back and eyeball one another in the privacy of our own home.'

'You make it sound like the prelude to some esoteric martial art,' said Coral as they accompanied her out to the car.

'That's what it feels like sometimes.'

'But not all the time, I hope.'

'No — no, of course not. It's just rather more life-changing than I imagined, or than I care to admit.'

'You and your pride. You're wonderful.'

Annet strapped the basket in the back. She and Marina kissed cautiously, she with a wary expression, Marina with a look of wistful tenderness.

'Don't leave it too long before you bring her over again — I *shall* be thinking of you both.'

'All, Mummy,' said Louise. 'Thinking of them all. David, remember?'

'Of course I remember, what are you accusing me of? But I do know a thing or two about mothers and daughters and it's a very close and special private bond, that's all I meant.'

'Thank you mother,' said Annet. She kissed Louise, and then Coral, who gave her shoulders a little pat. And said into her ear, just before she started the engine:

'I hope it's not all grief, because we're thinking of adopting one.'

Chapter Six

'Really?' David was gently sceptical. 'She wasn't winding you up?'

'I'm sure not. She *is* a bit of a wind-up merchant, but I got the impression this was something that had been discussed between them, and she lobbed it in at the last moment to avoid mother knowing too soon.'

'But Marina was there, surely.'

'She didn't hear. It was for my ears only. I thought I'd ring later and get more details from Louise.'

They were in the drawing room after supper. Miraculously, Freya was asleep upstairs in her room. The *Nine o'clock News* was on with the sound low, so that they could hear her minute sighs and grunts over the intercom. Privately David disliked this gadget – he had contended, vainly, that without it they'd still hear her if she cried, but without suffering this continuous state of low-level alert. The news vis-à-vis Louise and Coral was a welcome distraction.

'I can't believe they'll succeed,' he said, to himself as much as to Annet, but she was quick to pick it up.

'Why shouldn't they?'

'For obvious reasons.'

'They'd be model parents.'

'They might be,' he said. 'That has yet to be tested. After all, we're finding out how hard it is.'

'Sure, sure,' Annet waved this aside, 'but anyone could have predicted that. We're too old and hardworking, we weren't ready. They're just the right age, motivated as hell and Louise has a starred first in the domestic arts.'

He gave a little laugh, and touched her hand to show that it was not only because she was funny, but because she was more her old self. He ventured a tease.

'That means nothing. *We're* clever and motivated and know how to boil an egg but it availeth us nought.'

She looked incensed. 'We're coping!'

'Just about.'

'Speak for yourself. Anyway we're not the point at issue. Anyone with half a brain can see that Coral and Lou should be allowed to have a child.'

'Except that they're gay, so chances are they won't be allowed to adopt.'

'I know *that*,' she said stormily. 'I do wish you'd stop presenting the given factor as though it were an argument fresh minted by you.'

'Sorry, but one should never ignore the obvious.'

'Nor should the obvious be automatically regarded as right!'

'I was merely being pragmatic.'

'Merely?' She was aghast. 'Gimme a break.'

He pushed an arm round her waist and kissed her neck, just below the cat-like angle of her jaw. 'Any time.'

They made love urgently on the sofa, partly because they were uncomfortable and partly from a fast-establishing habit of seizing the moment. But still Freya didn't wake, and David, loth to let his wife go, lay with his arms wrapped round her and his trousers round his ankles like some teenage swain caught in the act.

After a few minutes Annet said: 'Sorry darl but my leg's going to sleep,' and he struggled to sit up.

'That was lovely,' he said. 'Wasn't it lovely?'

She gave him the cowboy look. 'It was many things darl, but I don't know about lovely.'

'Not?' He was crestfallen, and she cupped his cheek in her hand.

'Ask yourself would it have looked good on film?'

'That's a bit of a tough one, surely. We weren't going for an Oscar.'

'Exactly. It *felt* sensational, but Scorsese it wasn't.'

As if to emphasise her point she leaned forward and yanked on the waistband of his trousers. 'Nought point one for artistic impression.'

He got dressed, and Annet took their wine glasses out to the kitchen. and put the kettle on. While she was making the coffee the phone rang and she called 'I'm there!' Then he heard her say 'Oh, hi . . .' and there was the scrape of a chair as she sat down. The conversation seemed to be fairly onesided because there followed a long period of silence broken only by murmurs and muted exclamations. After five minutes he got up and went into the kitchen in search of the neglected coffee. As he picked up where she'd left off she waved a hand and mouthed 'Sorree!', pointing at the receiver and also mouthing: 'Mother!' which told him all he wanted to know. He leaned over and kissed her neck again and she raised an absent-minded hand to touch his face. He liked that, it carried with it a pleasing sense of returning normality.

Taking his coffee with him he went upstairs to check on Freya. They usually turned the landing light on when it became dark, but had omitted to do so tonight. Remembering why he was swept by happiness. He left the light off and walked in the gentle dark into the baby's room.

It was full of the faint scent he had come to associate with her – that odd mix of the sweet and the pungent, the infantile and the womanly. Even slumbering his daughter exuded a powerful presence. Almost reverently he went to the side of the cot and looked down at her, deep in that silent, motionless near-death of baby sleep. Compelled, as he and Annet both still were, to check that she was breathing, he leaned over the lowered side of the cot until his face was close to hers. Now he could detect the minutest sound, a tiny pulse or tick that seemed to come from deep inside her head. Her hand lay on the sheet and he thought he saw her index finger tremble. He was moved to think that he could have woken her in an instant – he had the size, the status, the wherewithal – but she held all the power.

Satisfied that she was asleep he straightened up. As he did so, something brushed his face and the side of his neck. He had the overwhelming impression that someone had been standing so close beside him that his movement had caught them unawares. There was a waft of scent, fine and subtle, quite unlike that of the baby. For a split second every hair on his body stood erect, the scent in the room made him nauseous. Giddy, he grabbed the corner of the cot with both hands and stood clasping it, swaying slightly.

The landing light came on. 'David?'

It was Annet, in the doorway. 'Why didn't you – darl, are you all right?'

He drew a deep breath. 'I gave myself a fright.'

'You look ghastly. You should have turned the light on.'

'I didn't want to disturb her.'

'I'm not sure anything could tonight.'

'No ...' He let go the cot and moved towards the door. His legs felt weak, but he could feel the warm blood returning through the layers of flesh and bone to his skin, each tiny hair softening and sinking back. 'God almighty ... what a funny turn.'

'Must be neonatal neurosis of some kind.' She slipped her hands beneath his arms and up around his shoulder blades, a nice feeling. 'Still – shows you're a proper new man.'

As they left the room he looked over his shoulder and saw, hanging over the cot, the Chinese mobile of paper angel fish, the first thing they'd bought when Annet found she was pregnant. Thank God, he'd forgotten about that. Almost imperceptibly the fish turned, surrendering serenely to some undetectable movement in the air, just as they must have done when they brushed his face.

Annet went down the stairs ahead of him. As he emerged on to the landing he was aware of the difference in the atmosphere: plain, clear — unscented.

'Tell me,' said Annet, pouring him a Scotch. 'Did you ever get in touch with that woman?'

Still in the wake of one shock he now experienced another. 'Who?'

'You know — the one you knocked off her bike.'

'Thanks for reminding me, I'd forgotten. I'll do it tomorrow.'

She put the Scotch in front of him, laid a hand on his shoulder. 'That's not like you.'

'I'd like to think not. I will call tomorrow.' Feeling scrutinised, he changed the subject. 'What did your mother want?'

'Oh ... she'd had a passage of arms with Louise.'

'With Louise?' He was incredulous. 'Is that possible?'

'Apparently.' Annet sat on one chair and swung her feet up on to another. 'But remember this is mother's side we're getting.'

'What about?'

'I was wrong about her not hearing what Coral said.'

'You're joking.'

'No.'

'I take it she's not happy?'

Annet covered her eyes with her hands, then dragged them down her face in a gesture of despair. 'What she can't face is the truth, and everyone else knowing it. That Lou and Coral are a couple.'

'She seems to accept it,' he said doubtfully.

Annet shook her head. 'Only because she pretends they're friends, that Lou's just slumming till something more suitable in trousers comes along. But if they have a baby, there's no escape. People will talk. She'll have to think of them *touching* each other — imagine!'

David, who had shamefacedly entertained such thoughts himself from time to time, couldn't find it in his heart to condemn Marina too harshly on this score.

'To think positively,' he said, 'once there's another baby in the frame – another grandchild – she can't fail to be happy.'

'But that's a long way off, if it happens at all. The thought of the grief she's going to hand out between now and then turns my stomach.'

'You mustn't let it,' he said. 'Bottom line is, it's not our problem.'

At this, the look she gave him said it all.

When they went up to bed, there was one of those little scenes so trite, so straight-off-the-telly that David almost felt his lines had been written for him. His pen had leaked a small black splodge on to the lining of his suit jacket. Annet said she'd take it to the cleaners, and began to remove things wholesale from the pockets.

'So who's the lady?' she asked.

He saw with dismay that she was holding Gina King's letter. 'Sorry?'

'Who's the lady writing to you?'

'Oh – Gina King.' He managed an insouciant tone, though he felt anything but carefree. 'That girl I had to sack?'

'Oh her—' To his astonishment Annet took the letter from its envelope. 'What's she on about?'

'A reference.'

'She's got to be joking. I do hope you didn't give her one?'

'I regret to say I haven't even replied.'

'Regret nothing. God, this is so creepy . . .' She read with one hand to her cheek, a finger in the corner of her mouth. 'Who does she think she is?'

David got into bed. His head was starting to ache. 'I don't know, using a bit of initiative, I suppose. Can't blame her for trying.'

'I can.' Annet tore the letter in half and dropped it in the wastepaper basket. 'I do.'

He flinched, swiped by an emotion he couldn't place. 'That was a bit sweeping.'

'Well – silly cow. OK, sorry, here you are.' She retrieved the torn letter and tossed it on to the bed, casually dismissive rather than angry. 'I mean, which brain cell was she using when she sent that?'

He decided that to discuss the matter further was to court more of this nameless discomfort. Fortunately, Freya began at last to cry and he was content to let his wife fetch her.

The letter was back in his briefcase the following day, but he didn't refer to it. Instead, he looked up Jean Samms and rang her from the office at lunchtime. Accustomed to wait for an obligatory few rings he was surprised when she answered at once.

'Hello?'

'Is that Jean Samms?'

'Speaking.'

'This is David Keating. The man who so stupidly caused you to fall off your bike?'

'Oh, yes?' Her tone was polite, but guarded. She might have been talking to a cold-sell conservatory salesman.

'I just wondered how you were.'

'Fine thank you.'

'No ill effects?'

'No, none.'

David realised with embarrassment that he had been expecting warmth, pleasure. Certainly not this distant civility.

'Right . . . Well I won't waste any more of your time. I just wanted to check that, you know, that all was well.'

'Yes, thank you.' She replied formulaically, as though he'd asked a question. He wanted to prod her into a more animated response.

'I really do apologise for what happened.'

'That's all right.'

'It wasn't like me. I'm a quite maddeningly careful driver as a rule.'

'I'm sure.'

'But of course you've only got my word for that.'

'I believe you.' For the first time there was a note in her voice of something other than mere politeness, the hint of a laugh. He pressed his advantage.

'It's true. It's my wife who's the speed merchant.'

'Oh dear!'

'And she runs a faster car. But she has a completely clean licence – there's no justice.'

'There isn't, is there? I confess I did have a stiff knee for a couple of days, but that was all.'

'You're made of stern stuff then, it was a nasty fall.'

'I've had worse.'

He was hugely, irrationally pleased to have cracked her reserve. 'Whereabouts are you, by the way? Did you have far to go when I so rudely interrupted you?'

'Oh no, not far – only round the corner, Rustat Road.'

'Good, because I felt bad driving off and leaving you to it.'

She didn't respond to this: she probably considered she'd said too much, been forward, perhaps even laid herself open to some nameless danger. He felt compelled to confide in her, in order to explain himself and allay her fears.

'In my defence,' he said, 'I was suffering from sleep deprivation. I've become a father for the first time at a somewhat advanced age.'

'Congratulations.'

'Thank you. Yes, she's enchanting, but I don't think I bounce as a younger man would.'

Her small laugh acknowledged the truth of this. 'Nor me.'

'Well,' he added, 'I won't take up any more of your time.

I'm so glad you're all right, it makes my conscience a bit easier.
Take care.'

'Goodbye.'

As soon as he'd hung up he scribbled 'Rustat Road' on the
nearest piece of paper.

That afternoon, a little self-consciously, Annet took a fretful
Freya for a walk in the buggy. The weekday village was still
strange to her and she suspected that those by whom she was
observed might be taking a certain evil pleasure from seeing that
opinionated woman from Gardener's Lane pushing the baby out
with bags under her eyes.

To make matters worse, term had just begun, and she had
inadvertently chosen the end of the school day when parents,
grandparents and the odd paid help converged on the gates
of the local C of E primary to collect their charges. So she
found herself part of a general procession of scarily-youthful
women in jeans and trainers, many of them with a toddler by
the hand and a baby in a pushchair. One or two, she noticed with
awe, were pregnant as well. She could only conclude that such
courage and resilience were functions of embarking on a family
in one's twenties. She had always regarded herself as tough in
mind and body, but theirs was real stamina.

She felt out of her element, but took only small comfort
from the presence of another outsider: a man she dimly recognised sat at the wheel of a yellow Mazda sports, one finger
tapping to a dim, thunderous backbeat. She remembered, now,
the meeting about parking rights, arriving late from London,
heavily pregnant but booted and spurred, not giving a damn,
cutting the crap, making heads turn ... At the end he'd shaken
her hand, asked her if she hired out by the hour ... Talk about
before and after.

To her dismay, as she tried to slip by with her head
down, the beat was snuffed out, and he lowered the window.

'Hello there. Put the fear of God into any parish councillors recently?'

She gave a lemony smile. 'No.'

'You've been a bit tied up since the last time, I see.' To her embarrassment, he got out of the car with the air of one ready to talk. Smiling indulgently, he indicated the buggy. 'Boy or girl?'

'This is Freya.'

'How old?'

'Two and a half weeks.'

'Congratulations.' He stuck out his hand. 'Harry Bailey by the way. I know who you are.'

He was a square-shouldered man no taller than her, possibly a little younger but dressed too young, receding hair cut Bruce Willis short to show he didn't give a stuff. Something in his manner, allied to the statement-making hair, the white collarless shirt and leather waistcoat, not to mention the yellow sports car made Annet's heart sink.

'The complainer from hell?' she suggested, proffering and retrieving her hand in a swift, seamless movement.

He gave a grunting laugh. 'You were taking no prisoners. It was a pleasure to watch you work. Mind out, they're coming.' As he said this he laid one hand on her arm and the other on the buggy handle and to her annoyance moved her and it firmly to one side as a crocodile of small children were ushered through the playground gate towards the amenity bus.

'The barmy army,' he commented. 'Thank God they have mothers to love them.'

'But I'm not one,' she said, 'not one of theirs. So if you'll excuse me I'll press on and get out of the way.'

She matched the action to the word. 'Take it easy,' advised Harry Bailey, stepping aside, raising his hands as if she were travelling at speed. 'See you around.'

Not if I see you first, she thought. From a distance of about a hundred yards she glanced over her shoulder and saw him still standing there, talking to a couple of laughing young women, his hand resting on the bowl-cut blond head of a small boy. She pictured him saying 'Hello girls,' and shuddered. The workplace, in which for this purpose Annet included a wide spectrum of wine bars, tapas joints, theme pubs and internet cafes, boasted any number of Harry Baileys — a particular type of well-heeled, moderately successful, hard-to-place man, probably pretending to be more classless than he was and with dependants, if there were any, safely distanced by divorce. The type who could initiate affairs for fun, and surf unscathed over the fallout ... The type, in short, capable of having a field day with the young mothers of Newton Bury.

She increased her pace to the junction at the end of the road. Here, the choice was between an uphill route in the direction of the ridgeway, or a gentle downhill one which led to the village high street. To put as much distance as possible between herself and the school-gate crowd she turned up the hill and was at once reminded of how unfit she'd become. The safe exercise routine undertaken on the bed and the bedroom floor had done nothing to prepare her for this unforgiving gradient and the weight of the buggy. Her weakness annoyed her and she forced herself to push harder, though her arm and leg muscles screamed for mercy.

'Care for a lift to the top?' The yellow Mazda hovered next to her, with Bailey leaning on the open window.

'It's OK thanks ...' She fought for breath. The blond boy was in the passenger seat, tinkering with a plastic space-lord.

'I won't tell anyone.'

His accurate assessment of her pride incensed her. 'I'm fine thank you.'

Disarmingly, he added: 'You're a damn sight fitter than me then,' before accelerating away up the hill.

Half a mile up the ridgeway she was sweating and her chest was heaving, but she kept going at a steady pace until everything calmed down. She told herself she was going to have to locate some sort of local sports club with a gym and a pool before she went back to work, or there were going to be comments.

Piers mocked her for being an exercise junkie, but he'd mock her even more for turning into a slug.

She'd anticipated the lane that wound back down to the village being an opportunity to freewheel, but the effort of acting as a brake on the buggy was almost as great as that of pushing it, and it was a relief to get back on the level. Outside the post office stores she met Karen, with her two-year-old grandson Damian in the kind of mobile micro-environment which made Freya's buggy look like a shoebox.

'Fancy meeting you here!' cried Karen. 'I'm doing my Nana bit like a good'un.'

'So I see.' Annet gazed on Damian. He looked enormous, terrifyingly male and mature, far too big even for the state-of-the-art chariot in which he rode. She would not have been surprised to see whiskers on his upper lip.

'He's lovely,' she said, adding tentatively: 'Is he big for his age?'

'Big?' Karen rolled her eyes in a gimme-a-break way. 'You should see his father. Not that this one's ever likely to.'

'He was tall?'

'Brick shithouse, and thick with it,' replied Karen cheerfully. 'Worst day's work Jules ever did.'

'How is Julie?' asked Annet. She had never met Karen's daughter but the hearsay had been sufficiently detailed for her to feel she knew her.

'Not too clever,' said Karen, 'which is why I've got the old boy for the afternoon.'

'Nothing serious I hope . . . ?'

'No, no, girls' stuff. Here—' Karen unzipped a funsize chocolate snack with practised dexterity and handed it to Damian – 'there. Peace perfect peace.' She shot Annet a conspiratorial glance. 'Saw you talking to Harry Bailey.'

This, thought Annet, was the price you paid for village life.

'Yes, I can't say I'd have recognised him, but he reminded me that we met at an acrimonious public meeting a few months ago.'

'He's lovely, isn't he.' This surprising remark was presented as a matter of indisputable fact. So much so that Annet only just in time prevented herself from agreeing with it.

'Is he?'

'You know who he is, do you?'

'No idea.'

'He works for Chris Harper. The singer?'

'Sorry.' Annet shook her head emphatically. It was a lie and a mean-spirited one, but she didn't wish to be impressed by Bailey's provenance.

'Yes you do.' Karen warbled: '"Thought it was over, thought that I'd won, but now that I see you I'm back to square one . . ." *You* know.'

'It rings some sort of bell,' Annet conceded grudgingly.

'It should do, he sung at the Prince's bash,' said Karen for all the world as though she'd been there. 'He and Lindl whatsit bought that stately home place up the road.'

'Lindl . . . ?'

'That Swiss model – famous bottom – You know,' said Karen for the second time.

'No,' said Annet. But a sneaking pride persuaded her to add: 'By stately home you mean Stoneyhaye, do you?'

'Socking great place. We took this one to the horse show when the other people were there.'

'Yes, I'm with you, My husband dealt with the sale.'

'Did he? You never said. Did he meet Chris Harper?'

'Of course. We're like that with the rock aristocracy, Karen.'

'Jesus, I don't know . . . !' Karen was happily despairing. 'Anyway the point is, Harry Bailey's Chris Harper's main man.'

'Really.'

Karen shook her head slowly. 'Not impressed, are you?'

'Not by Mr Bailey, no.'

'He's lovely, though, the way he looks after that kid.'

Annet's curiosity was momentarily piqued. 'That boy he was meeting from school – he's not his?'

'No way, Jay belongs to Lindl.'

'And – forgive me if I'm being slow – Chris Harper?'

'No!' Karen gurned in horror at this suggestion.

'So – again, forgive me—?'

'Who knows? Don't suppose she does. Too many contenders for the title, poor little sod.'

'I see. So among other duties Mr Bailey does the school run.'

'Right. And he does all sorts for the school, my friend's three are round there and she says he's an absolute diamond.'

'Presumably,' said Annet drily, 'he's the power behind the cheque book which doesn't hurt either.'

'Too bloody right.' Karen was nothing if not pragmatic. 'Go on, see if you can get us an invitation to the stately home.'

'Forget it,' said Annet. 'We don't know them socially.'

'Oo-ooh!' jeered Karen. 'Bet you wish you did!'

Just the same, there seemed to have been enough of a coincidence to warrant mentioning it to David over supper.

'Tell you who I bumped into this afternoon when we were out for a walk.'

'We?'

'Me and Freya, darl, who do you think. Someone called Bailey who works for that pop star, the one who bought Stoneyhaye.'

'Oh yes? What does he do?'

'He probably has some kind of smart title but from what Karen tells me he's a well-paid gofer. He was collecting the woman's child from school.'

'Lindl Clerc.'

'Probably. Some model or other. The child isn't Harper's.'

David appeared to think, briefly but carefully, before commenting: 'Harper left his extremely gracious and beautiful wife for her, so she must have something.'

'I'm sure she does, and we can guess what it is,' said

Annet acidly. 'Anyway, Karen and the school mums think Bailey's sent by God, but I formed the opinion he was a fairly standard prat.'

This made David laugh, as she'd hoped it would. 'Poor Bailey ... poor bugger.'

'Karen thought we should cultivate him – get ourselves asked up to the Big House for a cup of soup.'

'Why not?' mused David to get a rise out of her. 'I saw quite a bit of Harper at the time and he didn't strike me as a bad sort of chap. I imagine they can afford a decent cook.'

Annet laid a threatening hand on his neck. 'You're joking, I hope.'

When they went to bed, David returned from an abortive attempt to calm Freya, who was working herself into a frenzy in the other room, and discovered Annet standing in front of the wardrobe mirror in her underwear, with an expression of cold concentration that repelled advances. He caught the angry eye of her reflection.

'All right?'

'Why shouldn't I be?'

'Whatever it is she's after,' he said apologetically, 'I couldn't provide it.'

Annet didn't react to this, but pinched her waistline. 'I'm fat.'

'No you're not.'

'Fat and disgusting and middle-aged.'

'That's not true,' he said quietly. 'And you know it.'

'It depresses me.'

He stepped into his pyjama bottoms, not looking at her. 'Everyone carries more weight when they've just had a baby.'

She gave an acid, sniffing laugh. 'How would you know? And what's this "everyone"?'

He got into bed, picked up his book and laid it still closed on his knees. 'Anyway, it's sexy.'

As soon as he'd said this he realised he'd got it wrong.

'Who for?' She pulled off her underwear with careless, dragging movements, took a clean nightshirt from the drawer (less from necessity than from the desire to avoid him, he knew) and began brushing her hair as if administering a beating. Freya's cries had taken on a tremble of hysteria.

'I mean,' said David gently, 'that I quite like it.'

'Well dream on, because it's going.'

She left the room and after a few seconds the tone of the crying altered slightly as she picked the baby up. She did not, however, return, so he opened his book and stared miserably at the rows of print.

He didn't hear the crying stop but it must have done because the next thing he knew Annet was getting into bed and switching her lamp off. He turned to do the same and the book fell to the floor. In the sudden dark and silence he lay very still, trying to gauge her mood. He knew she was nowhere near sleep. After what seemed an age of harrowing tension he moved on to his side, his face inches from her back, wanting more than anything to put his arm round here and draw her against him, not to invade her angry privacy but to show his respect for it, and his love for her.

Suddenly and distinctly she said: 'Sorry.'

But then, as his hand touched her shoulder: 'No.'

There remained three weeks before Annet returned to work. Three weeks which David began to see as a countdown. It was not so much his period at home he dreaded as Annet's departure. If he himself had experienced return to work as a sort of release, how much the more would she? She had already begun to wean Freya on to a bottle, and to phone Piers twice a day: revving up, as he saw it, for the great escape. The soft curves which had so moved him were being determinedly eroded by lengths undertaken three evenings a week at a local pool. The advent of the bottle meant that if Freya woke during these times he was able to feed her. For the first time he found himself fearing his wife's compulsive drive to independence. It wasn't that he didn't trust her, he told himself, but that he didn't trust his own ability to let her go. For a short while, since Freya's birth, the dynamic of their relationship had altered – he had felt himself to be indispensable to Annet in a real, practical sense as well as an emotional one. Soon she would again be fighting fit (a peculiarly apt phrase), and once the nanny was in place and they became full-time working parents that tender balance would be thrown out in favour of the steady pull of opposites. It was no comfort to know that Annet probably welcomed this as much as he dreaded it.

At work, the dead zone at the end of summer meant there wasn't much doing. He looked up Samms, J. J., in Rustat Road and sent a modest bouquet Interflora. After a token round of interviews the temp Jackie got the secretary's job and initiated a major rationalisation of the filing system, both hard and computerised. She also reordered her own office according to what he was surprised to discover were *feng shui* principles – he wouldn't have taken her for a new-age type.

'Do you think it will make a difference?' he asked politely. 'It certainly looks nice.'

'Thank you,' she said. 'Looks are important. And if a setting is balanced and harmonious that can only be good.'

'True.' He couldn't resist asking: 'So what do you think of my office?'

But Jackie, for whom correctness was like breath itself, was not to be drawn. 'It's fine,' was all she would say. 'Very businesslike.'

He was due to go and look at a farm property that afternoon. Before leaving he wrote a short, handwritten note to Gina King, using the address at the top of her letter, which he'd painstakingly Sellotaped together.

Dear Gina
Thank you for yours of the 24th. I'm sorry that for a variety of reasons
I was unable to provide you with a reference, but I hope you got the job,
and please accept my best wishes for the future.
    Yours sincerely
    David Keating

First time round he had signed it simply 'Yours', but then thought better of it. He was pleased to have written the letter and to have struck what he believed was the right note. All the same he didn't leave it with the other mail for the franking machine, but took it with him to post when he left the office.

The property was an estate to the north of the town. He drove out through the least prepossessing of the suburbs – retail park, football ground, sewage works, a low-rise huddle of light industry, haulage firms and lock-ups. Roundabout followed roundabout, interspersed with frustratingly short bursts of dual carriageway. The farm itself was only a mile off the road, and visible from it, the undistinguished yellow-brick Victorian house flanked by a cluster of giant metal barns and siloes. This was no rich townie's fantasy of rural life, ripe for a national debtsworth of New Labour renovation, but a hard-nosed business venture, one of several owned by P. J. Hibbard and Sons. Hibbard, in no need of further income, was offloading Aston Lane Farm. The trick as far as Border and Cheffins was concerned was going to be the dividing of the property into parcels, to maximise profit on the house and garden, the outbuildings, and the several thousand acres of prime arable land.

David rather dreaded dealing with the abrasive, cash-driven owner, who didn't sound the sort to take any prisoners. On the other hand, the exchange was at least likely to be crystal clear.

A large, unsympathetic sign proclaimed the farm entrance, and indicated the direction to be taken by farm vehicles, business reps and visitors to the house respectively. Not without a tremor of uncertainty, David took the route to the house, and was

rewarded by the sight of Hibbard alighting from a parked
Land-Rover in which he'd clearly been awaiting his arrival.

'Land agents? Paul Hibbard. Shall we get on with it?'

Everything about this opening sally put David's hackles
up: the assumption that even following a reasonably lengthy
telephone conversation his own name had not been worth
remembering, and the note of impatience in spite of the fact
that he was scrupulously punctual.

'We'll do the house last if you don't mind,' went on
Hibbard. 'It's the least of my worries.'

They crossed the yard to the first of the barns. The
pale new concrete was traversed by runnels, currently awash
with a watery slurry. Hibbard, in tractor-soled boots, splashed
carelessly through these, leaving David to hop about to avoid
getting soaked.

'These are working buildings,' said Hibbard ominously.
'Functional, built for the job. No chance of turning this place
into a leisure facility in my view, but if some clown with more
money than sense turns up with the necessary I shan't argue.'

This remark set a tone from which Hibbard did not deviate
during the rest of the tour, which took in all the barns, the
glittering siloes, endless uninteresting acres of arable enlivened
by occasional patches of carefully-husbanded set-aside, and, of
course the house.

In spite of Hibbard's dismissive remarks it was the house, as
always, which David found most interesting. In this case it didn't
represent the must-buy factor in the deal, but at least it had some
atmosphere and individuality. Alarmingly, since David knew he
didn't live there, Hibbard let himself in at the back door, and
led the way through a well-equipped utility room in which two
washing machines burbled and churned, into a large kitchen of
which the predominant motifs were white Formica and stainless
steel. Cups, sugar bowl, milk jug and a slab of cherry-studded
cake stood on a broad breakfast jetty (the word 'bar' wouldn't
have done it justice) which jutted into the centre of room. A
good-looking ruddy-faced woman in jeans and a Guernsey sweater

was pouring boiling water on to grounds in a cafetiere as they entered. Having positioned the plunger she advanced and held out a hand to David.

'Perfect timing, give it a couple of minutes. I'm Hilary Bryce. Mr Border?'

'No, actually, David Keating – his partner. How do you do?'

'Mrs Bryce is the power behind the throne around here,' said Hibbard, heaving himself on to one of the long-legged chairs that surrounded the jetty. 'Dear God – speaking of which – but these are uncomfortable.'

'Rubbish,' said Hilary Bryce. Adding, with a surprisingly pretty smile in David's direction. 'And anyway, they're not for sale.'

'This is a magnificent kitchen,' he remarked, vouchsafed a sudden insight into the relationship between his hosts.

'Yes, it does the job,' she agreed. 'And since I knew he'd bring you in at the back door I thought we might as well start in here with some coffee.' She poured. 'With or without the doings?'

'Neither thank you.'

She handed him his, and poured a second – both 'doings' added without consultation – for Hibbard. The coffee was fiercely strong and aromatic, which caused David to entertain the fleeting, unbidden thought that Hilary Bryce was a tiger in the sack. This was the exact phrase that came into his head, though he could not remember a single occasion in life when he had actually used it. He experienced something close to his imagined idea of a hot flush.

'My husband's not about,' she said. 'So you'll have to make do with me.'

She took David round the house like a true professional while Hibbard retreated to his car phone. Like the kitchen, the rest of the house was immaculate, functional, giving nothing away. It appeared the Bryces had two grown-up children, one travelling in Indonesia, the other a GP in Wolverhampton, neither the least interested in farming.

'Which is fine, actually,' Hilary Bryce pointed out, 'because we only lease this place from Hibbard.'

The abrasive use of the owner's surname confirmed David's view that she and her landlord were on intimate terms.

'So what,' he asked cautiously, 'are your plans for the future?'

'None really,' she said. 'Geoffrey's retiring, but we certainly shan't be doing nothing. We're going to Darby-and-Joan it in our little place in North Yorks for a bit while making a plan. I have a yen for Australia, but we'll have to see.'

'It'll be a pretty big change for you both.'

'And a well-earned one,' was her spirited response. David considered that the biggest change was going to be separation from Hibbard, and wondered at the emotional and physical toughness of the landed types of which she was a paradigm.

As they went back down the stairs they could hear voices in the kitchen, and David was introduced to Geoffrey Bryce, a pale, distinguished-looking man more like a don than a working farmer. Hibbard had obviously accompanied him in, still carrying his mobile.

'Sorry I've not been here,' he said. 'Have you managed to see everything?'

'I believe so. It's a very impressive property.'

He turned to his wife. 'Did you show him the shop?'

'I thought I might do that on the way out.'

'Lot of nonsense,' put in Hibbard, but perfectly affably. 'That'll go when you do.'

Hilary didn't seem to take this amiss. Geoffrey Bryce pleaded paperwork, and she and Hibbard came out to the yard.

Hibbard stuck out a hand like a shovel. 'Well I'll let her show you the dried flower section. Perhaps you'd contact me as soon as possible about price, I want to be shot of this lot in short order.'

'Tomorrow morning.'

'That'll do.'

The other two said goodbye to each other like the intimate strangers they were, and David followed her to a Nissen-hut structure to the side of the house which he'd taken to be some sort of domestic annexe.

'Hibbard's right really,' she said. 'The shop's an amusing sideline for me, but it doesn't make any money . . . I say that, but lookee here, we've got a customer.'

A red Micra was parked at the far end of the hut. The double doors stood open on a fairly predictable array of jams, cakes, vegetables, pottery, stuffed toys and the aforementioned dried flowers. Behind the counter a grey-haired woman sat doing a magazine crossword.

In the middle of the room, studying a display of corndollies was Gina King.

'Good heavens—'

He hesitated for a second, and what happened next can only have taken another two, though it seemed longer. The woman at the till looked up and smiled at Hilary, who half-turned to introduce him. Gina left the corn dollies and walked straight towards the door, towards him. He began to say something, and may have done so, but although she passed within inches of him she didn't respond nor show any sign of recognition. A whiff of her familiar cheap, demure scent marked her passing . . . And then she was gone.

'This is Mr Keating,' said Hilary, 'from Border and Cheffins.'

When a couple of minutes later they went back outside, the Micra had gone too.

'Your customer didn't buy anything,' he ventured.

Hilary Bryce pulled a wry face. 'They mostly don't, except for Christmas and Easter. It's just idle curiosity, really.'

Geoffrey Bryce came out to see him off. 'Sell anything?'

'Of course not,' replied his wife.

'I only wondered, because that Micra was here when I arrived. Thought it might be worth a hand-thrown coffee mug at least.'

It began to rain on the drive back to town, so heavily at one point that the windscreen wipers couldn't cope, and David pulled into a layby with the water hammering down round him. During the few minutes that he was there a red car pulled in behind him. His scalp prickled with apprehension, but as the rain abated it drove off and he saw that it was a Mondeo. He did not realise he'd been holding his breath until, with a rush, he exhaled — but whether from delight or despair he couldn't say.

After that he didn't return to the office, but went straight home.

Chapter Seven

David didn't tell Annet that he had seen Gina King. The fact was that within an hour of leaving the farm, and certainly by the time he got home, he was by no means sure he *had* seen her. If it was her, she had not displayed the faintest sign of recognition. In fact, the curious thing was that she – whoever she was – had looked directly into his face as she walked towards him, but in such a way that he might not have been there at all. He had not been cut, but simply looked through. It was an odd sensation and a chastening one. He remembered with a frisson the figure in the lamplight opposite Bay Court ... the frightened, pale face of the person he'd almost run over the night he took Freya out ... The biblical expression 'through a glass darkly' chimed persistently in his mind. When he held his daughter in his arms he felt, among the now familiar welter of mixed emotions, a new fear – that of growing old, and mad.

Annet, on the other hand, was forging ahead, and away. When he mentioned his fears in what he hoped was a suitably light-hearted way she gave them short shrift.

'When she's sixteen, I'll be a pensioner,' were his exact words. 'It's a chastening thought.'

'So what point are you making?'

'That it may be a doubly difficult time.'

'Or easier. All that wisdom and experience, darl ...! Anyway, I refuse to start worrying about it now.'

Nor did she. She seemed stronger, both mentally and

physically, with each day that passed. She was keeping up with the exercises and the swimming, and was much less easily brought low by the demands of Freya, who was now fed from a bottle except at night. Annet had a further consultation with Lara McKay, the nanny, who was due to move into a shared house in King's Newton any day, and pronounced herself well satisfied with her own earlier judgement.

'I think we lucked out there. She's a nice girl.'

David, who had got home just as Lara was leaving, was slightly less sure. 'She's fairly overpowering.'

'That's just nerves. Meeting you for the first time.'

'I scarcely opened my mouth!'

'I'd much rather have chatty and open,' said Annet, 'than silent and secretive.'

'That isn't necessarily the only alternative,' he pointed out.

'Are you saying I made a bad choice?'

'Good heavens, no. I'm just wondering how she and I are going to shake down together when she starts. Without you here.'

'You'll be fine,' Annet assured him. 'But remember to let her get on with it. She'll be conscious of you hanging about the house, and she'll need some space to find her feet.'

'I'll be no trouble,' he promised drily. 'Lara can rule the roost.'

'No need to overdo it,' said Annet.

It also appeared that a long overdue boost was to be given to their social life.

'We should have a do,' Annet announced the following Sunday afternoon as they pushed the buggy round the lanes. 'I'm fed up with wandering the streets of this darn town like a stranger.'

He reminded her gently of the corollary of this. 'How many people do we know to ask?'

'Maurice and Marsha, those people from down the road, the Borders, Harry Bailey—'

'I thought he was a prat ...?'

'I've seen him once or twice since then at the leisure centre, and he's perfectly supportable, at least he'd leaven the mix. And maybe if we ask him we could invite the pop singer and his bit of stuff.'

'I scarcely know him,' David reminded her, 'and her not at all. He was just a client.'

'But you said you and he got on rather well. Be bold, darl. And we might as well include relations because then that's done.'

He was awed by the energetic ruthlessness of her approach. At the thought of Marina, not to mention Coral, let loose on their village acquaintances, he could feel his head beginning to ache. 'You think that'll work?'

'They're all adults for goodness' sake, it's up to them. We'll buy the drink, lay on the eats, open the doors and let them get on with it. Like we always do.'

Did, he thought: like we always did. They hadn't had a party of any sort since leaving London. The working week was so intensive and the weekends so precious that they hadn't felt inclined to do anything more than invite the odd one or two to supper now and then, a state of affairs which suited him down to the ground. He had never been a party person, but now he could see that it had only ever been a matter of time before Annet got the urge to fill the place with people.

The form which it was decided all this should take was Sunday lunchtime drinks the week before Annet returned to work. Because of the relatively short notice they invited people by phone. David adopted a slightly apologetic tone with Tim and Mags.

'It's a devil of a long way to come for a glass of wine, but I'm sure we could offer a plateful of something afterwards and we would very much like to see you if you can make it—'

'Whence all this diffidence?' cried Mags. 'A party's a party, we'd love to come.'

'Good, splendid.'

'There's just one thing.'

'Yes?'

'Would you mind if we brought Sadie and Luke? I really wouldn't be happy leaving them with the teenagers, even if it was legal.'

'Of course you must bring them,' said David, whose knowledge of his older nephew and niece, Josephine and James, would have resulted in pretty much the same conclusion. 'No question, it would be nice to see them.'

'Sadie would adore to help with Freya. She's at exactly that *Little Women* stage.'

'Even better.'

David was pretty sure that his brother's response to the invitation would be less enthusiastic. He could imagine the exchange all too clearly: 'Tool all the way up there for Sunday drinks, but we've only just been!'

And Annet's reaction to the prospect of the children's attendance, was also perfectly predictable.

'For goodness' sake, I'd have thought they could have been farmed out with friends.'

'It is Sunday.'

'They're going to have to toe the line.'

'I'm sure they will. Whatever their faults, Tim and Mags have got their kids pretty much to heel, the younger ones anyway. And Mags said Sadie's into babies.'

'So is my mother.' Annet slid him a look. 'In a straight fight between Sadie and Marina I know who my money's on.'

Annet called Harry Bailey at Stoneyhaye, but there was no one there, and since it was his voice on the answering machine she left a message. In spite of her earlier reaction she'd begun to like him. They'd become friends in a casual, undemanding sort of way. Far from being the smart-alec, cheap-feel poser she'd taken him for, his manner with her was affable and laid back. He seemed to enjoy her company, but wasn't pushy about it.

They'd had a drink on a couple of occasions after swimming but only if their schedules coincided: he didn't lay claim, or hang about. Curiously, although to all outward intents and purposes he and David were chalk and cheese, Bailey reminded her of her husband. Without ever referring to it, he seemed instinctively to understand something about her that not everyone did.

But the superficial differences amused her. When he remarked, over one of their low-cal beers, on the improvements currently underway at Stoneyhaye, she couldn't resist teasing him.

'Does it need improving then?'

'Come on – it's a dump. A grand old dump, but still a dump.'

'If it's that bad why did your boss buy it?'

'Because your old man sold it to him – no!' He put up his hands. 'Low one. No, every casting-couch tart wants to do Shakespeare, every pop singer wants to be a lord of the manor. Class at any price. Then when he gets there he wants to turn it into South Fork. But you won't catch me complaining, I'm a creature comforts man.'

She laughed. 'I must come and see all this.'

'There's a gym,' he said. 'When you're ready.'

When Bailey called back, Annet was upstairs bathing Freya and David, who had just walked in at the door, picked up the phone.

'Hello?'

'Um . . . now then . . . I wonder if I could speak to the lady of the house?'

David's antennae picked up some unwelcome signals. 'My wife's upstairs with the baby, this is David Keating, can I help?'

'David, my apologies. She called me about a party?'

'Probably. And forgive me – you are?'

'Harry Bailey.'

David's hackles stirred. 'We haven't met, but yes, we're having a few people in for drinks on Sunday week. Would you be able to come?'

'Most definitely. All of us. The full shebang.'

'So that's you and who else?'

'Hope I'm not speaking out of turn but your wife mentioned Chris – Chris Harper, I think you know him – and his old lady. They're keen to meet a few of the locals, integrate a bit.'

David murmured something about that being delightful, and poured himself a large Scotch.

'What on earth possessed you,' he asked Annet when she came down, 'to invite that bunch from Stoneyhaye?'

'I said I was going to. You mean they're coming?'

'So it appears. Bailey returned your call. They're complete strangers, not our type.'

'So we're going to get to know them better. Extend our horizons. Unknit that threatening unkind brow, darl, it's what parties are for!'

Of course, everyone accepted. It was that time of year, summer gone and Christmas not yet a gleam on the horizon: people were pleased to be asked. In a belated attempt to keep his end up, and in what-the-hell mode, David rang Hilary Bryce.

'Only a spur of the moment thing,' he explained diffidently.

'Yes . . . !' she sounded bright and amused. 'It makes a change beng invited somewhere where you're never likely to see anyone again. Just think, I could insult everyone in the room. Don't panic.' She gave an infectious, husky laugh. 'I shan't.'

'Well?' asked Annet, listening in.

'They're coming,' he told her.

'Good,' said Annet. 'Whoever they are. See how openminded I am? The more the merrier.'

The weather turned dark and sultry on the party weekend, the second in September. It was a toss-up whether they'd be able to use the garden or not. For the previous two nights Freya fretted and fussed in the unseasonal humidity. It seemed to David that Annet was less concerned these days: it was he who walked the floor, rocking and humming, and who lay, eyes wide open, waiting and hoping for peace to break out. It was apparent his vigilance got on her nerves.

'Settle down darl,' she grumbled. 'There's nothing left to do.'

'I can't settle if she doesn't.'

'Je-sus . . .' she moaned. 'Count me out.'

The result was that by the morning of the party he was tattered with lack of sleep. Freya, having been wakeful most of the night, slept placidly in her pram on the terrace while he and Annet set things up. Annet had a peculiar thing she did with glasses, a procedure handed down by Marina. After taking them out of the cupboard and washing them all she lay them on their side on a table cloth and dried them with a hairdrier. This ritual preceded each occasion that they entertained. He had stopped commenting that the glasses were clean anyway, that wasn't the point. It was what the Holbrooks had done, the only behavioural quirk, so far as he knew, which Annet had inherited from her mother.

'How many is it in the end?' he asked, aware of not having been much involved.

'About – twenty?' she said airily. 'Twenty-five?'

'OK.' David was wary of that vagueness; nor did he dare to ask how that number had been reached when he himself had only made three phone calls. Even allowing for his natural dislike of parties, this gathering had from the first instilled an ungovernable dread. He did not want the ground floor of his house to be full of people, two thirds of whom he scarcely knew and the remainder of whom (in the main) he did not wish to know or didn't want to see anyway. Most unsettling was the way his own diffidence seemed to feed Annet's enthusiasm. He could not dispel the idea that the influx of guests would drive them still further apart, and not just physically.

He was anxious on another count, too.

'I'll make it my business to keep an eye on Freya,' he suggested. 'With a party going on we might not hear her if she cries.'

She gave him a look that contrived to be both sympathetic and mocking. 'Between the two of us darl, I'm sure we'll see her right.'

It didn't take him long to get ready. Karen and Julie (Damian having been left with his grandfather) had been engaged as hired guns for the day, so feeling there wasn't much he could do he went to sit outside near the pram. Already the sun was appreciably lower and the patio was bathed in an almost gaudy brightness. But the sky over the ridgeway was a threatening navy blue, and at one point to the west a pile of inky clouds swirled up from the horizon like the plume of some predatory dark knight, distant but closing fast.

At ten to twelve Annet came out to join him, glamorous in black leather jeans she hadn't been able to wear since long before the birth, and an ice-blue satin shirt. She glanced into the pram and then bent to kiss his cheek, engulfing him in a wave of Nina Ricci.

He eyed her wistfully. 'You look wonderful.'

'Thanks. These trousers are a statement. Still snug, but a statement.'

He glanced down at his all-purpose, all-weather navy-blues. 'Neither of which descriptions could be applied of mine.'

'Cheer up,' she said, 'it's meant to be fun.'

He caught her hand. 'I know. I'm sorry.'

'Three hours from now and they'll all be gone.'

'I know.' Three hours? he thought. Dear God!

'Right.' That was as much reassurance as she was in the mood for, and her relief was palpable when at twelve sharp the bell rang. 'There's always one who has to be dead on time!'

In fact there were four – Tim, Mags, and their two younger children.

'I know, I know, don't say it,' said Tim irritably, 'but look on the bright side, we've had the drive from hell or she'd have had us here even earlier.'

'And anyway,' added Mags with the frayed air of someone who'd been looking on the bright side for the past several hours, 'we thought you might like these two keen young assistants before everyone else got here. They're eager to help, aren't you, chaps?'

'Are you?' asked Annet. 'Are you really?'

Sadie, ten, nodded, but Luke, a couple of years younger, made no reply and wandered dejectedly out into the garden. He wore camouflage trousers and outsize Nikes which emphasised his skinniness.

'Just ignore,' advised Mags. 'He was car sick, but he'll be fine in no time.'

'Anyway, it's great to see you,' said Annet, swinging into action. 'Let me alert the wine waiters.'

David was about to say he'd see to that, but Sadie sidled up to him. She was a pretty little girl, dressed in horribly unflattering baggy trousers with knee-level pockets, and a skimpy T-shirt – a look he dimly associated with some female pop group though the T-shirt bore the legend 'Boyzone'.

'Where's the baby?' she asked.

'Outside.'

'Ask Uncle David to introduce you,' said Tim, adding: 'Your daughter's the only reason she came.'

David led his niece out to the pram. Luke was mooching amongst the fruit trees at the end of the garden, determinedly not looking their way. David wondered if he'd been sick again, and if so where. Sadie was in raptures.

'Oh . . . !' she gasped. 'Oh she's really, really *sweet* . . . ! She's really, really beautiful . . . ! Can I look after her while you do the party?'

David could have wept with appreciation.

'Of course,' he said. 'That can be your job.'

Sadie put her hand into the pram and stroked Freya's head. David noticed with a pang that each small nail had a perfect

Beavis and Butthead transfer on it. Still stroking she looked up at him. 'Can I take her for a walk?'

'Well ... I don't see why not. Just round the garden.'

'OK, cool, where's the brake? Got it.' With a swift, natural expertise she released the brake and pushed off the stones and on to the grass with a murmur of 'Wicked ....'

The doorbell rang, but Annet called 'I'll get it!' and Mags appeared at David's side.

'Sadie's off – that's one guest happy, anyway.'

David considered that a little payment in kind was due. 'What a delightful daughter you have.'

Mags sucked in her breath thoughtfully. 'Delightful when she's not being diabolical. Luke looks a bit more cheerful ... I do hope that doesn't mean he's thrown up over your perennials. Best check.'

Glass aloft, she picked her way over the grass towards her offspring and David retreated to the house. The new arrivals were Marina, Louise and Coral. For what he and Annet had made clear was an informal party Marina was winsomely elegant in the sort of fitted suit that used to be called a costume, and which needed only frilled organza gloves and a cocktail hat to complete the picture. Her hair was crisply coiffed, her nails immaculate, her still flawless though finely-lined complexion made up to a creamy perfection. Though he could see why she riled Annet, he himself was quite fond of his mother-in-law, and rather admired her attention to turnout

'Hello my darling,' Marina said, laying butterfly hands on his shoulders as he stooped to kiss her. 'I don't see nearly enough of you ... Now where's the little one?'

She was off, pausing briefly to take delivery of her gin and dubonnet (provided specially) from Julie. Louise patted his cheek and followed. The bell rang again and as Annet answered it Coral came to stand before him in the ever so slightly challenging way she had. She was wearing a long dark red skirt and a red-and-blue waistcoat.

'How are you?' she asked simply, as though taking for

granted a whole mass of shared information and understanding.

'Fine.'

'In that case I'll say it, you look shattered.'

'I'm a bit tired. Freya hasn't been sleeping well.'

'Your wife, on the other hand, has rarely looked better.'

'Yes ...' He looked appreciatively at Annet – now surrounded by a group of guests, and holding the door open for others coming up the path – 'Yes, she's right back on form.'

'That's encouraging. Because you know we're going for IVF?'

He winced. 'I thought you wanted to adopt.'

'We did, but we thought better of it. Why expose ourselves to possible calumny and humiliation when there's a better way ... my God, there's a famous face, I'd better leave you to it.' She grinned and laid her index finger on his chest for a moment. 'We've chosen the father – loins of a lifetime, Paxman meets Irons – to die for.'

As time drew on, David came to think it was just as well that this exchange had taken place early on in the proceedings, because nothing that followed was any less disconcerting. Within fifteen minutes of its taking place he had met, greeted or otherwise acknowledged his twenty-odd other guests and felt himself to be a stranger in his own home.

The famous face to whom Coral had referred was that of Chris Harper. David had mentally rehearsed some line about not being remembered, but in the event this proved unnecessary, because Harper – a sad-faced man not far off his own age, in Armani tailoring, but neither shaven nor shirted – came straight up to him, transferring a tumbler of orange juice from one hand to the other.

'Put it there. Got to tell you Stonehaye was the best day's work I ever did.' He had the kind of untraceable, elided accent which could have been travelling either way on the social scale.

'Really? I'm pleased to hear it.'

'You too, I hope.'

'Most definitely. So you're happy there?'

'Yup—' Harper extended an arm, fingers clicking. 'Lindy—! Did you meet Lindy?'

'I don't believe so.'

David had seen pictures of Lindl Clerc in the paper, but none of them had quite done justice to the extremeness, the unsettling *completeness* of her beauty. It was all you noticed about her. He supposed, as he shook her long, boneless hand, that professional beauty was not just a gift but a job. She almost certainly needed no make-up to look beautiful, and yet her face was exquisitely painted: the eyelids soft butterfly wings of shaded and graduated colour, the cheekbones gleaming, the cheeks subtly shaded, the lips a glistening coral, exquisitely outlined. She was a work both of nature and of art. For the moment that her hand lay in his he was conscious of the whole limber, nearly six foot, of her, the sleek, careless curves beneath the ochre-coloured dress. Her hair, which might or might not have been blonde anyway, was bleached almost white and lay in whispy mermaid fronds against her neck. Her long toes in thonged gold sandals were slightly grubby as though she'd recently been barefoot. She didn't appear to have a drink, but she was smoking — David wondered in passing whether Annet had noticed this.

'Hello,' said Lindl. 'Thanks for asking me along.' She had a pretty, pouty French voice tinged prosaically with Essex.

'He didn't,' said Harper. 'His old lady did. Your wife knows my man Harry Bailey, right?'

'Right,' agreed David, realising that the phrase 'my man' had undergone a kind of quaint renaissance between Wodehouse and the present day. 'I think they encountered each other at some agitprop meeting or other. And now at the pool.'

'Mine'll be done by Christmas, she must come over and use it. And yourself, if you're into all that.'

'I can't say I am.'

Harper seemed already to have lost interest in the subject,

and was gazing upward. 'This is nice though. Mind if we look around?'

'Help yourselves.'

They were gone at once, with the world-weary savvy of the rich and famous, leaving David feeling strangely abandoned at his own party. It was with relief that he caught sight of the Bryces in conversation with Maurice Martin. Hilary Bryce wore the frill-necked jumper and culottes which she clearly considered suitable for the occasion but which didn't become her half as well as her jeans and Guernsey.

'I can't tell you what a hoot this is,' she told him. 'Geoff and I haven't met anyone new in ten years, and now blow me down there's a whole roomful when we don't need them.'

'Steady on,' put in Maurice in his personable way, 'you might meet us on the way down.'

Geoff Bryce looked across at David. 'I can't say I know Newton Bury well, but I did used to come across someone from here when I was in Rotary. Robert Townsend, mean anything?'

'It rings a bell . . .' David frowned. 'But we're shamefully guilty of not having mixed enough since we got here.'

'Too late anyway, poor chap died,' said Maurice. 'I took his funeral a few weeks ago. Standing room only in the church — not that he was a churchgoer, but he was a man who lived life to the full, and was taken in the midst of it.'

Geoff and Hilary murmured something appropriately regretful. But David was assailed by the memory of that afternoon only a week after Freya's birth. He could almost feel the still heat of the sheltered churchyard . . . see the drift of just overripening flowers and smell their dying sweetness . . . and the woman in the floppy hat, sitting on the bench . . . .

'I remember,' he said.

Maurice gave an apologetic grimace. 'Parking difficulties?'

'No . . . no. I think I read something.'

Hilary started in on how parking and potholes were the

abiding issues in village life, and David began to move away, then paused to ask Geoff:

'How well did you know Townsend?'

'Not well. Fellow Rotarian, no more than that. Immensely likeable and energetic. Never still. Never off, if you know what I mean.'

David considered this assessment as he wove his way through the chattering groups, noting the doctor, their neighbours, one or two half-recognised others. He accepted a top-up from Julie and a filo parcel from Karen who enquired confidingly: 'Enjoying yourself?'

'Yes indeed.'

'It'll be nice when it's over I expect,' she said, displaying an uncomfortable degree of intuition.

'Not at all. I think it's going rather well.'

She leaned her head towards him. 'You got the old rocker and his missus out then.'

'That was Annet.'

'I told her to give it a go. Bit of a result.'

'Is it?'

She batted his arm with the back of her free hand. 'Course it is. You can tell the others are fit to be tied, or they'd all be staring.'

This *aperçu* was echoed by Tim, who having negotiated his way out of the drive home was taking full advantage of the refreshment opportunity.

'How do you know old red eyes? The housewives' choice?'

'Through the housewife,' said David drily.

Tim barked with laughter. 'I'll tell her you said that!'

'It's true. Annet met his amanuensis at the school gate.'

Tim massaged his brow. 'Stop, stop, this is all too complicated for me.'

'Good,' said David. 'Now is there anyone I can introduce you to before I come up for air?'

'Well ... Would the rock chick be entirely out of the question? She really is something special.'

I did ask, thought David as they went into the garden, so I can hardly blame him for giving a straight answer. Marina, Mags and (curiously) Chris Harper were at the far end of the lawn, talking to the children in charge of the pram.

Luckily for Tim, Lindl Clerc sat alone on the edge of the terrace, still not drinking, still smoking. She seemed almost to be killing time, but without signs of impatience. It struck David that the apparent self-sufficiency of beauty isolated the possessor, and that unlikely though it seemed he might be doing her a favour by introducing her to his brother. And Tim, to be fair, was nothing if not pleasantly and openly admiring.

'How do you do, it's a real pleasure. I was getting bored with worshipping from afar, OK if I join you?'

'Sure ...' Tim's reward was a smile, tired but friendly. And a little gesture of tucking her skirt to one side as if making room.

'May I get you a drink?' David asked her.

'No thanks. I hardly ever do. Don't worry I'm quite happy.'

'You run along and enjoy your party, bro,' said Tim pointedly. 'I'm here now.'

He left them to it, trying to picture Mags' potential role in the mix, which in turn made him wonder what had become of Annet. His thought was answered by Karen, emerging from the drawing room with a half-empty tray of eats, and a smile on her face, a huge burst of laughter eddying behind her.

'She's in good form,' she said, 'keeping them all amused.'

He paused in the doorway and there indeed was his wife, glass at the high port, hip cocked, one eyebrow slightly raised – the cowboy look, but warmed by a nice chewy Bergerac and an appreciative audience. An audience comprising – he flashed a look round – Doug and Marsha Border, four locals including the neighbours, Hilary Bryce, and a dapper (one might almost have said spivvy) individual whom he took to be Harry Bailey.

Hilary caught sight of him. 'What a hoot she is, your wife!'

'It's the way she tells them,' he agreed with mild pride.

'I should say so – *and* looking like that only five weeks after having a baby, it's not fair.'

'She's been working on it. She goes back to work in a week's time.'

Hilary directed a series of interested blinks his way. 'Nanny all lined up?'

'Oh yes ... Jolly New Zealander, and jolly competent with it, you know the kind of thing ... I expect to be marginalised instantly.'

'Just so long as she's nice. May I go and look at your garden? I enjoy grubbing about and we're about to get a proper garden again in North Yorks, having been in the wilderness for years, so I'm picking up tips wherever I can ....'

People seemed always to be leaving his side. He was aware of his own apparent dullness next to Annet's spirited sociability, and turned towards the group, intending to identify himself with the main attraction.

Doug Border interposed himself and slapped him on the shoulder. 'So, my old mucker, how does it feel to be the host with the most?'

'If you mean Chris Harper, it had nothing whatever to do with me.'

'I never assumed it did. It's clear Annet's been networking like a good'un during her maternity leave.'

'Speaking of which,' declared Marsha *en passant*, 'I'm going to get some cooing done.'

'You mean that Bailey chap?' said David. 'Yes, she disliked him on sight but she seems to have got over it.'

Doug sucked his teeth leeringly. 'Never a good sign, early antipathy. Light blue touch paper and retire.'

'I wouldn't know.' David was deliberately cool, he didn't care for his partner in full man-of-the-world swing. 'I haven't met him before today. Still haven't, actually.'

'If you're interested,' said Doug, pointing over his shoulder 'they went thataway. I'm going to see if Harper and his totty want a Granny annexe.'

David waited till he'd gone and then went in the direction of the hall, where he'd pointed. They weren't there, but he could hear Annet's voice from the kitchen, and then Julie's giggle, just before she almost bumped into him in the doorway.

'Sorry — on my way!'

Bailey was perched on the edge of the kitchen table with his arms folded and ankles crossed. Annet, pink-cheeked and animated, was filling her glass from a bottle on the table. Without looking at him she said: 'Hi darl, anything I can get you?'

'No thanks.' He extended a hand to Bailey. 'How do you do?'

Bailey at once sprang to his feet and replied, in the American manner: 'Good, thanks,' which inclined David to the view that Annet's first impression might have been correct. But the man's handshake was firm, and his brown eyes — David arrived unwillingly at the word — cheeky, rather than shifty.

'I understand you're building a swimming pool up at Stoneyhaye,' he said, sounding stuffy without meaning to.

'Chris is up to all sorts,' confirmed Bailey, watching as Annet poured more wine into his glass. 'I was saying, you must come up and use it any time when it's done.'

David noticed that he looked extremely fit, in the bunched, tensile, rather pointless way of people who worked on muscle groups.

'I suppose there's already a gym?'

Bailey nodded. 'We put some air machines and weights in one of the rooms, but it's a shame I reckon to fill a beautiful space with that crap. I think they might do something with the stable block.' The words 'beautiful' and 'crap' sat side by side easily in this observation, gaining lustre from each other. 'But the pool's the main thing. Jay's going to enjoy that.'

'Jay's Lindl's son,' explained Annet. 'Remember I met Harry when he was collecting him from school . . . ?'

David was comforted by this reference designed to establish the openness between them.

'You're a man of many parts,' he said. He seemed unable to open his mouth without sounding pompous, but Bailey jerked his head in acknowledgement.

'You said it. IT, contracts, blagging, bullshitting, moving, shaking, childcare, that's me.'

Annet, on her way out of the room, leaned towards David. 'I've told him to let us know if he's free. We could do with an understudy for Lara.' She winked. 'I'm going to check on Freya.'

David found himself alone with Bailey, who seemed more at home in his kitchen than he did.

'So where's your charge today?'

'Gone to a friend's. If we'd known there were going to be other kids we'd have brought him along, but there you go.'

With Annet's departure, David's resentment had largely evaporated, to be replaced by curiosity.

'Do you have any children of your own?'

Bailey shook his head. 'Two wives, didn't get that far with either of them.' He glanced meaninglessly at his watch. 'Shame, because I like kids – I mean I really do. I like their company, I like the way they think. Shouldn't say this but I like the way they look.'

'They're not all the same, surely?'

'Right, but there's something the same about the way they're different.'

This seemed to David to be a point well, if allusively, made. 'Yes.'

'And I like it,' Bailey repeated.

'I hesitate to say this,' said David, 'but perhaps if you had one of your own you might not feel like that.'

As soon as this remark left his lips he regretted it, feeling it left him open to an obvious accusation which Bailey, to his credit, did not make.

'You could be right – not much point in speculating.'

'No.'

'How's your little girl?'

'Doing well.' David sensed Bailey's eyes resting on him, waiting for more. 'A big change in our lives, naturally.'

'I can believe it.'

'But one for the good.'

'Sure.'

There followed a short pause, more relaxed on Bailey's part than his own, before David said: 'I'd better return to my guests.'

Bailey gave another glance at the Rolex, more meaningful this time. 'I'd better return to your guests and all. And get going while you still have some Sunday left.'

Back in the drawing room the drift towards departure had begun. Annet was standing near the door, without her glass, acknowledging thanks and farewells. Luke was on the sofa drawing something on the back of his hand with a red biro. Marina, still with glass in hand, had cut off the Borders at the pass which caused David a certain quiet satisfaction.

He wanted suddenly, urgently, to hold Freya — to confirm to himself, and her, that the house was theirs again and the invasion over. But on his way to the garden door he was accosted by Hilary Bryce.

'Thank you so much, it was the greatest fun.'

'I'm glad you could come. I'm only sorry it's hello and goodbye, rather.'

'Paths cross, you never know, I'm a great believer in coincidence ... and by the way I like your careless garden.'

David wouldn't have been entirely sure how to take this, but then Maurice Martin, at his elbow, delivered himself of a slightly extended version of the same comment.

'This is how a country garden ought to be. Which of you's the expert, or is it a joint effort?'

'Joint, but neither Annet nor I would claim to be experts. It was pretty much like this when we came, and we were told to leave well alone for at least a year to see what was here. So idleness and expediency came together nicely.'

'Take it from me, it paid off. Marsha and I tend naturally

towards regimentation. Lamentable, but a habit that's hard to kick.' He clasped David's hand. 'It's been a very pleasant interlude, you must come to us as soon as we can summon a comparable number of amusing and witty people. Or since we'd like you to come in the forseeable future, even if we can't . . . .'

David emerged on to the terrace. Harry Bailey was escorting his charges up the lawn. At the far end, David noticed, Sadie (happily accompanied by Louise) was sitting on the bench on the far side of the pram, holding Freya.

'So you'll come and check out the pool then,' said Harper. 'We don't give parties, so no use waiting for an invitation.'

'We'll certainly drop round, thank you.'

Lindl gestured towards the pram with her cigarette. 'She's such a darling baby, so good. Jay never stopped crying.' She flashed him her sweet, unfocused smile. 'Neither did I!'

'Nice people,' said Harry Bailey. 'Nice party.'

David should have felt patronised, but didn't. He stepped back inside and encountered Coral, who took him by the shoulders and pressed a smacking kiss to either cheek.

'Darling heart, we're off.'

'Must you?'

'No, you're right, may we stay the night?' She waited for the dismay to show itself before adding: 'Settle down, we're going.'

'Marina still has a glass.'

'She can take it with her, for all I care, we're still going.'

David felt a surge of affection for Coral. 'So when's the big day? We'll mark it in the calendar.'

'Her indoors already did. October twenty-eighth.'

'Good luck – does one say good luck?'

'Say what you like, but—' she pushed her face towards his – 'be on our side.'

'I am,' he declared.

She went over to where Louise stood with Annet, and placed an unself-conscious arm around her waist. It was perhaps two seconds before he grasped the implications of this, and less than one before he was out in the garden. It was empty, but for the pram.

With an effort that almost burst his lungs he ran the length of the lawn. When he reached the pram his legs were shaking with strain.

The pram was empty. Freya, crying feebly, lay in the long grass beneath the bench.

'I haven't been down there for half an hour,' said Louise to Coral, as though David weren't capable of hearing.

'Sadie!' Tim crouched down by his daughter. 'We aren't cross—'

'Yes we are!' said Mags.

'We're not cross with you, but you mustn't ever, ever put a little baby on the ground like that.'

'Da-ad ...' Sadie's impatient whine had the terrifying ring of honesty. 'Get off, I didn't!'

'Then who the bloody hell did?' enquired Annet furiously over Freya's head. 'Luke?'

Mags reddened tigerishly. 'Come on Annet, don't pick on him, he's been loafing around up here for ages.'

'If there's nothing we can do ...' said Coral, with a well-judged ellipsis. 'Come on Lou. Marina?'

David, gazing out of the window, didn't move. Behind him his daughter, and the battle, raged. Outside, it was beginning to rain. Great slow drops fell heavily, and the pram was still standing, uncovered, on the grass.

'I put her in the pram!' protested Sadie. 'And that other lady was going to look after her.'

'Which other lady?' asked Annet.

'That blonde one.' Sadie's voice quietened at the possibility of being taken seriously. 'That friend of Uncle David's.'

The rain intensified with abrupt fury, and David, charging out into it to rescue the pram, chose not to hear Annet's question.

Chapter Eight

It was one of those things that in the end they had to let go. Freya after all was unharmed, and there seemed to have been no malign intent – whoever had put her on the ground had left her sheltered beneath the seat, and must certainly have known that she would be found within minutes. Disturbing though it had been at the time they agreed that they could hardly ring round everyone who'd been there and question them. Indeed, another bizarre aspect of the incident was that no adult had noticed anything untoward, or commented on the strange female guest.

Annet's money remained firmly on Sadie.

'It's all right, I'll never mention it again,' she said later, with a twist of anger still in her voice. 'But I think she was lying. Children do lie. She's a nice kid, it's not the end of the world, but I fully expect Mags at some point in the future convenient to her of course, to tell me that's what happened.'

'Maybe,' said David. 'I still think we should put it behind us. Try to forget it.'

'We can hardly do that,' snapped Annet, 'when it was plainly our responsibility – our fault for allowing a young child to be in charge of our baby. What on earth were we thinking of?'

She meant it was his fault, and was giving him the opportunity to admit as much. But he was afraid the fault might be much greater than she knew – and so sidestepped the issue.

'We didn't put Sadie in charge,' he said, 'we indulged her. With her parents' blessing.'

'Quite,' said Annet with a sardonic smile. 'We sure as hell have to accept that parents are always to blame in the end.'

This he conceded was probably true, and on this grimly philosophical note discussion of the matter finally fizzled out.

It nonetheless cast a shadow over Annet's return to work. He brought Freya, heavily muffled in her cot duvet, down to the hall to see her off. At the eleventh hour, on the doorstep, Annet hesitated.

'Pretty silly I know but I don't want to do this.'

'Yes you do.'

She put down her briefcase and held out her arms. 'Give us a go.'

He handed Freya to her. It was early, the sky still grey, with a premonitory breath of frost. David noticed his wife's hands, immaculately manicured, the nails painted a military scarlet for work, an asymmetrical silver ring he hadn't seen for weeks.

'You'll be fine,' he said, 'and we'll see you later.'

She gave the merest nod, holding it together with difficulty. Her size ten, dark-suited smartness reminded him of how far she'd travelled to get back to this point and he felt a familiar pang of love for her gallantry.

'Come on, off you go.' Gently he prised Freya away from her. 'Being late on your first day back won't help.'

'No.' She kissed Freya, David, Freya again. 'Y'all look after yourselves.'

'We will.'

He stood on the chilly threshold and waved her off. When he closed the door he sensed the whole realm of the place he called home, waiting for him – or more accurately lying in wait, to see what he was made of.

Freya gazed up at him, her small body-clock ticking away relentlessly. It was barely seven o'clock. In honour of Annet's departure he'd picked her up, although she hadn't started to fuss. He realised that by doing so he'd probably deprived himself of a precious half hour of peace and quiet. It was their — Annet's — usual practice these days not so much as to enter Freya's room until the summons became impossible to ignore. He couldn't put her back in the cot now her day had started. Wrily, he reflected that this might be the first and most valuable lesson of infant care: that it was always earlier than you thought.

But, he reasoned, even if she couldn't go back to her cot he could probably go back to his for a while. He carried the car-seat from the hall to the kitchen, and put her in it very gingerly in the hope that she might not notice. To his relief she remained quiet, squinting at her small red fists as he made himself a mug of tea. Then, carrying the tea well away from his body, he picked up the car seat in the other hand and took it upstairs. The decision remained whether to take her out of the seat and into bed with him, so risking disturbance, or place the seat with her in it somewhere adjacent. In the end he compromised and put the seat on Annet's side of the bed, facing him, and with pillows on either side of it.

He turned the radio on and heard the voice of a minister in trouble adopting that familiar of-course-this-is-unpleasant-especially-for-my-family-but-I-have-a-job-to-do-and-I-would-welcome-the-opportunity-to-do-it tone. David had never had much sympathy with philanderers and adulterers, particularly those public figures, like the minister, who should have known better, but this morning the whole thing seemed so removed from reality that he couldn't even summon a little token disapproval.

'... offered my sincere apologies to my wife, my children and my constituents, and they have been gracious enough to accept them. The Prime Minister, as you know, has given me his full support and I owe it to him to justify his faith in me and to discharge my responsibilities to the very best of my ability ....'

How did people get to be so pompous? David wondered. Whence all the sonorous humility and sense of destiny? Were certain individuals born this way and drawn to certain professions because of it, or did they learn these dubious but useful skills on the job? Listening to the minister draw to a dying fall, he concluded that it must be a mixture of the two.

The next item was one of those state-of-the-nation reports, this time on paid child-minders. The presenter – male and from Northern Ireland, a double-whammy of political correctness – pointed out that in Scandinavian countries the notion that a small child should spend most of its time with its mother was not just foreign but antipathetic. A child so reared would be considered deprived of essential socialisation, and its parents destructively burdened. Phrases such as 'no-win' and 'coming and going' flitted through David's mind as he put down his empty mug on the bedside table and turned his attention to Freya.

Annet had printed off an exhaustive list of requests, suggestions and instructions on the PC. It was a document as clear, comprehensive and carefully prioritised as any office spreadsheet. Reading it, David tried not to harbour resentful thoughts on the subject of the nanny's proposed autonomy. She after all was a professional, he a mere father. Some of the list, to be fair, took due account of his techno-blindness and led him gently through the programmes of the washing machine: 'Do everything on G, but keep dark blues/reds/other separate'. Others dealt with the almost insultingly obvious: 'Use the zinc and castor oil cream, not the nappy rash cream, it's too expensive to use as a preventive measure.' Friday, he noted trepidatiously, was 'baby clinic in village hall annexe, 2 till 4 p.m., better attend'.

He understood, of course, that the list had as much to do with his wife's anxiety as his own perceived incompetence. She did trust him, she knew he would cope and that all would be well – that was precisely the trouble.

Not that he felt over confident. He had never given very much thought to time and the way it passed. That it passed differently on different days and in different places was axiomatic. He'd found that the week of Freya's birth. And then ordinarily mornings were quicker than evenings, weekdays quicker than weekends and so on, perhaps because memory made them so. But now he was aware of time as a vast featureless space to be traversed without the benefits of landmarks or compass — to be made something of, from, as it were, a standing start. Also, he was sharing this uncharted waste with his daughter, who had no concept whatever of time as it was generally understood. Her needs had to be supplied more or less instantaneously while all the time aspiring to maintain a viable adult timetable.

These musings induced a more charitable view of Annet's spreadsheet. Perhaps after all he needed it in a far more fundamental and specific way. After all, here he was at eight-forty-five, still in his pyjamas, holding Freya, also in her sleepsuit, and lacking any immediate stimulus to action. It wasn't Karen's day, and there was nothing and nobody out there who needed him to put on a shirt and trousers and look lively.

A warm dampness on his shoulder and a familiar cheesy smell alerted him to the fact that his daughter had regurgitated a small dollop of semi-digested formula. The impetus thus provided, he went upstairs and laid her in the centre of the double bed while he washed, shaved and dressed. She became fractious about half way through the first of these processes, and by the time he took her into her room to change her she was in full cry. He had her sleepsuit and nappy off and was attempting to function calmly against the wall of sound, when there came a long blast on the front door bell. Picking up the disposable nappy he placed it roughly in position, swathed Freya in a blanket and went down to answer the summons.

'Thought I was right. Dads R Us?'

It was Harry Bailey, in black jeans and a baseball jacket. 'Just dropped the old boy off at school,' he explained, reaching out to ruffle the back of Freya's head with his finger. 'Thought I'd drop by and offer a little male solidarity.'

'Thank you,' said David without warmth.

'Went back to the coalface this morning, did she?'

'Yes — oh — a couple of hours ago.' He supposed he should be inviting Bailey in but he was wrong-footed by the sudden arrival of this self-confessed lover of children. Thankfully Bailey didn't outstay his welcome.

'Well best of luck,' he said. 'Tell you what, I'd rather have your job than mine. Give me real babies any day.'

He got behind the wheel of his car and leaned out of the window. 'You know where I am if you want a bit of kitchen-table therapy.' He nodded at the crying Freya. 'She's giving it some, looks like you might need it.'

David smiled thinly. 'You never know.'

'No need to ring, just turn up, they don't know what time of day it is half the time.'

'Thank you.'

The Mazda zipped away leaving a couple of puffs of exhaust hanging in the air like a fast car in a child's comic-book illustration. When he'd gone, David realised he'd probably cut off his nose to spite his face. The mere fact of another person in the house – if not quite the male solidarity referred to by Bailey – might have helped the time to pass.

He took Freya back upstairs and got her changed into one of the outfits from the daytime drawer. She was still at the stage when her trendier clothes looked faintly ridiculous on her. David liked her in the snug, simple 'Swee'pea' suits she wore at night. The straps of the microscopic pinafore dress he'd chosen stood up in loops, and the tiny red tights refused to stay put even when pulled up to her armpits. The inevitable result was that the garments seemed to be wearing her. He did the best he could, topped the whole thing with one of Louise's hand-knitted cardigans, and kissed his daughter's cross face.

'One day my girl,' he said to her, 'you'll break hearts in black velvet.'

He then put her back in the car-seat while he tidied the kitchen. She usually had a sleep about ten, but it was half an hour off that now, and she was snickery. He'd picked her up again when the phone rang, and it was Mags. He was as pleased to hear her voice, at a safe distance, as he had been dismayed by the arrival of Harry Bailey.

'How goes it?'

'Nice of you to call Mags — not bad, but then we've only just started.'

'David love, you'll be fine, it's only common sense.'

He gave a short laugh. 'Why do I take no comfort from that?'

'Nonsense,' said Mags, 'now listen. Why don't you bundle Freya into the car one day this week and come and see me? It's ages since you were down here, and it doesn't take long if you leave after nine in the morning and get back on the road about four, which you'd want to do anyway. As far as I'm concerned I can't think of anything nicer.'

For the first time David had a sense of how true this probably was. Mags was an old-fashioned company wife who ran a reasonably tight ship given the number of occupants, gave good car pool and brought business entertaining in on time and under budget. But with the whole brood now at school, even allowing for the hospice library, the scanner appeal and the servicing of a mind-boggling range of extracurricular activities, it was hard to consider how her days were filled.

'That's awfully kind of you, Mags ... can I think about it?'

'Of course, as long as you like, but do try. You'd be amazed how beneficial a change of scene can be.'

'I wouldn't,' he said with feeling. 'Believe me.'

'There you are then.' Did he imagine a short intake of breath before she added: 'I don't suppose you were able to shed any further light on the baby under the seat mystery ...?'

'No. To be honest, there was no harm done, so we haven't tried.'

'All very strange.' She sounded relieved. 'And *very* upsetting for poor you and Annet.'

'Surprising, perhaps,' he said.

'I want to say, David, that I do understand, and I'm sorry if I was snappish.'

'We all were.'

'You with rather more justification than me.'

'It's all over and forgotten,' he said firmly. 'Look, I must go, but I'll give you a ring tonight or tomorrow.'

'Yes, yes, we'll have a word, off you go.'

He put the receiver down and held Freya out at arm's length. Her legs pedalled energetically. Her neck was getting stronger and she held her head up for a few seconds, albeit at a rather tortoisey angle, to return his stare. For a moment he had a sense of the daughter rather than the baby – his daughter, the schoolgirl, the teenager, the young woman she would be. He wanted more than anything to hang on to the sensation or at least a clear memory of it. He brought her face a little closer to his and gazed into the opaque brightness of her eyes, trying to distil something of the essence of her, that unique part that would become her grown-up, black-velvet self. But she at once reverted to discontented infancy, unwilling and unable to hold his gaze.

He put her against his shoulder and fluttered his hand gently against her back.

'So what are we going to do then?' The 'then' was added involuntarily, it was a meaningless, soothing suffix that he'd heard Mags, Karen and Marina, even occasionally Annet herself, use when addressing the baby. It was odd to hear it on his own lips. Did one naturally begin to do these things when you became a parent or was it, as he'd heard people say on television, a 'learned behaviour'.

Either way, Freya had no answer and her mood was not improving. Jiggling her abstractedly, he referred to Annet's list. There were assorted commissions to perform in town, including the purchasing of a set of 'cheap, *stacking*, white microwave dishes *with lids*', dry cleaning to be taken and films to be collected. Also, he remembered, a couple of books on drawing that he'd got out from the library, now several weeks overdue.

He looked at his watch: the time had snailed forward to nine-forty. By the time he'd got Freya into the car it would be ten to ten, and by driving slowly via a scenic and circuitous route he could make the drive last half an hour, during which time, with luck, Freya would go to sleep. If she did, he decided, he would contrive to leave her undisturbed for as long as possible, even if that meant driving round for a bit longer. He realised this was not a viable or sensible option on a daily basis, but his job as he saw it at the moment was to keep his daughter happy.

Still holding her, he copied the relevant items off Annet's list on to another piece of paper and stuffed it in the breast pocket of his shirt. Then he locked up, turned on the answering machine, and introduced the protesting Freya first into her all-in-one suit and then into the car-seat before discovering that the harness needed adjusting to accommodate the suit. The adjustments, made with Freya in situ, caused a further deterioration in her mood and David's, so that by the time he'd been all thumbs with the car safety belt, started the car, and run back in to collect the cleaning and the film docket off the kitchen notice board, she was beside herself.

The car did, however, have its usual calming effect. Halfway up the ridgeway road David realised he hadn't brought a spare nappy with him, but this small risk, weighed in the balance against the huge one of his daughter waking up again, counted for nothing, and he pressed on.

This was a very different drive to the one he'd undertaken early on, in Annet's car. The Volvo was as powerful, but heavier and less nippy, and there was no temptation to speed. The threatening scintilla of frost had gone now, to make way for an indeterminate autumn day, of dim colours and soft edges. This most homely of the Home Counties was sodden and quiescent, nothing much on the roads, nobody much about — nothing much doing, in fact. David had to remind himself that while he was here, driving at thirty miles an hour, cornering like a nonogenarian, with the radio turned down to barely audible, other people were out there in what he now saw as the heady maelstrom of the workplace, subject to pressures, organising meetings, demanding pay rises, fiddling expenses ... Even idle talk in office corridors (of which Border and Cheffins had more than its fair share) seemed, from his new, outsider's perpective, to be a hectic and influential activity.

Not that this marginalisation was entirely unpleasant. As he cruised along the crest of the ridgeway he began to see himself as part of another, broader and more tranquil constituency. The 'out there' crowd might be the waves and the white horses, but the 'back here' people were the tides and the deeps. Happening upon this metaphor gave him great satisfaction.

The radio was playing some ballet music that he recognised but couldn't identify: a seductive melody full of unashamed sentiment and tremulous, swooping glissandos. Greatly daring he turned the volume up slightly. He glanced at Freya but she remained profoundly, soothingly asleep . . . .

What happened next was so sudden that for a split second he thought that the noise – the synchronised blare of engine and horn, the shrill gibber of brakes – was his doing, and automatically turned the volume knob backwards. But in the same second, with one hand still off the wheel, he smelt the tyres and felt the crude shock of the wing mirrors colliding as the other car, coming from behind, missed him by inches. In a vortex of terror he pulled the wheel over with his right hand, hauled on the handbrake with his left, pushed the brake to the floor, but he still seemed to mount the verge at terrifying speed, the car juddering and bounding, a heap of metal out of control.

When it finally stopped he was shocked to discover he'd travelled several hundred yards from the point of impact. Sweating and trembling he looked over his shoulder. Behind him were twin arcs, like a black rainbow, on the road, and a churning wake of mud and torn grass marked his sickening progress over the verge. Of the other car there was no sign except mirror-image skid marks swirling back and forth in ever shallower parabolas before being reabsorbed into the calm tarmac.

Still in shock, he was assailed by a new and worse terror. Freya. Incredibly, her eyes were still shut. His heart raced – how often had he thought of her sleep as a small death? How many times a day – and night – had he and Annet checked that she was still alive, then prayed she wouldn't wake? Fumbling with fear, unable properly to focus, he undid first his own safety belt, then her straps, with nightmare clumsiness. The engine had stalled, but the music, idiotically, played on in waltz-time.

He released her and held her cradled in his arms, her face cupped between his fingers and thumb.

'Freya?'

Her skin felt warm, and she was unmarked, but her eyes remained resolutely closed. Her babyhood suddenly made her an alien — foreign, distant, incommunicado. He had literally no idea if she were injured or not. Utterly dependent but utterly separate, she kept her secrets from him.

Fighting down panic, clutching her, he got out of the car. The air was cool and still. Every sound — his shoes on the grass, the rustle of his clothes, the muted bump of the car door swinging back on its hinges, even his breathing — was magnified. Eerily, he had not seen one other car on the ridgeway before or since the incident.

Lifting Freya against his shoulder he walked up the road, in the same direction he had been driving. To break what seemed like some sort of spell he began to sing, at first under his breath and then more loudly: "'I'll sing you one-oh, Green grow the rushes-oh, What is your one-oh? One is one and all alone and ever more shall be so! I'll sing you two-oh ...'" He didn't know where this particular song had sprung from, his schooldays probably, since when it must have waited, perfectly if unwillingly assimilated, to be brought forth when occasion demanded. By the time he reached seven-oh, he was singing so loudly and walking so fast that he didn't at once notice that Freya was moving. But when her head lurched unsteadily backwards he caught it in his palm and stared at her as he had earlier that morning, for signs and portents. She blinked and blenched, dazzled by even this muted light after the darkness of sleep.

'Freya?' he said again, almost ecstatic with relief, and was rewarded by a series of the small guttural clicking sounds that preceded complaint. Let her complain, he thought, let her cry, let her bawl her eyes out – she's alive!

As he turned to go back to the car it became clear how out of it he had been. For one thing, he had covered several hundred yards, and was as far from the Volvo now as it was from the original collision point. Also, a blue van had pulled up alongside and a man, the driver presumably, was standing on the verge between the two vehicles. He was looking towards David and now he called something, held up an arm as if to advertise his presence.

David quickened his pace and as he did so felt weak and nauseous. The strong, seismic shuddering of a few minutes ago, part of the impulse to survive, had been replaced by a sick trembling that threatened to take his knees from under him. It was as if he'd been sucked momentarily into another dimension where every atom of energy had been focused on his daughter, and had now been hurled brutally back into the real world with depleted resources. By the time he got to the van he was staggering, and his face and hands were ice-cold.

'This yours, mate?' asked the man. 'Nasty, you all right? How's the littl'un – want to give her to me? There you go ... You sit down, get your head down, that's it ... Go on, that's right, I'm a family man too ....'

David didn't know whether he answered this stream of kindly platitudes or not. The man smelled of paint. One shovel-like hand scooped Freya away from him, the other grabbed him under the armpit as he subsided on to the grass. It then applied a comforting pressure to the back of his neck, and rubbed him between the shoulder blades as he first gagged, then retched and threw up. When he'd finished the man moved away and came back with a bundle of white material in one arm. Still holding Freya, who was perfectly quiet, he shook this out and spread it over David's shoulders, applying little thoughtful tweaks and adjustments like a mother putting a child to bed.

'Sorry about the dustsheets ... You're in shock, mate. Anyone called an ambulance?'

David shook his head. 'Not necessary . . . .'

'Okey dokey, no worries, I got the mobile in the van . . .'
David could tell the samaritan was thinking fast, whereas he
himself could barely think at all.

'Tell you what we'll do,' said the man, 'In a tick when you're
up to it, you take the little lady and I'll move the car back on
the road. Then I'll give the police a tinkle, better tell them it's
here, then I can run the both of you over to the hospital.'

The word 'hospital' worked on David like a cold douche.
He'd had an accident! No sooner had Annet walked out of
the door than he'd crashed the car. One second's lapse of
concentration and he'd risked his daughter's life – and everyone
was going to know it.

With a superhuman effort he marshalled the strength to
say: 'Really there's no need for that. I just need a couple of
minutes . . . .'

'I know, I know,' the man was soothing but firm. 'But you
ought to get checked out. Especially the baby. After all she can't
talk, can she – can't tell us about it, can you, mate?'

With difficulty, David raised his head to look at her. 'My
daughter . . . does she seem all right to you?'

'Oh yeah.' The man crouched down next to him to spare
him further effort. 'But better safe than sorry – best to let the
experts take a look, right?'

David nodded miserably.

'How you feeling?'

'So-so. I'm sorry about all this.'

'No worries. You up to taking her while I move the car?'

'Of course.'

'Back up a bit and you can lean on the van.'

'Thank you.'

He allowed himself to be repositioned, and took Freya,
conscious that the man placed her in his arms with great care
and deliberation.

'Thank you,' he said again.

'Keys in there?'

'Yes.'

'Won't be a tick.'

He was aware, now, of a car passing, slowing down fractionally to take a look. How many others had there been in the past few minutes, that he hadn't noticed? How many people from Newton Bury who would go back and say 'You'll never guess what I saw on the ridgeway this morning . . .'?

The minute he had hold of her Freya began to squirm and grunt. He didn't have the van driver's soothing touch, or perhaps — a nightmare scenario of internal injuries and delayed reactions filled his head. He kissed her repeatedly, in desperation, but the kissing only made her worse. The sudden noise of the car engine startled both of them — he burst into a sweat, and Freya's arms jerked upwards. The noise rose and intensified as the wheels failed to get a purchase in the mud. He closed his eyes and rocked the crying Freya back and forth, more for his comfort than for hers.

'Sorry about this . . .' The driver stood at the side of the road, just in front of them, and flagged down the next car that passed. With a humiliating sense of his own helplessness David listened as 'a bit of a push' was elicited, and given, the engine switched off at last, and an exchange took place sotto voce in which he sensed he himself featured.

'OK, cheers!' The second car drove off and the van driver returned.

'All done. How you doing?'

'Not bad, but she's beside herself.'

'Pissed off, can't say I blame her. Here—'

He took Freya again, hooked his arm under David's and pulled him slowly to his feet. 'All right?'

David's head swam. 'I will be, give me a second.'

'All the time in the world, mate.'

The man was an exemplar of patience and kindness. To hell with Lara, David found himself thinking, this chap had missed his vocation. Now he helped him over to the van.

'You be all right in the back? You can lie down. Only she ought to go in her seat.'

'Of course.'

The back of the van had, he guessed, been hastily reordered to accommodate him, with plastic crates full of brushes and paint tins moved to the side, and the dustsheets spread out.

'Stretch limo it isn't,' said the driver.

'Please – I really can't thank you enough.'

'Won't take us more than fifteen minutes, just sing out if you want to stop.'

He strapped Freya's seat in, and tested its secureness, with a series of enviably brisk, decisive movements.

'Right then,' he said, rolling down the window and pulling out. 'Let's get this show on the road.'

They seemed to go at breakneck speed, but this may have been because David couldn't see. Freya had gone quiet again, but he told himself that she always did in cars.

'By the way, I got your car keys,' said the driver into his mirror. 'Don't let me forget to give them back.'

'I won't.'

'You're not legal in there, but if we're stopped it's an emergency, I reckon, yeah?'

'Certainly.'

They hurtled in silence for a while, before the driver asked: 'Mind the radio?'

'Not at all.'

He turned on Classic FM, *Fledermaus* sung by a soprano like a dentist's drill on speed. David was reminded of Kenneth Tynan's description of Anna Neagle, 'shaking her voice at the audience like a tiny fist', but the driver was enjoying it, and even turned the volume up slightly and tapped his fingers on the wheel.

The man's prediction as to time proved correct, and they arrived at the entrance to the hospital just before eleven. David carried the sleeping Freya in in her car-seat. He hadn't been near a casualty department in thirty years – not since he'd scalded himself with boiling milk in his shared flat in NW10 – and it was depressing to see how little things had changed. There were the rows of hard chairs, their cracked plastic seats sprouting occasional shoots of stuffing ... the table littered with dog-eared magazines ... the notice board warning grimly of everything from veruccas to meningitis and the detection of same ... the tropical fish ... the crate of grubby-looking children's toys surrounded by a litter of Stick-a-bricks and wax crayons ... the dozen or so unhappy patients ... The only difference that he could see was a display unit in moving lights forbidding the use of mobile phones, and the fact that the nurse behind the desk wore trousers.

'Now look,' said the van driver as they waited their turn, 'will you be OK?'

David was humbled by his kindness. 'Absolutely. I can't tell you how grateful I am.'

'Only I'd better get along to my job.'

'God, you must have lost hours, is there someone I can talk to you on your behalf?'

'I'm self-employed. Anyway,' the man looked at his watch, 'What – forty minutes, tops? I can make it up easy.'

'I hope so.'

'You'll be able to sort out getting your car back? No damage as far as I could see. By the way, I never asked – was there anyone else involved?'

'No.' It was an auto-pilot lie, spoken before he thought of it. 'No, I must have had a lapse of concentration. Entirely my fault. The person behind did have to swerve to avoid us but that wasn't surprising.'

'Never stopped, I suppose ... ?' The man shook his head in gentle despair. 'Never thought to see how you were?'

'No, but you did, thank heavens.' He fished in his pocket and took out his wallet. 'Please – will you let me reimburse you for your petrol?'

To his considerable relief, the man took the note without demur and made a small saluting gesture with it.

'Cheers. Appreciate it.'

When he'd gone, David felt bereft. It was a long time
– since childhood, probably – since he'd experienced such a
solidly comforting presence. On the other hand the samaritan's
departure had the salutary effect of making him think for
himself. There was a process to be undergone. The nurse on
the desk peered at Freya and asked if she'd been awake since
the accident.

'Well – naturally,' he said.

'Why naturally?' She was on her mettle.

'I mean, another car struck my car. It was a pretty disturbing
experience.'

'I see. So she's been crying and so on, behaving normally?'

'Yes, but obviously I can't be sure—'

'No, quite, we'll take a look at her. And what about you?'

'I was in shock. I felt faint, and I was sick, just afterwards,
but left to my own devices I'd have gone straight home. I was
persuaded to come here because of Freya.'

'You did the right thing,' conceded the nurse, scribbling on
a form. 'How old is your granddaughter?'

'My daughter actually.'

He had to hand it to the nurse, she thought on her feet.
'You can't tell these days with granddads getting younger all
the time.'

David was still smarting from this when he sat down. It
was true, grandparents *were* getting younger – you had only to
look at Karen – so it was an understandable mistake. But the
damage was done. Coming so soon after the accident, in his
already weakened state, he felt stricken.

He studied the piece of paper he'd been handed. In the
top left-hand corner was stuck a pink disc. Next to the disc
was printed the information: 'The coloured disc here indicates
the approximate length of time you can expect to wait. Green
= fifteen minutes, Pink = half an hour, Yellow = 1 hour, Red
= possibly more than an hour.'

He debated going back to the desk and complaining about
this prediction, but a cursory glance round revealed that several

other patients had pink stickers, which suggested that it wasn't an indication of perceived urgency or the lack of it, but simply the order of the day.

In the end it was only twenty-five minutes before he and Freya were summoned, and shown into a curtained cubicle where they were at once shut in with a whisk and a rattle. While they sat there for a further ten minutes Freya finally woke up, but as she didn't cry he decided against taking her out of the seat right away, on the spinning-things-out principle.

Eventually a frighteningly young Scottish intern swept in, aglow with brisk, no-nonsense bonhomie. He left the curtain open, as if to show that while waiting was a private activity, consultation was not.

'So, bit of a bump on the roads? A bit shaken up, the two of you I have no doubt?'

David confirmed this. 'I was, but I'm fine. It's my daughter I'm concerned about,' he added, to make the relationship clear from the outset.

The intern, whose badge proclaimed him to be Dr C. McPhail, folded his arms and stared down at Freya.

'Quite right, very sensible. Nonetheless, since the young lady's good as gold for now I think we'll start with you.'

David answered questions, and then lay on the couch while his joints were flexed, his stomach kneaded, and a light shone into his eyes and ears, after which he was declared sound in wind and limb. He then sat on the edge of the hard chair while Freya, curiously unprotesting (McPhail seemed to have the same effect as the van driver) was subjected to the same process.

'Is she always as good as this?' McPhail asked.

'No. She yells from time to time. She's our first,' David explained, 'so we don't have anything to compare it with.'

'But she's cried since the accident?'

'Oh yes.' He realised now what they were getting at. 'Oh yes, she protested violently when – earlier on.'

'Fine . . .' McPhail tweaked Freya's tights up and her dress down, and handed her over. 'Fine. I'm going to chance my arm and say I don't think there's any need for either of you to hang around here.'

David wasn't wholly reassured by the choice of words. 'You're sure? I mean about Freya? Because——'

McPhail shook his head, eyes closed. 'I'm sure.' He went to the entrance of the cubicle and stood there, seeing them out. 'Though it goes without saying that if you're worried about the least little thing you should consult your own doctor. And in fact even if all's well, as I fully expect, make an appointment with your GP for, say, the end of the week or beginning of next just to get the rule run over her. And you, if necessary.'

As if to prove a point Freya started to grizzle while he rang for a cab. It didn't seem appropriate to worry Annet with news of the accident on her first day back, and he didn't feel that he knew anyone in the village well enough to summon them, especially as he didn't wish this escapade to be common knowledge.

When he'd finally got through, and replaced the receiver he found a young nurse hunkered down by the car-seat in a squirrel-like attitude – a baby-lover if ever he'd seen one.

'Ah . . .' she said, 'd'you think she's hungry?'

He glanced at his watch. 'She could be, but there isn't much I can do, I didn't know we were going to wind up here,' he expained, 'or I'd have brought the life-support systems.'

She looked up at him, holding Freya's hand in hers. 'We've got some formula in the fridge, you know, we keep it in case it's needed. It's made up fresh every day.'

'Really?' He found himself thinking, what would Annet do? but banished the thought instantly. 'That sounds like a good idea.'

'I'll get some.' She stood up. 'How long will your taxi be?'

'Twenty minutes he said.'

'Why don't you go and get a coffee in the WVS shop and I'll bring her a bottle?'

She was so keen and sweet, so unaffectedly eager to help, that he did as he was told. In the shop – he'd have called it a café – Freya's yells were met with equal indulgence by the green-clad ladies behind the counter. As he paid for his coffee and Kit-Kat the woman at the till asked:

'You don't remember me do you?'

He looked up cautiously. This, like 'how old do you think I am?' and 'have you stopped beating your wife?' was a question to which there seemed no reply from which one could emerge with credit. But the moment he saw the speaker, he mercifully did recognise her.

'I'm so sorry – I do apologise – I was in a world of my own.'

'That's hospitals for you,' said Jean Samms. There was no one else in the queue, so she added, raising her voice slightly above Freya's. 'Are you visiting, or . . . ?'

'I was involved in a minor road accident, but we've been given the all clear.'

'That's good.'

He jiggled Freya. 'Do you work here every day?'

'No, no. I work at the library but Monday's my day off and I do the morning here.'

'That's very noble of you.'

'Not really.' She pulled a rueful face as if to say it was little enough. 'What else have I got to do?'

Without enough information even to hazard a guess, David didn't reply, and now the little nurse came into the café carrying a bottle of milk, and he raised a hand to attract her attention. 'That's for us, I'd better do something with it for everyone's sake.'

He found a table and sat down. Freya seemed to leap on to the teat like a salmon. She was still small enough for him to balance the bottle in his left hand and lift his coffee cup with his right. Peace, along with nourishment, spread through both of them. When he got up to go he waved to Jean Samms.

'Goodbye. It was nice to see you again.'

'Bye-bye,' she said, and made a small waving gesture towards Freya – the gesture, he suspected proudly, of a person who didn't have children.

*   *   *

In the minicab he strapped Freya's seat into the back and sat next to her. the driver was uncommunicative, which suited him fine. All he wanted now was to get back to the car, and then home. But as they left King's Newton behind and headed out towards the ridgeway, images of the accident burst in his head like fireworks

Getting back behind the wheel he experienced a lurch of queasy anxiety, and not just at the prospect of driving again. He remembered now – the car that hit his had been small and red, a young person's car. A Fiesta perhaps. Or a Micra.

Of course he was going to tell Annet – how could he not? He mentally rehearsed various approaches. These ranged from the casual; 'Some idiot clipped my wing mirror on the ridgeway this morning, we were lucky that was all'; via the righteously indignant: 'It was sheer, blatant hit and run, and not a thing I could do'; to the pre-emptively breast-beating 'I feel so responsible ... it makes me feel quite sick to think how much worse it could have been'.

But none of these felt quite comfortable, possibly because none took account of the small, cold fact that it had been partly his fault. He came down in favour of spontaneity – he would mention the day's events when a suitable opening presented itself, in whatever way seemed appropriate at the time.

What he hadn't anticipated was no opening at all. Freya had fallen sweetly and obligingly asleep over her post-bath bottle, but he kept her downstairs for Annet, and was still carrying her about when his wife finally got back at half past seven, wired.

'Talk about a shock to the system, you wouldn't believe the crap that's been going down in that place for the past couple of months, or maybe you would, but at least when they say they missed me I believe them ....'

She was marching to a different drum, and its fast, excitable beat drowned his own more hesitant rhythm.

'. . . oh look, sleeping like an angel, you are clever, darl. I'm sorry I'm late but you know what it's like.'

He wasn't sure that he did. He had never been charged up by his work in the way that Annet was. She took Freya up to bed and then came down and stood in the kitchen, drinking four glasses of wine, displaying the miniature denim jacket purchased by Piers at Baby Gap, and talking non-stop while he dished up a smoked-fish pie disinterred from the freezer. He noted that she seemed to have grown back into the sharp suit and high heels, so that whereas this morning they had appeared almost poignant, now they were a symbol of her invincibility, hot from the battle. Next to her in his weekend clothes he felt soft, rumpled, vulnerable as a mollusc without its shell.

'Don't worry,' she assured him, 'I'm not going to be this late every day, this was exceptional.'

'Of course,' he said, 'bound to be.'

Unexpectedly, she came and stood behind him, putting her arms round him and exerting a strong pressure over his heart. He knew this embrace, knew it was a demand for unqualified understanding as well as an expression of affection. He covered her hands with his.

Against his back, she said: 'So come on darl – tell me about your day.'

His hesitation was so small she wouldn't have noticed it. 'Oh,' he said, turning to take her in his arms. 'There's nothing to tell.'

Chapter Nine

———◇◇◇———

Lying to Annet, or being even slightly duplicitous with her, had been until recently a new experience for David, and he was profoundly uncomfortable with it. He couldn't pinpoint precisely when it had begun, but the cause had something to do with Gina King. The unhappy girl's short time in his employ, her dismissal and her subsequent refusal to, as it were, go away, all preyed on his mind. Once he'd entertained the notion of her being involved in the day's events the idea took root, and made it still more difficult to talk about.

A dozen times during the course of that evening he readied himself to say something like: 'Actually, when I said there was nothing to tell about our day I wasn't being entirely accurate ...' But on each occasion the words failed to find a voice. It never seemed to be quite the right moment to rock the boat and spoil Annet's mood, particularly since Freya (for the second time in her short life) appeared to have suffered no ill effects from her accident. The baby clinic on Friday would soon enough tell him if something were wrong. In the interim, he reasoned, it was a case of the most good for the most people.

During supper he was only too happy to let Annet do the talking. When pressed again for detail he told her about the rest of the day – the visit from Bailey, Mags's invitation, the work he'd done in the garden that afternoon while Freya slept in her pram. Suddenly drowsy at around ten, Annet had propped her head on her hand and said, round a yawn:

'You know, I think you could take to this.'

'It's fine,' he said. 'Except that it exists in a different time zone.'

'How do you mean?'

'More time,' he explained, 'but less possibility of doing anything with it.'

'You found out.'

'I was going to go into town to knock a few things off your list,' he said, 'but it didn't happen.' That close. He was that close.

'Oh, the list . . .' she chuckled. 'I'm sorry about the bloody list, darl, don't let it tyrannise you.'

'I won't. I could do with a bit of structuring.'

'I think I was having trouble letting go. Handing over.'

'Perhaps,' he acknowledged carefully.

'But not now.' She hiked up to him and kissed his cheek, then his mouth, amorously. 'I'm so lucky . . . .'

A few minutes later, going upstairs to join her, he told himself that he was too.

She was lying naked in bed with her hands linked behind her head, watching him as he entered the room. Her bedside lamp was off. The duvet had slipped down to reveal one breast, and as if to emphasise the point the sleeve of her nightshirt trailed wantonly from beneath the pillow: not wanted on voyage.

She flicked the other side of the duvet back and stretched her arm out on the sheet.

'Hurry up, I thought you'd never get here.'

He was acutely aware of her watching him as he undressed. Because she had been out in her other world, he felt more naked than usual, exposed to comparison. As he got into bed he switched off his lamp, but she at once reached behind her and switched hers on.

'No you don't . . . .'

He knew that a large part of her excitement was due to adrenalin, that she felt (ghastly modern word, but so true of her) empowered. But that didn't stop it being wonderful when she was upon him, hands sliding and grasping, legs twining, mouth finding him out ... He gasped.

'Hey ...' She paused, leaned back slightly to focus. 'What's this?'

'What?' He put his hand beneath her hair and tried to pull her back.

'Here.' She pressed the side of his arm, just below his shoulder.

He winced. 'Nothing.'

'Nothing, schmuthing, have you been consorting with rough women?'

'Chance'd be a fine thing, they were all out at work ....'

'This is a nasty lump, and a bruise ... Poor darl, I leave you alone for two minutes and what happens ....'

She wasn't that bothered, her fingers ran back and forth over the place, rubbing it in, reminding him. As her breathing quickened he felt the sad, shaming retreat of his own body. Concern over his small injury had fuelled her desire, but quenched his. He fought to revive it, he clasped her and found her mouth with his, tried to draw the feeling back into him, but it was impossible and she sensed the desperation in his kiss.

'Darl ...?'

'God. I'm sorry.'

'No, no, don't, it's OK ...' She dropped light, comforting kisses on to his face, her unexpected tenderness was heartbreaking. 'I don't care ... I understand ....'

'Do you?' he mumbled, knowing she couldn't, possibly.

'M-hm.' She nodded as she slipped on to her side, her shoulder tucked beneath his, her head on his shoulder. 'I think so. Being stuck at home's not very sexy.'

He couldn't bring himself to answer, but laid his arm over his eyes.

She added: 'Doesn't mean I'm not disappointed, though ....'

'I'm so sorry. I love you. I've missed you.'

'I know.' She caught his other hand, the one furthest from

her, and pulled it gently so that he rolled to face her. 'So it's not the end of the world.'

She guided his hand down between her legs and he heard her catch her breath, but her molten heat couldn't warm him.

'There you go,' she murmured, moving his hand, drifting. 'See what you're missing . . . ?'

Moments later she gave a little cry, and fell asleep almost at once, as though shot by a dart.

After a while he moved his arm from under her and she lurched away, still deeply asleep, snuggling beneath the quilt like a child. David did the same, so they lay back to back. The scent of her was on his fingers, but in his mind, for an hour or more, was the image of the speeding red car, and the fierce whine of its engine as it passed within inches of his life, and that of his daughter.

The next morning was qualitatively different in several respects. Annet was terse and preoccupied not, he knew, because of his failure, but because of her own perceived moment of weakness. To underline this regrouping she was up first and brought him Freya, already clean and dressed, while he was still struggling out of sleep.

'Present for you.'

'Lord, is that the time . . . ?'

'I heard her snuffling, so thought I might as well save you the bother.'

'Thanks.'

She wasn't so much helping, as stealing a march: he understood that, and didn't resent it. She knew from her own experience and his comments last night that the last thing he needed saving for him was time. Freya stared fixedly up at him. The clock read six-twenty-five.

'Look,' she said, 'I'm going to make an early start, try not to be so late back.'

'You get going.'

She dropped a kiss on each of them, and was off, rattling down the stairs at speed. It was a trick she had perfected. He remembered the first time he'd gone out with her they'd run down an empty escalator for the tube and she'd seemed to fly ahead of him, her feet barely touching the steps, reaching the bottom when he was barely halfway down.

He'd asked her then: 'How do you do that? It's not natural.'

'Clever, huh?' The cowboy look, sidelong, teasing. 'My secret.'

Ten years later he knew how she did it, though he still couldn't do it himself. It was a question of taking most of the weight off your feet and virtually sliding down the rail, resting on your hand. But it was an act of faith as well as of balance and these days he didn't have quite sufficient faith in his co-ordination.

'Bye!' she called now from the hall. 'See you later!'

'See you . . .' He wasn't sure that she heard, he hadn't liked to raise his voice too much and startle Freya. The door shut briskly behind her and he and Freya, eyes locked, listened as the Toyota started up, revved, then gave a little whoop before pulling away.

'There goes Mummy,' said David. 'Now how are we going to spend our day?'

In spite of the earliness of the hour, the start of the day seemed easier than before. He concluded, as he sat in his pyjamas giving Freya her bottle, that this was partly because he was that bit more prepared for what lay ahead, and partly because Annet's departure had been less of a trial, more of a release. Her restless energy allied to the strain of deception had been the cause of last night's disaster, he was sure of it. He salved his conscience, and soothed his injured *amour-propre* by deciding that he'd definitely tell her about the accident this evening.

Annet had dressed Freya in dark red velour dungarees, but the legs had to be rolled up several times and he soon found that they came unrolled all the time because of Freya's habit of rubbing her feet together like a grasshopper when she was in her seat. This mightn't have mattered except that she then managed to get both legs over the baggy crotch and down one trouser. Forseeing an ongoing problem he took her upstairs and put her into a babygro with yesterday's perfectly clean pinafore over the top. This he considered a masterstroke – the babygro was snug and neat, while the pinafore provided the requisite fashion note.

Karen, when she arrived, wasn't so sure.

'What's your daddy put you in?' she chirruped over the seat while David made coffee. 'What's he doing to you?'

He tried to conceal his irritation. 'Don't you think it's nifty? I'm rather pleased with myself. Prevents midriff separation.'

'It does that all right,' she agreed. 'Don't know what Mummy would say though, do we?'

He realised it was only babble, but the assumed sisterly solidarity between Karen, his daughter and the absent Annet, got on his nerves.

'Mummy,' he said, 'is far too busy to give the proverbial, I imagine. Can't remember if you take sugar?'

Afterwards he rather regretted having been sarcastic with Karen who was to all intents and purposes a treasure, but she seemed either unaffected or not to have noticed. Mindful of Annet's injunction to let the professionals have their heads, he deemed it best to stay out of her light and work out a plan for the day. This involved performing the errands in town (on the get-back-in-the-saddle principle), and in the afternoon if it remained sunny, driving out to Stoneyhaye. At the very least he could take Freya for a walk in the grounds. And if he was honest there would be a certain satisfaction in being first to respond to the open invitation.

Before setting off he laid Freya on a blanket on the living-room floor and rang Mags.

'How about Thursday?' he asked.

'Thursday it is!' She sounded ridiculously pleased. 'Can you remember how to find us or shall I fax a map?'

'I'm sure I shall remember when I get within striking distance, but fax a map anyway.'

'So you'll come sort of mid-morningish?'

'That's the plan.'

'Yippee,' said Mags, 'what fun!'

David put the phone down with the gratifying feeling that he'd done his sister-in-law a favour rather than invited himself to lunch. With today and Thursday as it were taken care of, he decided to devote Wednesday to some yet-to-be-decided-upon project around the house or garden, a surprise for Annet. It occurred to him that he might even do some drawing while Freya had her naps: perhaps try and draw her, though babies were notoriously difficult. The thought of retreating to the little room under the eaves set aside for the purpose, with Freya snoozing peacefully, and his pencils and cartridge paper to hand was immensely attractive. Time, thus planned for, seemed shorter. Yesterday was over. He was on holiday after all. The Hoover was going, so rather than call he took Freya upstairs and waved to Karen from the bedroom door.

She switched off, smiling. 'What can I do for you?'

'Karen, we're going into town.'

'"We"!' It seemed to amuse her.

'What?'

'You make it sound like you discussed it. I can just hear Freya going "Dad, I need to pick up a few bits and pieces in the Formby Centre"!'

'Yes ...' he chuckled, conscious of his earlier grumpiness. 'Well, anyway we're going and we shan't be back till you've finished, so I wanted to say thanks and remind you the necessary's on the table in the kitchen.'

'Cheers then. Have a good morning – drive safely!'

As she uttered this entirely casual advice she switched on again, so didn't notice David's fleeting double take.

Freya was tranquil this morning. She didn't even fuss when he put her outdoor suit on, and as a consequence he managed both that and the seat harness with the greatest ease.

The morning was perfect – the sky like a blackbird's egg, the air sweetly disarming, the sheltered grass brushed with secret frost, but an almost glittering green where the sun fell on it. Yesterday, with its muffling cloud cover and disobliging events, seemed aeons ago. And yet as David loaded the buggy into the boot he scraped his arm on the door brace, and winced: the bruise was still there.

Just the same his mood was cautiously optimistic. As a precaution, he selected a tape of Celtic music before starting the engine. Freya fell asleep to the tune of whistles, drums and fiddles. Up on the ridgeway the scars of yesterday's events were still plain to see – the careering skid marks, the furrows on the grass verge – and he superstitiously anticipated some sort of after-shock. But he drove steadily on, and nothing happened.

In town he collected the film, picked up the cleaning and put it in the car and then took his two overdue art books back to the library. When he'd paid his fine at the returns desk he asked the girl: 'Is there someone working here called Jean Samms?'

'Yes, Jean's here.'

'I'm an acquaintance, I wanted to say hello.'

'She's replacing stock in the children's section.'

He found her sitting on a tiny stool with a pile of picture books on the floor next to her.

'I'm not following you,' he said, 'I had some books to return and I remembered you said you worked here.'

'No, it's nice to see you.' She got to her feet, heavily but with dignity. 'I've probably seen you in here before without realising.'

'Not necessarily, I'm not much of a library-user I'm afraid, but I do sometimes take out books about drawing.'

'You're an artist?'

'No, I'm an estate agent.' He hit her with the proscribed term but she didn't flinch. 'Drawing's what I do purely for my own pleasure.'

'We're putting on an exhibition here in early November,' she said. 'You ought to take part.'

'I doubt you'd have me.'

'Not me, there's a committee. Come.'

She led him back to the desk and handed him a leaflet. 'Nothing ventured.'

After the library he had a cappuccino at one of the faux-New York coffee bars in the Formby Centre. He'd brought survival kit for Freya in a bag on the buggy-shelf, but she remained quiet, gazing at her surroundings. It was while he sat there that it occurred to him to take her into Border and Cheffins. He wouldn't make a big thing of it, just pop in at the front door as though he was passing anyway. It was no more than a ten-minute walk and he liked the idea of the receptionist, and Jackie and the other women clustering round admiringly as he'd seen them do with the new babies of other staff members.

Leaving in the direction of the office, he passed the fountain, and saw the same rough quartet there: the unprepossessing girl with the lyrical voice, the two sad-eyed soaks with their patient dog lying alongside. This time the girl was singing. 'The first time ever I saw your face' and he was ensnared by the soaring longing of the tune, the romance of the words, the pathos of the singer herself ... But Freya wasn't so sure and began to grizzle, so he reluctantly moved on.

Pamela on reception gave him the welcome of his dreams.

'Oh, Mr Keating, is this her? Oh but she's *beautiful*, you must be so proud! Hello darling – it's Fiona, isn't it?'

'Freya.'

'Freya!' Pamela crouched by the buggy, showing an acreage

of smart black leg beneath her tailored skirt. 'A goddess, and quite right too – am I allowed a hold?'

'Of course.'

'Aren't you gorgeous,' crooned Pamela. Basking, David stood back and let her get on with it. He was getting used to the idea that young, single women, especially attractive ones, whether unconsciously or no used babies as a sort of corsage – something fresh, alive and beautiful to enhance their own beauty.

'Look!' Pamela cried now as a trio of girls from admin. came down the stairs. 'Look who Mr Keating's brought!' And in no time there was a sweetly pretty flurry going on as Freya was fussed over and fawned on and passed from hand to hand. He suspected that Annet would have found the whole thing nauseating, but he was moved that these predatory, tight-skirted, modern girls should be so charmed by his daughter.

Pamela favoured him with an almost flirtatious look. 'Are you in charge then, Mr Keating?'

'I am.'

'What, all day?'

'All week.'

'Goodness!' She made round eyes. 'Your wife's gone back to work then, I take it?'

'Only yesterday. So it's my turn for a few days, and our nanny arrives next Monday.'

'Are you going up to see Jackie?' she asked. 'Only if not I'll give her a buzz so she can come down?'

'Well, if you think she won't mind.'

'Mind?' Pamela laughed and waved her hands to show the sheer madness of that idea. 'She'll go ape if she finds out she's missed you.'

David couldn't imagine Jackie going ape about anything, but no sooner had the admin. girls regretfully handed Freya back than she emerged from the lift: Pamela, back behind her desk, pointed.

'There she is, isn't she lovely?'

'Well,' said Jackie, taking one of Freya's hands and wagging it gently. 'Welcome, Freya.' It was typical of her that she didn't need reminding of his daughter's name. 'She looks like you,' she added, the only person to have said so.

'Most people think she's like Annet.'

Jackie nodded. 'How is Mrs Keating?'

'Fine. Back at work this week.'

'By the way,' Jackie let go Freya's hand to signal something more businesslike. 'A woman rang for you this morning and wanted to know if you were all right because she thought she saw your car broken down by the side of the road yesterday – I explained you weren't in this week and that I didn't know anything about it, but since you're here I thought I'd mention it. We were cut off and she must have been on a mobile because I couldn't call her back, so I'm afraid I don't have her name.'

'It doesn't matter,' he said hurriedly, 'it was nothing to worry about. Probably some acquaintance from the village.'

'She was only young,' added Jackie. 'More of a girl, really.'

As he left, Pamela called after him: 'I think you're a bit too good at this. You won't want to come back!'

David considered this possibility as he walked back to the Formby Centre. Today, with the sun shining and Freya at her most amenable he could almost imagine being a full-time father, or at least (he corrected himself) a father in full-time attendance. But Jackie's message and the attendant confused fears had taken some of the gloss off the day.

Annet's day had had no gloss to begin with. The autumn round so accurately predicted by Piers had begun to materialise with a vengeance, and Piers himself, not a stoic at the best of times, had developed a cold.

'I shan't come near you, never fear.'

'Good.'

'I'd never forgive myself if through my agency you carried back this vile infection to your new baby.'

'I wouldn't either, Piers.'

'Should I go home, do you think?'

'No! Just keep your distance.'

He did, but his snuffling, coughing and nose-blowing almost drove her to distraction, as did the way he ostentatiously raised his voice to cover the *cordon sanitaire* being mantained between them.

'Did Freya think her jacket was cool and groovy?'

'She did. That was nice of you, you shouldn't have.'

'I told you no little friend of mine is going to be stylistically disadvantaged while there's breath in my body . . .' he swallowed painfully, 'which may not be much longer.'

There were days when Annet might have found these antics amusing, but this wasn't one of them. It looked as if she was going to have to make at least two overseas trips in the next six weeks, one to Dusseldorf for the Graphics Fair and another to discuss a household energy symposium in the Hague. Both dull, both threeline whips. Even so, these trips used to be one of the perks of the job. She'd enjoyed the travelling, the meeting people, the buzz . . . Now she realised she was dreading them. And that was apart from Norwich, Glasgow, and Plumbing of the Future at the NEC.

At lunchtime, Piers having decided that his cold would benefit enormously from a curry, she sat with a sandwich at her desk and phoned home. But there was no one there.

David got back just after one to a clean, tidy house, and Annet's voice, with a slight edge, on the answering machine:

'Only calling to see how you were doing. I might ring again this afternoon but things are silly here so if I don't speak to you I'll see you later. Take care, I miss you . . . .'

Before giving Freya her bottle he took her upstairs to change her. There was a pile of sweet-smelling folded washing on the bed in their room, courtesy of Karen, and the baby's room had also been subjected to her professional touch, with soft toys arranged more appealingly, the cot bedding freshly changed and the rag doll rug subtly repositioned to signal hoovering thoroughly done. In an unexpectedly poetic touch she'd laid a sprig of lavender at the head of the mattress.

All this order and tranquillity, however, seemed not to agree with Freya, who turned increasingly crotchety. A couple of dud disposables which David could not persuade to stick did nothing to improve her humour, and although she sank her formula as though it were her last, most of it came back fifteen minutes later in a manner that redefined the term projectile.

Changing both her clothes and most of his own to an accompaniment of loud and furious crying, David reflected grimly that this was all it took to wipe the silly smile off one's face. Time, in the shape of the afternoon, once more reared up before him like the north face of the Eiger. He had been doing so well, the day had been half over and matters pleasantly accomplished. Now the remainder of it seemed almost unimaginably long. He was not optimistic about the chances of Freya falling asleep, because she'd napped in the car on the way to town and on the way back. This particular bout of yelling would have to be seen out one way or another, the worst case scenario being that she would sleep later from sheer exhaustion, and then be unwilling to do so this evening when Annet returned, hyper and hassled, from the office . . . .

He carried the protesting Freya into the garden and walked her round a few times to the tune of 'All things bright and beautiful' — another blast from the past that formed on his lips without apparent reference to memory. The singing, if you could call it that, was to calm him as much as his daughter. He wondered if the focused people of the world, the achievers and fast-laners like yesterday's straying politician, would be so susceptible to infant moods, or whether part of their genetic inheritance was the ability to rise above such things.

After a couple of circuits he sat down on the bench at the

end of the lawn, and laid Freya down on his lap, her head on his knees, looking up at him, a position that often seemed to amuse her for a few moments. Not that on this occasion she did look at him, or at anything: her face was contorted and her cries were taking on the vibrato of real distress. David thought of grim press stories about lone parents holed up in tower blocks, and could clearly appreciate why such people might become desperate. Theirs was a situation which could spell utter loneliness: sole responsibility, without recourse, without rules and possibly without moral support. He had a car in the drive, cash in his pocket as well as in the bank, several efficient means of communication – and Annet, with whom he could at least share the trials of the day later on. And yet he had rarely felt more helpless than in the face of this incomprehensible micro-storm.

He folded each of Freya's small, bunched fists in his hands and swayed her gently to and fro, trying to slow the rhythm of her cries. As he did so he gazed back at the house. This was its most pleasing aspect. From the confines of the road, hemmed in by hedges and walls, it could seem frowning and narrow, the interior darker than it really was. From the garden, viewed across the undulating expanse of grass and the shallow step of terrace it looked wholly benign. He admired the robust brickwork which glowed pink in the early afternoon sun ... the steep, twin gables and dignified chimneys ... the stately garden doors with their shutters folded back like wings ... the long, shining sash windows ....

His eye ran along first the ground floor, then the first-floor windows, matching them to the rooms inside, thinking of the quiet and comfortable spaces inside which had seen many occupants, and now saw them, David and Annet Keating. The sense of continuity calmed him, and he realised at the same time that Freya had gone quiet. Almost frightened to look he glanced down and saw that her eyelids were drooping. He kept up the movement, not daring to breath. The garden was very quiet, too; and not simply quiet, but silent – still. David felt embraced by the stillness. The village with its solid old buildings, and the shallow hills that shielded it, seemed to hold their breath with him. His heartbeat was like the tick of a clock through a pillow. He could hear no birds, but in the blue above the chimneys a sparrow hawk trembled fiercely far above its prey. He watched it for a second until it simply disappeared, the speed of its descent seeming to snuff it out.

His eyes moved back down to the house, and to the two small windows under the eaves. The one to the left was a box room, the place where they kept suitcases, and Annet's skis, and boxes of as yet unhoused books and old vinyl LPs, and cans of paint so they could remember the names of the colours. He glanced across to the right. This was the room where his drawing things were: where he proposed to retreat and sketch his daughter as she slept.

So far the room had remained almost empty – freshly painted, and with the floor sanded, but without either curtains or furniture apart from a trestle table and a rush chair. In truth they both rather liked it that way. David went up there occasionally not to draw but just to feel its airy lightness, and to look out of the window towards the hills, as he supposed some daydreaming maid or weary cook-housekeeper must have done during the house's heyday.

It may have been the extreme quiet and stillness, or his solitude, or both, which made him at once aware of someone looking back at him – not simply gazing out of the window but staring fixedly in his direction. David remained motionless: the watcher too. Freya slept, he could scarcely feel her hands in his. The air around him was like a cobweb in which he was suspended. He narrowed his eyes, but the focus didn't alter – the figure at the window was no clearer. He could make out the pale disc of the face, and curiously the eyes, or at least the intentness of the eyes, fixed on him. This was a presence – he would have said merely a presence, but that its force-field extended to where he and Freya were – androgyne and concentrated. While it stared, he believed himself unable to move. His body and limbs were not so much heavy as weightless, without the function provided by gravity: by normality. He tried to clear his throat, simply to be aware of himself, but the will to do so was not enough, his brain seemed to be uncoupled from the rest of him.

How long this altered state lasted for he had no idea, but there came a point where Freya moved slightly in her sleep, and her foot nudged his thigh gently. At once it was as though his ears had popped. The sticky caul of unnatural silence gave way to the noisy peace of Newton Bury on a fine autumn afternoon – a bird twittered, a distant car droned, the whispering breath of vegetation and animal life flooded into his system like strong drink. And as if he'd taken a strong drink his eyes watered and the blood pulsed in his face. He had never felt more alive, which made him wonder if perhaps he had been dead.

There was no longer anyone at the window. Freya slept on.

He was less shaken than curious. When he looked at his watch he saw that no more than five minutes had gone by, and yet the afternoon ahead no longer seemed an insuperable obstacle. He was energised. Firmly, without anxiety, he picked up Freya and, carrying her in the crook of his arm, went into the house. Its utter normality was cheerful as band music. He climbed the main stairs, and then the short half-flight to the top floor. The door of the little room stood open. There was no atmosphere of any kind, except the clean smell of the sanded floorboards, and that of his paper and fixative. He went over to the window and opened it. The garden seat looked surprisingly far away, further than he'd thought.

He stood for a moment, breathing in the sunny afternoon. Then he closed the window. As he did so he glanced down at Freya. To his surprise she was wide awake, her head turned slightly, her opaquely dark eyes fixed on some point behind him. She was completely relaxed on his arm.

'Hello,' he said aloud to her, to hear his own voice. 'Back with us are you? Shall we go out and see what's what?'

In the doorway on the way out he thought he caught a whiff of some flowery fragrance, but it was gone before he could identify it.

When he put Freya in her buggy she smiled at him, for the first time. A smile of such perfect confidentiality and delight that it brought tears to his eyes.

They went for a long walk, out of the village and along the footpath by the little River Nevitt – the 'Newt' in Newton. The footpath began as quite a tidy affair but even when it degenerated into a bumpy track Freya seemed not to mind. It may have been the smile, or simply that they had spent more time together, but he thought of her for the first time as real company, a person with a definite and individual presence. Once or twice as he pushed along he looked down and found her gazing up at him, but although he was tempted he didn't, out of respect for this new turn in their relationship, try to make her smile again. Let her give her favours freely, he thought, and not in response to her father's vanity.

At the point where the flanking undergrowth – dock, dandelions, nettles and bramble – rendered the footpath impassable for the buggy even at this time of year, he turned back. They'd come a good mile, and the village was picture-book pretty ahead of them, a tumble of ancient roofs from which the church tower emerged, glinting like a stone periscope. He decided to go back that way – he liked the church, and the route would bypass the centre of the village with its clutter of school mums.

When he did reach All Saints he found he was not alone. There was a truck parked by the gate and a couple of young men, the regular contractees, at work in the churchyard, one perched on a motor mower, the other, in a perspex mask, sweeping a strimmer back and forth around the edges of the older gravestones. Until recently this task had been performed by members of the congregation, but it was a sign of the times that the average age of those available on a weekday had risen, and this was a lot of grass to keep down ... Hence R. D. A. Garden Services of King's Newton.

The two men, cut off by the noise of the machines, didn't spare him so much as a glance as he walked up the path. In the porch he put the brake on the buggy and lifted Freya out, to give her a change. The main door was heavy and stiff and he had to push with his shoulder to budge it, but he closed it after him to shut the noise out.

Here, too, he was not alone. Maurice Martin was kneeling precariously on the edge of the pulpit putting a bulb into the wall light. He glanced very cautiously over his shoulder, without moving the rest of his body.

'Good afternoon whoever you are.'

'It's me, David Keating.'

'David, my dear chap, since you're here could you take this off me ... ?' He held out the old bulb at arm's length.

'Here.' David relieved him of it.

'Thanks. One less hazard to contend with. And could you possibly just switch this on for me to check? It's the left-hand switch by the vestry door.'

David obliged, the light came on, and he turned it off again.

'Good. Now for the undignified business of getting down.'

Back on terra firma, Maurice dusted his hand on his trousers. He was in mufti – cords, desert boots and a fleece – a bulky, strong-looking man who coached football (both sexes) at the primary school and wielded a useful middle-order bat in the Newton first XI.

'Of course this is your week for the joys of fatherhood. All going well?'

David liked Maurice. 'I'd hate to appear over confident, but rather better than expected.'

'So you didn't come in here to plead for strength and guidance, then?'

'No, no particular reason. We went for a walk up the river and came back this way.'

Maurice gazed around fondly. 'Place is a sort of magnet, isn't it? I mean, if you're at all susceptible. I know you could say I would, wouldn't I, but there are plenty of times when I come in just to be here – nothing to do with the job.'

'I'm sure.'

'Not today though!' Maurice jerked a thumb in the direction of the churchyard. 'Their last session this year. I'm afraid I rather unworthily make a point of stopping by when the R. D. A. chaps are here. Finding some pretext or other ... I've no reason not to trust them implicitly but it does no harm to show the flag – make it clear this is a place where people come and go.' He put his finger into Freya's furled palm. 'So you turning up adds a bit of credence to that.'

They strolled companionably down the centre aisle.

'Annet happy to be back? Or torn?'

'Both, I think.'

'It must be hard. Della and I were saying after your party – good fun, by the way – how much we admired your approach, the two of you. It's not a dilemma the clergy have to face much. Clerics work flexitime by definition and very few clergy wives go out to work, even in this day and age. Nothing to stop them I hasten to add, but the ministry has a way of expanding to employ the people available.'

They reached the cross aisle.

'Thinking of getting Freya baptised?'

'Thinking of it, yes.'

'Bone of contention?'

'Nothing as definite as that. I tend towards it, Annet doesn't, so we dicker.'

'Hm.' For only a second David caught a flash of something less than entirely genial. 'Apathy, the old enemy. Anyway—' Maurice slapped his hands together – 'is it just me or is it getting chilly in here? Were you going to sit, or shall we return to the sun?'

David might have sat, but the meeting with Maurice had made him slightly self-conscious.

'The sun beckons, I think.'

Maurice moved to the north door. 'Let's go this way to escape the racket, I've made my point.'

R.D.A. had already seen to this half of the churchyard, skirting, with jobsworth accuracy, the more recent graves so that the plots were like islands in the calm sea of shorn grass. The more kempt among them benefited from the comparison, but David couldn't help noticing that Robert Townsend's had been let go, the spanking new gravestone obscured by a shock of long, pale, autumnal weeds.

Maurice remarked: 'Sad when they're not looked after, isn't it?'

'I was thinking the same thing.'

Maurice went to Townsend's grave and began tugging at the weeds, which being half-dead came out easily, in handfuls.

'Not my business, I know, but the poor chap's only been gone a couple of months and already he's a mess.'

'Perhaps people feel – perhaps the grave depresses them.'

Maurice straightened up, grasping a shock of weeds. 'They can always go for a neat little urn.'

'That's true.'

'Still, judge not.' He was angry again about something. 'Cheerio. See you again soon.'

He went off in the direction of the compost-bin, and tossed the weeds into it. David, returning to the south porch to reclaim the buggy, felt more saddened than angered by the neglected resting place of Robert Townsend.

True to her word, Annet was home at six, less elated and more weary than the previous evening. She kept him company while he bathed Freya, sitting on the lavatory seat nursing a vodka and tonic, not talking much. Afterwards David put on k d lang, and Annet gave Freya her bottle, sitting with her feet up on the sofa.

He didn't go into the kitchen but lit the fire and sat with them, half-looking at the *Standard* she'd brought with her.

Once she looked over at him, and said: 'Nice.'

He couldn't bear to spoil things, when there was no need.

She put Freya to bed, and then he heard her winged feet flying down the stairs.

'David! I got a smile!'

'Did you?'

'A real, beaming smile, not wind, right at me!'

'That's fantastic,' he said.

Laughing, she splashed more tonic into her glass. 'Not fair is it? "Absentee mother gets first smile" ...?'

His heart gave a little skip.

'There's no justice,' he said. 'How about "Careworn father gets big kiss"?'

Chapter Ten

The next day was fine again, and still unseasonally warm. They both slept well and woke at the same time, and David went to fetch Freya for her early bottle while Annet had a shower. When she came back wrapped in her old robe she didn't at once start to dress, but perched on the side of the bed with her arms folded, watching them with a softly indulgent air.

'You're good at this,' she commented, like Pamela.

'You think?'

'Better than me.'

'Scarcely. It's not a case of better or worse, anyway, but of different styles. It isn't a job.'

'Exactly. Proves my point, darl. You're more temperamentally suited. To me it *is* a job.'

'You mean you're a perfectionist.'

'Don't tell me what I mean!' She grabbed her hair in exasperation. 'I'm not a perfectionist, but neither am I a complete idiot!' She heaved a short, pointed sigh, collected herself and went on: 'I wasn't making a value judgement. It's simply that in my opinion we confound the gender police on this one. I may well be more efficient, but you're more intuitive . . . or something . . .' She caught his eye and they exchanged a look that stopped just short of a laugh.

'Pax.'

'Ditto.'

As she stood in front of the long mirror doing her make-up

– he'd never realised she wore any till they were married and didn't know why she bothered – he asked:

'Where do you stand on ghosts?'

'You what?' She paused with the mascara held at eye level.

'Ghosts. Do you believe in them?'

She shook her head, smiling into the mirror in utter disbelief. 'What on earth brought this on?'

He opted for transparent simplicity. 'I thought I saw one.'

'And did you?'

'That's it, how would I know? I thought you might.'

She dabbed some mascara, got some on her cheek, said 'Damn!' and added as she applied a tissue: 'Wouldn't have a clue. So tell me.'

He described the face at the window, the deep silence, the sensation of time standing still. As he talked she finished her make-up, put the mascara away, and came back to sit on the bed, fixing him with a detached, quizzical look, as though sizing him up for a part in a play.

'How real was it?'

He considered. 'It seemed – unreal as a matter of fact, but to be actually happening.'

She slapped the duvet, got up again. 'Good answer. But I still don't know what to say. I accept what you saw. But what's the objective truth? If I'd been standing in the empty room at that time, would I have seen this person – this thing's – backview? And if I wouldn't have done, does that make it less real?'

He shook his head. 'Exactly.'

Suspecting that she was a natural sceptic, he was touched by the unexpected thoughtfulness of her answer, and its evenhandedness. He watched as she brushed her hair, which crackled and reared with static electricity.

She put the brush down and turned to face him, shrugging on her jacket.

'Were you frightened?'

'No.' He shook his head. 'But I was transfixed. Compelled to look.'

'Tell you what,' she came over and kissed him, then Freya, in her usual way, 'let's see if we can find something out about the house. Maybe there's something we should know that the wicked estate agent wouldn't tell us.' She ruffled his hair. 'We all know what bastards they are.'

'Whatever it is,' he said, 'it's not malign.'

'I'm glad to hear it.' She was beginning to lose interest, to move towards her day. 'I need a coffee.'

He looked down at Freya. The bottle was empty but she was still sucking sporadically on the teat. He put his little finger in the corner of her mouth and detached her with a slight 'pop' – it was surprising with what strength and tenacity she tried to hang on. Her eyes, which had been closing, flew open at this outrage.

'Let's go with Mummy,' he suggested.

They went downstairs and into the kitchen. Annet was pouring water into the cafetiere. 'Tell me,' she said, 'has it put you off that room?'

'No, not at all. As a matter of fact I went up there afterwards. It felt exactly the same. Peaceful.'

'Maybe it was a sign.' She put the cafetiere on the table. 'You should get back to your drawing.'

'I'm going to,' he said. 'I was in the library yesterday and they're putting on an exhibition of local artists.'

'Go for it. But not that one of me – I don't want that exposed to public view.'

'I know.'

He'd been unable to keep the note of disappointment out of his voice. 'You must have had it in for me that day,' she protested, pouring, 'you made me look like a mad woman.'

'Rubbish.' He took his coffee. 'Thanks. Don't make yourself late.'

This deserved the cowboy look and got it. 'Careful darl, you're beginning to sound like a wife.'

*   *   *

For an hour in the middle of the morning, between Freya's early nap and her midday bottle, he laid her on a rug on the drawing-room floor and played with her – dangling his keys, letting her grip his fingers, applying a light pressure to the soles of her feet with his hand to test her kicks. Twice, she smiled and his spirits leapt like flames in a draught – but when he tried to bring back the smile she gazed back at him blankly, and then grew impatient, as though the effort were simply too great. Out of respect for this he gave up, and carried her about with him for a while as he took things out of the freezer, discovered a map from Mags on the fax, and took a call from Doug Border.

'What do you mean by coming in and not coming to see me?'

'It wasn't a state visit. I was passing and thought the girls would like to see Freya.'

Doug grunted. 'Oh they did, they did, and they think you're the very model of a modern, caring daddy. If I hear the word sweet applied to you or your daughter one more time, I'll barf.'

David was flattered in spite of himself. 'What can I say?'

'Nothing, take it like a man, now listen – have you got five minutes?'

David glanced at Freya. 'I should think so.'

'At your party – nice do, by the way, we enjoyed ourselves – I got talking to Chris Harper, and bugger me it turns out he *is* looking for another property for his parents. Goes to show these things are always worth a try. His old man's got a dicky ticker and everyone would be happier if they were a bit closer.'

'With a place like Stoneyhaye,' said David, 'you'd have thought they'd go for a conversion.'

'Well, yes and no ... Who knows what goes on around there, and anyway the place is probably crawling with unsavoury types already. He's after some nice cottage in a village that has all the amenities. Expense is no object, a listed building with all mod cons would be great, or I gather he'd be interested in building them something if the perfect site came up, I warned him that planning regs were prohibitive in this area, but it's a possibility.'

David said: 'What would you like me to do? I don't want to point out the obvious, Doug, but I do actually have my hands full on the domestic front this week.'

'I know, I know, I fully appreciate that, your saintly status is quite safe with me, there are half a dozen females in this place who'd tear me apart if they thought I was interfering with your paternal duties ... But since you're on good terms with Harper and right there, I wondered if you could maintain a bit of a watching brief. Newton Bury's the sort of village that would do Harper's mum and dad nicely I'd have thought. We've got nothing on the stocks there at present, but if you're going to all those coffee mornings you might hear of something.'

'I'll keep an eye out.'

'Thanks. Are you likely to be seeing Harper in the forseeable?'

David considered the trip to Stoneyhaye. 'It's a possibility.'

'Great,' said Doug. 'Only if we can keep his ill-gotten bucks circulating via B and C it's good for us all.'

'Quite.'

'So!' Doug's tone became determinedly hearty. 'How's it going otherwise?'

When David had put the phone down and was warming Freya's bottle in the kitchen he told himself not to be so damn snobbish about Doug. Doug paid his not inconsiderable wages, and was a smart operator. That was how people got to be successful in business, by never doing anything else, by seeing every occasion and chance meeting as a potential business opportunity, by spotting the main chance. Though it was in his mind to visit Stoneyhaye this afternoon he himself shied away from the idea of discussing properties with Harper.

He took Mags's fax with him while he fed Freya on the sofa. It was detailed and enthusiastically over-annotated, with injunctions to 'ignore first turning, it's all round the houses', and 'pub sign obscured by tree, so slow down!' He was looking forward to tomorrow, to getting away from this area and, perhaps because he felt more confident, was not dreading the prospect of his sister-in-law's breezy expertise. On the bottom of the map she'd written: 'Sadie has the dentist tomorrow a.m. and is angling for the day off, hope that will be OK,' which he took as an indication that the party incident was forgotten.

Freya fell asleep before finishing the bottle. He put her in her pram near the garden door and made himself a sandwich. As soon as he'd eaten he went up the two flights of stairs to the top floor and into the studio room, as if trying to catch something unawares.

If that was what he'd hoped, he was disappointed. The room was light, bright and uncommunicative. He opened the window, and Annet's remark about objective reality came back to him. It was typically pertinent, but she had put the proposition in an open-ended way, not in the expectation of a particular answer. Nor was any forthcoming.

He glanced out of the window and found he had a good view of Freya down below in her pram. Contentedly, he sat down and opened one of his folders, spreading the drawings over the table, pleased that some of them weren't all that bad . . . .

It was three quarters of an hour later, and he'd even done some desultory free-hand sketching, when he went back downstairs. He locked up, loaded both the buggy and the papoose into the boot, transferred Freya with the greatest care from her pram into her car seat and was on the road by two. The route to Stoneyhaye lay in the opposite direction from town, not up on to the ridgeway, but due south-west along the river valley. For the first mile or so – the section that he and Freya had walked earlier in the week – the Nevitt was some distance from the road, dawdling but keeping pace between its threadbare autumn willows, shocks of bullrushes and ramparts of brambles threaded with willowherb. Here and there cows grazed, corralled by electric fencing.

After a couple of miles, the road crossed the river. Upriver of the bridge, to David's right, were two swans on an island of shingle. The hen sat with her head beneath her wing, the cob stood faithfully in attendance on a single shiny black leg.

Road and river kept each other company for another couple of miles, then David turned south into a lane that wound away first through the water meadows and then into the shallow, premonitory undulations of the South Downs. It was a day of clearness and clouds, with shadows trailing across the grey-green flanks of the hills above the treeline and a cold sharpness to the horizon. It was a pleasure to be driving on such a day, and David felt an exhilarating sense of freedom – the freedom that he imagined Annet relished in returning to work. Except that next to him lay his sleeping daughter. He was tempted to think of her sleep as trusting, but corrected himself: trust didn't come into it. Even had Freya been old enough to understand the concept, he recognised ruefully that he had done precious little to inspire trust. He reached out and touched the pure, fragile curve of her cheek, promising that he could and would do better.

A few miles down the lane he slowed down and began to watch out for the Stoneyhaye turning. He thought maybe he'd missed it – one of the charms of the house was its seclusion, an important factor in its appeal to Harper. A tractor appeared and he had to reverse as far as a gateway to let it pass. When it drew level he wound the window down and signalled the driver, who removed his headphones and leaned down, hanging on by one hand. David shouted over the noise of the engine, and the man pointed further along the road, hooking his finger round to the left and mouthing 'Not far'.

David thanked him and continued, but the exchange and the tractor engine had woken Freya. She didn't cry, but her startled gaze was fixed on him as if demanding an explanation.

'Sorry,' he said. 'Horrible racket.'

Even at twenty miles an hour he almost overshot the entrance to the house. This first gate was no more than two mossy pillars –

you had to look hard to see that they weren't treestumps among the beech and oak that surrounded them. He reversed and turned in, the car pitching and rolling slightly on the less even surface of what was scarcely more than a cart track. After a couple of long ox-bow bends that almost doubled back on themselves — he'd probably travelled no more than a hundred yards from the lane — he found himself confronted by the first of Harper's security arrangements. As checkpoints went it was tolerably unobtrusive, an apparently simple wooden barrier with equally unthreatening post and rail fencing stretching away from it beneath the trees. No barbed wire or Rottweilers, David noted gratefully. The barrier wasn't manned that he could see, and he was about to get out and look for some way of identifying himself when the barrier lifted. There was something almost eery in this bland acceptance of him — it raised the disturbing likelihood of an invisible watcher — but he drove on without further interruption, and as the trees began to thin out so the house came into view.

Stoneyhaye was built of mellow brick, a Georgian gentleman's residence rather than a stately home, its proportions not grand but graciously domestic. Much of the walls were covered with flame-coloured creeper. Because it sat not on rising ground but in a shallow valley its presence was benign and welcoming — a house with sufficient confidence to allow the visitor to look down on it. This approach led through open parkland, but behind the house the woods drew in again — it was here that the Nevitt's smaller sibling, the Prinn, provided the trout fishing which had been one of Stoneyhaye's major selling points (though not, David suspected, as far as Harper was concerned).

Accustomed by training and experience to spot unsympathetic adjustments and near-the-knuckle extensions, he could see nothing to affright the eye. Except perhaps the helicopter, perched like a bluebottle on the grass before the main entrance.

At the bottom of the hill the drive swept round to bring him in at right angles to the house. He slowed down respectfully as he approached the house. In the stableyard to his left he saw two Mercs, one black and one violet, both limited edition sports models, a Rolls Royce Corniche, a muddy Land-Rover and Bailey's yellow Mazda. All were untidily parked, with an air of having been simply driven in at speed and left where they came to rest. For some reason this struck him as the most obvious manifestation of casual wealth that he had yet seen.

Here a young man in a Donegal tweed jacket and open-necked shirt halted him with an upraised hand and a disarming, almost apologetic smile.

'Mr Keating?' He was softly and well spoken.

'Yes.'

'I'm sorry to bother you with this, but do you have any means of identification on you?' The question was tactfully phrased, with the emphasis on the 'have', as though conceding that it was a slightly unreasonable thing to ask, and accompanied by a quick smile in Freya's direction. Ageing rocker he might be, but Harper clearly had an astute grasp of what was required front of house.

'I might have, I don't know . . .' David felt in his pockets, then checked himself. 'Hang on – you know my name.'

The young man, whose lapel-badge proclaimed him to be Simon Acourt, laughed charmingly, allowing the stupidity of the whole charade. 'Well actually we know your car.'

David remembered the eerily-rising barrier in the woods. 'I see. How's that?'

'We have your registration down as a possible visitor.'

'Heavens, what thoroughness.'

'Thorough but discreet. And sadly necessary.' With this, the merest glint of steeliness accompanied the smile.

'Will a cheque card do? I'm afraid it's all I have on me.'

'Cheque card's fine.' Acourt took the card and subjected it to a lightning inspection. 'Thank you.' As he handed it back he nodded at Freya. 'Your baby?'

'My daughter, yes.'

'My Cleo's eighteen months, and already I'm putty in her hands. Park wherever you like Mr Keating, and if you want to leave the keys with me I can always move it if necessary.'

David felt he'd been subjected to one of those comedy taps on the shoulder, invited to turn one way only to find the person on the other side. Nothing was quite what it seemed including, these days, himself. And he was getting old.

He popped the boot and took Freya out of her seat. The young man came briskly over to him, no longer the security guard but the meeter and greeter.

'I expect you know Chris is away this week in Hong Kong.'

'I didn't actually. He and – um – Mr Bailey—'

'Harry, yes.'

'They were both kind enough to extend an open invitation to my wife and myself.' Acourt's bland smile prompted him to add by way of explanation: 'I work for Border and Cheffins. I was instrumental in helping Chris Harper to buy this house.'

'Right.' The young man glanced around. 'Splendid, isn't it? My uncle's got a place of this general feather in County Clare. It's a house that lives in you as much as you live in it. Gets in your bloodstream.'

'I can imagine.' David felt unable to cope with much more of this gilded youthfulness. 'Is Harry Bailey here?'

'He is, but he's a bit tied up right at this moment. And Lindl's here, but I don't know where – would you like me to check?'

'Please don't worry. Would it be all right if we went for a bit of a walk?'

'We—?'

How odd, thought David, that even this young father discounted the baby's presence. 'Freya and I.'

'You and your daughter – of course.'

'Then if someone could tell Mr Bailey I'm here I might be able to see him before I go – it's purely a social call, I don't want to keep him from what has to be done.'

'That's cool.' The young man's hunt-ball vowels made the phrase sound quaint. 'I'll let him know.' He swept an arm through three hundred and sixty degrees. 'Wander where you will.'

As David sat in the back seat of the car and went through the manoeuvres involved in getting Freya into the papoose and on to his back, he saw the young man speaking into a small black object which he thought was a mobile phone until he considered that it was held in front of his face, and was therefore a walkie-talkie. So the 'liberty hall' angle was part of the staff briefing: he was going to be watched.

When he'd locked the car and was setting off, the gadget had disappeared, but he was sure it had been used to apprise various other smart cookies that an elderly chap with a baby on board was roaming about, and could do with keeping an eye on.

On the way out of the yard, he said to Acourt:

'I'd quite like to explore the woods at the back . . .'

'Sure, just go across the front of the house, and round the side and you'll hit the path that follows the river. Then you can take it upstream or down, and in both cases there are crossing places if you feel energetic and want to climb the hill.'

'Thank you.'

He set off at a brisk place. It was a while since he'd used the papoose and it was strange not to be able to see Freya's face, but he enjoyed the feel of her clinging Koala-like to his back. Reflecting on the gently-born Acourt and his walkie-talkie he formed the opinion that those who worked here probably started out with the idea they were on a cushy number, and soon learned otherwise. He was prepared to bet that Harper was a ruthless boss. Anything other than exactly what was required would be a sacking offence. This impression was reinforced when he stopped to admire the helicopter and saw a girl in a grubby white boiler suit cleaning it as one might a family car, with a bucket, a rag, and something in a can. Absorbed in her task, she paid him no attention, but he saw the black stalk of another two-way radio sticking out of her back pocket.

He followed the path, past the secretive flank of the house. where he almost tripped over a child's trailbike, and into the edge of the woods. It was quite chilly here in the afternoon shade and he put a hand behind his shoulder to touch Freya's cheek. But it felt warm, and her head nodded, relaxed, against his fingers.

He felt the spell of the house, commented on by everyone who came here. Stoneyhaye was a spellbinding place, its magic for him only intensified by the occupancy of this bizarre, money-hardened bedouin. The complete otherness of the owners and their retinue, coupled with their straightforward admiration for the house, he found moving. It was the very opposite of the visceral attachment of the previous owners, but none the worse for that.

The woods that accompanied the Prinn, en route to its assignation with the Nevitt, were not that large, but they had a wonderful wildness. The woods had always been part of the Stoneyhaye estate, they had seen few people, and those they had seen had belonged here. Yet he didn't feel like an intruder; rather the reverse, as though these trees had known only gentleness and expected nothing less. The quiet that enveloped him and Freya was not secretive and sinister, but an embracing peace.

Now that David was out of sight of the house – although realistically, recalling the walkie-talkie, he realised his progress was almost certainly being monitored – he slowed his pace. When he came to the river he found that at this point it was wider than the Nevitt, but very shallow. It seemed scarcely to be moving, so leisurely was its progress, and when he stood on the grass at the edge he could easily see a group of brown trout hovering in the lee of the bank, only the wavering of their tails betraying the current.

He followed the river for a hundred yards or so till he reached one of the crossing places mentioned by Acourt. It was no more than a tree trunk, planed off and laid across the water at its narrowest point, which was also its deepest, with a rope handle slung above it. It didn't look awfully secure, but he walked over quickly, keeping his eyes on the far bank and his objective. He could see where another path led away at right angles to the river, presumably towards the open hillside – the path began to rise very slightly at its furthest visible point.

He was immediately attracted by the idea of climbing the hill and looking down on Stoneyhaye from a new vantage point – to see the valley as only those who lived here saw it. This notion made him wonder whether in fact the new owners or their staff ever did walk up here, or whether the land that surrounded the house was simply treated as a no-man's land, protecting their hard-earned privacy.

No sooner had he thought this than he glimpsed someone amongst the trees ahead and to the right of him. Stupidly, it made him jump – the back of his neck prickled and he felt a flash of adrenalin. For goodness' sake, what was the matter with him? He was on private ground, a whole colony of people lived at the house and could presumably go where they liked; added to which it was entirely possible that one or two had the responsibility of patrolling the woods to keep an eye on outsiders such as himself.

He kept walking at a steady pace, and didn't see the figure again for a minute or two, until suddenly she – for he saw now that it was a woman – crossed the path ahead of him. She had maintained the distance between them and was too far away for him to see her face, but for a second she glanced in his direction and he saw that it was Gina King.

He didn't doubt his judgement even for a moment. It had been her. The look, at once deferential and insinuating ... the long fair hair ... the rather hesitant stride. Neither was he surprised to see her here. This, he now realised, was because she had come to occupy some place at the back of his mind, constantly. She seemed to be with him always, so to see her quite clearly in return, even here at this moment, was perfectly natural. She was showing herself.

'Gina ...?' He didn't so much call her as speak her

name in acknowledgement of her presence. But having heard his own voice once he felt braver, and raised it enough to be heard.

'Gina!'

He walked faster until he reached the place where she had crossed the path; the trees thinned out here, and he could clearly see the open hillside beyond, but there was no sign of her. He turned quickly in the direction she'd gone and at once stumbled and nearly fell into some sort of drainage ditch. Freya let out a wail of fright as he staggered to right himself, and he sat down heavily and awkwardly to avoid squashing her, chastising himself for his foolishness and giving his back a painful tweak in the process.

'Who is that? Oh, hi . . . !'

Lindl Clerc was standing on the path looking down at him without surprise. She wore fawn cord trousers, so tight he could see the indentation between her legs, and was carrying a white plastic bowl.

'Hello!' He struggled to stand, but couldn't get a footing on the sharp slope.

'Want a hand?'

He would like to have declined, but was in no position to do so, especially with Freya on his back. He clasped the forearm that she extended, and clambered back with giant ungainly strides on to the path.

'Thanks. I wonder – stupid question but you can see better than me, is my daughter all right?'

Lindl took a look. 'She's a little cross—' she pronounced it charmingly, 'liddle' – 'but she's fine. I was picking blackberries,' she explained, holding out the bowl, 'you want one?'

'I won't thanks.' He dusted at his knees, his backside, fussing and discomforted. 'You must wonder what on earth I'm doing here.'

'Not at all. You wouldn't be here if you weren't meant to be.'

This struck him as a curious form of words, implying

perhaps unintentionally that destiny, and not just an efficient security system, was at work.

'We were taking a walk, and then I was going to call in and say hello to Harry Bailey. I understand that your – that Chris is away.'

'That's right.' She began to walk slowly down the path, the bowl clasped to her midriff with both arms. 'Hong Kong.'

He wondered, though was too polite to ask, why she hadn't gone too.

'I hate Hong Kong,' she said, mindreading, 'so I let him get on with it.'

'He's doing a concert?'

She shook her head. 'Private party. That man who makes the jeans . . . ? It's his anniversary or something . . . I don't know. Fancy taking Chris all the way over there to play at a party.'

David wasn't sure if this was a comment disparaging extravagance, or the dragging away of a family man.

'Is your son at school?'

'Yes, I'm going to collect him now. He plays soccer on a Wednesday. Normally Harry goes, but he's kicking ass.' She used this phrase in the wholly unironic way of someone for whom even the most scatalogical English was not a first language. She turned her wrist and leaned over the bowl to look at her watch. 'I'm going to be a little late, I don't like all those mothers.' Her tone suggested that she was using the word in its unflattering American sense.

'Villages are gossipy places,' he agreed. 'Being high profile must make you feel very exposed.'

'Yeah . . .' she nodded. 'I'd prefer the city—' siddy – 'but this is Chris's dream.'

He found himself liking her. This afternoon, without make-up but if anything more beautiful, there was a kind of no-crap directness about her that was endearing. He realised that this must simply be because her lifestyle required no crap: she asked, it was done; she desired, and received.

'Is Jay happy at the school?' he asked.

'He loves it. He'd like to live there.'

'And later — when he gets to eleven — what will you do?' He asked in a spirit of genuine enquiry, interested these days in the decisions people made about their children.

'Who knows?' She pouted and lifted her shoulders. 'Who knows where we'll be?'

Her frankness shocked him, reminding him as it did that not only was she not married to Chris Harper, but that Jay was not Harper's son. Sentimentally, he had assumed that the two of them had entered into some sort of pact, but now that assumption was well and truly rattled.

'Of course,' he murmured. 'Of course . . . .'

They reached the river and she walked ahead of him across the log-bridge with a practised lack of concern, pausing at one point to look down into the water. On the far side she waited for him.

'It's steadier than it looks,' she told him.

'I'm being careful because of the backpack.'

'She's a good baby.'

'By and large.'

Lindl gave a little sigh. 'We all have to cry some time.'

They walked on for a minute or so, and then she asked: 'Who were you calling?' She turned to look at him. 'You were calling someone, back there?'

'Yes — it sounds ridiculous but I thought I saw someone I knew. I mean, how could it have been? Anyway, it turned out to be you.'

'You know me,' she pointed out. 'And I live here.'

'Exactly. I think—' he paused, trying both to get it right and to finish this particular line of conversation. 'I think sometimes when a particular person happens to be in your mind and you see someone who resembles them . . . well, you see what you're expecting to see.'

This begged a question, but happily she was too discreet or too uninterested to ask it.

*　　*　　*

She led him back to the house the other way to that by which he'd come, rejoining the drive at the far side of the stableyard. Of Simon Acourt there was no sign, and David recalled how he had seemed to materialise out of thin air. By the violet Merc she stopped, handed him the bowl of blackberries, and thrust a long finger and thumb into her hip pocket to produce a car key.

'Nice seeing you again,' she said. 'Do you mind putting those in the kitchen on the way through?'

'Of course not. Where am I likely to find Harry?'

'Just go in here, kitchen's second on the left, Lily will know.'

He fell in with her implied assumption that it would all be as easy as winking. Against the smooth crackle of the Merc pulling away, he went into the house. Curiously there had been no attempt made to turn this side door into anything other than a tradesman's entrance. It was not locked, and opened into an uncarpeted passage. The first door on the left was a cloakroom with a tiled floor, a lavatory with a mahogany seat and a pile of magazines on a whiskery rush stool. David could see a gold disc on the wall – presumably the platinum ones enjoyed a more elevated position elsewhere in the house ... In the kitchen, which was large, spotless and Provençale in tone, a young woman in leggings and a long white apron sat at the table reading a fat Penguin classic. She wore half-moon glasses and when David appeared in the doorway she looked over them in his direction in a professorial manner.

'Good afternoon.' Her voice had a similar timbre to Simon Acourt's, freighted with taken-for-granted breeding. 'What can I do for you?'

'My name's David Keating – I was looking for Harry Bailey, and Lindl suggested you might be able to point me in the right direction.'

'Sure.' She laid the open book – it was *The Brothers Karamazov* – face down on the table. 'He's in the office, Mr Keating. You go along here to the main hall, left after the staircase, hang a right and it's at the end on the left. Quite a distance,' she added with a smile, 'it'll take you a couple of minutes.'

'Thanks.' He handed her the blackberries. 'Present for you.'

'Oh, lovely.'

It was becoming obvious to David as he followed Lily's instructions, that this upstairs/downstairs social inversion was a thread running right through the household. When he reached the hall he could make out a distant heartbeat of music from the upper reaches, and a burst of laughter somewhere at the back of the house. He remembered the girl in overalls cleaning the helicopter: this wasn't simply a domestic dwelling, it was a whole community in miniature. Stopping to admire the far-off, ornately decorated ceiling, he noticed the dark eye of a security camera gazing watchfully from a corner. Opposite him was a long, elegant room, opulently furnished in cream, gold and pink. Who had chosen those brocades and velvets and silk rugs? he wondered. Lindl, of the almost-obscene cord jeans and the dirty feet? Chris Harper? Or one of the smooth, top-drawer functionaries who fixed things for them and for whom Sotheby's was the corner shop?

The office, when he reached it, was not an office in the usual sense at all, but another vast reception room this time with a clubby feel — a billiard table at the far end, and some heavy oxblood leather sofas nearer the door. Against the wall to the right was a computer whose sleekly minimalist outlines declared its cutting edge status. Harry Bailey was perched on the edge of one of the sofas, with a slew of papers on a large teak chest in front of him. He looked up only briefly as he greeted David.

'Terrific, come on in, Si said you were here.'

'Thanks. I didn't mean to disrupt your work. I can't stay long, she'll be getting hungry — but we just had a nice walk.'

'Up the woods?' Bailey leaned back, rubbing the side of his face with his hand.

'That's right.'

'Nice up there — as far as I can remember.' He made

a wry face. 'I don't get out as much as I'd like. Coffee? Cup of tea?'

'No, I'm fine.'

'Take the weight off your feet why don't you. And off your back.'

David slipped the papoose off and took the sleeping Freya out of it. Bailey watched him, leaning back with his hands clasped behind his head.

'So how's it going back on the ranch?'

'Pretty good. I apologise if I was less than hospitable when you called round the other morning, I was in what you might call a period of adjustment. We're shaking down together now though, I'll be quite sorry when the nanny takes over.' This made him think of something. 'I met Lindl a moment ago – does she employ anyone? I mean to help with the little boy?'

Bailey prodded a thumb at his own chest. 'You're looking at him. Informal arrangement, but you know . . .' He looked at his watch. 'Which reminds me I wonder if she's remembered to go down and pick him up from footie.'

'She has,' said David. 'She mentioned it. And I saw her go.'

'Late, I bet – she can't be doing with the other mums. Doesn't bother me, but then I'm not coming from the same place she is.'

'No.' David had never been comfortable with this laddish kind of talk, which reminded him of Doug Border. 'I can understand her point, though. I expect she feels watched – talked about.'

'She should be so lucky. Pretty ladies no longer getting work need all the talk they can get.'

This struck David as unnecessarily harsh, especially when addressed to a comparative stranger. He changed tack. 'She says Jay likes school – so he doesn't get teased or anything?'

Bailey shook his head. 'No way. In the blackboard jungle, money can buy you love. Slightest sign of trouble I take the little bastards for a Happy Meal in the Roller and it's cool.' He gave a short laugh. 'Anyway, who am I kidding? I love it.'

'It's still a chastening thought.'

'Not really. They're just more honest than we are. You wait till the pool's up and running, Jay'll be Mr Big then all right.'

'I can imagine.'

'Want to look around?'

'If you've got time.'

'I've got the time if you've got the inclination!' Suddenly energetic again, Bailey slapped his knees and jumped up. 'Let's go.' At the door he said. 'I need a breath of air, I'll show you the pool first. Blokes aren't there this arvo.'

'Why's that?'

'Waiting for materials.' Though David had said nothing, he added: 'Yeah, I know, tell me about it, but you want a pool that looks like a Roman bathhouse you pay for it. And you wait. And the longer you wait the more you pay.'

With David carrying Freya they went back into the hall, and turned right, past the long sweep of the staircase, towards the back of the house.

'I can't imagine,' said David, 'that your boss would easily allow himself to be ripped off.'

'Oh, he won't. We keep a log, it's all on disk. There won't be much fuss till they've finished, then we'll take them to the cleaner's.'

The pool was situated in the right angle formed by the back of the house and the stable block. For now it was untidily covered with a kind of thatch of scaffolding and green plastic, but as Bailey explained it was destined to have a retractable roof, solar panels and daylight lighting, so the position was more for planning reasons than any other. The plastic meant there was a dim, green light, like being under water. Along one side were a row of changing rooms with arched doorways, decorated with a vaguely Roman pattern of intertwined laurel wreaths; at the end a shallow platform almost like a low stage, with built-in rostra, cylindrical and rectangular, presumably for sitting and eating. In the empty pool the Roman theme continued – shallow steps led down into different levels, separated by islands and promontories, and a large, fiercely-spined, turquoise fish with glaring eyes adorned the floor, surrounded by an ever-thinning shoal of smaller fish in bright colours.

David peered at the fish admiringly. 'That looks like mosaic.'

'Because it is. All Italian marble and mosaic, no messing. Look and weep.'

'It's going to be quite magnificent.'

'But OTT is what you're thinking.' Bailey cast him a knowing look. 'I mean come on, how much of this is going to be reflected in the price of the house when he sells it? Not that he's going to, but supposing he might.'

'Quite a lot. A pool, especially one with all-year use, is a huge selling feature.'

Bailey was over the other side now, he raised his voice slightly. 'Yeah, but you could get a terrific family pool with all the trimmings for a fraction of what this poncey lot is costing.'

'It depends who you're selling to,' David pointed out. Not knowing how much would get back, he didn't wish to be lured into discussions of taste.

Bailey pointed at the bottom. 'Want to go down and take a proper look? It may be a waste of money but it's shit-hot work.'

'I wouldn't mind.'

'Here,' Bailey walked round the other side of the pool to join him. 'My chance to hold the princess.'

'Are you sure? Thanks.'

David handed him Freya, and started down the nearest steps. It was strange to be down there with the steep sides of the pool all around him, like being a spider in the bath. Thre was a click and light flooded round his ankles.

Bailey called: 'Take your time. Your daughter likes me.'

He crouched down by the great fish, astounded by the level

of workmanship, each tiny piece blending with and completing its neighbour, the melding of colours, the breathtaking detail — the irises of the fish's great eyes were striped and mottled like a girl's, each of its huge sail-like fins was patterned with a web of veins, hundreds of scales overlapped and seemed to shimmer in the light. On the walls the smaller fish glowed dark and bright as jewels.

Fascinated, he must have been down there for ten minutes, perhaps longer. When he started up the steps again the plastic tent seemed dark after the bright light at the bottom of the pool. He was slightly disorientated, and couldn't see Bailey anywhere. Hearing voices — low, conversational, laughing — he headed for the open side, where the sheeting was looped back.

What he saw was a sort of family group — parents and child — heads together, the man holding the baby, the woman kissing it. It would have been an affecting tableau had not the man and the woman been Bailey and Annet.

'Here he is,' said Bailey to Annet. And then to him: 'Your missus turned up.'

Annet, still smiling about whatever it was, came to meet him and gave him a peck on the cheek. 'Hello darl, fancy seeing you here.'

Annet made various suggestions — if he could hang on for a while, or he could leave Freya and the car-seat with her ... But she must have known none of them were practical, Freya was now wide awake and needed her bottle. And besides David was on his dignity.

How weird, she said, she'd decided to leave work an hour early and check out the gym, and see the pool, and it had just happened to be at the same time as he was here. Two minds with but a single thought, she said, two hearts, etcetera. He had found it impossible to share her amusement at the coincidence.

On the way up the drive he met the violet Merc coming the other way. As they passed each other at a sedate pace Lindl gave him her come-day-go-day faint smile and raised her hand from the steering wheel for a second.

Jay, on the other side of his mother, dragged down his cheeks and tugged his mouth with his fingers, like a gargoyle.

At home, he noticed inconsequentially that the pram was standing inside the garden doors. He clearly remembered taking Freya out of the pram, in its present position. And he recalled putting the pram out on the terrace while he went upstairs — looking out of the studio window to check on Freya.

What he could not for the life of him recall was bringing it back in. But there it was, so he supposed he must have done.

Chapter Eleven

The proposed visit to his sister-in-law's in Chichester the following day helped to dispel the slight shadow cast by David's visit to Stoneyhaye.

When Annet returned home only an hour after him, she had seemed unaffected, laughed again about the coincidence of it all and whisked Freya off to bed, suggesting he go and fetch a takeaway instead of slaving over a hot stove. His response to this had been less than gracious, and he'd wound up cutting off his nose to spite his face, producing a less than successful risotto but not allowing Annet to say it wasn't as bad as he made out.

'Watch it,' she teased him, 'you're turning into a house-wife again.'

'Not on the strength of this,' he replied, prodding the risotto with his fork.

'I'm not talking about the cooking.'

He was stung. 'What then?'

'Never mind.' She reached out and took his hand. 'I didn't mean it.'

But he knew she had, and was right. If even then he'd been able to mention how troubled he'd been by seeing her with Bailey – how confused and vulnerable, how sick to his stomach – if he'd been able to do that he might still have dispelled some of his anxiety. But though fiercely real to him he feared that to her it would seem only foolish, and so he'd kept silent, and suffered. When that night she'd caressed him amorously he was once again unable to respond and she had snuggled philosophically beneath his shoulder and fallen asleep quickly, without asking for more.

With Mags the shadows were well and truly beaten back. Not it had to be said because she herself was all sunshine and light. When David and Freya arrived at eleven-thirty hers had already been a trying day.

'You simply would not believe the havoc that can be caused by a child mislaying something,' she declared, kissing David's cheek and automatically taking Freya from him before heading for the kitchen. 'Quite apart from the general inconvenience there's also this attitude that it's bound by definition to be my fault. "Where did you put my" are the words I dread most around here, they always seem to herald hours of unseemly wrangling and shouting. And the trouble is if I find it, which as we speak I haven't, that's always taken to prove the point! Talk about a no-win situation – coffee?'

'Thanks.' He took Freya back while Mags filled the kettle. 'So what's gone missing?'

She flapped a hand. 'Oh, some form James needs to fill in for his hockey trip, I'm perfectly certain I've never seen it and it will be lurking in the bottom of some disgusting bag with lots of other things he'd far rather I didn't see, but his attitude is "I gave it to you, I said it had to be done by Friday, what the hell have you done with it?" And if I start looking for it in any of the obvious places then of course I'm invading his privacy.'

David said, before she could: 'I suppose I've got all this to look forward to.'

She smiled tensely. 'Not necessarily, girls are so much easier in most ways. Until puberty,' she added.

At least this grim warning provided an opportunity to change the subject. 'Where's Sadie? All go well at the dentist?'

'Fine, only a check-up, we were in and out in a flash so I

insisted on school I'm afraid. Another example of mother as wrecker of lives.'

This was so unlike the breezy, advice-dispensing Mags of a few weeks ago that David had to laugh. 'Poor Mags. If it's any consolation I think you do an amazing job.'

She put the coffee on a tray. 'I hate to say this David but you speak from a position of ignorance. Come through.'

They went to sit in the family room which adjoined the kitchen. David sat Freya in her seat and Mags got down heavily on to the floor next to her. She was about the same age as Annet but her figure was fast becoming matronly. They were almost a different species from one another. His wife was unmistakeably a sexual being; Mags, increasingly, a domestic one.

'Tim OK?' he asked.

'Actually he's coming home for lunch, almost unheard of, but maybe he thought we'd be up to no good!' She chortled. 'No, things are quiet at work at the moment and he'd like to see you.'

'Good, that'll be nice.'

Mags unstrapped Freya and laid her on the floor. 'Do you mind? It's good for them to kick.'

'Be my guest.'

'It's only cold for lunch, I thought then you could go ahead with feeds and whatever and not worry.'

'Thanks. She usually has a bottle around twelve and then sleeps, but as she's slept all the way in the car that may not happen.'

'No,' agreed Mags, 'you could be right there, but she is *so* adorable. We might take her for a walk this afternoon. In fact what would really make Sadie's day would be if we took her to the school gate so she can push back, then you can jump straight in the car if that's what you want.'

'Sounds fine. Yes, I'd like to see the kids.'

She pulled a face. 'Up to a point Lord Copper. You don't want to see James, take my word for it, especially when he's in major recrimination mode. It's not a pretty sight.'

'The form will turn up, surely.'

'Yes, indeed it will, and if he finds it it will simply appear on the kitchen table without explanation or apology.'

Conversation moved on to the imminent arrival of the nanny, and Mags's intention (declared as David recalled at fairly regular intervals over the past three to four years) of getting a job. As his sister-in-law ran through the modest range of options he noticed for the first time that she was not at ease. This might have been simply due to the irritations of the day, or seeing her in her own home, or because over the past few days he himself had become sensitised to the currents and pressures of a different sort of life. He had always regarded Mags, not without affection, as a kind of necessary evil, his brother's helpmeet and the competent parent of his nephews and nieces. She was a woman who simply forged ahead along her chosen path in an unquestioning manner which, though slightly blinkered, was curiously comforting to the rest of them. Good old Mags, she was bossy and annoying and quick on the draw with the advice, but then that was all she had to think about. Also, if the truth were known, David had never really been able to understand what his younger brother saw in her. Even at the wedding where he had been best man she had seemed to be a young woman entirely without mystery, and consequently without allure.

All that might or might not have been true of her: he'd certainly believed it. Now he wasn't so sure. As she played with Freya and nattered on about earning some 'pin-money' – surely one of the last women of her age and class to think in such a way – he suspected for the first time that there was more being left unsaid than said, and the suspicion made him feel more warmly towards her. It also inhibited him. The terms of their relationship had shifted slightly where he was concerned and would have to be reconsidered.

At twelve-fifteen they went back into the kitchen and he fed Freya while Mags laid the lunch and opened a bottle of Chilean white.

'There's a perfectly good box of El Tesco Blanco on the go

in the fridge,' she told him, 'but Timothy's got a thing about getting it out in company.'

'I'm hardly company.'

'No, but you know what I mean.' To David's disappointment she replaced the bottle in the fridge. 'He's concerned about appearances.'

This remark, taken all in all with Mags's wild hair and straining stirrup pants, was giving David pause when Tim himself arrived through the back door. He wore a grey suit in need of pressing, and it may have been this that made him look older. His smile, though, was one of genuine warmth.

'Good to see you, don't get up.' He came over to where David sat and placed, fleetingly, a hand on his shoulder. 'She's grown, but turn your back for two minutes at this age and they do.'

Though David knew the shoulder-touch had been in lieu of a handshake, it still had the power to move him. He and Tim had never exchanged more than the most formal expressions of affection. 'Manly' was how their father would have described these exchanges, usually in the context of describing the alternative as 'unmanly', but David had never subscribed to this view of manliness. If Tim's simple gesture could induce this response in him, it could scarcely be considered anything other than right and feeling.

Tim made a gusty noise, something between a sigh and an exclamation, and hung his jacket on the back of one of the chairs.

'Hello!' cried Mags, who was slicing tomatoes. It struck David that she was over-projecting. 'I opened a bottle as instructed, it's in the door of the fridge.'

'Cheers.' Tim fetched the bottle and poured himself a glass. 'Did Sadie go in?'

'Yes.'

'Thank God for that.' He took a mouthful. 'I'd walk through fire for my offspring, but one of the pleasures of coming home to lunch is that we have the place to ourselves.'

Mags made a big-eyed face over her shoulder at David. 'Whatever you're thinking, that's not it!'

Tim continued as if his wife hadn't spoken. 'Looking forward to going back in next week? Or are you all for cancelling the help and doing this full-time?'

David was getting used to this question and a little tired of it. 'Somewhere in between the two it would be fair to say. I'm enjoying it, but I can understand why women get browned off.'

Mags gave a shrill little laugh. 'Hear that, Timothy? He understands. By the way is anyone else allowed a drink?'

'Believe me,' said Tim, pouring, '*I* understand. I should do, you've explained often enough. I just don't know what I'm expected to do about it.' He smiled sourly at David and added: 'Everyone around here's under the impression I leave the house at seven-thirty every morning in order to engage in non-stop fun and frolics. Instead of which I'm brown-nosing half the palsied house magazines in the south east in an attempt to persuade them to print with us—! Sorry.'

David, looking at Mags's furiously chopping backview – she'd moved on to cucumber – chose his words carefully.

'It's extremely hard to assess the level of someone else's pressure, that's for sure. I'm finding this. On the face of it I'm on holiday, nothing to do but mind a tiny baby all day, and yet – something you two will recognise – the sense of being on call permanently is exhausting. I seem to have time for very little else and I sleep the sleep of the utterly knackered.'

He fancied he had done his best to align his brother and sister-in-law with each other, if not in opposition then at least in contrast to himself, but they seemed determined to remain resolutely unaligned. Mags placed a bowl of salad on the table with more force than was strictly necessary.

'Think, David,' she said, 'at one point I had two under five and two at junior school, is it any wonder I'm a trifle careworn?'

'Get away Mags,' said Tim, 'you loved it.' The words were teasing, but the tone bordered on bitter.

Mags, very bright-eyed, looked at David and pointed at her husband. 'He would know of course.'

David attempted to laugh, but no sound came out. Mags opened the fridge and removed a bowl of potato salad covered in clingfilm.

'I should have taken this out earlier, it won't taste of a thing.'

Tim prised off the clingfilm. 'It'll be fine, stop apologising.'

'I didn't apologise, I made an observation.'

'Don't worry about it.'

She leaned her face down beside his. 'I've heard you sound off about chilly cheese often enough.'

David got up. 'I'll fetch Freya's seat.'

As he went into the family room he was aware of a brief, muted altercation behind his back. When he re-entered the kitchen, having taken a diplomatic extra couple of minutes changing Freya's nappy and eliciting smiles, plates of cold chicken were in place, glasses were charged and Mags held the breadknife poised over the baguette. He sensed a standoff, negotiated in his absence on grounds of politeness.

'Will she be all right down there?' asked Mags as he placed the seat on the floor. 'She's awfully good, bless her. If she gets fed up I want to pick her up.'

'Be my guest.' David turned to Tim. 'How is the print trade, anyway?'

'Pretty crapulous.'

'I'm sorry.'

Tim shrugged. 'I don't think it's terminal. I hope to God not. Middle management's last in and first out under those circs.'

'But surely you'd be safe? With all your experience, and so many years with the company?'

'There are no brownie points for loyalty. In fact in some quarters these days it's seen as a positive disadvantage – evidence of an unwillingness to try anything new, timidity, dullness, all that unsexy sort of thing.'

'If that's how people do think, I think it's completely out-rageous,' put in Mags, pinkly. 'My father got a gold half-hunter for being with Micanite and Insulated for forty years, and that's how it should be. It's like lack of respect for the old.'

'Anyway,' said Tim, closing the brackets on this intervention, 'don't let's get too gloomy. Nothing cataclysmic has happened yet, we're just a bit short of orders.'

But Mags was not to be deflected from her proseletysing course. 'You know, I often think how simply awful that must have been for you, David, when you were put out in the cold. You were so good and calm about it all but there must have been some terrible dark nights of the soul. And *we* were so busy trying to keep you cheerful we never really let you be miserable.'

'Bloody good thing,' said Tim. 'No disrespect bro, but being miserable should remain a lonely vice.'

David acknowledged this. 'And I was fortunate not to be out in the cold for long. Given my age I might easily still have been out there now.'

'How long was it?' asked Mags.

'A couple of years. Long enough to be shall we say character-forming.'

Tim tore another piece off the bread. 'Must have been, didn't you meet Annet during that time?'

'That's right.'

'So unemployment didn't diminish your pulling power.'

'I don't know about that. I mean I'm not sure I exactly pulled . . . .'

'No, correction, I don't think Annet is a woman susceptible to pulling, but anyway, low ebb notwithstanding you got together with one of the most glamorous women I know.'

At this point Mags abandoned what was left on her plate and picked Freya up, making a great business of patting her back and adjusting her clothes.

'Are you going to look like your mum?' she enquired rhetorically of the baby. 'Hm? Or be tall like your dad . . . ?'

David had the uneasy feeling that he had become the ball in a dogged baseline rally.

'Most people,' he said firmly, 'think she looks like Annet at the moment. She's got her dark hair and eyes, but that could all change.'

'Damn right. All ours were born with hair but bald as coots by three months,' commented Tim. 'But not smoothly bald, you could never say there goes that good-looking, bald kid, it came out in fits and starts, they looked as if they were suffering from creeping alopecia or mange or something.'

'Justin had eczema as well,' Mags remembered fondly, 'so you can imagine.'

'She's had a bit of nappy rash,' admitted David, keen to join in with anything that had a bonding effect on his hosts. It seemed to work, because both of them laughed.

'Unclean! Unclean!' cried Tim. 'If that's the worst you can come up with you're having one hell of an easy ride, bro.'

David smiled, pleased that they were pleased. 'I know.'

The rest of lunch passed perfectly pleasantly, with them running David through a familiar repertoire of stories of family life intended to divert rather than depress him, towards the end of which Freya began to complain.

'I'm going to take my niece for a stroll round the garden,' announced Mags. 'I don't want coffee, so you two go ahead.'

When she'd gone Tim upended the bottle over David's glass. 'You polish this off. I have to drive back.'

'So do I.'

'I'd forgotten – but not for a while, surely.'

David said: 'You're not seriously worried about work, are you?'

Tim tapped the end of his knife on his plate, gazed out of the window. 'Seriously, but not very, if you understand me. There are real worries but I wasn't flannelling you when I said they weren't going to bring us to our knees.'

'Good. Mags seems eager to aid the war effort, anyway.'

'There isn't any war effort!' Tim's voice was scratched with irritation as he slammed down the knife. 'I've got nothing against her working, bloody good thing, she's obviously climbing the walls around here, but she doesn't have to, financially. I get a little tired of this plucky little woman thing of hers. She should get a qualification of some sort, learn how to do something. The thought of her pratting about in some supermarket fills me with complete – I don't know.'

'If that's what she wants to do, surely ... does it matter?'

At this, Tim turned to look at him, and it was like the touch on the shoulder, suddenly and almost unbearably intimate. Though not, this time, amicable.

'It matters to me, David, though not for the reasons you think. I don't give a toss about the status or how it looks. It's not a case of "no wife of mine is going to stack shelves" – I want her to pull herself together.'

Although he knew Mags was out of earshot, David lowered his voice. 'That's a bit harsh. She's been primarily a wife and mother all these years, and a jolly good one, you can hardly expect her to go straight out and become a nuclear physicist.'

'No. Forget it.'

'She seems a little on edge,' ventured David. 'She just needs to get out, make a start. Anyone as demonstrably competent as Mags is going to find interesting employment in the end.'

Tim got up and began stacking plates, the cutlery clutched in one hand. 'Sure.'

'The kids are great. They do you credit.' He went for a white lie: 'After our little party we were saying as much. You could take Sadie anywhere.'

Tim slammed the plates in the sink and leaned on the edge, his shoulders hunched. 'Yeah.' After a pause he turned back, put his hands over his face and said in a tired voice: 'We're in trouble, though.'

Dread clutched at David. 'What sort of trouble?'

Tim shook his head, massaging his eyes. 'Not financial — not yet. I've been reasonably prudent.'

'Then what?'

'Christ . . .' Tim dropped his hands and sat down on what had been his wife's chair. He slumped, and David noticed with a pang that his younger brother had a paunch. 'Do I have to spell it out?'

'Everyone goes through sticky patches.'

'Not one lasting five years.'

David was humbled. 'I see.'

'We've been together nearly twenty you know.'

'That long? I suppose it must be.'

'Twenty years. Four kids. Three houses. Two decades. Too long.'

'It's great,' David tried for a positive note. 'A triumph. You should be proud.'

'Of what, for Christ's sake? Staying the course?'

'If you want to put it that way.'

'What other way is there? We're not exactly a couple of turtle doves. When I look at you and Annet, I — comparisons are odious I know, but it makes me want to weep.'

'We have our problems too,' David said quietly.

'Yes, yes, but you know you're *alive*.' Tim was impatient with him. 'You have something going on. The two of us have lived with sins of omission so long we've forgotten how — or why — it all started. Or I have. I'm on hold, David. Don't feel a thing, how's that for sad?'

The use of his name brought David up short. Yet another sign, if one were needed, that some dangerous corner had been reached.

'I'm so sorry.'

'Yes, me too. Sorry for me. Sorry for Mags. I don't love her any more.'

'Don't say that.'

'She doesn't love me either if that makes it sound any better.'

'It doesn't. And I don't believe it's true – of either of you.'

Tim gave him a mocking, twisted look. 'It's not up for discussion. As the person most affected, I'm telling you.'

'Love changes,' said David desperately. 'It has to change.'

'You're saying it alters when it alteration finds?'

'That refers to romantic love. Married love is different.'

'No, no—' Tim put up a hand as if warding off a blow – 'No! It won't do. We haven't had sex in two years, can you imagine that? I doubt it. Look at your wife, and then look at mine. Look at *me*, for Christ's sake. It's not a pretty sight.'

David remembered his mental comparison of Mags with Annet earlier in the day and was momentarily silenced.

'What do looks matter?' he muttered

Tim gave him another sneering glance. 'We both know what I'm saying bro. Mags and I may never have won any beauty competitions, but we've stopped trying for one another. She doesn't care what I think of her, and vice versa. Lack of self-respect. Lack of respect for the other person. QED.'

'But easily remedied,' suggested David.

'You mean she greets me in a suspender belt and fluffy mules and I bring her a bunch of flowers?'

'Something like that.'

'You have to want to do it, bro. It starts up here.' He tapped his head. 'And that's where we haven't got it. Not any more. Perhaps we never had enough of it to last, never enough lift-off.'

A terrible thought struck David. 'Is there anyone else?'

'No.' Tim gave a grunt. 'Wish there was.'

'That's an awful thing to say, Tim.'

'But truthful. The fact is, one chance and I'd be in there. But I'm too chicken-shit to instigate anything and not a good enough prospect to attract offers. It'd be funny if it wasn't so fucking tragic. I find myself looking at perfectly ordinary, not very bright girls in the office and imagining what they'd be like in bed. Do you do that?'

Dumbfounded, David shook his head.

'I thought not. You have Annet. You and she have each other. You have a *relationship*. Bit of an overused word, but believe me it's like reputation – when you don't have one any more, you realise what you've lost.'

David found his voice again, but seeing Mags cross the lawn, happy with the baby, lowered it. 'You two have a relationship. But a different one. You're different individuals, you've been married a long time.'

'Tell me about it.'

'Perhaps – perhaps you need a holiday.' The moment he'd said this David realised how trite it sounded. And the fact that Tim chose to ignore it completely confirmed him in this view.

'I wonder whether the kids notice,' said Tim. 'That's the bottom line, when your children start to suffer.'

On this David did feel confident. 'Don't be ridiculous, your children are the best-balanced lot I've ever come across.'

'Forgive me, but you don't come across many – no, sorry, thanks, but who the hell knows what effect we're having? I mean they're on about influences in the blasted womb these days, by the time they get to Josie's age Christ knows what must be going on in their heads.'

David said: 'But you and Mags aren't cruel to each other, or to them, you don't swear and throw things, I don't see how they can possibly know there are difficulties, let alone be affected.'

'I don't know ... I think they might feel it in their water.'

'Mags is a really good person. Genuine. Industrious. Sympathetic.'

'Jesus wept——!' Tim leaned back, slapping his hands to his head. 'That's supposed to make me feel better?'

Mags pushed open the back door. 'What's so funny?'

A little later, when Tim had returned to work, David and Mags put Freya in her buggy and went to meet Sadie and Luke from school. They attended the local church primary, not so very different from the one in Newton Bury, except newer and larger.

The walk from the Keatings' enclave of 1930s villas to the school was a busy bustling one, rife with hazards.

'Not very scenic and not very safe,' said Mags. 'Can you wonder I pick them up? I'd normally bring the car. But since we're walking we can come back via the park and let the sprogs let off steam on the swings and slides.'

They were five minutes early at the school gate and Mags got talking to some other parents. David stood a little to one side, idling the buggy back and forth with one hand. He found something touching in the school mums, including Mags. Tim's desperate confessions rang in his head, but he found these women warmly attractive, and even admirable. With his tiny stock of experience he could appreciate the small quotidian acts of courage, the resolve in the face of tiredness and boredom, the bread-and-butter love that was the staff of life. Who cared if they wore joggers and were too fleshy for elegance? And what did it matter if their perms and tints were growing out? He honoured their lack of vanity. Not only was it comforting, it was – the only word for it – womanly.

Sadie was enchanted. 'Can I push? Is it OK if I push her Uncle David?'

He hesitated, not wanting to give offence but not sure it was such a good idea either. Mags came to his rescue.

'When we get to the park. Hello champ,' she kissed Luke. 'OK? Good day?'

'Fine.' He said the one syllable long and bored, like a yawn.

'I haven't got the car, so we'll go back via the swings.'

'Yay! Can Sean come?'

'Of course, is his mum here?'

Mags and Luke went to extend this invitation. Sadie put the brake on the buggy and crouched down next to Freya, who at once beamed.

'She smiled at me! Was that a proper smile?'

'Definitely. She does quite a few of them these days. But not for everyone, she obviously likes you.'

Sadie rewarded him with a look of delight, scrunched with delicious embarrassment. 'I like *her*. I want to be a nanny when I'm older.'

'Do you remember Luke when he was a baby?'

'Yes but he was really gross.'

'How do you mean?'

'He was really *ugly*. And he cried all the time.'

'They all cry sometimes.' He was picking up the jargon. 'There isn't much else for them to do.'

'I picked her up when she cried at your house, at your party,' said Sadie. 'But I didn't put her on the grass.'

David's heart skipped a beat. 'No, you said. You said my friend did that.'

Whether she would have responded to this he couldn't tell, because Mags and Luke returned with the friend Sean, a tough-looking character with a ledge haircut. They set off for the park with David pushing the buggy, and Sadie walking alongside with one hand resting on the metal shaft. The boys alternately scuffled behind them and charged in front, while Mags kept up a barrage of warnings and instructions. 'Look out, look what you're doing, there are other people – I'm so sorry, they don't *look* – stop at the road! Did you hear what I said? That is dangerous, *wait* for me at the road. Press the button, well he's done it now, you press it the next time. Now we've got the green man, now we can go across. Sean – not a good idea. Yes, but only one tube each and not if there's any more fighting . . . .'

'They're a pain,' confided Sadie to David.

'They're just boys,' he suggested, adding: 'You may find this hard to believe but I was a boy once.'

She gave him another of her squeezed-with-delight grins. 'With my dad.'

'With your dad, exactly. And little horrors we were.' He wasn't sure how true this was – Tim had been a rumbustious child full of devilment and explosive energy, but he himself had been cautious and quiet. 'It would have been nice to have a sister,' he said.

'I'm a sister,' said Sadie. 'I've got *two* brothers.'

'Too bad,' he agreed.

They paused at the sweetshop for something called Big Blasters ('they're on the telly' Mags explained) and then went on to the park. Once through the gates Sadie took charge of the buggy and the boys hurtled away, yelling at the tops of their voices.

Mags pulled a cringing, apologetic face. 'Why must they do that?'

'Because they must . . . ?'

At the play area they found a seat. David took Freya out of the buggy and Sadie sat with them holding her for a while, before the urge to let off steam overcame her.

'Is it OK if you take her now?' she asked David.

'Of course. Off you go.'

Mags held out her arms. 'My turn, may I?'

He handed Freya over. Although she was quiet at the moment, lulled by the fresh air, the noise and the activity, Mags held her up against the side of her face, cradling her head with one hand and rocking slightly back and forth. There was an easy grace and tenderness about her dealings with the baby which was missing most of the time. He remembered reading something about women dividing into mothers and lovers. If that were true there wasn't much doubt which Mags was, but it still occurred to David that it was herself that she was soothing as she rocked.

When they got back he declined tea in the interests of getting back on the road before the work traffic. The children were watching television as Mags came to see him off.

'It's been so nice,' he said.

'Hasn't it?'

'And an unexpected pleasure to see Tim.'

'Oh, he wasn't going to be left out.'

He put Freya in the car. 'Thanks, Mags.' He kissed her cheek and thought he heard her make a small sound in her throat − of gratitude? of pleasure? − as he did so. With his hands still on her shoulders he asked: 'Everything all right?'

She smiled, too much and her eyes were pleading. 'Of course! How do you mean?'

'I don't know . . . You're obviously pretty tired. Tim too. I can see why.'

'We're *fine*. We're always tired, it doesn't mean anything.'

'Good.'

Perhaps to preclude any more questions the children were summoned to make their goodbyes. His last impression of Mags was of her standing sturdily amongst her brood, bending to engage in a swift, fierce remonstration with Luke, shaking his wrist, then straightening up with a brave face on, to wave cheerily.

Not waving, he thought, but drowning.

That evening Annet was out of sorts and Freya wouldn't settle.

'What on earth's the matter with her?' asked Annet, walking up and down in between him and the *Nine o'clock News*, jiggling and patting impatiently, probably making things worse. Already he noticed in himself a dismaying tendency to find fault with her handling of Freya.

'I've no idea. She's been good as gold all day.'

'That'll be it then. One sniff of her mother, shattered and shot at, and all hell breaks out.'

'Don't be daft.' He switched off the TV. 'Do you want me to have a go?'

'No thanks. How were they anyway?'

'Worn out.'

'I fully sympathise.'

'They could probably both do with a holiday.'

Annet jerked her head in exasperated disbelief. 'Gimme a break! I mean, their kids are all at school, Tim earns a good screw, they have a bloody nice house, what's their problem? I mean what does Mags actually *do* all day for heaven's sake?'

The fact that he'd often asked the same rhetorical question, or something like it, made it no easier to answer.

'I think – from what I can gather, though of course she didn't confide in me – that it's more a case of what she's been doing for the past twenty years.'

'Her choice.' Annet plumped down on the sofa and began undoing her shirt. 'Sorry, desperate measures.'

'Is there any there?'

'I doubt it, and it'll be a pretty vinegary brew after today's shenanigans, but any port in a storm.'

Freya latched on optimistically and Annet said: 'Mags needs to get a life.'

'I think she'd agree with you.'

She slid him a tired travesty of the cowboy look. 'You *have* been having heart to hearts.'

'Not at all. Not in the way you mean. She's an extremely loyal woman.'

'Ah, now we come to it. And Tim's not so loyal?'

'Let's just say he and I did have a heart to heart.' On an impulse he reached out and caressed her arm that cradled Freya. It felt firm and muscular. 'He envies us.'

'Really.' It was a sceptical comment, not a question.

'He thinks we have something going for us.'

'I should damn well hope so.'

'Well, do we?'

She kept her eyes on the baby's face. 'Of course.'

'I hope so too.'

'What, you have your doubts? Look darl, I really don't need this. I'm knackered, she's in a strop, and you seem to be saying we're all washed up—'

'I never said any such thing, on the contrary—'

'You don't want to start sitting about at kitchen tables with disaffected wives, it's unhealthy.'

'I didn't. We didn't—'

'Or husbands. In fact now I come to think of it that's worse.'

It was almost funny, and he would have laughed except that he so urgently wanted – needed – her to understand.

'All I meant was, it shook me to the core to think of those two having difficulties. I've got used to regarding them as completely solid and immutable, and now it turns out they're not. That Tim thinks *we're* the ones who've got it right.'

She sniffed, mollified. 'Solid and immutable?'

'No.' He cupped his hand over Freya's head. Thought of Annet and Bailey, and said gently: 'Just the opposite.'

When he looked through the curtains before going to bed, Gina was there.

The following day was Friday, and rainy. David could scarcely believe he'd reached the end of the week, the last day he'd spend on his own with Freya. On Monday the nanny would arrive and the process of handing over would begin.

This knowledge, and Gina's image, cast a wistful light on the day to come. Annet, misinterpreting his mood, said on her way out: 'Cheer up, darl, you'll be off duty soon.' But he couldn't help it, each thing that he did with and for his daughter had a tender, valedictory quality. When it was time for her morning nap, he put her in her Moses basket and took her up to the studio with him. For an hour he sketched as she slept, but although he enjoyed the process – the quietness of the room, Freya's company, the small sensuous pleasure of pencil on paper – he took no satisfaction from the results. She was still too little, he couldn't catch either her likeness to Annet or her fierce individuality. In fact, the most successful sketches were those which didn't attempt either, but which suggested, in a few swift lines, her sleeping form, her hands and hair, the cross-hatched texture of the Moses basket.

When she awoke he stayed up there for a while. He had the impression, fanciful probably, that Freya responded to the room in some way: that she understood it to be a place separate and distinct from the routines of the house. Perhaps they were both haunted.

This impression was reinforced when he went downstairs and she at once became cranky. The phone rang and it was Annet, sounding subdued.

'Oh God, bad moment?'

'Hang on.' Prioritising, he laid Freya back in her basket. 'She's only just started.'

'What's up, do you think?'

'Nothing much, that's for sure. She's been in the studio with me good as gold for the past hour and a half.'

'Look,' she lowered her voice, 'I only wanted to say sorry.'

'What for?'

'Saying lousy things about Tim and Mags.'

'Some of which were true,' he said.

'That's not the point, I was being the bitch from hell and we both know it.'

'I know no such thing.'

'Hmm . . .' He could picture the expression that accompanied this, and anticipated the swift change of gear that followed. 'OK, better let you get on. Bye, have fun at the clinic.'

As fun, David concluded, the baby clinic was right up there with clipping nose hair. As a quaint exemplar of village life it was more interesting. A trestle table in the hall annexe was manned by representatives of the church and the ruling classes in the respective shapes of Della Martin and Diana Fox-Herbert, armed with Dickensian-looking ledgers, a large box of mansize tissues and a set of scales. Around the edge of the room sat some half-dozen mothers with their offspring, of whom Freya was by far the youngest.

In spite, or perhaps because of this, the indignity of being dumped, naked, in a cold plastic dish caused her first to empty her bladder extravagantly (so explaining the tissues) and then to set about making a din that silenced all competition and gave rise to a litany of stock comments about sturdy lungs and the need to air them. Della told David he was a brave man, Diana Fox-Herbert said either that or a very foolish one, he said he just did as he was told, which gave rise to disproportionate hilarity all round. Freya continued to bawl as he got her back into her clothes, bawled as he took his place on one of the black plastic chairs beneath the indulgently smiling scrutiny of the mothers – and bawled for Britain in the presence of the youthful health visitor, who quickly pronounced her fighting fit and showed them the door.

The very instant David put her in the buggy and made good his ignominious escape, she fell fast asleep.

It had emphatically not been fun. But if there were one cheering aspect to the whole grim business it was that by the end of it he was beginning to regard the arrival of the nanny in a more positive light.

Chapter Twelve

Lara McKay, a light heavyweight from Cooney Bay near Auckland, five eleven in her Reeboks, arrived at speed, entered on a tidal wave of energy, and took charge. David had persuaded himself that his memory must have been playing tricks about her size: respectfully he had now to acknowledge that it wasn't. She was an Amazon, with hands twice the size of his own, thighs like bolsters, and shoulders to make a navvy envious. Her Medusa-like hairdo alone was so big it seemed to brush the sides of the hall.

'Mr Keating, here I am at last!'

'Hello Lara.'

'How you doing?'

'Fine,' he replied meekly, already sensible of an imbalance in this exchange.

She slapped her hands together. 'Where's that baby?'

'Asleep in her pram. Look,' he went on in a delayed bid for the initiative, 'why don't I make us some coffee and we can have a talk before she wakes up?'

'Great! Coffee sounds great! Kitchen's through here, right?'

He followed her in, glad that he'd put everything ready so she couldn't take over.

'This is a beautiful house,' she said, 'how old is it?'

'Not very, it's Edwardian. But they knew a thing or two about proportions back then.'

'Didn't they just?' she sighed 'I like old houses. My parents' house is old by New Zealand standards, but it's all, like, wood? It's got a verandah, it's pretty. But this is just so substantial.' She slapped the chimney breast with her huge, spatulate hand. 'Feel that. Magic.'

'Built to last,' he agreed. 'Sugar?'

'Fraid so, yeah, I know, but I do. And milk if you've got it.'

'There we are.' He put the mug down in front of her and, as an afterthought, the biscuit tin.

'So,' she said, removing the lid. 'How do you want to play this? I mean I know you're off work for a while yet and I don't want to cramp your style or anything, but I can't wait to get my hands on your daughter!'

The conversation seemed yet again to be getting away from him slightly.

'As far as I'm concerned,' he said, 'we can look on today as a handover period — and of course I'll be here for another few days — but after that I shall let you get on with it.' Thinking this might sound as though he were over-eager to pass Freya over, he added: 'To be honest, it'll be a bit of a wrench. I feel as if I'm just beginning to get the hang of it.'

'That's what I like to hear,' said Lara. 'Good on you. But I like to work as part of a team. I'm not taking over, you know, I'm making a contribution.'

This sounded so eminently sensible and reassuring, that he found himself wondering if nannies were taught to say such things: 'Never usurp the parents, girls, or look as if you intend to'.

Lara lent some credence to this suspicion by standing up, taking another biscuit, her third, and announcing: 'Sorry but I can't stand the tension — can we go and say hello to Freya?'

It was, he realised as he sat in the study after lunch, a rite of passage, and as such was bound to be uncomfortable. For one thing it was weird to hear someone else thumping around the house – and Lara did thump – making themselves at home. He wanted her to feel at home of course, had himself spent some time this morning showing her the ropes, but the speed with which she was adjusting to her new surroundings was alarming. He would have preferred to be up at the top of the house in the studio, where he could have amused himself with some drawing in relative peace and quiet, but felt he should at least try to look busy. In the end, having called the office and spoken first to Doug, then to Jackie, paid some bills and played two games of patience on the computer, he decided to remove himself from fretting's way, and go out.

Emerging into the hall he found Lara in the act of hoisting the papoose on to her back with frightening ease. David was unsettled not just by this, and its implications – that she too was going for a walk and it might be impossible for them to avoid one another – but by her assumption that it was OK to use the backpack. He had imagined her pushing the buggy, or perhaps even the big pram, not using this, a piece of equipment which he'd come to see as his preserve, the emblem of the special relationship between father and daughter.

'OK if I use this?' enquired Lara breezily, extending the waist-strap and snapping shut the clasp. 'Thought your daughter could show me round the neighbourhood.'

'Yes of course,' he said, knowing he hadn't the least grounds for refusal or complaint, but put out nonetheless. 'As a matter of fact I've got a few things to post and some stuff to collect, so I'm going to pop into town. I shan't be more than an hour or so. Will you be all right on your own?'

'Right as rain,' declared Lara. 'Might as well start as we mean to go on. Okey dokey, let's get this show on the road . . . !' And with this she was off, leaving David dazed and bereft.

Still, he thought, I'm the one in charge. Annet and I pay her wages. She's here to assist us and we must learn to take advantage of that. Suddenly he thought of something and rushed to the front door.

'Have you got a key?' he called. 'Because I shall lock up!'

In answer she tweaked a loop of string from the neck of her fleece and waggled a key at him. 'All set, thought of everything!'

Despondently he told himself that this was good, it really was. So far she had shown herself to be friendly – perhaps a little too friendly but not unpleasantly so – adaptable, enthusiastic and competent. She had shown initiative. Annet had made an excellent choice and he was going to have to wear it.

In town he posted the bills and then went into Border and Cheffins.

Jackie told him that Mr Border was out, and added slightly reprovingly that everything was under control.

'I don't doubt it for a moment but since I had to come into town ... I don't want any nasty surprises waiting for me.'

'We've had a couple of people interested in the farm since you rang,' she said pointedly, 'and at round about the right price, which is encouraging. You probaby know Chris Harper's looking for a property for his parents.'

'Yes, I went over to Stoneyhaye a couple of days back but he'd left for Hong Kong.'

'There are one or two places already on our books which might be suitable, can I give you copies?'

'Thanks. I'll be back on Thursday as you know.'

He said this to remind himself as much as her. As he waited for her to run off the copies, the expression 'the first day of the rest of your life' sprang into his mind. From Thursday the new dispensation would begin – the way it was going to be from now on, with short breaks for holidays, illness and so on. He and Annet would work, and Lara and her successors would look after Freya most of the time. It seemed like a heavy decision freighted with moral issues, and yet parents, either singly or together, were making it all the time. He would be here, at Border and Cheffins; Annet would be in London, forty miles away. And their daughter would be in Newton Bury with Lara who in her turn was several thousand miles from where she belonged. Try as he might he couldn't get a satisfactory handle on it.

After the office he went to pick up the photos he'd brought in the previous week, and sat down on a seat in the Formby Centre to look at them. When he slid the twenty or so snaps out of the folder, he found that they covered both before and after Freya. The first eight pictures were of the holiday he and Annet had taken in June. They'd rented a *gîte* in the Dordogne – two weeks of blissful heat and seclusion. In one of the pictures Annet was sunbathing in a deck chair, one hand resting on a tilting wine glass in the grass, her T-shirt hitched up to expose the smooth dome of her pregnancy, gleaming with Factor 15. In another, she was at a restaurant table, groomed and elegant in a black dress that showed off her ripe decolletage. Her hair was pulled back tightly from her tanned face, and she wore shining long earrings that reached almost to her shoulders. A waiter had been commandeered to take the second picture, which showed the two of them together, David smiling into the camera, Annet laughing and looking away. He knew that attitude, it wasn't bashful, but comically despairing, probably over something he'd said. He remembered where they'd been when the photos were taken, a jolly little place down a side street, bourgeois and value-for-money rather than smart. It had been an unusual pleasure on that holiday to take Annet out to eat without watching her punish herself the next day. This was the summer she'd finally given in and relaxed. He found her fecund fatness arousing, and once she'd accepted it she did too. It had been a high summer of slow sex.

There were a few more shots of the cottage, and the view, and one of David arriving back the morning he'd decided to walk down the hill – more of a small mountain really, to get the bread and coffee, instead of taking the car. Annet had been laughing so much the camera shook, but the out of focus picture reminded him of how ghastly he'd felt – heart hammering, face clammy, lungs heaving, the classic picture of a middle-aged man who'd overdone it. And only middle-aged, he reminded himself sternly, if he were destined to live to a hundred and two.

The next picture was also of him – one taken in the labour ward. He was holding Freya (not that she'd been Freya then, just 'a girl!') and his face looked equally blotchy and distressed, though his eyes were wide, pupils dilated. His daughter was a small, scowling person wrapped in a pink blanket, her hair still sticky. He peered intently at the picture, reliving the feelings of that moment. Successive pictures showed Annet with Louise and Coral; Louise holding Freya; Annet holding Freya, flanked by Louise and Coral ... He himself featured in only one of this batch, sitting alongside Annet's pillow with his arm round her shoulders, wearing a rather wary smile. Then there were a few of Freya after they'd brought her home, lying on her mat, in her cot, in the crook of some unidentified arm. He could scarcely believe how far the three of them had travelled since then.

Shaken, he put the photos away. He was sitting not far from where he'd seen Gina King the day he'd come to find where she went in the middle of the day ... Involuntarily he scanned the faces of people at tables, on the fountain wall, milling about in shops. Though he didn't see her he was sure she was there, and could see him. He realised that he had become used to the idea that she was never far away. Since the day she had left his office – the day they brought Freya home – she had been a presence in his life. There were times when he was not sure whether this presence was in or out of his head, but it remained real. The notes and messages, the scent he so often caught in the house, the face at the window ... The face at the window? That was something he still couldn't account for. But another thing of which he was sure – the red car which had so narrowly missed his had been Gina's.

As he got up and left the Centre in the direction of the car he wondered where she was watching him from at this moment. The thought made him straighten his shoulders and quicken his stride.

Once out of the Centre there was no escaping the relatively

depressed nature of the rest of the shops in town. Within a hundred yards there were two closed-down businesses, the second of these currently housing a charity shop. When at work he quite often popped in here to look at the secondhand books – it was surprising what bargains could be found amongst other people's weedings-out or, in some cases, the contents of entire bookcases being energetically got rid of by the relatives of the deceased.

'Morning!' the pleasantly-spoken retired man on the till recognised him. 'Haven't seen you in here for a few weeks.'

'I've been off work,' said David. 'I have a new baby daughter.'

'Well I never – congratulations.'

'Thank you.'

'Don't suppose you've had much time for reading, then,' went on the man. 'You're out for the count the moment your head touches the pillow, if my memory serves me.'

'Pretty much,' David agreed.

'Anyway, we've had boxloads in recently, so you might find something . . .' the bell on the door tinkled again. 'Morning!'

There were certainly a lot more books than usual. Some of the bric-a-brac and china which usually occupied the shelves had been moved to accommodate them. And in a pleasant change from the paperback novels which ususally predominated there were dozens of hardbacks in good condition, many of them with the dustjackets still on. They were mostly non-fiction – travel, gardening, biography and diaries; a few local interest books, with a self-published look. He spent a tranquil half hour browsing amongst the former, and selected four: the autobiography of a general with a reputation for literacy and broadmindedness; an American journalist's treatise on 'The Real New York' which he thought might amuse Annet, whose favourite city it was; another slightly older book about the Dordogne, written by a painter of whom he'd never heard, who'd owned a pretty house there in the fifties; and the notoriously scurrilous diaries of a blue-blooded cabinet minister.

SARAH HARRISON

He wasn't going to bother with the local history, upon which in his experience, the dead hand of worthiness and wordiness invariably lay, but then his eye was caught by the mention of Newton Bury on one cover, and he drew it out. *Sheltered by Hills — a portrait of the village of Newton Bury* by D. M. Cartwright. The dedication read: 'To English village life, long may it thrive!' which made him think the author might be a woman, and the date of the book's original publication was 1970. Out of idle curiosity David turned to the central section of illustrations. All the obvious subjects were there – the church, the pub, the school (in its old, brick gabled building, now the home of a computer salesman), the rectory and even 'the secret manor house of Stoneyhaye, seat of the Wycherley family'. But most surprising was to find his own house, with the caption 'Bay Court, source of one of the village's many colourful stories'.

He added the book to his collection and took them to the till.

'So you did well then,' said the man behind the counter.

'You were right, there was plenty of choice today.'

The man wrote the prices down on a piece of paper and began adding them up, but David put down a ten-pound note. 'Please, don't worry about it, they're cheap at the price.'

'Thank you, I shan't say no, that's most generous.' He put the books in a crumpled carrier bag and handed them back to David. 'Actually, it's rather a sad story. The owner of all these was a patron of ours, absolutely first-class chap called Robert Townsend. The hospice is going to miss his energy and commitment very badly. His wife – widow – is thinking of moving I understand. She brought these in only yesterday.'

'What a strange coincidence.' David took the Newton Bury book out of the bag. 'We live in this village. I didn't know Townsend, but he was obviously very highly thought of.'

'Very, oh yes. Good example of "if you want something done ask a busy person". Always had time, always went that extra mile. Lovely man.' He held out his hand for the book. 'May I?'

David gave it to him and he opened it at the flyleaf. 'There you are.'

There were actually three names on the page, and a faded bookplate opposite which proclaimed that the book had originally been a school prize. 'To Audrey Collins, for Essays.' The other two had been Jane Douglas and K Smith, under which was the next in line, signed simply, in blue ink: 'Robert Geoffrey Townsend'.

'I'm pleased to have found that,' said David. 'What's more there's a picture of our house in it.'

'Good . . .' The man was rummaging for something under the counter. He produced an A4 printed leaflet and opened it on top of the counter, tapping a photograph with his finger. 'That's him, Townsend, at our patrons' lunch in May. That's Mary next to him. They were such a delightful couple.'

David studied the photograph. Townsend was younger, or younger-looking, than he'd anticipated – a big, vital man with crisply curling hair and a broad smile. Beside him his wife appeared tiny – a well-groomed doll of a woman, standing in her husband's shadow.

'Did they have children?' he asked.

'Yes, and grandchildren. He was a great family man.'

'And his wife?'

'Mary? I didn't know her but she seemed charming – rather reticent and retiring, but then he was such a ball of fire, perhaps somebody had to be: they made a good team. She's taken it very hard, as you'd expect after thirty-odd years.'

David handed back the newsletter. 'It's a pretty drastic step to move house so soon.'

'I thought that. Didn't say anything of course. As a matter of fact I was shocked by her appearance. I don't believe I've ever seen such a dreadful change in a person. He was her life, I suppose.'

On the drive home David thought about Robert Townsend. From that hot day following the funeral, this man he'd never known had insisted, like Gina, on recognition. And yet there was some aspect of Townsend's story that troubled him. The uncared-for plot that had so dismayed him and Maurice, and the traumatised widow described by the man in the hospice shop – there was a clear contradiction that he didn't understand.

It was strange, when he got home at four, to hear Freya complaining, not very seriously, upstairs. His first instinct was to go straight up to see her; his second to leave well alone. But Lara called cheerfully down to him:

'Is that you, Freya's dad?'

'Yes.'

'We're up here getting changed.'

For a moment he entertained a disconcerting vision of Lara in her underclothes, before realising that she was using the transferred royal 'we' that other people, especially women, used with babies.

He accepted the implied invitation and went up the stairs and into Freya's room. His daughter was lying on the divan while Lara popped the trail of press studs round the inside leg of her dungarees.

'Hi—' she glanced up at him – 'I think I walked a bit too far, she was soaking wet when we got back.'

'Where did you go?'

'Gosh, now you're asking, all over ... I set off round the village, getting my bearings, you know? Shops, post office, pub, school, community hall ... suppose I should say church, but I don't go to church.'

'I don't, very often. But you ought to take a look. You like old buildings and it's extremely historic'

'Better give it a go next time then.' She picked Freya up and passed her to him. 'There you go Dad, while I straighten things out.'

Perhaps he should have been put out by her breezy familiarity, but it was so much a part of her it seemed churlish to object. She seemed unaware that there was any other way of doing things apart from this matey and democratic one, nor as far as he could tell was there a mean bone in her body. As she bounced about the room, throwing discarded clothes in the washing basket, picking up rubbish and 'straightening' as promised, he saw how quickly she had colonised the space. She seemed already to inhabit it more fully and easily than either he or Annet, and he found that he didn't resent this as he might have expected to. An entirely congenial working relationship seemed suddenly to be on the cards.

'I like that picture,' she said now, pointing at the drawing of Annet. 'It's Mrs Keating, right?'

'Yes.' Encouraged he allowed himself the small vanity of confessing: 'I did it as a matter of fact.'

'Did you . . . ?' she breathed admiringly, going to study it more closely. 'Good on you. It's brilliant.'

'She doesn't like it.'

'No well it's like photos isn't it? The camera never lies, that's why we never like photos of ourselves. I think you really got her.'

He was genuinely gratified. 'Thank you.'

'You're welcome. Now then,' she said, holding out her arms. 'Shall I? It's what you pay me for.'

He handed Freya back. 'You seem to be on top of everything.'

'Yeah, doesn't take me long, I get the feel of things pretty quickly.' She walked past him and began going downstairs. 'Do you mind if I make myself a cup of tea, and I might give this young lady a spot of juice at the same time?'

At once David was on the alert. 'I'm not sure she has juice . . . I don't think we've got any.'

'You have now, I took the liberty of picking up some rosehip at the little store?'

'I'm not aware,' he said, slipping into that pompous style that seemed to take over when he was anxious, 'that she's ever had it.'

'I expect you're right, but no time like the present . . . Unless you have any objection?'

They were in the kitchen now, and she looked directly at him, eyebrows raised, as she ran the tap.

'No,' he said, 'none at all, but maybe you should run it past my wife first.'

'Sure, you got it, but I don't think it's a problem. When we last spoke she was all in favour of developing a routine. And now,' she switched the kettle on, 'I'm going to be *really* cheeky.'

'Yes?' He asked warily, and she burst into a jackassy laugh.

'Your face! Don't worry, I was only going to ask if there was somewhere where I could watch TV for half an hour while we have our drink?'

'By all means – the TV's in the drawing room.' He made a mental note to rent a portable at the first opportunity. 'I shall be in the study.'

'That's really kind. I'm not that addicted to the goggle box, but I love that quiz programme where they have three lives . . . ?'

'I don't know it,' he said.

'That doesn't surprise me. Daytime TV's a girlie ghetto. No, carers' ghetto – nannies, mums, granny-minders, love it.'

She took a bottle out of the steriliser, added an inch or so of boiled water and shook in a few drops of pink juice. Then she made a pot of tea, and put a cosy over it – an item he vaguely remembered seeing in a kitchen drawer over the years but never before put to use. The cosy was in the form of the famous Dürer hare, he suspected Marina's touch. At no point did Lara put Freya down, and he noticed there was no crying. Her boundless confidence was catching.

'Okey-dokey,' she said, 'we'll get out of your way if that's all right.'

When she'd gone he poured himself tea, and as he carried it across the hall to the study he could see that she was sitting on the floor with her back against the sofa – the sunburst frizz of her hair was outlined against the screen.

In the study he took the secondhand books out of their bag

to examine them more closely. He'd pretty much accepted that he wasn't going to work for these next couple of days, it was to be an acclimatisation period, so he might as well enjoy it.

The New York book had no inscription, so he wrote one himself: 'To whet your appetite for a nice, grown-up, long weekend when the Little Apple of *our* eye can safely be left ... XXX, D.'

The painterly memoire of the Dordogne had itself been a present, but the message wasn't what he'd expected. 'To my darling Mary, to remind you of a magical holiday in a magical place, All my love Robert.' So the grief-stricken widow had got rid of this, too. Had the memories been too painful? Possibly, but he found that he still didn't care to think of the New York book, or any one of dozens of others chosen with care and given with pride and love, meeting a similar fate.

The military biography was the newest of the books, a Christmas present from a son: 'Dear Dad, Have a good one, love Roger' with the date beneath. The price had not been snipped off the inside front cover – £19.99.

Aware that he'd been saving the best – or at least the most interesting – till last, he picked up *Sheltered by Hills* and began reading. He found himself gripped: the pages, and with them the minutes, flew by. Not that there was anything exceptional about it. The writing was solid and competent, with occasional forays into pedestrian humour. The research – so far as David could tell – was adequate but well-larded with opinion. Many of the photographs seemed to be taken from postcards: a small printed legend was occasionally visible where they had been insufficiently cropped. The fascination, he decided, was in viewing a place that one knew through the lens of another's perspective.

Newton Bury, it seemed, was mentioned in the *Domesday Book* under the name of Nevitt's Burye and interestingly had had about the same population then as now. The main difference in the aspect of the village in those days was its position. Several centuries ago, according to D. Cartwright's sources, the buildings were strung out along the river valley, clinging to its banks rather than turning their backs on it. 'The ancient manor house,' she wrote, 'was located where the telephone exchange is now, and the walker sufficiently intrepid to hack their way through the brambles at the back of the exchange will be rewarded by a clear view of the submerged remains, now no more than a tantalising pattern of ridges and mounds beneath the grass ...' David decided to be that intrepid walker in the not too distant future: with autumn approaching the brambles would be a less daunting obstacle. The present arrangement of the village had apparently been arrived at over hundreds of years, dictated by transport, changes in farming methods, and the lessening importance of being near the water supply. 'The church of All Saints,' wrote Cartwright, 'is the oldest building in Newton Bury, with the oldest section of the church being the north wall and door which date from the eleventh century. But its origins go back even further, and it is generally thought that a place of Christian worship has stood on this site since St Augustine walked our green and pleasant land ...' This provoked something of a 'yeah, yeah' response in David. He was beginning to form a picture of the author as an enthusiastic but an imaginative woman in sensible shoes, eager to imbue her little book of local history with the Christian message. This was not a message towards which he felt any antipathy, rather the reverse – in animated discussions with Annet he invariably found himself the champion of organised religion – but D. Cartwright's writing had a pedagogic flavour which he found irritating.

However, about halfway through the book, just after the section of black and white plates featuring Bay Court among others, she embarked excitably on a quite different tack.

'For a small village Newton Bury boasts more than its fair share of old and interesting buildings, to many of which curious stories attach. It is not my job to comment on their authenticity, and I shall not do so, but it would be a shame in the context of this book if the rich oral tradition which brought us these stories were to be ignored in the interests of strict factual accuracy.' In other words, thought David, time for a little slumming.

The pub, apparently had been one of eight licensed premises in the village, and although the most enduring had not been the most notorious. That distinction was reserved for the long-defunct Moon and Stars, which had occupied the building now known as Green Lane cottages. Legend (and D. Cartwright) had it that a villainous multiple murderer, an eighteenth-century serial killer named Abel Flack, whose victims were young girls, had been a regular drinker there and been protected for many years by the landlord and regulars who would hide him in the bread oven. This oven, David read, had been where the attractive conservatory of 3 Green Lane Cottages now stood, but the present owners had not reported any strange smells or sinister sounds as they sipped drinks on a summer's evening! Cartwright had a firm belief in the power of the exclamation mark.

There was also, naturally, the church, with its plague corner 'where the compost tip now stands', and its quota of mad, bad incumbents including one Micah Dawson who was rumoured to have bled the poor of the parish dry and used confirmation candidates for his own pleasure. Stoneyhaye got a mention in connection with a society hostess, 'whose hospitality had extended well beyond what was dictated by politeness and friendship!' and on account of a phantom huntsman said to gallop with his red-eyed hounds across the deer park when danger threatened.

The reference to Bay Court was so brief, a mere sentence or two in parenthesis, that he almost missed it. But there it was: '. . . the attractive Edwardian villa of Bay Court, built by the publisher John Latham in 1905 is also said to have a ghost, of a purely benign kind, but anecdotal evidence suggests this may be the sort of paranormal phenomenon generally seen after closing time!'

His heart pounding, David turned back to the photograph. It was quite old – the trees, including the eponymous bay tree which Annet so disliked, and the laurel hedges were less mature, the driveway wider, and there was no gate, only a couple of rather jolly pillars topped with balls. The paintwork on the window frames seemed to be of a different colour, not the fresh white that they were now.

Well, he thought, he and the benign ghost had gazed into one another's eyes, and it had only been two in the afternoon.

'Boss!' called Lara. 'TV's off – it's quality time!'

She explained to him that henceforth there would be a pattern to the day. There was no reason why they as parents should stick to it, but it might prove a useful framework.

'Afternoon tea, playtime, bath, supper, bed!' she declared. '*I*'ve never stuck to a routine in my whole life, but for babies? Every time.'

'I'll defer to your superior judgement on that,' he said, and she smiled.

'You're not a lawyer are you?'

'No, I'm a property agent.'

'It's the way you talk – the perfect English gent.'

'I'm glad you like it.'

Lara chuckled. 'There you go again!'

They attempted playtime together in the drawing room. Freya lay on her plaid rug with Lara sitting on the ground next to her and David perched slightly awkwardly on the edge of the sofa.

'She needs something to look at,' said Lara 'other than us two, gorgeous though we are. Do you have one of those activity frames?'

'I don't believe so. If we have it'll be upstairs. I suppose we thought she was a bit young for toys.'

'And you were dead right. Don't want to get into all that stinking commercialism too early. But you can get these dinky little A-frames that you can stand over them? They can, like, focus on different things, and try to reach out and grasp the handles?' She must have seen his baffled look. 'Shall I get one? They only cost about a fiver.'

'Do, it sounds a good idea.'

He was fascinated by how many different strategies she had for playing with Freya, from simply holding her hands, to lying on the floor beside her. And singing – she appeared to have an inexhaustible supply of nonsense songs with lines like 'Bodger, bodger, the old codger, what a lodger, my oh my!' When he asked her about these she said she'd learned them from her granddad who'd been a first generation immigrant from Bethnal Green.

At around five-thirty, when she'd gone upstairs to bath Freya, the phone rang, and it was Annet.

'Sorry darl, I'm going to be late, tonight of all nights, I am just so pissed off about it – how's Lara?'

'She's great. Getting on with it, as you said she would. I like her. Freya likes her – I felt a bit displaced when she first arrived, but we're shaking down a treat.'

'I'm so glad.'

'She gave her rosehip syrup, was that all right?'

'Did Freya like it?'

'I don't know that she didn't.'

'Then it's OK. Is there any chance of a word with her?'

'I should think so. Hang on.'

He went upstairs and took over, while Lara went down to talk to Annet. By the time she returned he'd finished, and was buttoning Freya into her sleepsuit.

'Blimey O'Riley, you're a dab hand!'

'So I should hope.'

'Most of the fathers I've dealt with are half your age and only half as nifty. If you don't mind my saying,' she added quite unapologetically.

'Not at all. The older the fiddle the better the tune.'

She cackled with laughter. 'OK. Give us it here.'

'Look,' he said, 'don't worry. It's been a long day and we're nearly at the end of it. You knock off and I'll put her to bed. Annet's going to be late as she probably told you.'

'Sure? If you say so.'

He was pleased that she didn't demur, another sign of her

straightforwardness – she wished to be taken at face value, and would do the same with him.

Freya went down quietly – he took it as another good sign – and he poured himself a beer and took it, and D. Cartwright, into the drawing room. Lara had folded the plaid rug and laid it over the arm of the sofa as if to say Freya lived here too.

He was almost at the end of the book when he heard footsteps in the drive, followed by the clap of the letter box. Going into the hall he found the parish magazine, *Outlook*, lying on the mat. He opened the door and saw Maurice on his way to the gate.

'Maurice!'

The rector turned and took a few steps back. 'Sorry – did I disturb you? My lady what delivers is off sick.'

'Fancy a swift one?'

'You twisted my arm.'

Maurice accepted a beer and David poured himself another.

'Where's Annet?' asked Maurice when they were both seated comfortably. 'Not still at work?'

''Fraid so, she rang to say she'd be late.'

'She works hard, your wife.'

'Yes – but then it's what she enjoys. Maurice—' he hesitated, picked up the book, put it down again. 'This is going to sound pretty ridiculous.'

'My dear chap, I shouldn't think it'll even register on the scale where I'm concerned – remember my line of business.'

'For that very reason.'

'Spit it out.'

David laid his hand on the book. 'I picked this up in a charity shop in town. There are two strange things about it.'

'And the first?'

'The first is that this and some other books I bought, all belonged to Robert Townsend – I gather his wife took them in herself a few days ago.'

'Yes, that is a coincidence,' agreed Maurice blandly. David waited, but it was obvious that was all he was going to get, so he went on:

'The second is that it mentions this house – it's a work of local history you understand – and says there's some sort of ghost story connected with it. It isn't in the least specific, and the author's fairly dismissive of the whole thing, but purely out of scientific interest I wondered if you'd ever heard anything ...?'

'I can't say I have. I'm trying to think, but I don't remember anything, even of the public bar kind. Why – cold spots? Crying in the night – sorry, bad joke ... Faces at the window?'

'I did see something like that,' said David eagerly. 'Or thought I did. A few days ago, before I got this book. Which is another reason I'd value your opinion.'

'Interesting.' There was a pause. Maurice clasped his hands around his glass. 'Fair enough, tell you what I think.'

'Please.'

'I'd never dismiss anything out of hand, with the proviso that I'm a Christian, so I believe in redemption. That doesn't sit well with the notion of wretched souls in limbo wandering around making a nuisance of themselves putting heaven, as it were, on hold. But if they're there, then I have every sympathy. And I believe some people see them.'

'A perfectly sensible and cautious reply.'

'What else did you expect?'

'Nothing.'

'One more thing, though, since you ask.'

'Yes.'

'In my view,' said Maurice, giving him a steady look. 'It's not places that are haunted. It's people.'

David waited up for Annet, but she wanted only to go upstairs to bed. By the time he'd locked up and turned the lights out she was asleep. When Freya woke at one-thirty he didn't like to disturb his wife, so went downstairs and gave the baby her bottle in the drawing room in front of the red-veined rubble of the fire. A slight wind had got up, and the sound of it fumbling around the outside of the house made the room seem cosy.

When Freya had finished he walked her about for a few minutes, humming softly. To the south of the house the wind was so strong that the curtains were moving, and a weaselly draught ran round his ankles, lifting the fringe on the Turkish rug. His mind running on what Maurice Martin had said he parted the curtains for a moment, wondering if he were not alone in looking out at the wind-maddened garden.

He did the same at the window at the front of the house and was not surprised to see, in the tossing lamplight opposite, a slight figure in a hooded coat, waiting patiently.

Closing the curtains, he went back upstairs and laid the dozing Freya in her cot. When he looked out into the street again, Gina was still there. She was the last thing he thought of before falling asleep.

Chapter Thirteen

Annet delayed her departure next morning in order to see Lara. When, over their coffee at the kitchen table, David showed her *Sheltered by Hills* she seemed impressed, peering closely at the photograph, and reading the brief entry on Bay Court with serious attention.

'Well I never ... So you were right.'

'I don't know about right. But at the very least it's an interesting coincidence.'

She looked at him, one eyebrow lifted. 'Any more paranormal experiences since that one?'

'No.' He decided against mentioning any vaguer and more general feelings on the subject. 'No, that was it.'

She handed the book back. 'What about little Miss King?'

His scalp crept for a second — what connections had been made in her mind between her last question and this one?

'Still haunting you?' she asked.

'No,' he lied. What point would there be in telling her? 'But I've got something else to show you.'

She evinced a kind of comical horror over the photographs. 'God, look at me!' she cried, 'I was the size of a house!'

'You looked incredibly glamorous, though.'

She put on a Mae West voice. 'You're saying I don't now?'

'You know I'm not.'

'Hm.' She laid the picture of them in the restaurant, and

the one of them with Freya in hospital, side by side on the table.

'Before and after,' she said. 'I'll put them in a frame.'

Lara turned up and reopened discussions on rosehip syrup and related matters, and Karen arrived half an hour later. Heavily outnumbered, David retreated to the study, telling himself that in default of some major crisis he would return to the office tomorrow, a day early.

Annet stuck her head round the door at nine-fifteen.

'I'm off.'

He held out his arm to her and she stooped to receive his kiss. 'What will you do with yourself all day?'

'I was just wondering the same thing. Treat it as a holiday I should think, but I might go in tomorrow all being well. On the understanding Lara can call if she needs to.'

At this Annet heeled the door to behind her and lowered her voice. 'I'd stick around this morning if I were you, darl – you may have the clash of the Titans on your hands out there.'

'Don't tell me they've taken against each other?'

'I wouldn't go that far. Quite. But they're two strong personalities and neither of them are what you'd call team players.' She grinned. 'Good luck!'

Fortunately for him the phone rang several times over the next couple of hours so his attention was distracted from listening out for ructions elsewhere in the house.

First was Tim, calling from the office.

'Got to be brief,' he said. 'Good to see you the other day.'

'For me as well. I've dropped you a note.'

'No need for that – look I can't talk, just wanted to say – my little outburst. It never happened, if you don't mind.'

'What outburst?'

'Thanks, I appreciate it.'

In view of this exchange David regretted mentioning the situation to Annet. But surely Tim would take for granted that he'd tell his wife ... He wondered whether this implied a retraction of Tim's remarks the other day, or merely regret over a perceived indiscretion. He hoped it was the former.

Next was Jackie, businesslike as ever. Another reason for getting back into the office was the unsettling notion that his PA might otherwise assume charge completely and render him redundant.

'Did you get a chance to look at those specifications I gave you?' she asked.

'Not yet,' he confessed.

'Mr Border wanted you to know that a nice new property's come up in your village. Alasdair's going out to do the spec., but Mr Border thought you might know it.'

'Good thinking. Do you have the details?'

'I do, have you got a pencil? It's called Orchard Mead ...' she paused for him to take it down. 'And it's in Orchard End, so that's easy. It's Grade Two listed so it might be the sort of thing Chris Harper's looking for. The owner's name is Mrs Townsend.'

As he made a note he told himself that it was hardly surprising that a listed property in a prime location should wind up with Border and Cheffins. 'I'll probably stroll round and take a look later today. And by the way I'm thinking of coming in tomorrow.'

'I'll look forward to it,' said Jackie.

The moment she'd rung off he picked up *Sheltered by Hills* and found Orchard Mead in the index. The page reference was marked with a small dash in pencil. He found it, and read that this fifteenth-century cottage was one of the oldest houses in Newton Bury; that it had one of the village's three remaining wells in the front garden; and that the thatchwork was among the finest to be seen anywhere in the county. There was no photograph, but he was pretty sure from this description that he knew the house.

A rhythmic rap on the door heralded Lara.

'Excuse me, sorry to disturb.'

'That's all right.'

'Her ladyship's having a nap, but when she wakes up I thought we might whizz into town and buy one of those activity frames.'

'Good idea.'

'Give me a chance to look around as well.'

'Good idea.'

'So, what I'll do, I'll take her bottle and stuff with me and we might have lunch out.' She must have noticed his fractional hesitation. 'If you're not happy with that I don't mind.'

'No . . .' He shook his head. 'I'm perfectly happy with it. After all, if I weren't here—'

'Exactly,' said Lara round the door as she left. 'If you weren't here I could have the rough trade in at all hours and you none the wiser.'

He smiled faintly, but for a second her silly joke resurrected his old misgivings about the situation, and how much of it depended on an act of faith. He was half tempted to call her back, and tell her that he didn't want her 'whizzing' anywhere in the car with his daughter, and what's more if he ever suspected – but common sense prevailed.

A little while later Karen, set-faced, brought him the post and some coffee, placing them on the desk with an unmistakable I-know-what-the-master-likes air.

'Thanks, Karen.'

'I wonder if we could have a word before I go?'

He leaned back welcomingly. 'Now, if you like.'

'Later on would be better,' she said.

'When you've finished then.' He hoped he wasn't going to have to intercede in some messy domestic altercation. This, he supposed glumly, was what you got for not doing your own dirty work.

The sight of Gina's letter, peeping shyly from amongst the junk mail gave him a shock. But not, he found, an unpleasant one. Before opening it he turned it over a few times in his hands, and sniffed it – the cheap lilac paper smelled of her scent, and boiled sweets. He slid his thumb beneath the flap of the envelope, not wanting to tear it.

'Dear Mr Keating,' he read.

'I was sorry you were not able to provide me with a reference for my job application, but of course I understand. As expected I didn't get that job but I am working in a car showroom now and am very happy there. I deal with the general public every day which I enjoy, although I do miss being in the centre of town. How are you? I often think of you and the new baby and wonder how you're getting on. Please give my best to Mrs Keating,

Yours Gina.'

Touched, he put the letter, with its quaint mix of formality and assumed intimacy, back in the envelope, which he then resealed and tucked in the inside pocket of his briefcase. That way he could pretend even to himself that he hadn't bothered to read it.

He was staring into space when the phone rang for the third time.

'David, it's Lou.' She sounded harassed. 'This is a longshot but is Annet there?'

'No, she's at work.'

'I tried her there but she hadn't arrived yet.'

'She wanted to talk to the new nanny so she left late.'

'It doesn't matter ...' Louise's tone belied her words. 'There's probably no point in worrying her at this stage anyway.'

'Anything I can do?' he asked warily.

'Not really, bless you David ... It's Mummy.'

'What's wrong?'

'She seems to have had some sort of fall.'

'Oh Lord — serious?'

'Not in the sense of any serious injury, no, just a few bruises. But it's the implications that worry me. It seems to have shaken her marbles a bit. She got to the phone, fortunately, and she's in hospital as we speak. They're going to keep her in overnight for observation. I am rather worried about what it portends.'

'I'm so sorry. Look, are you quite sure there isn't something I can do?'

'No, no, good heavens, you've got your hands full . . . .'

'The nanny's here now.'

He heard Louise heave a huge and slightly shaky sigh. 'No. I've got myself into a quite unnecessary tiz. There really isn't a panic. As Coral said, it's not a big crisis, this is the sort of thing that happens with old people on their own. It's just that Mummy's always been so sprightly.'

'She has,' David agreed, feeling remorse for several years' worth of small, ungenerous jokes at his mother-in-law's expense. 'She's wonderful for her age.'

'It's so good to talk to you. I feel better, actually. I needed to unload.'

'You've got it all on your plate at the moment. Would you like me to give Annet a call and get her to ring you at lunchtime? She'll want to know anyway.'

'Yes, but not when she's at work. I'll catch up with her this evening when there may be something more to report. And Coral can be the voice of calm and reason.'

Coral's name reminded him of something. 'Isn't it your big day fairly soon?'

Her voice lightened audibly. 'Yes, not long. I'm hanging on to that. We're both so looking forward to it, but this with Mummy has rather come between, if you know what I mean.'

'This too shall pass, Lou,' he said. 'And then just think, the four of us will be able to get together and talk babies.'

'David?' said Louise. 'You're a man in a million. If I ever turn from my present course it'll be you I turn to, and that's a promise.'

'I'll hold you to that.'

David's thoughts were preoccupied with Marina when at

half past eleven Karen's 'I'm about to go!' summoned him into the hall. If he'd been able to leave his sister-in-law a little happier it proved harder to do so with Karen.

'Karen, thank you.'

'Don't thank me, it's my job.'

'You said there was something you wanted to discuss.'

'I'll come to the point, then. Lara's very messy.'

'You could be right.'

'I mean she's a nice girl, very jolly and all that, but she leaves a trail of stuff wherever she goes. It doesn't make my job any easier.'

'I can see that.'

'The thing is when it comes right down to it you pay me to do your cleaning, not hers.'

'Point taken. I'll have a word. I'm sure she'd be appalled to think she was making life difficult for you.'

'To be honest I'm not fussed what she thinks,' declared Karen. 'I want to do a good job for you.'

Against this subtle blackmail David felt he had no defence but to say: 'I know, and we really appreciate all that you do, Karen. You leave it with me.'

When she'd gone he stood in the hall and breathed in the peace of the empty house. Before going out he retrieved Gina King's letter from his briefcase and slipped it into the breast pocket of his shirt.

On leaving the house he first walked across Gardener's Lane to the opposite corner and stood by the lamppost looking back towards Bay Court. The window of the main bedroom appeared surprisingly close. Anyone standing in the window, as he had so often of late, would be as clear and distinct as a framed portrait . . . .

As he walked on he thought of Marina and her fall. It was hard to predict how Annet (whom he had decided he would call at lunchtime) would react to this news. He feared a whirl of fearsome, largely futile, activity intended to assuage the guilt that was a fellow traveller in all his wife's dealings with her mother. His own view was that nothing much could be done while Marina was in hospital, but that there was a strong case for visiting her when she got home and taking the emotional temperature. He was sure that it was Marina's mental rather than her physical state that would be the issue here. If she had in any sense persuaded herself that the time had come for her daughters to take up the reins, then Louise and Annet would be left very little choice in the matter. Respectfully, he realised that he himself had been let off lightly in this department. His parents had both died relatively young, in their late sixties, his father of a heart attack and his mother two years after from what was referred to even by the doctor as a broken heart. She had simply turned her face to the wall, and faded away. At the time he and Tim had been devastated, but having since seen the years of terrible emotional attrition, resentment and remorse which attended the long deterioration of other people's parents, he was glad of it. Apart from anything else it meant that he retained a memory of them as whole, vigorous people in their prime, not rendered pathetic and querulous by the indignities of extreme old age.

He continued round the back of the village, on the opposite side from All Saints and the river. This took him via Green Lane Cottages, formerly the infamous Moon and Stars hostelry, and he slowed down to try and identify the conservatory where the bread oven had been. But since all three cottages now had conservatories of varying degrees of grandeur he was none the wiser.

He passed the school playground, currently swarming with mixed infants on their midday break. A few came to the brick wall and hoisted themselves up to lean on the top. A little girl with Baby Spice bunches called out.

'Hello, Mr Man! Hello Mr Man!' and then they all started

doing it. Rather embarrassed by the shouting, he went over to them.

'Hello. What are you doing?'

'Leaning on the wall,' explained one of the small boys with the blank air of one who couldn't quite believe he'd been asked such a stupid question.

'Had your lunch?'

'Yes!' they all chorused.

'And was it nice?'

'Yes!' It seemed to be developing into a game, and David felt quite proud of his own success.

'What did you have?'

'Packed lunch! Packed lunch!' they shouted, well away now.

'So the others are still inside are they?'

'Yes!' they shouted, and this time the Baby Spice girl added: 'School dinners don't come out till after.'

David made a mental note to repeat this wonderfully opaque observation to Annet.

'I see. Well, lucky you. So what was in your packed lunch then?'

This line of questioning proved a mistake, because it prompted each of them simultaneously to embark on a detailed inventory of the contents of his or her lunch box. David, smiling bemusedly, sensed things beginning to get out of control, and was rather relieved to see a fierce young teacher in a long skirt and ankle boots steaming across the playground towards them.

'Get down off there at once please. What's going on?' she demanded, hauling her charges peremptorily off the wall and glaring at David.

'I'm sorry, I asked them about lunch. It wasn't their fault.'

'I dare say. Go on off you go.' She shooed the children away and then turned back to him, bristling with the authority invested in her. 'They're not supposed to speak to strangers.'

'Of course.' He was mortified. 'I do apologise.'

'Do you have a child at the school?'

'No ...' He felt too humiliated even to embark on an explanation. 'Not yet.'

'If you did,' said the young teacher tartly, 'you'd appreciate why we have this rule and why we enforce it rigorously.'

'I perfectly understand.'

'Good. Excuse me I have to ring the bell.'

As he walked away, smarting, the bell clanged imperiously behind him. Ask not for whom the bell tolls ... So he had been taken for a potential child-abductor. It occurred to him that if he'd only had Freya with him in the pram, or had met someone that he knew outside the school, this appalling scene would not, could not, have taken place. The perfect rightness of the young teacher's case did nothing to soften the cruel injustice of her suspicions.

He was still miserably chewing this over when he reached Orchard Mead. By the look of the narrow lane he suspected it had been given its present name in the sixties, just before the publication of *Sheltered by Hills*, and around the time of the small modern development that clustered on its corners. He remembered now that the only other time he had been up here was when the charity for the homeless had asked him to distribute envelopes for voluntary contributions around the village, a humble but time-consuming task which he had since avoided.

Orchard End was well-named – the lane came to a full-stop at its gate. The well and the thatch were just as described, and a coven of stooped apple trees clustered crookedly around the garden path. But there was plenty of evidence of discreet modernisation. A rustic sign declaring 'private drive' marked the route to a detached double garage to the left of the house and the outside plasterwork was in mint condition. A dark red Citroën estate was parked outside the garage with the tailgate up, to reveal one or two supermarket carriers in the boot. As David stood there a black Labrador burst from the open back door of the house and charged the fence, leaping up and down and barking so frenziedly that he stepped sharply backwards. When a smartly dressed woman emerged from the house and ran across to restrain the dog, David felt like a felon for the second time that day.

'Sorry . . . he's perfectly harmless but a bit overenthusiastic. *Bad* dog Pluto, *basket* — I said BASKET!' She pointed, arm extended, in the direction of the house and the dog ambled off. It didn't actually go inside, David noticed, but at least it wasn't jumping for his throat.

'Sorry . . .' said the woman again. He put her in her late thirties, capable but harassed. 'Did you want my mother?'

'Is that Mrs Townsend?'

'That's right.'

'I wasn't intending to disturb anyone as a matter of fact. I'm David Keating of Border and Cheffins Country Properties.'

'I'm Sue Bentham.'

'How do you do. By the way, I live in the village — I was so sorry to hear about your father.'

She gave him a surprised, hopeful look. 'Did you know him then?'

'No—' He almost wished to qualify this, but checked himself. 'No, only by reputation.'

'He touched a lot of people's lives.'

'How is your mother?' he asked.

'Very bad.'

'Of course. I'm sorry.' He let this lie respectfully for a second, before going on: 'You obviously know that your mother's just placed the house with us, and I believe Mr Macky's coming to see you.'

'That's right, tomorrow.'

'I'm not here to pre-empt his visit in any way. I'm having a few days off and thought I'd refresh my memory of where your house was.'

'You were doing a recce,' said Mrs Bentham. 'No, no, that's fine . . . Do you want to come in? Mother's having a zizz.'

'I won't, thank you, I'll leave you in peace.' He gazed around. 'It is lovely, I must say, your mother's going to be sad to leave it.'

'I don't *know* ...' mused Mrs Bentham, and then added: 'Not as sad as you might imagine, I think she feels she has to move on.'

David tapped the top of the gate. 'I'll let you get your shopping in.' He extended his hand. 'It was nice to meet you, albeit under such sad circumstances. I'll be in touch from the office tomorrow after Alasdair's been, and we'll get things moving.'

On the way back down the lane he could have kicked himself for the way he'd spoken to her, so smooth, so – there was no other word for it – fatuous. Thinking of Robert Townsend's widow sleeping off another grain of grief on this sunny afternoon reminded him again of Marina. Annet considered her own mother's grieving to have been a charade, but one never knew.

Not wanting to appear a vulture for the third time that day, he avoided the school on the way back. At Bay Court the Metro had returned, and when he opened the door he could hear snickery pop music playing on the radio in the kitchen. In fairness to Lara this was switched off the moment he appeared in the doorway. She was sitting at the table, holding Freya, with a half-eaten sandwich and an open newspaper on the table in front of her. The empty formula bottle stood on the draining board.

'Hi!' she said. 'Excuse me carrying on, but I didn't know how long you'd be.'

'I think we have to operate as free agents, don't you? As a matter of fact you seem to be so on top of things, I thought I might go into the office tomorrow. You can always ring me if you need to.'

'Sounds good to me. Now ...' she hoisted Freya on to her shoulder and massaged her back, 'how are we doing ... ?'

She seemed, David thought, a little subdued. 'May I?' he asked, holding out his arms for Freya.

'She's all yours, literally.'

He took his daughter and held her in front of him for a moment.

'She holds her head well, doesn't she?' commented Lara.

'You'd know more about that than me, I think.'

'She's a strong girl.'

He liked that. And it was true, he could feel it. Already Freya was bigger and more active, her arms and legs were getting solid. As if reading his thoughts, she smiled at him.

'Ah, she recognises her dad,' said Lara. 'By the way,' she added, taking her plate to the sink, 'sorry if I upset Karen.'

'If you did,' he said carefully, 'we all realise it was nothing intentional.' He was relieved in a way that she had saved him the embarrassment of raising the subject. 'Karen's not used to having someone else around – I mean someone who's also got a job to do.'

'Yeah, I appreciate that. And I'm an untidy cow.'

He smiled. 'As long as you appreciate the situation that's half the battle. She only comes a couple of mornings a week. You might find it easier to be out at those times ... or whatever.'

'Don't worry, I'll make an effort.'

'I know you will. And Karen's not a bad sort, you know. Her heart's in the right place.'

'It's funny,' said Lara, in a slightly less penitential tone, 'the way people say that about people who are grumpy sods.'

He smiled. 'Fair comment.'

It may have been this which decided him to go and visit Marina that afternoon. That, and the fact that he was unable to raise Annet on the phone.

'She's like a headless chicken in here today,' Piers confided. 'We all are.'

'In that case, no message. Don't even bother to say I rang, it can wait till this evening.'

'Wise move,' said Piers.

Whether it was or not he didn't know, but he reasoned that a first-hand report on Marina's condition would at least give Annet the basis for a decision.

He left at half past one. As he drove out of the village and up on to the ridgeway he checked his rear-view mirror once or twice for the red car. The letter from Gina was still in his shirt pocket. She said she had a job, but he suspected that might not be true. If it was, how could she afford to spend all this time following him, observing him . . . ?

With a guilty pleasure he was too honest to deny, he admitted to being both disturbed and flattered.

True to form Marina, who could by no standards have been the sickest patient on the ward, had parlayed her way into an amenity bed. He encountered Louise outside the door of her room, carrying a pack of Evian water and some chocolate.

'David!' They exchanged a kiss. 'This is so nice of you.'

'Not at all. I wanted to, for Annet's sake as much as anything.' Today, the gratifying sense of doing the right thing made a pleasant change.

'Coral's coming over too, any minute now.'

'Will we be too many people for her?'

Louise pulled a face. 'Please, this is my mother we're talking about.' She put a hand on the door, but paused before opening it. 'Did you tell Annet?'

'I couldn't raise her, it's hell out there today according to her assistant. I thought if I'd been over I could give her my impressions.'

'You're probably right.'

They went in. Marina was leaning back on her pillows, her head turned towards the window. She wore a diaphanous bed jacket in powder blue, but her hands, resting on the sheet, though impeccably manicured as always, looked gnarled and old, the tendons standing out on the back, the joints sharply pronounced, the skin densely blotched with liver spots. Her beautiful rings, 'my precious rings' as she called them, looked too heavy for her fingers. Her hair too, without the usual level of attention lavished on it, appeared whispier. David was shocked to be able to see her scalp between the thin, expensively coloured strands.

'Mummy?' said Louise. 'Look who I've got.'

Marina rolled her head on the pillows. Her sweet, weak smile persuaded David that she was probably going to live. Mr Toad at his most outrageous had nothing on Marina.

'David, how lovely ....'

He kissed her. She had no make-up on but her skin felt soft and she smelled as always of some recherché scent.

'Marina,' he said, 'you know you really must give up all this wild partying.'

'I know, I know, what a foolish old woman I am.'

Louise put the water bottles on the locker and indicated the chair by the bed. 'Take a seat, I'll perch.'

'Annet would have come like a shot,' he said as he sat down, 'but I couldn't reach her on the phone at work. As I'm having a few days off I thought I'd come and run the rule over you first.'

In answer, Marina held out a frail hand and he took it in both his. Gestures which would normally have been foreign to him, came easily when dictated by Marina.

'Dear David ....'

'So what did you do?' he asked. 'What happened?'

'That's the trouble, I wish I knew ... One moment I was taking my coat off as nice as you please, the next I was horizontal.'

'It was incredibly fortunate for Mummy,' put in Louise from the end of the bed, 'that she fell in the centre of the hall, on the carpet, and close to the phone. If it had been the kitchen, or the loo, or somewhere with more hazards, it could have been a different story.'

Marina's eyes had not left David's face during this speech. 'She wants me to have a panic button.'

'It might be sensible,' he said. 'I'm sure Annet would say the same thing.'

'Have you seen one of those things?' She waggled her hand in his to ensure his full attention. 'They are perfectly hideous.'

'They're not supposed to be a fashion accessory, Mummy,' said Louise.

'I know, but really and truly . . .' Marina sighed, withdrew her hand from David's and let it fall lifelessly on to the quilt. 'Still I expect you're right.'

'I am.'

'How are you feeling, anyway?' asked David.

'Shaken, I must say. Very shaken, and very, very foolish.'

'There's no need for that. Anyone can have a dizzy spell.'

'How strange then that it is mainly silly old ladies who do,' replied Marina. It was one of those rare moments when he was vouchsafed a glimpse of something Annet and her mother had in common, though he doubted Annet would have admitted to it.

'But no bones broken,' he offered.

'This time,' muttered Louise.

'No,' said Marina. 'I feel as if I've been run over by a tractor, but the schoolboy masquerading as a doctor assured me that's only to be expected.'

'I'm sure he's right. But Lou tells me you're going to stay in overnight, so they'll probably slip you a Mickey Finn. You'll have a really good night's sleep and wake up feeling a new woman.'

'A new woman . . .' she gave a dry little laugh, and a glance in which he thought he detected the the origins of the cowboy look. 'Now that would be nice.'

The arrival of Coral provided him with an excuse to leave, and Louise saw him to the lift.

'So what do you think?' she asked. 'Be honest.'

'To be honest she seems in rather good form.'

'But so frail – or maybe I'm guilty of not having noticed how thin she's got.'

'Yes . . . but then old people tend either to spread or shrink.'

Louise laughed. 'And Mummy would never, ever, spread. Thanks for coming, David, you're a mensch. Give Annet my love, won't you and tell her I'm on the case – I don't want her dropping everything to harry the hospital authorities.'

'You think I'll be able to stop her?' He got into the lift. 'She'll be in touch.'

On the whole he was heartened by the visit to Marina. It would be pleasing to tell Annet, truthfully, that although frail her mother had been in better spirits than he'd expected.

He let Lara deal with bathtime, and put some effort into the preparation of supper, the Spanish omelette which was by way of being a speciality of his and a favourite of Annet's. Mindful of the fate of an earlier letter, he took Gina's envelope out of his pocket and put it in the drawer of his desk beneath Jackie's pile of property specifications.

When he went upstairs it was to find Lara sitting with Freya in her arms, a pretty picture with only the soft glow of the nightlight in the baby's room.

'Couldn't keep her awake,' she said quietly. 'Not even for her dad.'

'Nor should you. I'll put her down, shall I?'

He kissed Freya on the forehead and laid her in the cot. Strangely, as she grew almost before his eyes, so she seemed to him to be becoming more vulnerable: stepping out into the world. He thought of the child at the school wall with her bright 'Hello Mr Man!' and it squeezed his heart.

'She's a gem, your daughter,' said Lara, not joking, and so revealing the genuine niceness which silenced criticism.

Annet returned at eight-thirty. He turned the heat on under the skillet when he heard her key in the lock, and took the bottle of Murphy's Landing out of the fridge. He was determined that this should be a good evening, one that even the news about

Marina would not spoil. He was glad that he would be in a position to set her mind at rest about that, and glad too that he had tucked the letter from Gina where there was no chance it would be found . . . .

She put her head round the door. 'Hi there. I'm just going to nip up and see our little angel.'

She had a way of spiking her endearments with irony. 'Do that.' He lifted the bottle. 'Now?'

'When I come down.'

He heard her run up the stairs. You never saw Annet plod or trudge, it wasn't in her nature. She seemed always to have more energy available in her reserve tank than most people had at the start of the day.

She was gone about five minutes, and returned wearing jeans and the classic, drop-shouldered American football sweatshirt that she'd bought in Detroit. She exactly suited these clothes, and he went to put his arms round her as she reached for her glass.

'Mm—!' She held the glass out to one side. 'First things first!'

'That's what I was thinking.'

'Oh go on then . . .' She let him kiss her, not returning his embrace because of the glass, but pressing herself against him. 'Can't a girl even have a quiet drink at the end of a working day without being jumped . . . ?'

'Not around here she can't.'

'Look out, your pan's smoking.'

'Shit—!'

He rescued the skillet to the accompaniment of her laughter, turned the heat down and poured in the eggs.

'Smells nice,' she said. 'I am totally ravenous.'

'Busy day?' he asked, interested to see if her account accorded with that of Piers.

'Mad but not bad. Hard but not smart. I quite enjoyed it though. Had a fun stroppy meeting with the design people.'

She enlarged on this while he completed the omelette, and

he let her finish her story, her supper and her second glass of wine, before saying cautiously:

'This is absolutely nothing to worry about love, but Louise rang today. Your mother's had a fall.'

'Christ!' She actually whitened, and put down her fork with a rattle. 'What?'

'She's OK. No, really.'

'That's what Lou says, she doesn't want me to go over there, doesn't want to worry me, she can be so patronising—' She got up and flung down her napkin, which missed the chair seat and landed on the floor. 'Excuse me, I'm going to call her.'

'Don't – Annet, calm down.'

'Calm down? Get lost, darl, my mother's probably had a stroke and you're telling me to calm down?'

'But she hasn't had a stroke,' he got up and went to her, standing close but not touching, respectful of her mood. 'Louise took her into hospital, but it's only precautionary. They haven't been able to find anything except a few bruises, but they're keeping her in overnight in any case just to be sure.'

She looked up at him, her gaze flicking back and forth, scanning for duplicity. 'And who told you all this good, calming news? Louise?'

'She did, yes.' He played his trump card. 'But as a matter of fact I went over this afternoon and saw her for myself, and I can report—'

'You *what?*' Her fury was like a smack in the face.

'I went to visit Marina.'

She took a few steps away from him, held her brow for a second, turned back, hand still to head. 'You didn't think to call me?'

'Lou tried first thing, the office and here. I tried later and you weren't available. Piers said you were all having a hell of a day. I thought if I popped over to see her I could at least give you a progress report.'

'And if I'd been I could have seen for myself!'

He could scarcely believe he'd got it so wrong. 'Annet –

she's all right. She'd love to see you naturally, but there's nothing seriously wrong.'

'So why did she fall?'

'I don't know.' He realised how lame that would sound to her and tried to stifle her scorn. '*They* don't know. But Lou says they've established it definitely wasn't a stroke.'

'Jesus!' She slumped back on to her chair, elbows on the table, head in hands. 'I suppose it's too late to see her this evening anyway, they turn the lights out about nine in those places.'

'Yes.'

'Why didn't you *tell* me? Why didn't you get Piers to tell me to call?'

'I'm sorry.' He was sorry, but she'd got to him – he was also rattled. Not quite angry yet, but heading that way, his apologies were taking on a bitter note. 'I am truly sorry, I acted for what I thought was the best.'

She said something sotto voce, a furious mutter.

'What?'

Now she raised her voice almost to a shout. 'Why the hell did you take it on yourself to decide what was best!'

'If you hadn't been so late,' he heard himself say, 'you might have had time to see her.'

She shook her head with an expression of angry astonishment. 'I beg your pardon?'

'I mean where have you been since the fun meeting with the design people? Having more fun?'

'Yes, actually. I went to the gym at Chris Harper's. There was no one else there. I did half an hour aerobic and half an hour on weights and then I drove home. But it was still a bloody sight more fun than taking this crap from my husband!'

She got up and left the room. David heard the study door slam – she was going to phone Louise. He was riven with the shock of this row. It was the first they'd had, they were wary of confrontation. She was too quick to anger, he too slow, both had their dangers and they'd recognised them.

Till now. This time they'd blown it.

*   *   *

He was in the drawing room pretending to read the paper when she went upstairs. He called 'Annet—?' but she didn't answer. He heard Freya crying, and when he did go up Annet was sitting in her nightshirt on the chair where Lara had sat earlier, breastfeeding.

'Good night then,' he said.

'Good night.' Her voice was completely normal, but he didn't take that as a good sign. It meant she'd been thinking.

He read for about fifteen minutes and then turned his lamp off. She didn't come. Eventually he slept, and when he woke the green numbers read one-o-six. Annet wasn't in bed. He went to the door of Freya's room and saw that she was sleeping on the divan. Such a thing had never happened before. The clichéd brutality of the message cut him to the quick.

Instinctively when he returned to their room, he pulled the curtain aside. And there she was. His lily of the lamplight, watching over him.

Chapter Fourteen

He took comfort in small things. The journey in wasn't bad. The roadworks were gone. Even Doug Border was a breath of fresh air.

'Put it there, Davey boy, we've missed you!'

'I'm delighted to hear it.'

They were in Doug's office, and he thumped the back of a chair. 'Take the weight off your plates. Family well? No wrecks and nobody drownded?'

'No,' was all David could say to this.

'So – er – says he cutting to the chase – did you get a chance to take a peep at the Townsend place?'

David nodded. 'I did. It seems delightful.'

'It had better be, she wants three hundred thou. Alasdair's going round this morning to talk business with the poor lady. Or more likely with the poor lady's daughter who seems to be managing things.'

'Mrs Bentham, I met her yesterday. And there's no reason why we shouldn't get that sort of price. If the house is half as nice inside as out, it'll be worth every penny of that to the right person. It's certainly worth contacting Chris Harper about. I should think the family would be wholly delighted with a cash sale, no chain, and very possibly no conveyancing fees.'

'Yes!' declared Doug, bunching his fist. 'I feel a good day coming on!'

David did not, which was probably why he was relishing

the simple and entirely unforeseen pleasure of talking shop with his partner. He himself had always been the outsider, the man who didn't quite fit, the ringer (Doug's word) who was effective without anyone quite understanding why. Now suddenly he felt a kinship with Doug. Apart from his brief exchange with Maurice, and the longer but unhappy one with Tim, he had been surrounded by women for the past week. He liked women, and even preferred their company to that of men most of the time, but it was entirely possible he'd had too much of a good thing. He was still reeling from the row with Annet. Doug's uncomplicated blokiness, and his robust relish for business was as comforting as a bacon butty.

'So you'll liaise with Harper, then,' said Doug as he left. It wasn't a question. 'You're the one he knows, the one who hobnobs with the stars. He drinks at your house for chrissakes.'

'He has been once.'

'That's all it takes. I was impressed. Smooth operator or what?'

Back in his office, Jackie said: 'Mrs Keating called, I said you were in a meeting. But she said not to call her, because she won't be in the office.'

'Thanks.'

Annet had left the house early, without even her usual coffee. All the sounds leading up to her departure – doors opening and closing, her quick footsteps, the full-blast, two-minute shower, even the brisk crackle of her hairbrush – had seemed to David to speak volumes: she remained furious, and he unforgiven. The phone call reported by Jackie might have presaged a softening, but his unavailability would probably have blown that. She wasn't going to make it easy on either of them, and he smarted with the injustice of it. The whole wellbeing of their relationship had always depended on his adaptability, on second-guessing her moods and, if necessary, pulling his punches. Now, on the only occasion when he'd lost his temper he was being made to feel as if he'd done something monstrous. Perhaps he had. Perhaps the trouble with good behaviour was that it set you up for an almost inevitable fall. But of one thing he was sure – he didn't deserve this cold-shouldering

Only when he'd nursed his resentment for half an hour did he remember that of course Annet would be out of the office, visiting her mother. But he was still sore, and it was more out of duty than fine feeling that he eventually dialled Marina's home number. There was no reply. Jackie furnished him with the number of the hospital and he got through to the ward to be told the doctor was with Mrs Holbrook.

Jackie brought him a baguette at lunchtime, and he called Lara. As he waited for the phone to be answered he wondered why he couldn't leave well alone. When she did pick it up it was to a background of Freya's crying and the chitter of commercial radio.

'Boss—? Hang on – hang on – be right with you!'

The radio was turned off, there was some bumping and scuffling and one tremendous clatter – he guessed the phone had fallen to the ground – before Lara returned.

'Hell's bells, dropped the phone. Beg pardon, no damage.'

'I just rang to see how things were going.'

'And now you know, bet you wish you didn't.'

'A bad moment obviously.'

'Your daughter is one cross baggage today.'

David found this no-flannel assessment more reassuring than any soothing words. 'She can be.'

'She's going to be a woman of character. Still, there's only one way from here, and that's up.'

'I'm glad you're being so positive.'

'It's what you pay me for.'

'That's true.' He was starting to feel at home with her conversational style.

'And I bet you're glad you're in that office of yours.'

'Absolutely. But I'll be back by five.' There was something he had to ask. 'Has my wife rung?'

'Of course. She always does.'

Duly reprimanded, he hung up. He got Jackie to call Chris Harper, but she received the message that he wasn't answering the phone. After a brief consultation he took Jackie's advice and wrote a letter, rather than sending a fax or e-mail.

'You want to do the gentlemanly thing,' was how she put it. 'I think that would go down well.'

'I suspect you're right. Take a letter, Miss Jones.'

'Handwritten would be even better,' she said.

Once that had been done he tried Marina's number again, and this time it was answered by Louise.

'We just got back,' she told him. 'They've given her the all-clear but I'm going to stay here for at least tonight.'

'How does she seem to you?'

'A bit shaky after the journey, otherwise pretty good. We're having a drink as a matter of fact.' She dropped her voice fractionally. 'Annet's here.'

'I gathered she must be.'

'David, to say she's angry would be an understatement. Hopping mad would be a more accurate description.'

'I know. I feel bad about it. I obviously made a serious error of judgement.'

'We both did. Anyway it's Mummy who's getting it in the neck at the moment.'

'That's hardly fair.'

'It's all right, they understand each other.'

'May I have a word with her?' he asked.

'Hang on.'

He heard her call his wife's name, once clearly, from near the phone, once further away. When Louise returned to relay the message, her tone was carefully non-committal.

'David? She can't come now. She says she'll see you later.'

He'd had to be content with that. But he remained restless and unsettled. Once he'd cleared his desk – not an arduous task since Jackie had kept things up to speed in his absence – he prepared to leave.

'This won't be a habit,' he explained. 'I'm not officially back yet.'

'I know,' she replied, adding 'Till tomorrow,' which might have been an endorsement or a farewell, he wasn't sure.

In the car he set off in a northerly direction, following signs for the London Road. In his mind's eye he could see Gina King's address, in her round, even hand, as it appeared on the top of her letter. He was pretty sure he knew the area it was in: he just wanted to see her house, as she had seen his. The notion that she might even now be watching him, and might gradually realise what he was doing, was titillating. He was leading her on. As he left the city centre he discovered with a guilty pleasure that he was slightly aroused.

The area he was looking for was a large estate, the Egremont, completed about twelve years ago, with houses ranging from maisonettes and starter homes through to four-and-five-bedroom detached villas, all at highly competitive prices. Though they were not remotely in the Border and Cheffins bracket, it was common knowledge that they were a poor investment. The situation, between the local league football ground, the municipal landfill and the London Road was nothing short of horrible, a classic example of the rule 'location, location, location' being not simply broken but callously flouted.

He was, however, pretty sure that this was where Gina lived, for the simple reason that her house was in Raleigh Road, and the Egremont Estate abounded with names of the nation's explorers, inventors, philosophers and men of letters, perhaps in the hope that the aspirations and achievements of those it commemorated might rub off on the inhabitants.

Unfortunately, the modest prices ensured that those who bought houses here were not best placed in terms of time or money to absorb the influences of Britain's greatest thinkers. This was no sink estate, but as soon as David turned off the London Road there were the unmistakable telltale signs of lives lived close to the economic bone. He noticed the scattering of litter ... the occasional gate hanging off its hinges ... the pointy-faced dogs trotting about on the green areas, leaving mess and looking for trouble ... a vandalised and abandoned car with a POLICE AWARE notice on it. The gardens and outside woodwork of many of the smaller houses in particular were sadly under-maintained, with shreds of rubbish clinging to straggling hedges. So it was with Burns, with Shakespeare, with Byron, Dickens, Shaw, Wilde and a host of other literary luminaries.

When he reached Nelson Way the houses became larger, and he knew he must be closing on his objective. Traffic calming bumps meant that his slow progress wasn't in any way conspicuous. He cruised along Wellington and Montgomery, down Drake, round Scott and into Kitchener before spotting Raleigh Road on his left. He pulled up opposite the turning but couldn't see the red Micra anywhere and besides, he told himself, it was far more likely to be somewhere a safe distance behind him.

He turned into Raleigh. Here, there was definitely a tone being kept up – he noted net curtains, porch extensions, no litter, the occasional shock of pampas grass sprouting from tidy front lawns. A dog barked, but faintly, from behind double glazing.

He reached number twenty-three, but didn't want to stop. He decided to go to the end of the road, turn, and pull over a little short of the house in order to inspect it.

Not that there was anything much to distinguish it from its neighbours. David's searching eye spotted a satellite dish, a seasonally-bedraggled passion flower clinging to the front wall, a security alarm peeping from below the guttering, and immaculate paintwork. The Kings weren't people to let things go. On a lamppost next to him hung a yellow sign proclaiming Raleigh Road a neighbourhood watch area.

He was about to pull away when the front door opened and Gina came out. Her appearance was so sudden and unexpected, that he felt his palms break into a sweat and his scalp stir. He sat motionless, paralysed by this reversal of circumstances. He could only hope that she would not see him because she wasn't expecting to either. There again, had she been watching his progress up the road, and back to his present position, all the time? There was no red car in the drive — in fact no car at all. He didn't want to start up the engine and drive away in case that attracted her attention. So he watched, frozen, praying she wouldn't walk in his direction.

She was wearing a straight fawn skirt, high heels and a brown suede jacket with a tie belt that he thought he remembered. A neat white polo-neck showed above the collar of the jacket. Not a fashionable look but pretty and feminine. She carried no handbag, but seemed to be walking purposefully, carrying out some small commission or other. Mercifully she turned away from where he was parked and set off at a smart pace towards the T-junction with Kitchener.

He waited until she'd moved out of sight over the gentle rise in the road, and then followed. The safer option was to do a three-point turn and leave Raleigh at the far end, but he wanted to see where she was going. This left him with no choice but to drive straight past her.

On the corner of the junction was a letter box. She was posting her letters as he approached, and turned as he pulled up at the give way sign. He did not, could not look. Two maddeningly-spaced cars dawdled by over the sleeping policemen. His heart was thumping with the sort of thrilling fear that had accompanied dubious adventures as a boy. Without thought to his route he turned left as soon as he could. When he glanced in the rear-view mirror she was no longer there.

Flustered, his sense of direction gone, he took one road after another, the distinguished names flashing past in mockery of his shabby confusion — Rhodes, Livingstone, and then the shift back to Chaucer, Shelley, Tennyson, Burns . . . The series of roundabouts that formed the preamble to the London Road were so welcome that he inadvertently carved up a man in a VW, who quite justifiably treated him to an upraised finger and a volley of inaudible insults.

He was shaking by the time he reached the main road. He

turned north and pulled into the forecourt of a garage to take control of himself. Catching sight of his reflection in the mirror he scarcely recognised himself. There was his face, but it seemed to be inhabited by someone else – the eyes stared back at him excitably, there were new lines around the nose and mouth, scored by emotions he didn't care to identify. He wondered if he were going mad – but it was axiomatic that if he was, he would be the last to know it, if indeed he ever knew at all. He could have wept, but there was no one to weep to. Looking in the direction of the shop he saw the youth on the till staring curiously at him, and pulled away into the stream of traffic.

He was heading out of town, away from home, but decided – insofar as he was capable of a decision – to make a virtue of necessity and go round the ring road rather than take the short route back through the centre of town at a time when people would be starting to leave work. It was also the fact that he wanted to prolong the car journey. While he was driving he could not be required to do anything else – and so could do nothing else wrong.

It was at times like these when Annet realised that like it or not she and her mother were more alike than she cared to admit. There was a certain tactic, a way of deflecting concern and pouncing on weaknesses, which she recognised as one she used herself. This did nothing to improve her humour.

When Louise told her it was David on the phone, she simply waved her away.

'Not now.'

'Are you sure, he only—'

'Not now, Lou!'

The moment Louise had left the room, Marina asked plaintively: 'Why won't you speak to the poor man? What's the matter?'

Marina was also a past master at moving the goalposts. Annet ignored the second question. 'I'm talking to you at the moment.'

'Talking at me, darling. It's awfully tiring. And your husband is far more important, always, than your decrepit old mother.'

This was an observation of such breathtaking insincerity there was no point in arguing with it. 'I am trying to help.'

'I know but you're wearing me out. David was perfectly sweet when he came to the hospital yesterday ....'

Annet felt a headache start up with hammer-blow intensity. 'Bully for him.'

'He was at his most charming and gentle ... I thought it so kind of him to come.'

'He was off work,' pointed out Annet. 'I wasn't. And no one let me know about this accident or I'd have been over to see you.'

'Oh good Lord darling, work is work, I wouldn't expect it ....'

'No, work *isn't* work when my mother's had a fall, that's what I'm trying to explain,' said Annet through gritted teeth. 'I would have come, straight away, but I wasn't told.'

'Sorry,' said Louise, coming back into the room. 'My fault.'

Annet acknowledged the truth of this remark by ignoring it. 'But now that I am here,' she went on, 'I have to tell you I'm not satisfied with the doctor's analysis of why this happened.'

'I am,' said Marina, 'and as the person most closely affected I should have thought that was enough.'

'But you don't know what happened. You don't even remember feeling dizzy. I regard that as cause for concern.'

'It is a worry,' agreed Louise, 'but I do think we have to accept what the doctor says.'

'I'm not worried,' murmured Marina.

'Of course we don't, we could get a second opinion.'

'Please stop talking as though I'm not here.'

'I'm sorry.' Annet pressed her palms together. 'But we want to stop it happening again.'

'It is most frightfully inconvenient,' agreed Marina, with an edge, taking a sip of her gin and tonic. 'For everyone.'

'That's not what I meant and you know it!'

'I think,' said Louise, 'that for now we should look on this as a celebratory drink. Panic over, no harm done, and all that. Mummy – cheers!'

'*Salut!*' Marina bobbed her glass. 'Happy days.'

It was all coming back to Annet, she could feel the old, bad stuff washing through her like a sickness. Nothing could save her. Nothing could stop her reverting to the angry, left-out, misunderstood child of thirty-odd years ago.

'Am I the only person,' she demanded, 'who takes this seriously?'

'Darling . . .' said Marina sympathetically. 'It is beginning to look that way.'

It was as well Louise said something. Somebody had to and Annet was struck dumb.

'My turn to fuss,' she said, 'Mummy you should have a rest. Proper rest, feet up in bed. No arguments, I'm going to take some Evian and a glass up for you, and I'll come and fetch you in a moment.'

They were left together. Annet leaned her head back and closed her eyes to shut her mother out, but it wasn't so easily done.

'You shouldn't get so wound up,' Marina advised. 'It's too tiring.'

'For everyone, I suppose you mean,' suggested Annet sarcastically, which was the cue for Marina to look wounded.

'No, I mean for you.'

'I'm not tired.'

'You look it. It was the first thing I thought when I saw you.'

'Well I'm not.'

'Is Freya keeping you awake at night?'

'No. She still wakes up of course, but she doesn't keep us awake for long.'

'Because God knows, that's exhausting enough without having to go into work all day. I couldn't have done it but then it was a very different world when I was bringing you two up.'

'Mother!'

'Mm . . . ?'

Louise returned. 'Come on Mummy, let's be having you.'

'No peace for the wicked,' sighed Marina, wavering gracefully to her feet with Louise's assistance. 'Still, I know I must be sensible.'

On the way past Annet's chair, she leaned towards her. 'Don't worry about me. You concentrate on that nice husband and that dear little baby of yours.'

Coral's finger was on the bell as the front door flew open and Annet emerged, white faced, and stormed past her as though she wasn't there.

Louise and Marina were negotiating the stairs.

'Please,' said Louise over her shoulder. 'Don't ask.'

Because of the visit to Marina, Annet had driven into London that morning. Now she drove out at the sort of speed that brooked neither manners nor negotiation, let alone argument – she took every risk, played every advantage, pushed her luck at every light, used her indicator as a battering ram and changed lanes like an eel, half-hoping the worst would happen so she could legitimately scream a blue streak. She always drove fast, but generally speaking she considered herself a safe driver. This afternoon she drove like a pig. Like a bloody *man*, she told herself, though that was hardly fair since it was her mother that had put the tin hat on it.

She knew it was childish, but it seemed she could do nothing right. For God's sake, she had been *treated* like a child, information about her own mother had been withheld from her, and then to be accused of neglecting her family *by* her bloody mother – a blare of horns made her skin jump and her eyes prickle with tears, but she muttered, 'Fuck off!' and trod even harder on the accelerator, leaving the bastards for dead.

And David, what was he playing at? Where had he gone? There seemed to be some conspiracy against her, but she couldn't put her finger on its provenance, or who was involved. For so long they had been a good team, tongue and groove, sweet and sour, opposite and complementary, without ever having to make anything of it. They understood one another – or she had always believed they did. Now that belief was shaken. Incredibly, David seemed to doubt her, to be harbouring some sort of grudge whose source she couldn't begin to guess at.

And there was another thing. She had never known love like that which she bore her daughter – its fierce, visceral tyranny had humbled her, and she'd had to fight to reclaim herself ... But that she had succeeded didn't mean, as it seemed others might think, that the love was less. She hurled the car round a corner, too wide, too fast – what did they want, blood? She would not play their game, would not profess her love and whimper and whine because that was what they wanted to hear – she had never done so with David and she would not now with Freya. But if David of all people, the person who saved her from herself, who knew the passion and tenderness of which she was capable so that there was no need to speak it – if David were no longer there, she would be left alone with her failings. A phrase from some long-forgotten church service floated into her mind: '... manifold sins and wickedness'. She wasn't wicked, but her sins were as manifold, and a great deal more manifest, than the next woman's.

She compounded that now by going not home, but to Stoneyhaye. By any reasonable standard it was not just the rash but the wrong thing to do, but then Stoneyhaye was a place where reasonable standards did not apply. That was its charm for her at the moment, the reason she went so often. She could walk in there at any time and no one she saw gave a flying fuck about her manners, or her marriage or her driving or her bloody parenting skills. Why should they? They weren't exactly without morals, but theirs was the cobbled-together, quick-fix morality dictated by sudden silly money. If it worked, they went for it. If it sucked they threw it out. At Stoneyhaye she could enjoy the luxury of seeing herself as a woman of principle, and the even greater luxury of ditching the principles at will.

She justified her visits on the grounds she needed to work out, and today was no different – the endomorphine surge engendered by an hour in the gym would relieve her headache and ease, if not alter, her humour. These days she kept her sports bag in the boot of the Toyota, so the work-out was at least a possibility. But as the barrier rose as if in salute at her approach, she knew that as a serious likelihood it was dead in the water.

'Hi there *Daddy*,' said Lara. 'I'm awake this time!'

To his utter shame David experienced a thud of disappointment and must have failed wholly to disguise it, because Lara continued with tinkling irony: 'But since I've been a little so and so all day, maybe I'll pop off to bye-byes any minute now.'

He peered at Freya who was propped in the corner of the sofa surrounded by the armoury of amusements – scrunched up cellophane, a bendy pink panther, bells on a stick – with which Lara had been doing her considerable best.

'Have you been a madam?' he asked his daughter, joining in the game. 'Have you been giving Nanny Lara a load of gyp?'

'Yup,' said Lara cheerfully. 'Damn right I have.'

'Look,' he said, 'I'm going to get a drink and then I'll take over.' He hesitated, then thought what the hell. 'Would you like one?'

'I'd kill my granny for one, but no thanks. Not the time or place.'

He was obscurely grateful to her for this solidly correct reply.

'By the way,' she added. 'Check your machine, Mrs Keating's sister rang twice.'

He poured himself a beer and went into the study. The

first of Louise's messages was polite and straightforward. She was sorry Annet had had to rush off, Marina was having a good sleep and she and Coral were having a pow-wow; they'd welcome her opinion.

The second was a good deal less composed. 'Annet, I thought you'd be back there by now. I hope you're all right, you did storm out rather. Mummy's still being completely maddening but there's no point in rising to it, that just adds fuel to the flames, something you really ought to know by now. Do ring when you get in, I'm here for the night as you know. Love to David ... Cheerio ....'

The message tailed away rather despondently. So where had Annet got to? He glanced at his watch and realised that it was only six, so there was even a possibility she'd gone back to work.

He returned to Lara. 'My wife's mother had a fall, there's a bit of a panic on.'

'And quite right too,' said Lara. 'It goes with the territory.'

Annet was waved through, parked her Toyota next to Lindl's Mercedes and went into the house. There was a pervasive and delicious smell of frying bacon. The kitchen was full of people and smoke, a litter of beer bottles. Someone raised a hand.

'Lindl?' she asked. 'Or Harry?'

'Watching telly,' said someone.

She went through to the hall, and passed left of the stairs to the back of the house. Through a long, uncurtained window she could see the green plastic sheeting that covered the pool, it reminded her of one of those tents that the police used to screen bodies found out of doors.

In the television room, which was huge and sparsely furnished, Lindl and Jay were curled together on a beanbag sofa, tranquilly watching a barnacled alien direct a stream of sputum at a hapless American cheerleader.

'Come and join us,' said Lindl, waving her cigarette. 'It's absolutely revolting.'

'Apser. Fucking. Lootly,' agreed Jay. Lindl batted his knees with her hand, but neither of them took their eyes from the screen.

'I'll pass thanks,' said Annet. The cheerleader, screaming in agony, dissolved into a puddle of steaming green pus. 'They said Harry was here.'

Lindl shook her head. 'Try the studio . . . .'

He was in there. She saw him through the glass at the top of the door, sitting at the mixing desk listening to something, arms folded, chair swivelling gently, knee just moving in time to the beat. A bottle of Jack Daniels and a paper cup stood on the edge of the desk. The studio beyond the glass was in darkness.

She pushed the door open, and a torrent of noise burst over her, a rock-god at his most stormily passionate backed by whinnying guitars, an orchestra, a bass that made her intestines vibrate.

She flinched, and he must have seen her reflection in the glass, for he dragged a switch and the noise sank to a manageable level.

'Come on in.' Like Lindl, like all of them, he didn't seem in the least surprised to see her.

'Lindl said you were here,' she explained.

'I tell you what,' he said in his elliptical way, 'I wouldn't let him watch that.'

'He seemed to be enjoying it.'

'Exactly.' He picked up the bottle. 'Want one of these?'

She sat down in the chair next to him. 'Better not.'

He didn't argue with her. 'Going to the gym?'

'I might.'

'We all might,' he agreed. 'Unless we change our minds.'

She knew he wouldn't ask what other reason she had for coming, so she told him anyway. Already she was calmer.

'Harry . . . I hate my life.'

'No you don't,' he said placidly.

'I hate myself.'

'That's more like it.' He poured another half cup of bourbon as if ready to listen all night. 'Crap day?'

'You could say that. My mother had a fall, my sister considered that I didn't need to know, my husband agreed and when I did get to visit my mother she accused me of neglecting my baby and my marriage.'

'I'm sorry to hear that,' he said. 'How is your mother?'

She realised that she'd been reminded in the most laconic way of what the priorities were. In the shifting sands of Harry's life there were odd rootless certainties, the detritus of a solid upbringing.

'Unscathed apparently,' she told him. 'But the doctors don't seem to be able to shed any light on why she fell, so in theory it could happen again at any time.'

He gave a one-shouldered shrug. 'Old people fall over, yeah?'

'They do, but she's – has been – good for her age. Not in the least doddery. I sometimes wish she had been, she sends me ape.'

'No offence to your mother, but I saw her at your party – very pretty lady – and she enjoys a drink.'

'She does, but she's a social not a secret drinker.'

'How would you know?'

'Because my father was a serious boozer.'

'OK.'

They sat in silence for a moment. In the background the Pavarotti of rock growled into a ballad.

'You've probably gathered,' said Annet, 'it's the bad feelings with the others I can't stand.'

'Especially your David.'

The way he said this, as if reminding her of something, brought her close to tears. 'Yes.'

'Everyone has rows.' He jerked a thumb in the direction of the door. 'You should hear these two.'

'Don't make comparisons, Harry. There *is* no comparison. The two situations couldn't be more different.'

'I know that. There's no foundations there, unless you count shagging. You guys have got something going for you.'

She remembered David telling her that Tim had said much the same thing. 'So people seem to think.'

'What do *you* think?'

'I thought we had. But since Freya was born the balance has been upset. I mean, how dare he imply that I somehow avoid my responsibilities, that I'm running away? How dare he?'

'Perhaps he's hurting too?'

At this the dam burst, and she cried. It wasn't a pretty sight, she choked, sobbed and snuffled as if her heart would break, and muttered 'Shit!' as she rummaged in her handbag for a tissue. Harry didn't attempt to touch or even comfort her, and had no large clean handkerchief to offer. Instead he topped up his paper cup and listened to the music until she'd finished. Then he poured her half an inch of JD and pushed it over.

'Medicinal.'

'Thanks.' She gulped. 'Sorry.'

'Be my guest.'

She smiled angrily. 'This isn't something I do.'

'You just did.'

'It's such a bloody cliché.'

'Most things are. We all reckon we're different, but in the end we all go around behaving like everyone else.'

She laughed in spite of herself. 'That's true.'

He raised his paper cup in her direction. 'That's love.'

Chapter Fifteen

David's official return to work was qualitatively different to the day he'd simply chosen to return early. This seemed a solemn and irrevocable step, not back to normality but into uncharted territory. It was as if all the delicate membranes of his married life, already stretched to capacity, were being pulled painfully further apart.

On the face of it he and Annet were friends again but he was acutely aware, and knew she was too, that their sensitive understanding had been fractured. They were behaving well, but bleeding.

The night after she'd been to see Marina they'd made love, quietly. It was a cautious rather than a passionate reunion. After she returned Louise's calls she'd told him about the day, and about going to Stoneyhaye again to work off her fury in the gym. The brutal truth was he didn't believe her. His own deceptions had sensitised him to deception in her. She smelt not of the shower, nor even of the office. There was whisky on her breath and a hint of cigarette smoke in her hair. She was lying to him and he didn't know why.

When Freya woke in the small hours Annet stirred, but David said, 'I'll go.' Freya took a couple of ounces of the bottle that had replaced the night-time feeds and fell asleep again without fussing.

He looked out of the window on the way back to bed, but was devastated to see that there was no one there.

*   *   *

At Border and Cheffins it was business as usual. His new fatherhood was no longer news to the rest of them, and he no longer found Doug's management style refreshing. The thought struck David that this might well constitute two-thirds of the foreseeable future. He sat at his desk gripped by a glum panic. Redundancy had changed his life – for the worse, then for the better. He didn't care for change, and rarely initiated it – it had to happen to him. That was with the key exception of marriage to Annet, something he could still scarcely believe he had pulled off. He felt out of control – not in the sense that he might do anything, but that he was able to do nothing. It seemed he could only react.

And Gina was no longer there. Gone. It wasn't simply that she was not outside the window at night. He sensed that she wasn't around. She had withdrawn from him when he most needed her, as everyone seemed to be doing. He wished now that he had not avoided her when he'd seen her at the letter box, but had stopped, got out, thanked her for her letter, perhaps invited her for a drink ... In her case at least he had been looked up to and admired: he had the power to change things for her. Since that day everything seemed to have taken a turn for the worse.

His concentration was shot to pieces, but fortunately there were some positive developments at work which gave the illusion that his time there was being spent productively. Alasdair put together the specification for Orchard End, the board went up, and Harry Bailey called on behalf of his employer.

'He's in the studio till next week, but he's definitely interested. Any chance I could take a preliminary look round? I've got the minimum requirements off pat.'

'I'm certain it would meet those,' said David a touch frostily. Since his visit to Stoneyhaye he was even less comfortable with Bailey, for reasons he didn't care to rehearse.

'Course it would – but he wants to get on the case right away.'

'The specification's only been circulated today, and he's top of the list. But if you want to make an appointment ....'

'Tomorrow?'

David decided he could depute Alasdair to take him round, on the basis that one second in command deserved another. Chris Harper, on the other hand, would receive his personal attention.

The other good news was that Aston Lane Farm had gone for the asking price. Hilary Bryce dropped in to say goodbye and he got Jackie to make some tea for them.

'This is nice,' she said. 'I didn't expect hospitality.'

He didn't tell her that any diversion was welcome. 'You must be looking forward to your new life.'

'Yes—' she hesitated. 'We are indeed. George isn't well, and we need to be away from the pressures. I'm enormously fond of Paul – we both are – but he's a driven man. I suppose one doesn't get to be a millionaire without also being a taskmaster, both to oneself and others ... At any rate, off with the old.' She gave a strained smile.

'I'm sorry George is ill.' David was aware, not for the first time recently, of the barbed complexities of even the most apparently straightforward lives. 'Do pass on my best wishes.'

'I shall certainly do that,' her tone was bright, daring him to be too sympathetic. 'He's developing Alzheimer's, which is awfully sad, but he's aware of it, and we can laugh about it, so we're prepared. If you're ever in Yorkshire you must come and see us before too long – before we're both going about with our clothes back to front!'

Her gallant attempt at humour moved him more than he could say, so he let it pass. 'We shall certainly do that. But bear in mind we have Freya.'

'What could be nicer?' She rummaged in her bag for a second and produced a bunch of postcards held by an elastic band. 'There you are, our change of address. Keep in touch.'

At the door she said: 'It's not often one makes new friends through a chance meeting, but so nice when it happens.'

'I agree.'

He saw her downstairs. When he returned he caught Jackie's eye and unusually she offered a comment:

'What a nice lady.'

Because of her dependable discretion he was able to say, 'And a brave one,' confident that she wouldn't press him: nor did she.

David was shocked, though. He didn't know George Bryce's exact age, but even allowing for him looking a little older than he was, he couldn't have been more than sixty. At their first meeting, he had inevitably suffered somewhat by comparison with the bullish, virile energy of Paul Hubbard; but at their party he had been voluble and amusing. David remembered that it was George who had pointed out Robert Townsend's connection with the village. He could only suppose that such a condition did not proceed at a steady pace, but in fits and starts, like one of the terrible wasting diseases one read about. He tried to imagine the sort of difficulties Hilary had had to contend with, and those that faced her in the months and years ahead. And thinking back to his first impression of her he was sure she was making a bigger sacrifice than her husband could ever know in order to tend him, and grow a new garden, in Yorkshire.

At the weekend he and Annet were measured and polite with one another. It was a pact, but not their usual secret and intimate collusion: this was a truce based on damage avoidance, in which both of them knew there were unused weapons lying in the corner.

As always, they tried to do the weekend things they used to do, but more slowly and with greater difficulty because of Freya. They went to a farm auction in the morning and Annet bought a bike with a child seat on the back, but with Freya in the car the seat couldn't be lowered to accommodate it and they had to leave it for collection another day. Lunch at an old and well-appointed pub on the way home had to be curtailed because Freya's post-prandial battle with indigestion went beyond what could reasonably be tolerated by even a self-proclaimed 'child-friendly' management.

In the afternoon Annet and Freya slept on the double bed and David did some clearance at the far end of the garden, tearing at weeds, ripping out great spiralling ropes of ivy and hacking off suckers with a billhook. As a horticultural exercise it was a triumph: the effect was so startling, revealing all manner of stunted, light-deprived plants from the fleshy spears of autumn-flowering bulbs to the faded brown tangles of honeysuckle, that he wondered why he hadn't embarked on the project before. As sublimation, it was only partly successful.

On Saturday night they were invited to supper ('definitely not a dinner party', Della told them) at the rectory. Neither of them wanted to go, but in the end they did, because both recognised that it was preferable to sustaining an evening on their own without the presence of Freya as a lightning conductor.

So they could both have a drink they walked the short distance to the rectory, carrying Freya between them in the Moses basket. She wasn't asleep, and seemed to be staring up at the stars as she bounced along.

'Mind if we're not too late leaving?' said Annet.

'Absolutely not.'

'Who's going to make the first move?'

'You. Just tip me the wink.'

This leaving plan was something they'd always gone in for – who was going to make the decision and when, according to mood. Going through the motions of making the plan this evening provided the small but hollow comfort of familiarity, a reminder of a closeness they'd lost.

While they were there it seemed for a while to return. In the safety of congenial company and warmed by the Martins' easy hospitality they regrouped, conforming to their hosts' perception of them. Freya took a while to go to sleep and required another bottle to help her do so – 'I always find that,' commented

Maurice – but once she dropped off and was safely bestowed in Maurice's study with the baby alarm, she remained quiet.

Supper was at the kitchen table. Mediterranean fish stew of awesome authenticity (Della had a tame fish man in the market who got her things) and a strictly English cheese board with stooks of giant celery.

It was preceded by grace. 'For friends and food and decent but affordable wine we thank you, Lord,' intoned Maurice, adding fervently: 'From washing up deliver us.'

'You should start leaving that bit off,' said Della as they sat down, 'we've got a perfectly good dishwasher.'

'But he likes to leave it in,' protested Annet. 'Because it makes him seem like a regular sort of guy, aren't I right Maurice?'

'Damn – rumbled! And by a woman, too.'

There were a good many of these exchanges, because in this context Annet enjoyed the atheist's freedom to say pretty much what she liked as long as it was amusing, and Maurice took pleasure in playing up to her. Seeing his wife in good form was for David like watching her through glass – a strange and interesting phenomenon, no longer connected to himself. The best of her seemed always these days reserved for others.

After the stew, while the two of them were wrangling happily on the upkeep of church buildings, he helped Della clear. They carried the plates and dishes through into what had originally been the scullery, now a utility room. The Martins' Labrador rose from its beanbag to greet them and Della pushed the door to behind them. 'No you don't. Excuse the mess.'

Two cassocks were suspended on wire hangers from a pipe over the sink and there were animal dishes on newspaper on the floor into the largest of which Della scraped some leavings of bread and fish skin.

David stared doubtfully as the dog wolfed this offering down. 'Is that wise?'

'She'll eat anything. There were no bones in that lot. If there were some that by chance I missed we'll know all

about it come dawn patrol tomorrow. Or Maurice will –
he's got communion so it'll be his turn with the bucket
and cloth.' She pressed her hands together with a delighted
smile. 'Oh yes, I knew there was something I wanted to
tell you.'

'Unconnected, I hope?'

'Totally, that's how my mind works these days, or fails
to. Do you remember at your party we talked about Robert
Townsend, the man who died recently?'

'Yes – George Bryce knew him.'

'Everybody knew him. You know she's moving?'

'Actually we're handling the sale.'

'No—' Della was an incurable gossip. 'Curiouser and
curiouser.'

'Why?'

'A whited sepulchre.'

He had to smile at the unashamed relish with which this
judgement was delivered. 'Why?'

'He led a double life. Had a complete secret orchard in
town, for years.'

Instinctively, David believed this, but for form's sake said:
'May one ask what your sources are?'

'The best – queue at the village post office. I think the
Reverend knows something more officially, but of course he
wouldn't dream of mentioning it. I'm only saying this to you
like King Midas telling the ears of corn or whatever – I've got
to tell someone and I know you're the soul of discretion – but
isn't it fascinating?'

'It's rather sad. His poor widow.'

'May I say something? I never liked her. A cold, miniature
sort of person. Iced tea in her veins. Whereas he was lovely. I
just hope his other life made him happy.'

David returned to the table with plenty of food for thought.
Maurice got up to fill glasses. 'So what did you talk about?
There isn't a burning issue that hasn't received the lighter-fuel
treatment in here, I can tell you.'

'We were gossiping,' said Della, transferring the cheese from sideboard to table. 'MYOB.'

'I said people would start to talk,' said Annet out of the side of her mouth to Maurice. 'We mustn't make it so obvious.'

On the way home — it had turned so cold that they'd borrowed Della's quilted jacket to lay over the Moses basket — Annet asked:

'So what were you gossiping about?'

His decision was instantaneous, he was scarcely conscious of making it. 'She was joking about that. We were discussing dogs and their upkeep. She'd just given hers the remains of the fish stew.'

'And the best of British.'

'That's what I said.'

When they got home Annet took Freya upstairs. David found himself pottering a little longer than was strictly necessary. When he heard her go into their room, followed by the sound of the tap running, he waited another five minutes, then filled the kettle, a sound which bought him another two. When he eventually went upstairs her bedside light was off and she lay turned away from his, her eyes closed, hands folded child-like beneath her cheek. Her shoulder rose and fell evenly with her breathing, in a perfect — he hoped not practised — simulation of sleep.

More in hope than expectation he looked out of the window. The night was sharp and clear, the ground bleached with moonlight, the black sky littered with an infinite dazzle of stars. But there was no one out there, either.

On Sunday they were both suffering from a slight hangover, which had a temporary bonding effect. Freya woke at five a.m. in sparkling form.

'It's pathetic,' said Annet. 'Look at us, we're out of practice. We don't get out enough.'

'Pity poor Maurice,' David reminded her. 'He has to spread the good news in this condition.'

'Serve him right . . . .'

During the morning they passed the baton of responsibility back and forth while attempting to read the papers. In addition David took Freya up to the studio for a while and doodled, and Annet, silent and headachey, dried out a chicken and reduced sprouts to a pulp. Afterwards she confessed herself beaten and took Freya upstairs for a nap. David lay on the sofa with his stockinged feet up on the arm and prepared finally to complete the week's instalment of pitiless memoirs penned by the straying politician's wife. But over the ensuing quarter of an hour it was clear Freya was having none of it and he trudged upstairs.

'No go?'

'It doesn't look like it. I can't understand it, she's been awake for hours, *surely* she's knackered.'

'She'll drop off eventually,' he said, picking his daughter up, and addressing her: 'Won't you?'

'Don't bet on it.'

'I'll take her out for a while.'

'Would you, could you? I think I'll die if I don't close my eyes.'

'Go ahead. We'll go for a walk.'

As he went down the stairs he tried not to think of Annet's eyelids drooping as the delicious, warm tide of sleep washed over her, nor of the three thousand deliciously vengeful words left still unread on the drawing-room sofa. Since the birth of his daughter he had rediscovered, under threat of their loss, the keenest pleasure in small things. Bone-tired himself, he vowed that he would never again take for granted an afternoon nap, or nipping out to the pictures, or an undisturbed pint in the pub, or reading the Sundays . . . There had even been times, not so very long ago but scarcely imaginable now, when Sunday afternoons, drowsy with wine and food, had been occasions of sin.

Just the same there were compensations. Following a crescendo of disapproval as he put on her pram suit, Freya went quiet when laid in the buggy, and her quietness was like a blessing bestowed on all three of them.

So he was cheered, on setting out, to think that this simple exercise was enabling Annet to sleep.

It was cold and bright, not a day for dawdling, and he set himself a straightforward out-and-back along the Stoneyhaye road. There was scarcely any traffic, and the village itself was closed. He encountered a couple of serious walkers with dogs, and one group which seemed to consist of hosts and visitors, surrounded by a loose scrum of small children. This reminded him of Tim and Mags and their difficulties. He remembered with affection his bruising honesty and her loyal dissembling, the combined effect of which had been to make him think more, not less, of their marriage. Stupidly he had always assumed that his brother and sister-in-law were pre-programmed for the long haul, that perhaps (it made him blush) they were simply too unimaginative to see the pitfalls. That both these assumptions were false both shamed and moved him. Almost superstitiously he clung to the hope that they would come through their time of trial.

And then there was Gina. The idea was forming in his mind that he had to speak to her, to find out why she'd gone.

Long before he'd turned for home, Freya had fallen asleep and now that he felt warmer he slowed down and walked at a more leisurely pace through the village. He resisted a temptation to revisit Orchard End, and not just because he'd been caught snooping there once already this week. He recognised in himself the base instinct to revisit the scene of the crime – or to be more accurate, the scene of the crime's victim. It was true that he felt little sympathy for Mary Townsend. Not because of Della's brisk condemnation of her, but because in his view of the story she was not much more than a cypher: it was Robert Townsend that interested him. What was clearly viewed by the village as a betrayal of the grossest kind, one that made a sham of the marriage vows, he could not help seeing as a perverse, almost sacrificial fidelity. Fidelity to two women, it was true, but fidelity nonetheless, an honouring of those vows made in the face of God and passionate, private promises.

He did, however, pause at the school gate. Doing so now, with Freya, when the playground was still and empty except for a few yellowing leaves, went some way towards exorcising the ghost of his earlier humiliation. But the thought of how the incident would have been described by the young teacher in the staff room still made him acutely uncomfortable.

After stopping at the school he described a figure of eight and looped back towards the church. There had been a service there that morning, they'd heard the bells – electronic these days – pealing for about fifteen mnutes from nine-thirty. Early for some, but their day had felt half over.

Next to the churchyard from the direction in which he was approaching there was the field where the November the fifth bonfire was traditionally held – last year's site was still visible like a dark corn circle, and the parish council had already made a start on this year's bonfire with some old car tyres and a tepee of dead branches.

Also in the field were the Fox-Herbert horses, grazing peaceably. David wasn't much interested in horses, but these days they represented new possibilities as a diversion for Freya. She was a little young yet, but he could picture himself bringing her down here in the spring, perching her on the top of the gate to see them, perhaps bringing sugar lumps and bits of carrot ... He paused and clicked his tongue experimentally. To his slight consternation both the horses lifted their heads and trotted briskly towards him, snorting, ears pricked, tails waving like flags. As they came to the gate and stretched their huge heads towards him he backed off respectfully. He had forgotten – or more likely never properly appreciated – the sheer size of these animals, the great eyes fringed with luxuriant lashes, the cavernous nostrils, the bewhiskered prehensile lips that groped and trembled in expectation of a titbit. One of them began to knock impatiently with his foreleg against the bottom rung of the gate, a rung which David could see was already cracked presumably from this very treatment. A little anxiously, in case he'd accidentally perpetrated some frightful breach of rural etiquette, he glanced about. The banging continued, and the other horse nodded its head so violently that a shower of greenish spittle landed on David's sweater.

He withdrew, reminding himself that when he did bring Freya he should be extremely circumspect: gate-perching such as he'd envisaged would be out of the question. When he looked over his shoulder the horses were standing to attention, watching him go with ears still at the high port, incensed no doubt at having been led up the garden path.

Prompted by earlier reflections, David went round the church, towing the buggy behind him over the bumpy ground. Knowing what he now did, he wanted to see if Robert Townsend's grave was still so conspicuously neglected. But someone was there before him – a woman kneeling alongside the plot, flanked by a handbag on one side and a green refuse sack on the other. He paused, unsure whether a widow nursing not just a grief but a grievance would wish to be disturbed.

Just then she sat back on her heels, and at the same moment that he realised it wasn't Mary Townsend, she looked over her shoulder and saw him.

'Oh – hello,' said Jean Samms. 'You crept up on me.'

'I'm sorry.' He was disconcerted. 'Am I intruding?'

'It's common land as far as I know.' She got to her feet in well-managed stages and took off her gardening gloves. 'I was doing a spot of tidying.'

'It needed doing,' he agreed. 'It was looking pretty sad last time I was here.' He left the buggy where it was and went to inspect her handiwork. The plot was pin neat. 'Forgive my asking, but – are you a relation?'

'No. Just a friend.'

He watched as she tied the top of the refuse sack, which was full of weeds and dead stuff.

'His widow probably hasn't had much time,' he said, feeling it incumbent upon him as a resident to offer some excuse for the neglect. 'She's about to move house, and what with that . . . .'

'Yes of course.' She gazed thoughtfully at the plot. 'I might put a few bulbs in, do you think that would be taken amiss?'

He wondered why on earth she would ask him, a stranger, such a thing. He certainly had no idea what the protocol was in such matters, and confessed as much.

'Why not drop in on them,' he suggested. 'And ask.'

'No, I don't think so.'

'Mrs Townsend's daughter's staying with her at the moment and I'm sure she'd be perfectly straight with you.'

'I'm sure she would.' She smoothed her hair back off her face with her strong, plain hands. And with this simple, sensuous gesture, gave herself away.

'I'm sorry,' said David. 'I think—'

'Don't let's,' she said. She stooped to pick up handbag and gardening gloves, and he quickly took charge of the bag of debris.

'Allow me.'

'There's a bin next to the north porch.'

He collected the buggy and they dumped the rubbish and returned to the path that led to the lychgate.

She stole a look at Freya. 'Your daughter looks none the worse for her adventure the other week.'

'Quite the opposite. She doesn't give a damn for the grown-ups' day of rest. The price of this peace was a five-mile hike.'

She smiled. 'Still, you're lucky.'

'I know. I need reminding of that sometimes.'

'I consider I've been lucky as well,' she said. She said it firmly, meeting his eye squarely, quelling question or comment.

'Good.' With so much precluded, it was all he could think of to say. 'I'm pleased.'

A battered VW beetle chugged round the corner and pulled over a few yards short of them.

'My carriage.' She glanced at her watch. 'Well I never, perfect timing. Goodbye, it was nice to bump into you again. And the little one.'

'Goodbye.'

David found he could hardly bear to watch her go, with her story untold, their conversation stillborn. She got into the passenger seat of the beetle and sat with studied calm as it started and stalled a couple of times before moving off.

She didn't look David's way as they passed, but the driver did, bestowing on him the swift, uninterested appraisal of the young.

The face that David saw, studded with metal and shadowed with stubble, was that of a youthful Robert Townsend.

Chapter Sixteen

There had been a time, David clearly remembered it, when he'd feared the arrival of a nanny because of the possibility of her coming between them. Now that Lara was here, and quite unwittingly did, he was glad of it. Her large, benign presence interposed itself like a cushion, absorbing the tensions, deflecting the anxieties, stifling those antagonisms which at the moment stalked their every exchange, waiting to pounce.

The game plan, now that they were both back at work, was that Lara would arrive at eight-thirty, and that they would take it in turns to synchronise their departures with her arrival. In reality this meant that it was usually he who waited, because he had the shorter journey. The early mornings found him bleak and jaded. He tended to go to sleep wondering what had become of Gina, and wake up wondering much the same about his life. But the few minutes in which he handed over to Lara cheered him up, with the sense of the responsibility easing from his shoulders, and her unfailing breezy amiability.

Perhaps this was why, halfway through his second week back, he couldn't help noticing an infinitesimal cloud, not even as big as a man's hand, on her generally sunny demeanour.

'Everything all right?' he asked, as she cupped Freya's head beneath her chin, eyes closed, in the unashamedly tactile rapture that was one of her most endearing qualities. 'You seem a bit subdued if you don't mind my saying so.'

'Say what you like boss, you pay me,' was her predictable response, followed by: 'You could be right.'

He peered at her anxiously. 'You're not feeling ill, are you? Because if so I really think—'

'If I was ill I wouldn't come near your daughter.'

He stood corrected. 'Of course not.'

'No,' she said, 'my nan's sick. Back in New Zealand?'

'I'm so sorry.'

'She's just about my favourite person in the world. Always been on my side no matter what, and we've always had great laughs together. Haven't we?' She gave Freya a kiss to conceal another emotion.

'Is it serious?' he asked.

'I don't know ... I suppose when you get to seventy-something it's always serious. She got the 'flu and it turned into bronchitis. She's had to go into hospital so maybe she'll do as she's told in there.'

'Not a good patient?'

She shook her head and laughed. 'Not used to being a patient, at *all*. But the problem's pneumonia, isn't it?'

'With the elderly it can be.'

'Yeah ... So I guess we have to hope she doesn't get that.'

'I do hope so.'

On the way out, he added. 'Oh, Lara – if you want to make a call from here, to find out how your grandmother is, please feel free.'

'That's kind of you, but I wouldn't dream of it. I did take the liberty of giving Dad this number though.'

'Good.'

On the drive in to King's Newton David was moved by Lara's concern for her nan. He'd heard and read a good deal about the special relationship between grandparents and grandchildren, but had never experienced it for himself. His own grandparents had been very old and very distant, he'd found them creepy.

In Marina's case the brutal truth was that her children had left procreation so late that his own daughter, and the child which Louise and Coral hoped to have, might well not know or remember their maternal grandparent.

It turned out not to be a day when he could freewheel. As soon as he arrived Jackie reminded him he was due to take Chris Harper to Orchard End that afternoon. There was a job to do, because the visit of Harry Bailey with Alasdair had not been an unqualified success.

'It's a little tricky to say the least,' Alasdair had complained, 'showing someone round who isn't the putative purchaser, and when you don't know their agenda.'

David had divided sympathies. He was sure that Bailey considered Alasdair a chinless hooray, and that Alasdair had resented doing his stuff with a mere emissary.

'Did you meet Mrs Townsend?' he asked.

'No, it was her daughter who took us round. I'm afraid I thought that given the circumstances Mr Bailey was . . . let's just say there was no need to be so picky. My understanding was that he was checking the basics.'

That had been David's understanding too. But at least Harper was coming to see for himself. On his own account he rather hoped the daughter would remain in charge – he didn't relish confronting Mary Townsend after his encounter with her rival, especially as he couldn't help liking Joan Samms.

On the basis that forewarned was forearmed, he rang at midday. Susan Bentham answered the phone.

'Mr Keating, we're expecting you this afternoon.'

'Is that still convenient?'

'Perfectly. I suggest you and I show Mr Harper round. Mother will stay out of the way, she finds the whole thing a bit painful . . .' He murmured something soothing. 'But I'm primed to take questions, as it were.'

In terms of time, Chris Harper was the easiest client he'd dealt with. David remembered that the Stoneyhaye sale had been swiftly decided upon – it was the subsequent brokering and arbitration which had been lengthy. Susan Bentham either did not recognise him or did not concede that she had, and conducted the tour of the house at a brisk pace. Harper took in each room quickly and moved on with a perfunctory 'Thanks, right' or even just 'Yup'.

When they'd finished, she offered refreshments, which Harper politely declined.

'It's a nice place,' was all he would say.

Afterwards David suggested they went for coffee at the Anvil.

'So do you think it would suit your parents?' asked David. 'It is an almost perfect example of a house of that size and period, I've been reading about it in a local history book. The well's blocked now of course because the Townsends had young grandchildren, but I understand it's in perfect working order should anyone be moved to draw their own water. In fact the whole place is in excellent order, I don't think you or your parents would be inheriting any hidden costs.'

Harper listened attentively to all this, then said: 'No. I'm sure that's right. It's certainly what I was looking for.'

David heard the past tense as if he'd shouted it. 'Was?'

'Don't get me wrong, I wanted to see it. At my age, in my line of business property's always interesting.'

'But in general, you seem to be saying, rather than in particular . . . ?'

'I think so.'

David experienced a thud of disappointment. His time and energy and that of other people had been wasted on what now appeared to be a rich man's whim.

He said politely, understandingly: 'So Orchard End isn't the one.'

'It might be,' conceded Harper, 'but I'm thinking of moving.'

'I beg your pardon?' He was thunderstruck.

'I've drunk your wine,' said Harper in an almost old-fashioned way, 'I'll be straight with you. I'm selling up.'

'I see.' David gathered himself. 'But you've made such a colossal investment at Stoneyhaye.'

'In more ways than one.'

'Has it – not worked out as you hoped?'

'No.'

This could not have been plainer or less ambiguous, but David still shook his head in disbelief. 'What can I say ...? You and that house seemed made for each other. Would you care for a drink?'

'No thanks. Don't let me stop you.'

'No ... What about your parents?'

'Don't worry,' Harper glanced briefly out of the window, 'I'll take care of them.'

'Of course.' David felt he'd been reproved.

'But I don't want all that. Let alone,' he jerked his head, 'all this as well. I got back from the Far East and looked at it all and thought, what am I doing? Who needs so much responsibility? I like money for the freedom it buys, not the baggage.'

'I understand,' agreed David. Now he'd got over his surprise he was full of curiosity. 'So what might you do ...?'

'Downsize. Do what normal people do. Get a place where Mum and Dad can stay near their friends, pick up a nice flat in Docklands or somewhere where I can keep an eye on them. I don't have any friends I want to be near.' This last was accompanied by a thin smile.

'It sounds eminently sensible I must say,' admitted David.

'*And* get rid of most of the poxy hangers-on. I don't want to be a milch-cow for every Jasper and Emma on the make. I'm going to do them all a favour and relaunch them on the job market.'

'What does Lindl think?'

The question had slipped out almost without thought, and he wondered whether he'd overstepped the mark, but Harper now seemed in a mood to debrief.

'It won't affect her. She's moving on.'

There seemed no end to the shocks. 'Where?'

There was another flicker of a smile, somewhat sour. 'More of a who.'

'I'm sorry. I don't know what to say.'

He shrugged. 'Nothing to say. Shit happens.'

'And Jay . . . ?'

'She brought him, she's taking him.' There was a short, embattled silence. 'Don't get me wrong, I'll miss them.'

David had a sudden and unwelcome premonition of what was to follow, and took no pleasure in finding he was right.

'Still,' said Harper. 'Plenty more fish in the sea.'

'I did know actually,' said Annet when she got in that evening. 'Harry Bailey told me.'

David felt a humiliating stab of jealousy. 'I see.'

'I went to use the gym. He said it wouldn't be for much longer.'

'I suppose I find it shocking,' he said starchily, 'that a beautiful old house like that which has been cherished by generations of one family should be picked up and discarded so casually.'

'What makes you think there's anything casual about it?' If he was starchy, she was spikey, it seemed to be the way of things these days.

'It's casual by any normal standards, surely. He buys a place like that, for cash, embarks on all kinds of changes and improvements, changes his mind inside a year and bungs it back on the market.'

'Anyone's entitled to change their mind. What niggles you is that he has the money to act on it.'

He was hurt, because she was at least in part right. 'Why would that bother me?'

'I've no idea, especially as B and C are likely to clean up as a result.'

He told himself this was just her usual abrasive style, but he couldn't help taking it to heart. These days everything that passed between them was stained by what he could only describe as a lack of respect — Tim's phrase, come back to haunt him.

Over supper he introduced what he hoped would be the less contentious issue of Lara's grandmother.

'*Himmel*,' said Annet, 'no disrespect but I do hope she isn't going to feel compelled to fly to her bedside.'

'They were obviously very close.'

'Yes but is anyone that close to a grandparent? I'm not sure it constitutes a valid reason for compassionate leave.'

'Probably not, but there's no suggestion she wants to do anything of the sort at the moment, so don't let's wind ourselves up.'

'I wasn't. But one has to be practical.'

David wondered if, like Tim, he had simply stopped loving his wife, and she him. But if that were so, surely he wouldn't feel this pain? The effect was more as if they were trying to communicate with each other through soundproof glass, mouthing and gesticulating to no effect.

Annet seemed still to be humming with some nebulous antagonism when she got into bed. She lay on her back with one arm behind her head, staring at the ceiling, as he got undressed. When he got in next to her she said quite loudly as though they were in a boardroom:

'You know Lindl Clerc's been playing away from home?'

He was tempted to say 'Why would I? you're the expert', but resisted it.

'I wouldn't be entirely surprised.'

'Why?'

The now-familiar bad feeling churned in his stomach. 'You've only got to look at the setup over there to realise it's not exactly a testament to family values.'

'Maybe so,' she said, switching her lamp off. 'But at least they did their best.'

The following early evening after work David took the folder of his drawings, those he considered good enough and called in at the central library. For fun, he'd included the sketches of Freya in her basket, and out of curiosity (and a certain bloody-mindedness) the despised portrait of Annet. At the desk he asked for Jean Samms, but was told she was attending an information technology day at county headquarters.

'Can I help?' asked the young man. 'I'm assistant librarian.'

'Miss Samms told me about the art exhibition you're putting on here.'

'That's right. Faces and Places.'

'I've got some drawings I'd like to put in for consideration. Some of them are mounted, but I'm afraid there's only one that's framed at the moment.'

'Don't worry about that. First things first.'

'I'm pretty sure they won't stand a chance.'

'I'm sure they will.' The young man smiled encouragingly. 'Are you by any chance a member of the watercolour society?'

'No. Is that a problem?'

'Quite the reverse.' The young man dropped his voice and glanced from side to side theatrically. 'We're swamped with tasteful views of the Nevitt as seen from the churchyard and the church spire as seen from the water meadows.'

'Actually,' said David, 'I'm more of a faces man.'

'Ah!' The young man took his folder as though it contained precious stones. 'I don't want to build up your hopes or pre-empt the decision of our distinguished hanging committee, but I think you have grounds for cautious optimism.'

This small lift to his spirits was all David needed. On leaving the library he drove to Raleigh Road.

At this time of day it presented a rather different aspect from that of his previous visit. There were cars parked in most of the driveways, and people in the street, tired-faced walkers returning from work and children kicking footballs and careering dangerously about on bikes in the fading light.

He did not, on this occasion, hesitate. He parked in the first space he could find and walked steadily, head down, as far as the Kings' house, and up to their front door. Through the ruched nets in the front-room window he could make out the spasmodic coloured flicker of the television. He pressed the bell.

The door was opened by a stout woman in her forties, with the kind of looks which must once have been sweetly pretty but which had not been treated kindly by the advancing years. A winsome urchin cut did no favours for her grim, grooved face, and the girlish leggings and outsize angora jumper emphasised a weight problem.

'Yes?'

'I'm so sorry to bother you but I was looking for Miss Gina King?'

'Yes?'

'Does she live here?'

'That's right.'

David smiled in what he hoped was a friendly, confident manner, though his heart was pounding.

'It's rather a long story,' he said. 'Gina worked for me for a while at Border and Cheffins, the property agents. We've kept in touch and I was in the area – I wondered how she was.'

'I see. What did you say your name was?'

'I didn't – David Keating.'

'I'm her mother.'

'How do you do?' He held out his hand but she ignored it. 'Just wait there would you.'

The door was pushed to and he was left standing on the doorstep. The woman's expression hadn't changed one iota but he sensed that his name had rung some sort of bell. This, and the prospect of Gina's reaction, kept him from beating an ignominious retreat.

Fully two minutes later, the door was opened again. This time it was Gina who stood there, wearing pale blue ski pants and a white high-necked jumper – pretty, soft. Fluffy slippers, he noticed, with faces like little guinea pigs.

'Hello Gina.'

'Hello.' She sounded very quiet and shy.

'I hope you don't mind my calling on you.'

'Why did you come?'

He shrugged, with a smile, wanting to appear casual. 'I wanted to see how you were doing. I was sorry not to be able to give you a reference.'

'How did you know where I lived?'

'It was on your letter,' he reminded her gently. 'May I come in for a moment?'

She seemed to glance over her shoulder before saying: 'OK.'

He entered and she closed the door behind him. There was a faint, not unpleasant smell of convenience cooking – warm and oily, a hint of ketchup – but he still caught her scent as he passed her. A youth of about sixteen in stockinged feet and the black blazer of the local comprehensive appeared from the back of the house carrying a plate, and disappeared up the stairs without a look or a word.

'My brother,' explained Gina.

'I see.' The notion of siblings hadn't entered his head. For so long Gina had been a lone figure, watching and waiting.

'We can go in here,' she said, pushing open a door on the right of the narrow hall. As he went in he could see through the half-open door of the room opposite, the plump woman standing in front of the television, talking on the phone.

They were in the dining room. It felt chilly, and this impression was reinforced by there only being a single overhead light, which Gina switched on – a small chandelier twinkling like a cut-price constellation in a waste of anaglypta. The curtains were open but she made no move to draw them.

'Do sit down,' she said.

'Thanks.' He pulled out one of the hard chairs and sat down. In the centre of the table on a lace mat stood a basket of pink and brown dried flowers, further desiccated to the point where they'd shed a drift of brownish granules on to the surrounding surface.

On a trolley beneath the serving hatch was a pile of raffia mats. It had the air of a room not much used.

'Would you like a drink?' she asked.

The question made him realise how much he longed for one. 'Yes please, that would be nice.'

'Tea, coffee? Or we've got Coke.'

He tried not to show his disappointment. 'Are you going to have anything?'

'I might have a cup of coffee.'

'In that case, if you're making one anyway . . . .'

'I won't be a minute.'

She left, closing the door after her, and a moment later he heard her the other side of the serving hatch. Then she came back into the hall and he thought he heard her voice and that of the mother. On the wall opposite him was a painting, in acrylics, of the King's Newton church as seen from the water meadows.

Another couple of minutes and she was back, bearing a tray with two cups and saucers containing dispiriting greyish instant coffee, and a matching jug with milk already added.

'Do you take sugar?'

'No thanks.'

'There you go.'

She put the tray on the table and sat down in a chair at the far end, with her back to the hatch. It was an impossibly awkward situation for both of them, but he knew that it was up to him to breach the awkwardness. He felt his responsibility not as a burden, but as a privilege.

He said: 'I do hope your mother doesn't mind my turning up like this.'

She glanced towards the closed door as if checking. 'Oh no.'

'She must be a bit baffled – I'll have another word with her before I go.'

'It's all right.' She blushed slightly. He had forgotten how pale her skin was, her hair fine and light as a child's . . . Her air of demureness.

'Gina—'

'Yes?'

'I thought we needed — perhaps — to talk?'

'I don't know.'

'I meant it when I said I was sorry I couldn't help when you wrote to me.'

'It doesn't matter.'

'Obviously you've managed very well in spite of it,' he conceded. 'But I have thought about you a great deal.'

She didn't speak, but looked down at her cup, tucking the pale fronds of hair back behind her ears. Her cheeks coloured again. David was moved. He was so close now to the truth.

He said: 'I have seen you, as well.'

She was silent.

'It was you, wasn't it? Outside my house? Following me in the car? Gina . . . ?'

She murmured something that he couldn't hear.

'What did you want?' he asked. 'Was there something you wanted to say?'

Now she shook her head. Whispered: 'No.'

He was beginning to feel more confident. 'Then perhaps I could say something.'

Another whisper, which he didn't catch, accompanied by a quick, nervous glance towards the door.

'Don't worry Gina,' he said, 'I'm not about to say or do anything you wouldn't want your mother to hear. Quite the opposite.' He waited but she'd dropped her head again. Something about this shy, penitential attitude convinced him that he'd done the right thing in coming here. She was very young, and confused. If she felt guilty about anything, she needed to be relieved of that guilt. If she needed his help and attention, she should have it.

He leaned forward. 'I want you to know — it's important to me — that I wasn't happy about letting you go after your trial period at the office. I think we worked together well. We understood each other. We could have made a good team.

The whole episode was a very distressing one as far as I was concerned.'

She looked up now and he was surprised by how levelly her eyes met his. 'Was it? Was it really?'

'Yes.'

'But you had your new baby and everything.'

'Yes. That's true. Maybe that's why I didn't fight my corner strongly enough on your behalf. At any rate since then you've been in my thoughts a great deal – almost all the time – and I want you to know that if there's anything—'

At this point the front door slammed shut, and the dining room door flew open almost simultaneously, and with such force that the inside door crashed against the wall and bounced back. The man who entered stopped it with the palm of his hand. The effect was of a series of reports, like gunfire. David flinched with shock. Gina let out a little whimper and seemed to shrink in her chair.

'You,' said the man, pointing at David. 'On your feet.'

'I beg your pardon?'

'I said—' the man took one stride, grabbed David by the arm and hauled him out of his seat – 'up.'

'Gina . . . ?'

At the same moment that he spoke to her, a voice from the hall said. 'Gina, you all right in there?' and Mrs King came into the room. She went and stood next to her daughter, giving David a look of utter disgust. The man released his arm with a shaking motion, as if ridding himself of something sticky, vile. Worse than the violence was the loathing and contempt in the man's eyes.

'I'm sorry,' said David. 'Who are you?'

'This is my husband,' said Mrs King.

'Gina's father,' said the man in a mocking, bullying voice. 'You better believe it.' He turned to Gina. 'Is this him then?'

'It is,' said Mrs King. 'I told you it was, on the phone—'

'Is this *him*?' asked Mr King again, still looking at his daughter, but this time stabbing a finger in David's direction.

Gina nodded. 'Yes . . . .'

David was panic-stricken. It was like the worst sort of nightmare, a situation both terrifyingly dangerous and utterly incomprehensible, and over which he had no control whatever. 'Please,' he said. 'What am I supposed to have done?'

The man turned back to him, slowly, with an expression of sneering disbelief. 'Don't push your luck. The only reason I haven't called the police is because I don't want my daughter put through any more.'

'Any more – I'm sorry? Gina?'

She burst into noisy sobs. Her mother mouthed the word 'Bastard!' as if it were too foul for her daughter to hear.

The sobs, an expression of real feeling, made him foolhardy. 'Gina, tell me what it is I'm supposed to have done wrong—'

His arm was grabbed again, this time so hard that the fingers bit into him like steel teeth.

'Shut – the fuck – up!'

A small hopeful possibility occurred to him. 'Why *don't* you call the police? Then at least I can make a statement, we can all be clear, keep our tempers – there's been a misunderstanding—'

'No there hasn't!' Gina stood up, her chair crashing to the floor behind her. Her face was reddened and swollen with emotion but not, he noticed, wet with tears. 'You dirty liar! You know you've been spying on me! You got me dismissed and then you've been watching me, you found out where I lived—'

'Gina, you told me, it was on your letter—'

'No I did not! You found out and you came over here. I've seen you before, but the other afternoon you knew I'd seen you. You did! That's why you came back! And you've been coming on to me – he has!' She enjoined her parents. Mr King jerked his arm painfully. 'He's been sitting here saying how he's always fancied me, it's pathetic, I hate him, he got me the sack because I was on to him!'

'You frigging low-life,' said Mr King conversationally. 'I ought to give you a good slapping only I don't want to dirty my hands.'

'I hate him!' screamed Gina. 'I hate him, he's disgusting! I hate him.'

'Hear that?' asked King into David's ear as the tempest raged. 'If not, listen up: she hates you. You disgust her. She's not the only one.'

David may have said something, he had no idea what. All reality seemed suspended. The mother, too, was now screaming in a kind of parody of hysteria that would have been laughable if it hadn't been so terrifying. What was she doing? How could people behave like this?

'Come on – out!'

He was manhandled into the hall, and slammed up against a wall. The breath flew out of him and a muffled explosion of pain went off in the back of his head. So this, he thought wildly, is what it's like. You've seen it in films, but this is what it feels like – never forget. But that was nothing to what followed. King was pressed up against him, like the assailant in some bizarre sexual encounter, but now he had him by the balls, clutching and squeezing. David howled, then retched, and King released him abruptly, again with that shaking, throwing away action, which resulted in another excruciating stab of pain. Bile flooded his mouth. King opened the front door, returned, dragged him forward and pushed him out.

'Get out of my house you stinking creep, before you make a mess on my carpet. And if you get inside mailing distance of my daughter again your life won't be worth living!'

It would have been a small mercy, David remembered thinking, if King had followed this speech by slamming the door as he had on the way in. Instead, he held it wide, and stood watching him as he struggled to stand in the bright wedge of light, weaving and tottering with pain. Though he was unaware of any other spectators, he knew there must have been, and that for the first and only time in his adult life he was being deliberately exposed to public humiliation.

He made it to the car and leaned for a moment on the roof, his lungs heaving. His head felt as though someone were beating on the back of it with a hammer, and the contents of his stomach pressed somewhere just behind his throat, ready at any moment to burst out and add to his shame. When he'd summoned the strength to unlock the door and get in he saw that King was still staring. Only when he'd started the engine and begun to turn the car did the door of the house close.

It was a long and painful pilgrimage getting home. He did it in fits and starts, the frequent breaks necessitated by the need get out and gulp fresh air and fight back nausea. To weep would have been a comfort, but no tears came.

At one point on the ringroad he passed a police car parked in a layby, two bored officers in the front with nothing better to do than pick on motorists. The awful idea occurred to him that his slowness might cause suspicion and he be breathalysed, and he crept cautiously up to forty. For a moment at the Kings' house he'd have welcomed the police with open arms, as symbols not just of authority but of order: now the thought of being questioned about his condition filled him with dread. But they took no notice and when he was well past he slowed down again, to the annoyance of the haulage truck behind him.

The longed-for haven of home, when he reached it, presented a new set of problems. It was only six-thirty, but Annet must have got home early, the Toyota was parked in the drive. He switched off the engine and peered at himself in the driver's mirror. His head and his crotch throbbed. His face, though sickly, was unmarked, but his suit was muddy, and there was – he could scarcely believe it – a tear in the leg of his trousers where he'd crashed down on the Kings' front path. Between the jagged edges of the tear was a gleam of blood.

There was no escaping the need, yet again, to lie.

'No panic,' he said, filling the seconds of Annet's horrified reaction. 'A couple of lads duffed me up in the car park.'

*　　*　　*

It was impossible to tell whether she believed him or not. Untypically, she didn't ask a single question, so he provided the information anyway, putting the story on record. Keep it simple, he thought.

'They were about to break into the car. When I shouted at them they rushed over and did this on their way past. Just a couple of kids really, but quite big. I was scared half to death ... The whole thing only took seconds, there's no way I could identify them.'

He said all this as Annet helped him undress. Silently, without looking at his face, she unbuttoned his shirt, moved round him to ease off his sleeves, knelt to unlace his shoes and slip his trousers over his feet ... Freya, in her nightsuit, lay propped on the pillows on their bed, watching.

'They pushed me,' he continued doggedly. 'I came a hell of a cropper on the back of my head, and one of them kicked me in the crotch for good measure.'

She made only two comments. The first was to say. 'You should have gone to A and E you know.'

To which he answered, truthfully: 'I only wanted to get home.'

The second came as she noticed the bruises on his arm.

'They didn't like you, did they?'

'No,' he said, 'they did not.'

She put witch hazel on the bruises and bathed his cut knee with disinfectant, but held up her hands, literally, at the angrily swollen condition of his balls. She found some proprietary painkillers in the medicine cabinet and he swallowed a couple with a cup of sugary tea while she put Freya to bed. By the time she came back he was barely conscious, exhausted by fear, pain and tension, and muzzy from the pills.

She sat down on the edge of the bed next to him.

'I think you should report this.'

'Pointless ....'

'If everyone took that view these little thugs would never get their comeuppance.'

'I told you I wouldn't recognise them anyway ....'

'OK.' She gave his hand a brief squeeze and stood up. 'I'll let you kip. Light on or off?'

'Off ... thanks ....'

She switched it off and went to the door.

'At least,' she said, 'you're back.'

Chapter Seventeen

The next morning, after a wretched and largely sleepless night David felt as if he'd been put through a mangle. Specific injuries were lost in the miasma of pain, which the pills (repeated twice during the night) succeeded in distancing but not dispelling. Preferring full consciousness, he decided against taking any more: he wanted to maintain a hold on the sequence and detail of his story.

Annet saw to Freya, and brought him a cup of tea. When he heard her talking to Lara in the hall he struggled with agonising slowness out of bed, drew on his dressing gown as though it were barbed wire, and hobbled down the stairs.

Annet watched his progress with the same thoughtful expression she'd worn last night. Lara, holding Freya, was more expansive.

'Hell's bells!' she yelped. 'It's the dawn of the living dead!'

'Good morning.'

'Little bastards, they need a taste of their own medicine.'

'Yes,' he murmured, pleased at least that his story had gone into circulation. 'But I wasn't the man to give it to them.'

Annet met him at the foot of the stairs, gave him a peck on the cheek. 'You know my view, you should report it anyway.'

'We'll see.'

'And if you feel at all dizzy, or have any trouble with your vision – anything like that – you must call the doctor. Or ask Lara to take you to Emergency.'

'Don't worry,' said Lara, 'I'll have him in hozzy so fast his feet won't touch the ground.'

There was the merest suggestion of the cowboy look as Annet said: 'Good.'

When she'd gone, Lara was firm. 'OK Dad, you've proved you're tough, why not go straight back to bed? I won't tell anyone.'

'I haven't even called the office yet.'

'Let me do that while you crash out.'

He was sorely tempted but decided, on mind-over-matter grounds, to try and remain downstairs for at least the morning. Upstairs in bed there'd be nothing between him and the awful images of yesterday.

He lay on the sofa and attempted to read the newspaper, but the print jiggled before his eyes like a swarm of black insects. Lara took Freya upstairs, leaving him in peace – he could her her pottering about up there, singing, talking to the baby. At nine-thirty he got up – an exercise which made his eyes water – limped across the hall to the study, and rang Jackie.

She was horrified. 'That's terrible! Have you reported it? You should, you know. And don't even think of coming in tomorrow either, you must be in shock!'

It was the first time he'd heard her sound even remotely put off her stroke, and he was touched that it should be on his behalf.

'Don't worry,' he said, 'I shall be fine tomorrow.'

This was open to doubt. The pain, of course, would diminish. But the pain was a distraction. Even now, while he was still struggling with it, the memory of what had happened kept erupting, turning him weak and clammy with shock. The smells returned – the cooking, Gina's scent, the stale smoke on King's jacket ... And the sounds – her voice, harsh and coarse, screaming 'I hate you!' ... her mother's vulgar wailing ... the sickening bang of his head against the wall ... Worst of all was the endless, inescapable recreation of his humiliation on the front path ... It still seemed too awful, too alien, to have happened.

At ten-thirty, with Freya taking a nap, Lara brought him some coffee.

'I put sugar in,' she told him, covering his groan as he sat up.

'Thanks.' He tried to focus on matters other than himself. 'Has there been any news of your grandmother?'

'Dad called last night – early morning their time. He said she was peaceful. I suppose that means she's going to die.'

He was shocked by her bluntness. 'Not necessarily. How's her physical condition, did he say?'

'No worse, but no better either.'

'She's making her mind up,' suggested David.

Lara seemed to like this. 'That'd be right. She's a contrary old bird, it'd be just like her to keep us all guessing. If I was there I'd put a squib up her backside I can tell you.'

'Send her a telepathic squib. You're forceful enough.'

She laughed, and he felt rewarded. 'Right!'

Half an hour later, after checking with him, she took Freya out in the car to do some shopping. The house settled round David, solid and warm as a sleeping body. He still hurt all over, but for the first time in nearly twenty-four hours he began to relax, to contemplate the possibility of sleep. He felt as if he were dropping through the net of pain, feeling its rough touch as he went but gradually, steadily, sinking into some quiet, dark place beneath it.

It was when he was on the very brink of sleep, separated from its blissful oblivion by a single tenuous thread of consciousness, that he saw her.

There was nothing vague or amorphous about her presence. She stood near the window, looking over and beyond him in the direction of the drawing-room door, as if anticipating the arrival of a friend. She wore something plain and dark, but he couldn't have described it because his attention was entirely drawn to her face. It was a face handsome rather than beautiful – strong, intense, androgynous – with pale hair, it might have been fair or grey, swept straight back from the forehead.

David knew without a shadow of a doubt that this was the face that had stared back at him from the upstairs window that day. And also that he recognised it: it was familiar to him in some visceral way, the way – and the analogy sprang easily to mind – his newborn daughter's face had been familiar; as if somewhere beneath the surface that was hers alone her genetic inheritance lay like a reflection beneath ripples. And now he lay still and relaxed as a newborn infant himself, and perfectly, blessedly, pain-free. There was the sense he remembered of the air around him being a caul, enclosing and protecting him. He was certain that the woman knew he was there and might even be watching over him in some way.

This entire experience, complete and vivid as it was, could not have lasted more than seconds. The last thing he saw as he plunged into sleep was the hauntingly familiar face, still gazing over and beyond him with Red Indian-like calm. And just after his eyelids closed the faintest trace of some sweet, evocative scent . . . .

He woke, disorientated, to the sound of the phone ringing. It took him a moment to recall himself to his surroundings. The phone was picked up and he heard Lara's voice. Glancing at his watch he saw that it was one-thirty: he had slept for two hours.

Lara came into the room, carrying Freya. 'It's Mrs Keating, to find out how you are. I said you were asleep, but she's still on the line if you want to talk to her.'

'Yes – yes I will . . . .'

'Shall I bring it in here?'

'No, I should move. I'll come.'

'Okey-dokey, up to you.'

He heard Lara say: 'He's on his way, but you've got time to write that memo!'

Partly because he was stiff and a little muzzy in the head, but also out of curiosity, he paused near the window where the woman had been standing. But though her image in his mind was strong enough to have masked the events of the previous day, there was no lingering trace of her – all was bright and everyday. The caul broken.

'How are you doing?' asked Annet.

'Better, thanks.'

'Lara said you were having a kip.'

'I was. I went out for the count for a couple of hours and it's done me good.'

'Poor old darl.'

David's heart leapt. For the first time in days there was something in her voice – the ironic warmth, the mutuality, the recognition of how things were with them. Even, he dared to believe, the love.

'You know,' she said, 'you shouldn't do these things.'

'What things?'

'Go being a justice crusader. Picking fights with rough boys.'

He laughed, but his eyes stung. 'I know.'

'Anyway, so long as you're on the mend.'

'I am.'

'Don't do anything about supper, I'll call in at the Fortune Cookie on my way home, good idea?'

'Very good.'

That afternoon he slept again. Lara took Freya out in the backpack, and turned the answering machine on, but if the phone rang at all he didn't hear it. His sleep was deep and untroubled. He heard Lara return, and not long after that the front doorbell rang. This time he called: 'I'll get it!'

He walked stiffly but not quite as painfully to the hall, and opened the front door. There was an Interflora van parked in the drive, and the man on the doorstep carrying a large square box.

'David Keating?'

'That's right.'

'Present for you.'

David was left holding the box as the van disappeared. He closed the door and Lara appeared from the back of the house, carrying Freya, both of them still pink-cheeked from their walk.

'Hey — a secret admirer?'

'I somehow doubt it.'

As he began picking at the tape that sealed the box it crossed his mind that perhaps it was some appalling revenge device from the Kings. But when the two flaps swung open it was to release a huge heart-shaped balloon, in yellow and silver, which floated to the ceiling, trailing a kite-like tail decorated with silver bows. On one side of the balloon were the words: 'Keep your sunny side up!' and on the other a smiling, sun-like face.

'Wow, brilliant!' cried Lara. 'Who from?'

He rummaged in the box and found the card. 'To Mr Keating from Jackie and all at B and C'.

'Good on Jackie,' said Lara. 'She your secretary?'

'My PA, yes.'

'Sounds like you lucked out there. Look, look at Daddy's balloon ...!' She reached up and caught the balloon's tail, tugging so that it bobbed, beaming, across the hall. Freya, captivated, also beamed in Lara's arms as they chased it. The phrase 'a picture of happiness' seemed for David to have found its moment. He had to remind himself that Lara had her own worries, that she was simply doing her job.

He went to make tea. He was still sore, but his mood was so much restored that he ventured to say:

'Lara, why don't you knock off early? I think I've skived for long enough today. Annet won't be long.'

'Mrs Keating won't appreciate my going off and leaving you after your ordeal,' she replied doubtfully.

'You're Freya's nanny, not mine,' he reminded her gently.

'Yes, but leaving you in charge when you're groggy ....'

'I'm no longer groggy. I'm on the up. Honestly. Get on home

and ring your family. In fact—' he felt the warm, expansive glow of generosity – 'ring them from here before you leave. My treat – please.'

'I don't think so!' She studied her watch. 'It's five in the morning in Cooney Bay.'

'I thought you colonial types leapt out of bed in the small hours and bagged something furry for the pot before sun-up?'

'Darn, you're right!' she laughed. 'I'll do the tea, you do the quality time. Promise I won't be more than two ticks.'

He assured her she could be as many ticks as she liked, but she was barely one and a half. When she re-entered the drawing room he refrained from opening the batting in case it was bad news. She came and sat next to him on the carpet and ducked her fuzzy mop of hair at Freya to make her smile.

'Thanks boss,' she said, without looking at him. 'Nan's taking the lightly boiled egg as of last night. Dad says she'll live to get pissed at another Christmas dinner, worse luck.'

He was surprised at how delighted he was by this, almost as if he'd made it happen.

'That's terrific. Would you like a drink to celebrate?'

She grinned, a little misty-eyed. 'You keep trying that one, but the answer's still no.'

In fact, good girl that she was, she didn't leave until she'd bathed Freya and left David sitting by the fire giving her her bedtime bottle.

'Night, night,' she said. 'And now Lara's off to get lashed at the wine bar. See you Monday!'

Under the circumstances, Stoneyhaye was the very last place Annet should have visited. She knew that. But the house and its occupants had been on her mind since Harry had dropped the bombshell about leaving. And the very circumstances which should have prevented her, now compelled her to go for what might be the last time.

The attack on David had knocked her for six. These things

happened – you read of them in the paper all the time – but seeing the evidence on his body had been horrifying. She kept rehearsing in her mind the events as David had described them – the empty car park, the fierce, frightened youths, the sudden hail of blows and kicks – and it made her feel physically sick. But as usual her shock had rendered her undemonstrative, the more so because her current emotional turmoil was too large a beast to unleash. The more that needed saying, the less she could say it, it had always been that way and David had always understood. But had he, this time? His injuries were like a grim warning of the distance between them.

She understood him, too, more than he knew. The suspicion that he might be being less than truthful was like an open wound on her own heart, reminding her how much she stood to lose.

So the visit to Stoneyhaye was a farewell. She'd been able to leave the office even earlier than she'd anticipated on compassionate grounds, and it was still light when she reclaimed the car from the station car park. She went first to the Fortune Cookie and picked up a feast – a hostage to fortune, which she put in the boot of the Toyota.

The weather forecast on the radio was appalling – storm-force winds, especially in the south east, with a strong possibility of structural damage. But in a way she was glad of that, because the storms would drive her back to her husband and daughter, and sanctuary. In her rare moods of self-analysis Annet conceded that the phrase 'her own worst enemy' might have been invented for her. There were times when her wilful urge to self destruct was in indirect ratio to her ability to put the brakes on. She knew exactly what was happening, and did it anyway. In this instance the elements, already beginning to bully and threaten, were on her side.

She turned off the road into the secretive driveway. The woods on either side of the drive lashed and fretted and she could hear the angry rattle of the security barrier being shaken on its mountings. The wind was from the south west, turning the shallow valley of the Plinn into a natural wind tunnel. The grassy slope of parkland running down to the house seemed to stream away from her like water, and the Toyota wavered, its roadholding no match for the brute blast of the gale.

The only two cars in the yard were the Land-Rover and Harry's Mazda. Simon Acourt ran out, carrying a torch, the collar of his Barbour up round his ears, and yelled through the window at her.

'Hi! You must be mad!'

She lowered the window a chink. 'I know, I shan't be long – came to say goodbye!'

'If you want Harry, he's round the back with the others, trying to make the pool safe!'

'OK!'

She got out, and felt the wind smack against her with such force that she staggered for a moment, her mac whipped round her legs and her hair into her eyes as she fumbled to lock the car.

Acourt shouted something, produced a key and signalled her to follow. He took her into one of the open garages and unlocked the door at the back.

'Short cut – I'll leave it open for the moment, you can come back this way . . . !'

'Thanks!'

'I wouldn't be too long if you've got to get back in this – it's revving up for a shitstorm!'

As she emerged the other side it was starting to rain. Harry and some of the others, men and women, were fighting to secure the plastic covering over the still unfinished pool. Great green waves of the stuff reared up above them, snapping and booming in the darkening air. Harry and his team were like the crew of a sailing ship, struggling to hold course. She saw him coming towards her, leaning outwards against the weight of the sheeting. Intent on his task he expressed no surprise at seeing her there, braving the tempest in her work clothes and high heels. A loop of hard, wet nylon rope was thrust into her hand, his face came close to hers, eyes narrowed against the stinging rain.

'Grab this and don't let go! We'll start pegging from the other side!'

Instantly she felt the fierce tug of the plastic, and the rope seared her palms. She hauled backwards, her heels driving into the ground like tent pegs while the girl next to her slithered and staggered in trainers.

It was an interminable five minutes before the sheeting was all secured. Another two before Harry was satisfied and the soaked and shivering team were dismissed and ran, heads down, for the house.

He made a hand movement, yelling, 'Drink?'

'No thanks!' She shook her head. 'I came to say goodbye!'

It was around half past six when David noticed how hot Freya was. Sitting by the fire they had been cosy. As the wind got up outside it had been comforting not to know where his warmth ended and hers began. Only the thought of Annet out on the roads spoiled the snug peace inside the house. For the first time in weeks, when he parted the curtains to look out of the window it was in the hope only of seeing his wife.

Another reason that he hadn't noticed Freya's temperature sooner was that with evening his aches and pains returned somewhat – he had a dull headache, his crotch was still agonisingly tender and he was stiff. When he rose to take her up to bed he was obliged to creep the first few steps like an old man. and the effort involved in simply straightening up and taking his normal stride made him sweat.

It was one of those evenings when Freya hadn't finished her bottle, appearing to fall asleep with the teat still in her mouth. When he got her upstairs – an operation which tweaked a hitherto undiscovered injury in his back, presumably incurred on the Kings' front path – he laid her in her cot while he went to take some paracetamol in the bathroom. After the pleasant fireside fug of the drawing room it was cooler up here, he shivered as he ran a glass of cold water and swallowed the pills, and went to the bedroom to pull on a sweater before returning to his daughter.

Now, he noticed, she was not asleep. Her eyelids were lowered to reveal a mere slit of eye, and she lay perfectly still, her arms and legs in the unnatural akimbo position of a doll. Her cheeks were pink.

Aware of the smallest pinprick of anxiety he lifted her out and laid her on the changing mat on the divan. It wasn't strictly necessary to change her before putting her down for the night, but it was a process likely to elicit a reaction.

There was none. Or none to speak of – she made a couple of halfhearted little mewing sounds when his cold fingers removed her nappy and touched the hot skin, but she felt curiously limp (the word lifeless sprang to mind and he beat it back) and her slitted eyes seemed not to focus on anything. When he'd finished changing her he wrapped her in her patchwork shawl, bringing it up round the back of her head so that with the fronds of black hair on her forehead and her red cheeks she resembled a Russian doll.

He told himself not to overreact. She wasn't crying, so she wasn't in pain, and less than an hour ago she had been completely well, kicking and smiling on her rug. He must apply common sense. After all, he reminded himself, Lara had taken her out for a long walk in the backpack on an afternoon which even then had been windy and bracing – anyone would be flushed and soporific after such a walk. Or she might have caught cold in which case the time-honoured remedies applied – warmth, comfort, perhaps some more milk in due course since she hadn't finished her quota.

He carried her downstairs and laid her against the sofa cushions while he made up the fire. The strengthening wind was beginning to find out Bay Court's weaknesses, whining under doors and inserting sharp, scrabbling fingers of draught through the frames of the sash windows. In spite of himself, worry was beginning to drag on David's spirits. He did not yet feel justified in ringing the doctor, and wished Annet were here to share the responsibility ... It was then he hit on the bright idea of calling Mags.

'Hello? Oh, hello!' she said. 'We were only just talking about you.'

He noted the 'we' and was encouraged by it, but not enough to ask what they had been saying.

'Mags, I need your advice.'

'If it's mine to give, it's all yours.'

'Annet's due back soon, but it's extremely stormy up here—'

'And here, like banshees!'

'—quite, so she may be late. And Freya appears to have a temperature. Or at least she's hot and has a high colour ... is there anything I should be doing?'

'Not worrying, mainly,' said Mags. 'They run a temperature at the drop of a hat at that age.'

'What about speaking to a doctor?'

'I *think* a doctor would say the same thing at the moment. I mean she hasn't got a rash or anything has she?'

'No.'

'Vomiting, diarrhoea?'

'No.'

'Keep her warm and cosy and give her some water to drink, consult with Annet when she gets back – call the doctor on duty if you're really concerned a bit later.'

He felt calmer, and was grateful. 'Thanks, Mags.'

'My pleasure. One of us was going to be in touch anyway – not now but over the weekend, perhaps – with a ginormous favour to ask.'

'What's that?'

She laughed. 'Under the circumstances it'll keep! Tim and I are thinking of taking a long weekend together before Christmas, and we need to put a few backup systems in place ... We'll talk another time.'

'OK. We'd be glad to help.'

'Don't be too sure! Anyway, anon, anon. You go and look

after that little daughter of yours. But don't stay too close — a watched tot always boils!'

After he'd hung up he put on some music, *American in Paris*, to shut out the noise of the wind and establish a more harmonious mood in which to think sensibly. When he next studied Freya her eyes were fully closed, and he felt cheered by this small sign. Sleep after all was the great healer. If she could sleep she was all right, though her breathing was a little more pronounced and shallow than usual ... He longed for Annet's return. But in view of the weather and the fact that she was already later than she'd predicted, he was not optimistic.

In the end Annet accepted a shot of Jack Daniels in the kitchen, to counteract the effects of the cold and wet.

'Here's to you then,' she said, raising her glass. 'And good luck with everything.'

'Sod luck,' he said. 'Graft more like. I tell you what, I wish I could write the songs that make the housewives' hearts beat faster ... Anyway I'll be here while the house is on the market.'

'Has Chris already gone?'

He nodded. 'Back to London. And Lindy's in Switzerland with Jay.'

'You must miss him.'

'I do.' He swallowed the last of the JD and put his glass down with a bang. 'I will. But there you go, I brought it on myself.'

'How?'

He seemed to consider, briefly, what answer to give before saying: 'As the man said I can resist everything but temptation and this business is stuffed full of them.'

They ploughed heads down like Arctic explorers back to her car, and he braced the door open as she settled in the driver's seat.

'You know what,' he shouted against the wind. 'You and I are two of kind.'

She switched on the engine. 'Maybe.'

'Not that it's anything to be proud of!'

Their eyes met for a moment, before he slammed the door and raised a hand in farewell. By the time she'd reversed and turned, he'd gone.

The car shuddered and wavered on its way across the park, but driving through the wood was worse, like being below the surface of a rough sea. She flinched as the huge branches scythed back and forth, black on black, pouncing suddenly into the headlights and then disappearing. By the time she'd passed through the barrier and was back in the lane her heart was racing. She felt acutely vulnerable, and wanted to be home.

When Freya had been asleep for half an hour David lifted her gingerly and carried her upstairs to her cot, laying her on the mattress as gently as he could, still wrapped in the shawl, and covering her with the duvet.

He wanted to go into the kitchen, pour himself a drink, and see what if anything there was for a non-labour intensive supper since the prospect of the takeaway seemed increasingly remote. Also he suspected Mags was right: he was a little too close to Freya to be objective, constantly checking her breathing, her temperature and her appearance. He would hear her if she woke, and in the meantime it would be nice to have a break from this nibbling, low-level anxiety.

He still had the music on in the drawing room and so couldn't be quite sure when she actually woke up again, but it could have been no more than fifteen minutes before he became aware of small sounds from upstairs. His own injuries forgotten he dashed up the stairs and found her with the duvet kicked back and the crocheted blanket in a tangle, her face blotched red. The worst thing of all was that she wasn't crying properly, simply whimpering as though that was all she had the strength for.

Full of remorse, he scooped her up, bundling the blanket round her. The skin of her face scorched his, and felt slightly papery. Her weird, weak voice continued its eery complaint as

he carried her back down and into the drawing room, where he
turned off the music.

The wind was coming from all directions now, buffeting the
house in a blind fury; even the leaves on Annet's plants trembled
before its invasive breath. A distant clattering signalled some
wretched householder's dustbin taking flight. He crossed the
hall to the study. As he did so the lights wavered and dimmed,
but mercifully returned. Clutching Freya to his shoulder he
rummaged one-handed for the address book and found the
number of the health centre. A recorded voice said that in the
event of an emergency the number of the doctor on duty was
– followed by an eleven digit number he recognised as being
in town.

Never mind, he told himself, a tiny baby with a high
temperature *was* an emergency.

He was halfway through the number when the line went
dead.

'Damn! Damn, damn . . . !'

He began to dial again, but from the sound of the keypad
he could tell the phone wasn't working. Trying not to panic he
lifted the fax phone, but it was the same story. The wires must
be down – must in fact have gone down only seconds before. He
let out a moan of frustration. Freya leaned against him, emitting
her pathetic mewings of distress. As he stood there he heard the
splintering crash of a roof-slate falling on the terrace.

He returned to the drawing room and sat on the edge of the
sofa with Freya lying on his knees, trying to gather his resources.
Stupidly, he thought he could always call Mags again, and then
remembered why that was impossible. He supposed he could
put Freya in the car and take her to the hospital, leave a note
for Annet. But the conditions were atrocious out there. As well
as the wind there was now heavy rain battering on the windows.
The prospect of all three of them, incommunicado and out on
the roads in a hurricane, was not a happy one.

Somewhere, he remembered, Annet had a book . . . the new
mother's bible by some guru or other. Clasping Freya, beseeching

a God from whom he had no right to expect anything, he went upstairs to find it.

The tree fell almost slowly across the lane in front of Annet, but she had to brake violently to avoid crashing into it. It seemed to bounce slightly on landing, a shock of roots appearing on the bank to her right like electric wires. Standing in its rightful place, flanking the lane with the rest of its family, it hadn't seemed a particularly big tree: lying sprawled across the narrow space in front of her it was an obstacle akin to Beecher's Brook. Stunned by the closeness of her escape she sat with her arms braced on the steering wheel, and as she did so the tree rolled slowly, a half-turn like someone settling in bed. Instinctively she shrieked, and wrapped her arms round her head. Massive branches fell across the bonnet, pushing with dumb adamantine strength against the windscreen. Others, that she couldn't see, mashed into the front of the car, stoving in the radiator grill and killing her headlights.

'Well fuck you!'

Utterly enraged, swearing a blue streak she got out of the car – with difficulty, for a forest of sharp twigs impeded the door – and tried ineffectually to stamp the twigs underfoot with her high heels. In the confused darkness she could feel her tights being shredded, and the skin of her legs torn. Her clothes, already damp from their earlier outing, became instantly sodden and icy on contact with the wind and rain. Furiously she yanked at the branches that lay across the Toyota's bonnet, searing palms already sore from the rope, and coming away with no more than tiny handfuls of dead leaves. After no more than a minute she was drenched to the skin, cut to ribbons and had achieved nothing. She got back into the driving seat and was deprived even of the small satisfaction of slamming the door because of the spikey resistant twigs.

'Fuck!'

With wet, numb hands she located her bag, rummaged for

her mobile phone and dialled her home number with fingers that felt like lumps of wood. After getting the protracted 'not obtainable' tone twice she dialled the operator.

'I'm sorry but due to the adverse weather conditions there are lines down in that area.'

'So when are they likely to be working again?'

'I really can't say at present. There is a team out, but you'll understand the conditions are such that—'

Annet rang off, swore some more, drew a couple of deep breaths and found her wallet. By the tiny light of her car-key torch she picked out her AA card and dialled the emergency number. It rang perhaps a dozen times before anyone answered, and as she embarked on an inventory of details the signal began to break up. In an agony of frustration she raised her voice, as if that would make any difference, but the warning blips and the increasingly distant 'wha—?', 'Sorry—?', 'You'll have to – tha – 'gain' told her it was useless.

At this point she wept out of sheer frustration, swiping the tears off her face with what she knew were filthy hands.

'OK,' she said aloud after a minute. 'OK!'

She was not, she told herself in the Gobi Desert or on the Russian Steppe. She was no more than two miles from people, functioning phones and a bottle of Jack Daniels. She'd walk back to Stoneyhaye.

David went by the book. The author was not a professional, but a woman famous for having many children (and now grandchildren), who wrote anecdotally from her own experience, with the endorsements of various experts. He felt disposed to trust her judgement.

The gist of it was, not to panic. Almost every infant indisposition will go away of its own accord, she said, so not to worry if you can't get hold of a doctor right away. Don't wrap the baby up, keep her cool. Give her boiled water to drink. If her temperature gets very high, she may fit, though this is relatively

rare. If she does, chafe her and keep her limbs moving. Take
her to hospital. She'll almost certainly be fine. The author went
on to tell a story about one of her own daughters, 'a frequent
fitter' as she put it – very frightening at the time, but duly grown
out of, and the aforementioned daughter was now apparently a
strapping teenager crossing continents ....

He laid Freya on the hearthrug, unwrapped her and sponged
her gently with a clean J-cloth soaked in tepid water from
a mixing bowl. More than her heat, it was her inertia that
frightened him. When she was a little cooler he wrapped her
loosely in a Viyella sheet and tried to persuade her to take some
boiled water from a bottle. He was almost pleased when her face
convulsed with distaste and she arched backwards to avoid the
horrible thin stuff. But as she did so the sheet parted and he
noticed for the first time, with horror, a red stippling on her chest
between the tiny mauvish nipples. Swaddling her again he went
to the kitchen, he had some idea that Annet had brought back
a plastic card from the hospital which detailed the symptoms
of meningitis. Yes, there it was. He tried to make himself read
the whole thing, but the part that leapt out at him was the
tumbler test ... he'd seen it done on television. He fetched a
liqueur glass from the cupboard and pressed it to Freya's chest.
Her arms flew up in shock at this and she wailed, still feebly
but with a welcome hint of annoyance. Also, to his great relief,
the rash changed its complexion when viewed through the glass
– a good sign. However, the card indicated, the test should be
performed at regular intervals because in rare instances the rash
had been known to change.

He was astonished, when he looked at the clock on the
kitchen wall, to see that it was half past nine. Annet wasn't
back, he hadn't eaten, and he was exhausted with worry.

Freya appeared again to have gone to sleep, but he had been
lured once too often into a false sense of security. He took her
upstairs and laid her on the centre of the double bed, where she
looked tiny and vulnerable. He then went back down, buttered
a piece of bread and folded it round a piece of cheese, opened

a can of beer and put these items on a tray, along with Freya's water bottle, the damp cloth in its bowl, and the liqueur glass, which he carried upstairs.

Annet was dismayed at how short a distance it was before she had to admit defeat. Jesus, she thought, survivors of air crashes tramp miles through rainforests without food or water to reach civilisation ... snowblind mountaineers with limbs gnawed by frostbite struggle out of ravines and rejoin their companions ... perfectly ordinary couples go potholing and rock-climbing at weekends for *fun* ... and yet she, who thought of herself as fit and energetic, couldn't walk a quarter of a mile in the dark.

It was the dark that was the problem. Once she neared the woods it grew almost opaque and she became disorientated. She was wet through and shivering with cold and each blast of wind seemed to tear right through her so that her teeth chattered. She couldn't feel her feet at all and what with that and her unsuitable shoes she kept turning her ankle over and at one point went off the road completely and slid, her leg painfully bent, into the ditch at the side. Cursing roundly she struggled out, but a hundred yards later she was so cold and wretched and still nowhere near the turning to the house, that she gave up. After all, she reasoned, someone was almost certain to come along, if only a farm vehicle, and the worst that could happen was that she'd be there all night. It would be a sign of near-terminal decrepitude if she couldn't even contemplate spending the night in a car.

She returned, got in, locked the doors and decided to run the engine for a while to generate some warmth. She was going to need rescuing anyway so it would hardly matter if the battery was flat.

The engine failed to start. She got out again, fetched the sheet of brown tarpaulin from the boot, got back in, arranged it like a giant bib under her chin and over the rest of her, and prepared to stick it out.

* * *

For David, that night was like a long dark hangover of the soul. His own discomfort, along with anxiety about Freya, kept him from sleeping, and at those rare moments when sleep did seem to be overtaking him the slightest sound or movement from her would jerk him fully awake with every nerve tingling. On half a dozen occasions during those lonely, dragging hours he changed her, bathed her with the cool cloth and offered her the bottle of water. At around three-thirty, the digital display informed him, she finally accepted a drink, and swallowed steadily for some forty seconds, making him feel like a man who'd conquered K2.

Annet woke to find a stranger's face, streaming with rain and reddened with cold, grimacing at her from no more than a foot away on the other side of the window. Disorientated by a night of bitter cold and miserable discomfort she couldn't at first make sense of her surroundings. He beat on the glass and she could only stare back at him.

The gale was still blowing. The branches pinned against the Toyota's windscreen shuddered and vibrated, those further away tossed crazily against the churning grey sky of first light. The man was shouting something at her, she could hear his voice but not what he was saying. He wore a balaclava and a khaki cape, and seemed huge and menacing, a Magwitch-like figure. She hesitated and he rapped again with growing impatience.

Unable to activate the electronic window, she was obliged unwillingly, to unlock and then to open the door. The minute she'd done so the man pulled it right back on its hinges and she noticed that most of the surrounding small branches that had made her life so difficult last night had been cleared.

'Thank God for that!' he exclaimed with rough cheeriness. 'A couple of minutes back I thought you might be dead! Have you seen yourself?'

*   *   *

When David woke to find the bedroom in half-light, and the retreating rain and wind no more than a desultory patter on the window, his first thought was that Freya might have died while he slept.

He turned over cautiously in case he should roll on her, and propped himself up on his elbow. She lay there quietly, still and pale and – he touched her cheek – quite cool. Perhaps too still and pale, perhaps even cold! He picked her up and at once she registered her objection with one of those familiar movements, a twist and stretch, her mouth pursing, her small fingers clutching as if at sleep itself. Poleaxed by relief and gratitude he laid her down again and snuggled the duvet round her, a couple of pillows on either side to prevent the quilt from covering her face.

His relief was shortlived. The clock said six-o-five. Annet still wasn't back.

As good samaritans went, Annet's rescuer might not have got the role from central casting but he had the qualifications that really mattered – a tractor and chains, a functioning mobile phone, and an unfazeable wife who brought coffee and bacon sandwiches.

Her own car was towed on to the verge as though it were a dinky toy, but in spite of the arrival of farmworkers in a Daihatsu truck, armed with chainsaws and accompanied by a mad-eyed Border collie the tree was going to take longer. The police were informed, and Annet tried yet again unsuccessfully to call David.

'Your poor husband,' said the woman, 'he's going to be sick with worry. Why don't I just take you straight home, and you can take it from there? We can always tow the car back to our place.'

They had to take a long way round, some six miles off the usual route, through a trail of devastation. Branches were scattered about like kindling, there were at least three abandoned cars, one with its nearside wheels in a ditch, and here and there they were obliged to circumnavigate debris which had clearly travelled some way – bin-lids, broken glass, tattered remnants of fencing.

When they reached Bay Court the woman declined Annet's invitation. 'Only too glad to help,' she said, 'but I think we've both of us got plenty to do.'

David tried the phone, which still wasn't working. His bone-tiredness helped him to function, he hadn't the energy to panic. In less than two and a half hours Lara would be here, if she was able to get through, and he could hand over to her and find a phone somewhere else. If she didn't make it at the very least he could take Freya to Karen's while he found out what had happened. On the other hand the phone might be reconnected at any moment.

He splashed his face with cold water, cleaned his teeth, and went downstairs. The drawing room with its unguarded fire, the phone, the baby bible, Freya's blanket spread on the ground – all made him shiver with remembered anxiety.

He drew back the curtains. The front garden was like a battleground – shrubs flattened, twigs and branches scattered everywhere, stripped of their remaining leaves, a slab of corrugated iron roofing from God knows where, caught in the hedge as if left there by a receding flood.

And there, walking towards him, like someone emerging from a shipwreck – scarred, soaked and bedraggled but miraculously alive – was Annet.

His wife, returned to him.

They barely spoke. He took her in his arms and felt her relax, utterly against him. He made her tea, and ran her a bath.

In the bedroom doorway she picked up Freya and gave her a long kiss, her eyes over the baby's head taking in the tray, the half-eaten sandwich, the towel, the beer can, the liqueur glass, the damp cloth . . . .

'You got the loose women out just in time then.'

'I knotted a couple of sheets.'

She laid Freya back down, managed the ghost of a lopsided smile. 'Tell me later.'

'Plenty of time.'

He sensed that they both knew how much there was to tell, and how much time to tell it in.

While she was in the bath Freya woke, and he gave her her bottle and tidied the room. On her return he was about to take Freya downstairs, but she stopped him.

'Please don't go.'

'You'll want to sleep.'

She laid her hand on Freya's head, her own forehead on his shoulder. 'Please, darl. Lie down with me.'

They lay quietly, and slept – Annet first, then Freya. Even, eventually, David. Like lights being turned off, one at a time.

When the phone rang he awoke with a start and raced down the stairs, but Annet and Freya barely stirred.

On his return, Annet had her arms behind her head, and asked drowsily:

'Back in touch at last – who was it?'

'Louise.'

She sat up. 'Oh God . . . .'

'No. Marina's fine. More than fine, they all are. Louise is pregnant.'

She gave something that might have been a laugh or a sob. 'Just think, darl . . . All this is waiting for them.'

He sat down on her side of the bed and pulled her to him for a kiss. She sank into his arms, her mouth opening under his, a homecoming. Afterwards as he held her, her head beneath his chin he caught sight of their reflection in the wardrobe mirror. And glimpsed in their two so different faces, almost joined, the suggestion of a third face that he recognised but could not place ....

It didn't bother him. He had the peaceful certainty that in time the truth would out. He would remember the face.

The kiss he would never forget.

Chapter Eighteen

In the village of Newton Bury, the season turned.

Hallowe'en, with its attendant minor atrocities, became All Saints. On this, their patronal festival, Maurice Martin reminded his congregation of their duty to each other and the community, the wider family of which they were part.

In the field next to the church the bonfire grew tall with the wreckage of the storm, and the Fox-Herberts' hunters were led back to their stables until the fireworks were over.

In the churchyard itself, the plots took on a bedraggled autumnal appearance, except that of Robert Townsend, on which a small rose bush had been planted. At the parochial church council meeting the church warden wanted it minuted that it was a nice idea, when a family moved away and could no longer attend the grave, that they should leave a living memorial of this kind.

Orchard End was still on the market, because the price was too high, people said. But the manor house of Stoneyhaye was to be bought by a conservation trust, a great improvement on the last owners, whose hearts had never been in it.

Those who went to the art exhibition at the central library noticed the portrait of Mrs Keating from Bay Court. Apparently it had attracted a potential buyer, a Mr Bailey, but he'd been disappointed: it was not for sale.

Of course neither of the Keatings were great mixers, though they were devoted to that baby of theirs. She was a strange one, people said. But he was a nice man.